# THE GOLDEN AGE

also by michal ajvaz in english translation

*The Other City*

# THE GOLDEN AGE

a novel by michal ajvaz

translated by andrew oakland

dalkey archive press
champaign / london

Originally published in Czech as *Zlatý věk* by Hynek, 2001
Copyright © 2001 by Michal Ajvaz
Translation copyright © 2010 by Andrew Oakland
First English translation, 2010
All rights reserved

Library of Congress Cataloging-in-Publication Data

Ajvaz, Michal, 1949-
[Zlaty vek. English]
The golden age / by Michal Ajvaz ; translated [from Czech] by Andrew Oakland. -- 1st English translation.
p. cm.
Originally published: Zlaty vek, Prague : Hynek, 2001.
ISBN 978-1-56478-578-7 (pbk. : alk. paper)
1. Travel--Fiction. I. Oakland, Andrew, 1966- II. Title.
PG5039.1.J83Z39 2010
891.8'635--dc22

2009048556

Partially funded by the University of Illinois at Urbana-Champaign and by a grant from the Illinois Arts Council, a state agency

This translation was subsidized by the Ministry of Culture of the Czech Republic

www.dalkeyarchive.com

Cover: design and composition by Danielle Dutton, illustration by Nicholas Motte
Printed on permanent/durable acid-free paper and bound in the United States of America

*Without doubt, metaphysics has to do with everything that exists. However, the totality of what exists, including what has existed and will exist, is infinitely small in comparison with the totality of the Objects of knowledge. This fact easily goes unnoticed, probably because the lively interest in reality which is part of our nature tends to favor that exaggeration which finds the non-real a mere nothing—or, more precisely, which finds the non-real to be something for which science has no application at all or at least no application of any worth. [. . .] There is not the slightest doubt that what is supposed to be the Object of knowledge need not exist at all.*

Alexius Meinong, *The Theory of Objects*

*And they are each other than one another, as being plural and not singular; for if one is not, they cannot be singular but every particle of them is infinite in number; and even if a person takes that which appears to be the smallest fraction, this, which seemed one, in a moment evanesces into many, as in a dream, and from being the smallest becomes very great, in comparison with the fractions into which it is split up.*

Plato, *Parmenides*

*The whole thing looks senseless enough,*
*but in its own way perfectly finished.*

Franz Kafka, "The Cares of a Family Man"

# 1
# The second journey

Whenever I told my friends about the island in the Atlantic Ocean where in my travelling days I spent almost three years, it often happened that one of them would ask me to submit a written report on this little-known island which is known to its inhabitants by no name and which travellers through the ages gave a name according to superficial impressions, moods of nostalgia and the need to flatter the families of their rulers. I would be vexed by the thought of writing of a society whose mores and pleasures I barely understood even when I was living among them (although I succeeded during my stay in catching every sickness of its spirit). It seemed to me more agreeable and more considerate to this place to accord it the fate of other landscapes I passed through, simply to look on contentedly as its contours gradually dissolved in a haze created by a mix of memory, forgetting, and dream, a radiant mist which softens shapes, leaving phantoms of sense to wander among them, and soaks them with the breath of a conciliation which perhaps has its basis in fallacy and the long useless. I thought it perfectly appropriate for the island to live on only in the form of nameless echoes which are stirred in gestures, muted tones resonating in the meaning of words and utterances, phantom-like faces which flit past in the contours of things perceived, when the fluttering of time unlooses memories and their liquid quintessence seeps into the landscape of the present.

That I have now undertaken to make a second journey to the island is not because I have begun to feel regret that the memories of my last visit will soon dissolve. (Images must die so that they may help make new images and feats.) The taste and the courage for a new journey were born of other reasons. Only now, when the images are at last being swallowed by the confused jungle of the past, when they are almost entirely lost to the rainforest of the past which covers the greatest part of the territory of our consciousness, only now am I drawn to embark on a journey which promises to be as adventurous as a voyage across the seas, en route to the exotic lands of the past, to the tropics of memory of forgetting, where flashes of reality mingle with dreams and visions, images with the rhythms and whirls of forces, crumbling words with the unremitting hum of the consciousness and the tenacious glare of erstwhile gemstones and the painfully dazzling rays of an inner sun.

The aim of this expedition is not the conquering of images, nor the salvation of distorted shapes, nor the discovery of an order or a sense of the real. These wanderings have a purpose in and of themselves. Whatever aim this journey has consists in its futility. The aim of my return to the island is merely my private joy at a pointless resurrection, a parody of passion in which the dissolving phantoms of memory come back to life as the even less real and spookier ghosts of language, joy and comedy, in which the evermore elaborate maze of the past turns into a similarly elaborate and impenetrable maze of sentences, in which the questionable joys of language feed on the untrustworthy pleasures of memory and forgetting. Welcome to the show, dear reader. It is possible that some will think the celebration of the pleasurable rituals of futility the realm of less dignified literature; I would like to remind such readers that there are many books replete with wise thoughts and deep psychological insight which will no doubt satisfy their needs, and that there is no reason why they should read a travel book about an island unknown to them and its strange inhabitants.

The islanders would understand this; and I would surely not undertake such a journey if during my long stay on the island I had not become infected with the islanders' way of perceiving the world. On the island meaningfulness was taken as something base, almost indecent, and the islanders saw a great many shades of pleasure in the meaningless. So while others use words to build complex structures of meaning, I wish to devote myself to the joyful histories in which the maze of the island's life, which is without order and has no centre, is first transformed into the still more fantastic ruins of memory reminiscent of the sleeping Leviathan before it is overgrown with the jungle of language so completely that it disappears into it. I must admit that I am also driven to write by regret, by nostalgia, and the silent hope that as the sentences meander the smells of the island—from which once I had allowed one ship after another to leave without me—will waft in my direction, at least for a while. For the very reason that words do not always attend to our wishes, coming to us uninvited, serving to confuse us, out of landscapes unknown, for a moment their light can shine on lost treasures, treasures hidden from the memory.

When I confided in some of my friends my intention to write about the island after all, I was given various advice. There were those who advised me not to succumb to the prejudices of the society in which I live or to my own sympathies or animosities; I should keep a cool distance from my material. This is unproblematic for me, as I neither loved the inhabitants of the island nor did I loathe them (although there were times when I admired them and times when I felt for them contempt and perhaps even hatred). The islanders never did anything to harm me, but when I left none of them were particularly sad to see me go. I am not sure if my indifference—which is a product of my stay on the island, incidentally—will allow me to keep the scientific distance of the ethnologist, but at least it is a guarantee that I will treat even-handedly a people among whom I lived for three years and in whose language my dreams still speak.

It will be more problematic for me not to disappoint the hope of some that what I have to tell of the island will be enthralling. For certain life on the island was different in many ways from our life, but it would be difficult to find in its features any richness of colour or picturesqueness. The island was not adorned with any examples of natural beauty or historical monuments; it had no stories that boasted of glory or fame; there were no gaily-coloured festivals or folk costumes to charm the visitor, nor was there fineness in the ways or peculiarity in the character of the islanders. We might indeed describe life on the island as exotic, but this was an exoticism of elaborate ornament and oriental music that captivate at first by their unfamiliar shapes and sounds but after a while induce boredom, as they offer no instructions for their rendering in the language of our shapes and the language of our sounds. And I will disappoint those who enjoy reading tales of the adventures of travellers in distant lands: for several hundred years, since the time conquerors from Europe disembarked on its shores, nothing of note has happened on the island. It was one of the safest places on earth, but—for those with no appreciation of the strange pleasures of the islanders—also one of the most boring.

Some writers adopt the habit of describing a strange land by admitting or concealing their intention to demonstrate and criticise faults in their own society. I can assure the reader that he or she will not encounter any such bad literary practises in my report. On the one hand it does not seem to me that life on the island has anything to offer an understanding of our own world, and on the other I am not in the slightest tempted to exploit my encounter with another world in the service of something that interests me so little as a social or moral critique of our own society. (Although I have just expressed the concern that the reader will find a description of life on the island less than thrilling, I still think that learning about this most boring of foreign worlds is more interesting than a lesson in moral philosophy.) The reader need have no fear that he will be presented with some kind of social or moral ideal dressed up as description of an unfamiliar society. If I indeed held to such an ideal and wanted to communicate it to others, a description of my travels beyond distant seas would not be the way to achieve this. And if for whatever reason I decided to disguise my scheme as a tale of travel, I would certainly not make this nameless island, whose inhabitants fortunately were quite unusable for the communication of ideals, the subject of my book. One of their virtues was the impossibility of making of them citizens of some Utopia.

## 2
## The island

The island is about twenty kilometres in diameter and lies in the Atlantic Ocean on the Tropic of Cancer between Cape Verde and the Canary Islands. In the course of my stay I could only guess at its shape; on maps it always looked like a small circle. It seems that no publisher thinks enough of this region to commission the drawing up of a proper map. Only after my return did I first see a more detailed cartographical representation of the island, in a scale of 1:300,000; this was in a slim paperbound volume from late-nineteenth-century England which took the island as its subject. (For some reason it referred to it as St George's Island.) I found this book in an antiquarian bookseller's in Munich's Schellingstrasse; its leaves were falling out and tiny flakes of paper jumped from its pages as I turned them. I took it with me to a small Italian coffee house in nearby Türkenstrasse, where I sat over a sweet espresso and studied the map.

The island of the map was like a jellyfish, its waving tentacles the headlands and promontories of rock separated by wide, rounded bays. The eastern side of the island had been hatched by the cartographers of old with loving care almost in its entirety; this hatching, reminiscent of crumpled fabric, modelled faithfully the slopes and gorges of the mountain ranges, with the greatest peak marked on the map with a little white cloud and recorded as 3,400 feet high. As the mountains of the east dropped sharply to the sea, the hatching became denser, remaining so until it was cut off by the thick black line of the coast. In the island's centre the hatching suddenly disappeared for the stretches of stony upland plain which are overgrown with low bushes. The cartographer had represented with a small oval the cold lake that lies in a shallow depression, but the three mountain streams that rise in the slopes and whose waters are gathered in the lake perhaps seemed to him too paltry, and their beds, which the current fumbles to find in the rainy season, too uncertain to bother with. But the river, which flows out of the lake and on which lie both the island's towns, had been rendered conscientiously with all its bends. As the river approaches the sea its flow becomes lazy; on the map it seemed that the engraver's hand had faltered. West of the lake the hatching returned, now less dense than in the east; here were the slopes out of which the upland plain dropped to the coastal flats, the most fertile part of the island. It was here that I often walked under the trees; behind their greyish trunks was the dark-blue canvas of the sea, and against their dark leaves the berries shone yellow, red and orange. It was from these berries that the islanders made their celebrated jellies and pastes.

Someone who had never been on the island might be mystified by the place on the map where the hatching of its western side was intersected by the line of the river. Perhaps he would be unable to say what it meant; he might think he was looking at the rough traces left by a sudden mental disturbance on the part of the cartographer. In this place the hatching suddenly thickens, while the line of the river frays into fibres which get ever thinner, as if the river had decided to disappear, before the delicate lines gradually come together again. Into this tangle of hatches and threads a little black wheel is set, of the kind used on maps to indicate a town. The area represented by this jumble of lines is stranger still than it appears on the map. Here the gentle, fertile slopes of the west become a rocky scarp, through which the river cuts as it flows out of the lake; ledges of rock divide the river into many branches. On islets of stone between these branches the inhabitants of the island built the upper town, a kind of vertical Venice. Beneath this the waters of the river merge again in a single stream which flows unhurriedly to the coastal flats, through a corridor of high bulrushes which sway in the wind that never quite dies on the island, down to the lower town, at whose harbour it joins the sea. In the Munich coffee house my feet recalled the hot sandy earth of the coastal flats, how one's shoes would sink into it and dry, thorny stalks would keep cracking under one's soles. When I looked up from the book I saw on the white wall a faded film image of the sand lifted by the wind, like a yellow veil rippling over the ground.

The island's only road joins the lower with the upper town; in its final stretch it becomes nothing more than a widish path carved into the rock. On the coastal flats the road follows the river, and in stretches it is difficult to find beneath the sand scattered over it by the wind. But as there are no automobiles on the island, no one minds this. (The islanders know nothing about technology, and they dislike noise, speed and sudden movement.) Apart from two broken motorboats left by seamen in the harbour, the visitor will discover a single testimony to the modern world: one day a boat with a cable in tow landed on the island, since which time a telephone box has stood on the harbour's stone jetty. The only people to use this are the seamen from the boats; there are no other telephones on the island and the islanders know no one abroad whom they might telephone.

With the exception of the western slopes which extend between the coastal flats and the plateau, the island is not particularly fertile, but in many places its earth conceals colourful stones immediately below the surface. The mining and trading of precious and semi-precious stones is the islanders' main employment, and in the harbour of the lower town boats with British, American, Italian, Spanish and Greek flags—and, quite often, the gaily-coloured flag of some African state—are forever lying at anchor. The islanders obtain most things they need in exchange for precious stones. To this trade in export we can add certain culinary specialities and fine papers produced from reeds.

There is no money on the island, a fact which in the 1960s provoked a French writer of the Left to produce an article which makes a point of describing the island's society as a prototype for selfless brotherhoods of the future. The fallacy at the centre of his thesis is quite laughable: the islanders had not the remotest interest in philanthropy and humanism; indeed, their language possessed no words to give expression to these concepts. While the islanders' absolute lack of appreciation for the accumulation of money was estimable and did much to clarify their behaviour, it was also connected with features of their character which were more difficult to take and by which I was often exasperated. Money is nothing but a pile of memory and anticipation by which we unchain ourselves from our given circumstances; the accumulation of money is a form of asceticism which holds back forces so that these may later form new shapes and deeds. Time on the island knew no such barriers. It knew no lulls and hardships; it was a monotonous milling of many weak energies, all of which ran flat as soon as they emerged. What went on here was reminiscent of the endless rearrangement of the fragments of colour in a kaleidoscope; there were moments when I found these figures fascinating and more beautiful than anything I had seen in Europe, but there were others when they seemed to me superficial, disagreeable and boring.

I have mentioned already that the inhabitants of the island did not call it by any name. They did not like fixed names and changed their own with great frequency; in the course of his life, each islander had dozens of names. A new name might come into being by the bearer's accepting a corrupted pronunciation he had heard somewhere of the name by which he had gone up to that point, or he might adopt a name by which someone addressed him in error. At the same time the islanders understood names as things which established a certain dialogue with the things they designated. Names were saturated with the qualities of things, but they also worked on these things and transformed them. In this dialogue both names and things matured, underwent change and perished. Some people might think it strange that while on the one hand the islanders conceded so much power to the name, on the other they could quite light-mindedly accept as their own a name which had come into being by chance. But the inhabitants of the island believed that it was precisely names with their origins in errors, slips of the tongue or mishearings which in their dialogue with things had the power to surprise—that it was these names which embedded themselves in their unprotected side, from where their most interesting voice was wrung.

Whenever an islander accepted a name, he tended to adjust his behaviour so that it corresponded to the new name. Islanders also went through periods when they lived without a name. I believe that in the past the island, too, had various names, and it will surely have a great many names in the future, but my time there coincided with a time when the last name had expired and the next had not yet come into being. The islanders would forget the island's past names, just as they forgot the names they themselves had had in childhood and youth. I, too, had several names while I was on the island and I, too, have forgotten what they were, with one exception; this was a word which in their language designated a bird similar to a pelican, and perhaps I got it because my European name was similar to this word. In the time that this word was my name, I came to recognize in myself certain qualities I shared with the bird; already I was so steeped in the mores of the island that I caught myself imitating its strange walk and the timbre of its voice. Was it the name which had imposed these traits upon me or were they already present within me, waiting for discovery and restoration by the new name? But as others never gave a thought to such things, nor did I agonize over them.

## 3
## Murmurs and lights

In the slim volume from the antiquarian bookseller's in Munich I read that the ancestors of today's islanders built the upper town on the river where the rock drops sharply and the river frays into a maze of strands, and that they did so because water is in short supply for much of the year and to protect themselves from the pirates who once plundered the coast with great regularity. I believe that these factors may indeed have played a part in the founding of the town as it was; but the main reason for the islanders' remaining in this inhospitable, barren place is their liking for the soft water music that forever accompanies life in the upper town, just as in the streets and apartments of the lower town they like to hear the steady ripple of the sea. The islanders did not drink alcohol or use drugs (with one exception, of which I shall speak later), but their love of rustling and other quiet sounds, sounds which we rarely perceive, had something in common with an addiction to drugs: they were able to listen all day long to the rush of the sea or the sound of the wind through a crack in a wall.

The upper town is built into a waterfall. The roaring masses of water and the rapid, wild, swirling currents are impossible to imagine. Formations of rock divide the current flowing from the lake above the town into many strands, and these zigzag down the rock-face, beating into the shelf, dividing as they go into ever more strands. In the lower part of the town they begin to come together until they become a single stream again on reaching the coastal flats. In this way the river creates in the upper town a kind of double delta. The river's current is not particularly strong even in the rainy season. On the area of the upper town it is divided into so many weak strands that the water passing through the town only whispers in trickles, drips, rustles and ripples. At the beginning of my stay in the upper town all the sounds came to me as one, an indistinguishable murmur, but with time I learned to tell them apart—the sound of water flowing down the rock-face and the stone steps, the sounds of water columns and walls of water, fountains and individual drops falling on stone and on the surface of water. The monotonous murmur was transformed as if by magic into a musical composition played on a great variety of instruments by a full orchestra, a symphony without end whose movements traced out subtle differences in style, gave expression to the whole scale of moods and feelings of the phantom composer; it seemed to me that I could even hear in it various philosophical notions. This water composition was of varying quality: sometimes it came up with quite unexpected chords and original moves, at others it tended to repeat already familiar combinations of notes, yet never did it lapse into the banality and sentimentality saturating so many famous compositions from Europe. (When on the island I sometimes imagined an inverse world, in which concert halls would be turned over to the sounds of rain and the rustling of winds while in the treetops and on the weirs and behind the walls of factories, sonatas and symphonies would ring out; in a world such as this the damp on the plastering of walls would probably form coherent text while the pages of books would be covered with indistinct marks.)

The houses of the upper town are built on islands of rock among the branching currents. At their rear the houses are attached to the rock. The river splits into two above the roof of a house, and these two arms flow around it before dividing themselves up further; some of the new arms are drawn away before joining a stream grown out of other currents, while others come together again beneath the house, creating a circle of water around it. Sometimes the occupiers admit an arm of the river into their house, where it continues to fray. To begin with I thought they did this so the current could be put to work in rooms hidden somewhere in the house, but the islanders would likely grow indignant at such single-minded exploitation of this element whose quiet power they esteem so highly; they take simple delight in the coolness of the water and the sounds it makes, and sometimes they put drops of dye in it and watch the figures change and melt. (The islanders sometimes put me in mind of the Japanese, though the former differ from the latter in that they feel absolutely no need to create objects of beauty.)

The occupiers of many of the houses directed the water across the roof so that as it tumbled over the edge it became a lustrous curtain of water made up of several columns, in which threads of sunlight created the perfect illusion of sparkling beads of coral or a solid wall of water. (It may be that this feature of the island's architecture inspired Frank Lloyd Wright to design his unrealized house in the Arizona desert with its wall of water.) Naturally it was a simple matter to pass through such a wall of water, meaning that any intruder who chose to enter the house would be obstructed by nothing more than a brief dousing. But there was no thievery and murder on the island. Although morality and humaneness meant nothing to the islanders, they were strangers, too, to egoism, and they were too dreamy and lazy to do evil.

On the island I had a girlfriend. I shall refer to her as Karael, as this was her name at the time we first met. In her house, too, the bedroom was separated from the outside world by a murmuring wall of water. When at night I was unable to sleep, I would watch the wall shining magically in the moonlight and listen to the trickling of the water until sleep reclaimed me. Or I would watch the wall from the room as the sun was setting, when it seemed that the wall was composed of a liquid crimson glow. These moments of the day and night were for me the pinnacle of happiness: I would forget about Europe and all I still wanted to do there, about the stories and articles I was working on, about my friends and the countries I wanted to visit. I would forget, too, my constant objections to the islanders' way of life, which consisted of nothing more than bathing lazily in their perfect, unvarnished sense of the absolute, in the sea of bliss composed of lights and murmurs before these degenerated into shapes and words. And I would ask how I could wish for something other than this clear light, than this splendid, idle glow of the present.

Some inhabitants of the upper town distributed the water around their houses by a system of narrow gutters that trailed across the ceilings; the water would flow over the sides of the gutters, thus creating walls of water inside the house, too. The rooms in such houses would be separated from one another by nothing but these cool, translucent walls. The water would be drained from the house by channels in the floor. These half-transparent walls breathed out an exhilarating coolness even on the hottest nights, but they long made me feel uncomfortable as naturally they granted those who lived within them no privacy; behind the wall to a neighbouring room, objects and bodies appeared as deformed and imprecise shapes. I was taken aback that the islanders had no difficulty in performing the most intimate acts behind transparent walls, even when the room beyond the wall of water was full of people.

When I complained about this to Karael she did not understand why I was bothered by it. She said that nobody really saw us, that the people beyond the wall of water watched only the quivering shapes on the wall's surface, and although these resembled us a little, there were all kinds of things which resembled us, certain other people, for example, or our own shadows and pictures and photographs of us, and we did not identify ourselves with these things. I understood later that the islanders' perception of images on walls of water and reflections in the mirror is different from ours: they look at them as at independent objects that bear a certain relation to what is behind the wall of water or in front of the mirror, but this relation is no more remarkable than relations that exist among all things.

For the islanders the real presence of a thing was enough. For them shape and colour had an intrinsic longing to create a glowing carpet, and our gaze did them a great injustice by forcing them to become components of things, by attaching to them all kinds of doubtful phantom interiors and unverifiable backs; it seemed to the islanders an inexcusable impropriety to dispose of colours and shapes so that they represented other, remote things. When after my departure Karael telephoned me from the booth on the jetty, I had the impression she did not identify fully the voice in the sun-heated receiver with the foreigner she had known on the island.

The islanders did not bind images and reflections to things; they set them free, granted them lives of independence. I think they understood the relations between things and images as two-sided, believing that the shapes and motions of figures originated too in what took place on the surfaces of mirrors and bodies of water. On the island things and their images and images and their things conducted similar dialogues to those which existed between things and names. I observed that some of Karael's gestures and the agitated play of her fingers probably had their beginnings in the quivering images on the wall of water, that from the time she obtained an octagonal mirror of green glass, an olive tinge appeared in her dusky complexion. (I wouldn't like to speculate on whether this phenomenon was caused by the mirror's drawing my attention to something that had been there all along, whether the colour of Karael's skin changed as a consequence of a psychosomatic process, or whether there exists in obscurity some kind of mirror sorcery.)

When I was on the island I, too, gradually learned not to make too great a distinction between things and images, while the imitation of images by things seemed to me a truly banal phenomenon. Regrettably this inability to defend myself against the power of images has stayed with me: for example, I come home late at night and see in the hallway mirror that my face resembles the dim reflection in the window of the empty night tram; I see etched in my features a hint of the dark facades of the houses that passed by my face when I was on the tram. You would never get me into the labyrinth of crooked mirrors on Petřín Hill.

## 4
## Labyrinths, mirrors, precious stones

The walls of water had one more purpose: they served as clocks. On flowing into a house, water would enter a receptacle in which there was a cylinder composed of twenty-four layers. Each layer was made up of a dense aromatic essence, and the water which flowed through the receptacle dissolved one layer every hour. In this way the walls of water always expelled the fragrance of the hour so that in their every waking moment the inhabitants of the upper town knew what time it was. I found this particularly pleasant at night. Whenever I awoke in the middle of the night, the damp air would be replete with, let us say, the scent of vanilla and I would say to myself, "It is only two o'clock, I may sleep for a long time yet." Or else I would smell oranges and know that daybreak was at hand. Even today in my Prague flat sometimes I stir in the night and, neither asleep nor fully awake, sniff the air to determine the time, at which point the smells of the city break into my reverie through the half-open window. And I ask myself what strange hour is this before my disquiet wakes me properly and it dawns on me where I am.

How happy I would be if these lines of mine inspired someone to start producing aromatic clocks! I am convinced that it would not be too difficult. There is many a sleeper who awakes to the darkness, to be smothered in the formless matter of the night so that he cannot breathe; there is a soggy, amorphous mass on top of him, and the sight of the glowing face of his watch cannot save him as the black, liquid mud that stuffs itself into his lungs, ears and brain, refuses to have anything to do with phosphorescent numerals. But the night would be powerless to resist a scent effusing in the darkness, washing into all its bays; it would have to capitulate to this amicable foe, this kindly victor, to accept the segmentation the scent was offering, to submit to the bleary but precise arithmetic. Thus would the night lose its power over the wakeful, allowing them to return to the realm of sleep, of their desires.

The water flowing out of the lake above the town was divided into several arms that divided and frayed further until in several places—on tables of rock, in the moss, in the depths of a house—the current transformed itself into a fine capillary net before the strands were gathered together again. I would often study the places where the river dissolved almost to nothing; here were labyrinths of tiny, barely visible, dissipating threads of water, zigzagging, dripping, oozing underbeds, which rose and receded and evaporated. It seemed incredible to me that a flow of water which above the town and down on the plain moved in orderly fashion in a single direction and despite the shallowness of its basin earned the designation of *river* in every season of the year, should now and then transform itself into this tangled web that verged on nothingness. It seemed to me that by these muddled and fading movements it revealed its true nature, the well-concealed secret of its unity and calm. The capillary labyrinth was at the heart of the double delta that spread through the town, the secret heart of the river as a whole.

The rooms of the apartments of both towns had practically no furniture, although the inhabitants of the upper town had a liking for mirrors, which made up a large proportion of the cargoes which came to the island by ship. On the walls of stone and water of the upper town there were mirrors small and large, oval, round and rectangular, in which was reflected the maze of arms of the double delta, which itself was like a mirror image. In these mirrors the labyrinth was multiplied, it gathered to its arms new braids; it seemed as though some of the currents flowed into a dark sea concealed in the depths of the mirrors, while others rose from dream-like sources in the mirrors and gradually acquired substantiality as they went on their way. Waters that dissipated in the mirrors were constantly replaced by currents that flowed into reality from the world of reflected images.

In the rooms of the upper town it was difficult not to look at the world from the islanders' perspective, with no significant distinction made between things and images. The heart of the double delta, the fading capillary labyrinth, which itself was on the border where being and non-being collide, was not much more substantial than its mirror image. The muddled motions of the sources were no different in kind from the motions originating in the quiverings of mirrors suspended in draughts; the water threading its way down the curtains seemed to be heading for the fantastic, hovering lake that was also the destination of imaginary, reverse waterfalls ascending out of the depths. The lake was visible on horizontal surfaces beneath real walls of falling water, while the glass of the mirrors reflected walls of water that looked like half-materialized images. It was no simple matter to distinguish real water from its mirror image. After a while anyone living among the mirrors, in a world where the things reflected were so weak and insubstantial and reflections so disengaged from things, ceased to make too great a distinction between the two.

The upper town was also the centre for the mining of precious stones. I had heard something of the island's celebrated precious stones before I disembarked there. Down in the harbour I witnessed trading between seamen and islanders, and in upper-town apartments I saw decorations of small coloured stones set in stone walls as well as wavering figures composed of precious stones that were suspended on long threads in walls of water. I was puzzled not to see on the island anything that looked like a mine; indeed, I encountered nothing to suggest that the earth was dug. Once I got to know Karael, I asked her to show me a place where precious stones were mined. We were sitting on the terrace of her house in the upper town; she took me by the hand and led me through the wall of water into one of the rooms at the back of the house, which was up against the rock. She opened a door in the wall I had seen many times before and assumed led to some kind of closet or pantry. When she switched on the lamp I saw a narrow, damp cave.

Karael explained to me that every house in the upper town had such a door in the wall or trapdoor in the floor. The islanders mine precious stones at home. They have no regular working hours, but from time to time—typically several times a day—they go to the seams and tap away at the stones with a small hammer. There are not as many precious stones today as there once were (the rock's productivity has gradually fallen off), but the meagre yield is sufficient for the islanders, who also make use of many of the coloured stones to decorate their dwellings. It cannot be said that they work particularly hard, nor has their work yet made it easier for them to learn the lessons the rock has to teach them; they do not read in the rock's features which stones it is concealing and where these stones are to be found. I would maintain that the ease with which they earn their living has much to tell us about the islanders' characters, good traits and bad, about their generosity and nobility and their lack of interest in creation and in deeper and more systematic thought.

## 5
## Hot walls

As I was first approaching the island, standing on deck looking at the wide, straight streets and the sprawling palaces of the lower town, I was in little doubt that this was the capital city. But when I walked through these streets and saw that they were clogged with sand, that the interiors of the palaces were empty, their patios thick with vegetation and their facades covered over with climbing plants, I had to re-think: I now had the impression I had been washed up in a peopleless, dead town. I was to learn later that the lower town was the seat of the king and as such the island's metropolis, but the presence of the king, a figure confined to the background, served only to intensify the sense of emptiness in the lower town, making life there all the more dreamlike, making its streets seem all the more desolate. I learned, too, that the town was not as lightly populated as I had believed at first sight, although only a few of the houses were lived in and these were scattered throughout; their occupiers stayed in them only temporarily, for reasons of trade, or the proximity of the sea, or the need to be alone.

No one had his permanent base in the lower town. At any given time almost every house was empty and it was enough to pick one out for oneself and to occupy it. Should anyone wish to settle permanently in one of these dwellings he would meet no resistance, but I do not believe that any of the islanders ever thought of doing so; indeed, for their stays in the lower town they rarely used the same house twice. I, too, in the time before I knew Karael, lived in an empty house, on a square with an equestrian monument at its centre. There I would sit at the window for days on end, watching the stone horseman's shadow inching across the hot slabs in the manner of a great sundial. Then, out walking one day, I took a fancy to a house right on the edge of town whose windows gave onto the sandy plain; I moved into it straight away. And after I lived at my girlfriend's I returned to the lower town for a longer stay. All the islanders lived like this. The bonds between man and woman were not particularly strong, and it was a common occurrence that one of the partners would disappear to the lower town for a good long while and then return.

The uniformity and great width of the streets gave one the impression that the lower town was vast, when in fact it was possible to get from one end to the other in a quarter of an hour. The town was built to a regular ground plan shaped like a chessboard. The visitor walked long, straight boulevards, meeting no one. From cracks in the pavement, the kind of prickly stalks grew that are everywhere to be found on the coastal flats; every corner offered up the same monotonous view of straight, empty boulevards, broken at regular intervals by the shadowy mouths of cross-streets. These straight lines appeared to be hurrying into the distance, giving the impression they wished to guide the visitor to an important destination as quickly as possible, but at the end of each street all such a visitor would find was pale, rolling sand or a wall of rock. He would pass colonnades, dry fountains whose metal basins were overgrown with thorny stalks, the flaking facades of houses and palaces with yellow grass and other vegetation growing out of their crumbling eaves and sills. He would walk past hot walls, past series of high, paneless windows; the pleasant smells of empty rooms warmed by the sun would waft towards him. From the plain, the town was penetrated by the belt of high reeds that lined the riverbank. The visitor who chose to step into this thick, damp jungle was soon surprised to find statues of sphinxes and mighty, recumbent lions, coated in a sandy soil, rotting leaves and vegetation; there was a flight of broad steps that reached down to the river and some great metal rings set in granite slabs.

The lower town was not built by the forebears of the islanders: it was established on the site of a village in the port by conquerors who came to the island many years ago. I thought I saw in the decoration of the facades, in architectonic members scoured for centuries by a sand-filled wind, modified elements of Venetian architecture, twisted features of the Roman and the Spanish baroque. From these clues I composed a story for the town. I speculated on what the people were like who all those years ago landed on the island's shores and built these houses and palaces. I pictured them as sailors with dirty lace collars whose activities at sea were half-piratical, half in the service of their kings; I imagined these figures, each of whom was simultaneously traveller, brigand, engineer, discoverer and geographer, and I fancied that some of them had picked up something of the new philosophy in the salons of Paris or London.

Although they missed their homeland, they would not have been able to live in it any longer; they had become used to the vast expanse of the sea, to the heat which dissolved thoughts like alcohol, to the lure of coastlines that seen from the bow of a ship stretch out like so many marvellous flowers. They discovered new lands and plundered them to the glory of their king, who, being so far away, was easy to venerate, but they were no longer capable of being anyone's subjects or respecting anyone's laws. When they landed on the coast of this island, whose population was too mild-mannered to defend itself, when for days on end in the burning sun the colourful gemstones sparkled before their eyes, when the women they encountered were beautiful and submissive, they formed the intention to settle for good, to build their own kingdom here, to build a new home which they would likely call by the name of their own country or king.

As I studied the volutes with their exaggerated twists furling into one another, the luxuriance of the stone acanthi on the capitals of columns and the bizarre shell-like curves, it came to me that these monuments had been constructed in fits of homesickness, even though their builders—after years spent roaming the seas—had forgotten the order and dimensions of home. The breath of the South stretched and warped shapes into a dreamlike, joyless, ghostly, tropical rococo. Even today the walls of the palaces exhale pride, nostalgia, evil, daydreams and pain. The interior gardens of the palaces, their arcaded galleries overgrown with reeds, give away how much the foreigners hated the land of which they had become the lords, how they tried to conceal their memories inside their homes.

The wide, straight boulevards and right-angled crossroads were intended as expressions of the triumph of order. The Europeans wanted the inhabitants of the rocky dens of the upper town, whom they mocked as savages of the labyrinth, to be amazed by the sight of the regular chessboard of the town on the plain; they wanted the natives to feel humble whenever they walked its magnificent streets. But in the burning, blinding sun, all the geometry and symmetry acquired a hallucinatory character, investing the town with a dreamlike air; it was the same with the illusory interior gardens and the over-adorned facades, which betrayed their creators by befriending the shapes of the aborigine rocks and trees.

The islanders did nothing to resist the invaders. During my stay on the island I was forever bewildered by their placidity. When their property and lives were in danger this could manifest itself as an almost heroic calm, but at other times it could come across as a dull indolence and want of courage (though the islanders were no cowards). No one could take from them their treasures, which were embedded in the present, and they knew this very well; hence there was nothing for them to fear. The murmurs to which they listened, the tangled shapes whose script they read, these things they could find anywhere; I believe that they even imagined death to be some kind of murmur, and for this reason they had no fear of it. Yet their complaisance made me uncomfortable. One should bear in mind that in the end they triumphed over their conquerors; I believe that they knew from the very beginning of the magnificent victory to come. If their submissiveness was part of a highly successful strategy, I'm not sure this makes their attitude any more estimable or easier to bear.

As I got to understand the character of the islanders better, I was able to imagine what this secret war must have been like: evidently it was so inconspicuous that for a long time the conquerors had no notion that any kind of struggle was going on, let alone that their inglorious defeat was foretold from the beginning. I see the foreigners as they condescend to describe to the islanders the stories and dogmas of their religion, as they tell them of the latest advances in knowledge in Europe, as they speak of the natural sciences, the laws of mechanics and new teachings in logic and distinct ideas, as they demonstrate to the islanders the machines they use in their building and war-making. I imagine the islanders listening to them, repeating their concepts and theories, reciting their prayers. The foreigners sense that something is happening to their ideas and their faith, that they are undergoing some uncanny transformation, but they have no notion of what this transformation might consist in; after all, all the islanders are doing is repeating their utterances verbatim. As the Europeans see no place at which to strike, as they do not know what to forbid and what to eradicate, what to polemicize about and what to refute, they have no means of self-defence. The natives do not even have a god one could take from them. The islanders always repeat what they are told and are never silent; whenever the Europeans retreat to their patios with their fountains, the voices of the natives, buzzing like insects and repeating the words of the Europeans, seem to reach them through the thick walls.

When the islanders repeated the theories of the Europeans, they did not change in them a single word or concept; no article of proof was missing, nor were any laws of logic violated. Yet it seemed to the foreigners that in the act of repetition the logic they had used to this point was revealed to be a dreamlike game, its logical structures to be labyrinthine. Although the methodical approach was disturbed in none of its aspects, it was transformed into a ritual that hinted at sorcery. It remained the case that if man is mortal and Socrates is a man, then Socrates, too, is mortal, but suddenly it seemed that the mechanism that transmits to the conclusion by means of a central article the predicate of the upper premiss, was started up by a unknown force, a force that the Europeans had never before been aware of; now it seemed that behind the figures of their judgments they were seeing the outlines of mechanisms wholly different, driven by this force with the same willingness and perseverance; they also thought they glimpsed the contours of fantastic syllogisms in whose judgments the place of Socrates was taken by scaly, malodorous monsters and in whose conclusions were revealed flashes of venomous light and muted cries which, by some strange irresistible method, flowed out of the colours of sounds and the rhythm of premisses. It would have been bad enough if this transformation was just a sickness that afflicted logic in the tropics; but the Europeans felt an ever-growing anxiety that something worse was going on, that in this accursed place they had got themselves into a trap from which there was no escape, that logic had taken off its mask and with a grimace of irony exposed the true nature it had hitherto kept hidden.

## 6
## The secret war

Now the Europeans were coming to regret the vaingloriousness with which they had paraded their machines to the natives. The islanders turned the handles of the apparatus and machines brought to the island by the foreigners and all the components moved as predetermined, but everything was different. A machine performed the activity for which it had been built, lifting or beating, ejecting or grinding or turning, but suddenly these functions were no more important than all the other movements of the machine that made them possible, while these movements were no more important than the many small, pointless movements with which they were accompanied—the shaking and rattling and grinding of parts, the various vibrations for which there were no names. (Here the Europeans suddenly felt their language to be inadequate.)

Suddenly it was no longer possible to distinguish the purposeful movements from these others, and the unified process towards whose achievement all movements of the machine were joined was not the most important, nor even was it different in kind from the movements and processes going on around but apart from the apparatus, such as branches swaying in the wind or the rustling made by the sand as it recast its shape. All these movements became parts of some kind of cosmic ballet in which every part had an equal share, in which every part was equally important, equally nonsensical and had the same disturbing, bewitching gift for histrionics.

All this gave the Europeans bad migraines, which drove them into the gloom of their rooms and interior courtyards. They were alarmed to realize that they were beginning to look at the world through the eyes of the islanders. They were made nauseous by the world revealing itself to them, a world in which all sounds made a dreamlike music and all movements a monotonous, incomprehensible, melancholy ballet. On the island a great many things occurred which frightened them, but perhaps most frightening of all was the fact that in the depths of their consciousness they understood this singular world and actually liked it. They had grasped the extreme certainties of mathematics and faith but in so doing they had accelerated the catastrophe: to this presumed stronghold they had attracted demons who fell on the new prey with gusto and devoured its world. With the fall of mathematics and faith, the rest of the world, too, would go soundlessly into decline.

The Europeans continued to hold to mathematics, even after they began to perceive mathematical equations and calculations as bizarre dramas, as evidence of the work of the same blind forces as those that cultivated logical deduction and flowed through machines, forces which drove an unceasing, monotonous division and unification. The Europeans were made nauseous by multiplication because now they perceived it as a diseased swelling, a proliferation anterior to any kind of sense and order, a growth which had arisen by the dull repetition of the same numbers and their resigned coalescence in the whole; they dreaded division because in it they saw disintegration, made more horrifying still by the unnatural disintegration of wholes into parts of equal size. Addition was yet worse, as it meant a progressive decline in new units, heralding the destruction of all divided shapes and the enthronement of One that is nothing, the victory of the monster of the Whole. Subtraction was the saddest of all: they saw in it the falling off of sick pieces, a kind of arithmetical leprosy, a crumbling that turned shapes into dust, that led down another path to nothingness. They performed calculations because they sought salvation in exactitude, but at the same time they were horrified to perceive mathematical operations as movements of some monstrous figure; instead of considering the result of a calculation, the Europeans saw the choreography of a loathsome dance, a dance similar to that performed by the treacherous machines.

Having been betrayed by mathematics they turned to the saints of their prayer books, but now they had the impression that the sounds of the prayers were made up of some dark material which was not of their God's creation and which had so little in common with Him it could not even be said to stand in opposition to Him; indeed, He was indifferent to it. It was just that in His words resided the murmur of the ancient melody, a melody that sounded in the emptiness before the Word, that hummed quietly in the first word and in which the meanings of words are still dissolved today. And pictures of the faces of saints were lost in the labyrinthine pleats of the drapes, became nothing more than pleats in some fabric undulating in the cosmic wind, gathering then opening out as if in a dream, submerged in a spider's web of fine cracks that absorbed and devoured them, then spewed out the face of an unknown god or devil.

The islanders liked the barely perceptible shapes made by the waves of the sea and the leaves as they moved in the wind, but the geometry of the town the foreigners had built presented them with no problems; the straight lines and right angles seemed to them like the parting of the same forces that draw and then erase white figures of foam on the sea and wake in the treetops a silvery surf. These forces created all shapes and all shapes exhaled them; the forces were the same, whether they played with elusive traces of smoke or drew a straight line and then broke it into a right angle. Through the eyes of the islanders the straight lines of the lower town were transformed into a dreamlike web, whose lines sounded like thin strings in a music of empty, apathetic or liberated time that was heading nowhere. And so a town that was soaked in dreams when it first came into being, now lost its last remnants of substantiality: it transformed from a dream to a dream. For the foreigners it became a tormentuous labyrinth of hot walls from which there was no escape, while the natives were able to settle in, take walks about the squares, and relax in the shade of the great colonnades and on the magnificent granite embankments with their statues of sphinxes and lions.

The native women submitted to the foreigners, but the foreigners acquired the habits and the gestures of the natives and their children spoke the natives' language better than their own. It seems that by the third generation, the conquerors had merged with the natives: they had forgotten their language, abandoned their books, machines and their god, and were listening to the murmur of the sea and the scratching of the sand, or watching shadows move across walls on hot afternoons. All that remained of the foreigners were certain features in the faces of the islanders—like the letters of a forgotten alphabet, the sense of which has been lost. Of the foreigner's language, a few roots remained, which the language of the natives absorbed and used in its games; they were good for prefixes and suffixes. The shapes of the instruments the conquerors brought to the island can still be seen today in the adornment of facades—in simplified, distorted and endlessly repeated form. And thus the conquerors disappeared. What remained of them was the lower town—their dream of home that had become a stifling labyrinth, overgrown with reeds and smothered in sand.

I believe that this breakdown in the thinking of the foreigners after years of torment, homesickness and anxiety brought with it a deep, unexpected joy, and that in its final phase the foreigners accelerated the process themselves. To their astonishment and delight, they began to understand that the labyrinth they had built for themselves and that had them in its grasp, was after all the home they had yearned for while at sea, that it was more of a home to them than the distant cities of Europe whose systems had been dissolved for them beyond all reconstruction in the winds of the tropics. Out of the town the foreigners had built as a memorial, the natives had fashioned a new town—a labyrinth-town—in which, so it proved, it was possible to live in contented tranquillity; it was at once Ithaca and the island of the Lotus Eaters. But in the birth of the new town the foreigners also played their part—by how they saw it, by how they responded to it in gesture, by the paths they pursued in it. Now they saw the same town as the natives did. For the foreigners, too, all shapes had the same importance; their feet, too, made of the town's geometric ground plan an intricate mandala of futility. They came to understand that the force echoed in the motions of machines and the procedures of logic and mathematics could be accepted and delighted in, that the cosmic ballet they had had such an abhorrence of, could be seen as a performance of endless fascination. I imagine them sitting on the patios of their palaces, just watching, filled with a joy growing like the weeds and shrubs produced by scattered seeds, like the sand that blew gently into their living spaces. I think they forgot all about Europe, but the cities of the north were transformed in the joyful dream of the moment, which floated among the hot walls and was just as much a part of this place as the roar of the sea. A golden age began with stains, rustlings and aimless journeys.

I understood them because I, too, got a taste on the island of the lotus of effervescent chaos. Perhaps this was not even chaos, but something beyond chaos, a space of calm, swirling forces from which shapes, images and some sense of order rose up before sinking back without regret or memory. I would say to Karael almost daily how much I was irritated by the indifference and laziness of the islanders, but still I let one ship after another sail away without me, until the time arrived when I realized that my own transformation had progressed so far that in a few weeks or days I would be unable to leave the island, ever. So return home I did, but I will be forever marked by my stay on the island. I feel the island present within me still like an incurable disease a traveller brings back from the tropics in his blood, like a stifled fever that silently marks every gesture and glance. And I know that forever more every shape I see will be lost in the repulsive yet delightful network of mazy, tangled lines; forever more words will be somewhat higher waves on the endless, unbroken surface of the rustlings.

## 7
## The hidden king

I have already mentioned that the king had his seat in the lower town. It is a problem to identify the islanders' political systems. The ruler of the island was appointed for an indefinite period by means of institutions which were something between elections, dreams, referenda, small talk and a proliferation of knocks. In the conversations the islanders carried on within the family and among close friends, they spoke of who might be king; some of those present at these conversations were then present at other conversations with other people, at which suitable candidates for the post of king were discussed. The opinions expressed here were formed in other conversations still, were influenced by others still, and flowed into others still. In this spillover names broached the surface of the conversation and then disappeared again; a name would sound in almost every utterance but shortly thereafter it was no longer spoken at all, except perhaps in a rapid whisper. Names were spoken loudly and then more quietly, unambiguously and in vague observations and woolly allusions; names would gather in clusters, then disperse. All this would happen without more than three or four people ever having met at any one time.

As I said, the names of the islanders were often subject to change. These changes of name made the electoral process still more complicated as it was often less than clear who was being spoken about. One could say that many of the names were introduced in error, though of course it was possible to find in the tangle of echoes an element of truth which would serve to distort the error, and in any case the islanders considered error a sound reason for the existence of the things it begot. As a consequence of such errors, after some time people began to speak of a candidate for the post of king as of a person who did not really exist. Not even this did the islanders find alarming.

Naturally people nominated as candidates took part in the conversations; to greater and lesser extents they expressed resistance to the idea. I do not believe that any islander was too keen on the prospect of entering kingly office. All this was spread by means of knocks, tale-telling and indirect reports, which distorted both purposely and unwittingly what really happened and what was really said. But the islanders understood this distortion not as a malfunction of the electoral mechanism, but as something which was part and parcel of the royal election process. If the changing flow of names in conversation played its part in the appointment of a king, so too did chance and fate. And an argument founded in a slip of the tongue had a power equal to that invested in a discussion of character and achievement.

It cannot be said that this series of conversations had any kind of end. But there were moments when the process reached a phase where the powers effective on it were temporarily in balance. Many of the various strands outlined within it came together in a single person, and for a short time the pressure applied by the persuaders and the resistance put up by the subjects of persuasion, fuelled by fatigue, argument, error and slips of the tongue, cancelled each other out.

If a king were to be enthroned, the phase at which a fragile balance obtained needed to be exploited; if the opportunity were missed—not an uncommon occurrence—the knots would begin to work themselves loose, before tangling themselves up in confusion, forming once again many centres. And it would be necessary to wait for a new balance to emerge, for the tips of the star-shaped scales, with their many arms and pans, to meet once more, however briefly, and indicate a name. The islander who gained the impression that it was he who stood at the centre of this temporary balance of forces, took himself off to the royal palace in the lower town, where he performed the king's office until new conversations formed in him the impression that his government had ended.

Reports of or conjecture on the ascension of a new ruler were also broadcast as a network of echoes, knocks and confusing mirror images, and thus it could happen that conversations on the election remained ongoing several weeks after a new ruler had been installed in the royal palace; conversely, the impression could establish itself that the election had reached its conclusion—while the conversation petered out, the royal palace remained unoccupied. It is no wonder that in these circumstances the islanders were never quite sure at any given time who their king was, or, indeed, whether the island had a king. And as the kings themselves never made much show of being kings (I believe they were always slightly embarrassed by it), and as generally speaking their stays in the royal palace were interspersed with stays elsewhere (some kings visited but once a week), it might happen that an islander had no idea that the king was someone close to him, perhaps even a family member. Indeed, it might be the case that a wife did not know that her husband had been ruler of the island for several years.

The islanders were supported in such ignorance by the fact that they had little sense of family. The bonds they took on were loose, they never held for very long, and it was not required that they join two members only. This is not to say that the islanders did not know love, although they did not always distinguish the body from the landscape, so that their love contained much of the space and the moment. This sense of being rooted in the landscape saturated moments of love with precious essences, but one of its consequences was that the flame of love never burned long or strong. Connected with this was the fact that islanders—male and female alike—never declared fidelity; they made no attempt to conceal from their partners relationships with other men and women. At a sepia banquet, for example—of which I shall speak more later—Karael was surprised by my look of distress at her withdrawing to the bedroom (which was separated by nothing more than the wall of water) with one of the guests. The thought of being faithful to me seemed to her eccentric, but so as not to cause me pain she never embraced anyone else in my presence as other women of the island tended to do in front of their partners.

In a certain sense the power of the king was absolute, but in another he was practically powerless. In reaching his decisions he sought no counsel, but as his decrees were broadcast by the same network of whispers and allusions that had brought about his election, it was quite natural for the directive generated by the network to have little in common with the king's original command. The decrees of the ruler were put into circulation by the friends and relatives who visited him in the royal palace or in whom he confided when he was living in his own house. It was quite common that a decree took on a meaning which was the opposite of the one intended, as the islanders expressed negation by placing the particle *ul* before a word, something which was easily missed amid the background noise of the island; or it was heard in places where it had not been spoken. Hence the meaning could change many times in the course of one conversation, and if there was an even number of changes, the declaration or directive comprised the same words as those spoken by the king.

I had the impression that this strange sameness—which was dependent on an even or odd number of mistakes and mediated by many mishearings caused by the murmur of walls of water and the roar of the sea—actually set the utterances that finally reached me still further from the originals than would have been the case with a deliberate lie or a purposeful misrepresentation, as these might be pervaded with the (perhaps false) hope that the king's original meaning could be hunted down, while this network of haphazard, apathetic changes and shifts from affirmation to negation showed that the identity of the king's words and how they were differed from, was not important.

The network of falsehood also drew in the original utterance, which itself had arisen through mishearing and error. There was nothing one could do but listen in silence to words born out of mishearings and expiring in the murmur of the water and the wind, and, after the words had died away, listen to the murmur itself while dreaming a dream about a king in whose court one could find asylum, a dream which was so intoxicating because it could never become reality.

In the murmurs it was of course possible to hear all kinds of things, not least because the islanders spoke so quietly. Just as at dusk in the lower town crouching, elongated, emaciated, melting, delicate, fracturing figures would flit about in the cracks and stains of the walls, it was not unusual for the manifold murmurs to beget phrases which no one had uttered—known to the islanders as "the speech of the water"; in this way every conversation was a weave of real utterances whose wording was transformed by the rustlings and murmuring of the island and hallucination-like utterances made by the water or the wind, out of which often bad words and dark images would emerge. This was how words never uttered by the king could enter a conversation as a king's ruling. Whether or not this ruling had its origins in the words actually spoken by the king was of no great importance, as generally these were changed so radically that the outpourings of the speech of the water may have been closer to the king's intentions (at least to those of which he himself was not yet apprised).

These changes to the rulings of the king did not, of course, come to an end by the forming in conversation of some kind of final version. Rulings continued to change for as long as they were circulated in the conversation network, until they dissolved and died. Nor was it possible to divide this long series of changes into a phase of formation and a phase of disintegration; laws came into being, reached maturity and began to decompose in a single act. I could not reconcile myself to the fact of the islanders' unconcern that a ruling would enter a neighbour's house in a form different from—or, indeed, opposite to—the one in which it entered their own; it enraged me that they felt no need to investigate which of the versions was the true one, or at least which corresponded most closely to the words of the king; I found it astonishing that they did not attempt to get the two versions somehow to agree. All this might give the impression that the islanders' attitude to laws was a relaxed one and that they were not much concerned with upholding them. But this was not so: the islanders needed laws and had a highly developed sense for them. For the islanders there was nothing arbitrary about the wording of a law, its interpretation and the manner in which it was discharged. They were conscientious and meticulous in their attempts to interpret a law correctly, although this correctness was the correctness of a particular phase of the law's transformation; not only was there nothing in it to rule out the emergence in a later phase of a law of completely different character, it actually demanded this.

# 8
# In the royal palace

From all this it is easy to conclude why it mattered so little whether the royal palace, the seat of the ruler, was occupied or left empty. Rulings and laws were always generated in conversation, regardless of whether their origins were in the words of the king or the roar of the sea. In such circumstances the institution of king seemed to me to a great extent pointless. I wondered why it was that the islanders had not got rid of it long ago. Conservatism was not the reason, to be sure: the islanders were no respecters of history and tradition. It was not that they disliked the past, but for them it was nothing more than a dreamlike area of the present, populated with interesting, blurry ghosts. To begin with I thought the institution of king might be an expression of the islanders' subconscious desire for some kind of centrepoint and meaning, whose ever-beating pulse would underpin their love of chaos. But once I got to know the islanders better, I knew I was mistaken in this: I realized that the islanders' resistance to a fixed order was underpinned by a yet firmer resistance to order and an old, unassuageable distaste for meaning.

The real reason for the islanders' keeping the institution of king was most likely the sense it gave them that the absence of a centre would itself, if secure and neither disputed nor threatened, become a centre of a kind. Although for the creation of rulings and laws the conversation had no need of a king, if the only ruler was the hum of conversation, over time the illusion might spread that this state was a mere preparation for the establishment of some kind of centre and beginning, that the absence of a king was in fact a wait for a king. But because there already was a centre, because a king had his seat in a great palace in the lower town, the suggestion was made that this centre could exist as nothing other than an empty place in which every beginning was dissolved; as there was a king there already, it was evident that no one was waiting for the arrival of a king to fill the void, that the king could exist only as this veiled, dwindling figure and his laws only as the speech of dreams, phantom words quivering on the bottom of an echo, in the chatter of water; it was clear that there was nothing to hope for and nothing to fear.

When I talked of the island's monarchy in Prague, some of my listeners understood this order of government—in which it was possible to make contact with an unknown ruler only by means of a network of illusory echoes which knew no end—as the accomplishment of a Kafkaesque Atlantic vision. I tried to explain to them that the way things operated on the island was diametrically opposed to the world of Kafka. When I described to Karael the plot of *The Castle*, she was completely incapable of grasping it. On the one hand she considered the secrecy of the ruler as something altogether banal, on the other as something pleasing that was part and parcel of the good functioning of a state and the well-being of its people; with amazement she asked me why the land surveyor squandered so much energy on attempting to change this common, desirable state of affairs—wasn't the real, inaccessible Count Westwest better than the phantom in K.'s head, better than a bunch of village gossip?

I remember us talking about *The Castle* when we were having a picnic on the rocky headland by the lower town. We were sitting above the sea on a hot, fragrant rock; I was looking down on the town's first houses, into the empty, shadowy rooms whose windows were only two or three metres distant from the stony incline; I was looking at the wide boulevard, how it ended nonsensically at the foot of the rock, how it led somnambulistically in a single direction across the whole town until in the distance of the far side it sunk itself into the sand dunes. In the meantime I told Karael about the wanderings of the land surveyor in the snow-covered village. And I thought about how I could answer Karael's objections. By this time I had reached a certain understanding of the nature of the islanders, so I knew that there was no point in talking of a desire to hear the original word of law. So I said that at the very least K. was spurred on in his efforts by the ambition to perform the work of a land surveyor in the village. But Karael was surprised that he should think the work of the surveyor so much better than the work he was given, that of the school janitor.

I said to her, "Fine, I've been on the island long enough now to understand the point you're making, that a king's ruling is something created in conversation, that we need take no interest in the words the king actually pronounces. I also understand that this need not be important to the king himself, that he, too, finds his true rulings in words born out of the echoes of his words and the whisperings of the water and the wind. But this changes nothing in the fact that down there in the royal palace there lives—sometimes, at least—a real person whom you cannot identify. Perhaps the main reason for my wish to meet the ruler is curiosity, but I would say that curiosity is not the worst of all reasons on which to base a desire."

Laughing, Karael asked, "Would you like to pay a visit to the king today?"

"What nonsense is this you're uttering?" I was astonished. The island's king seemed to me such a vague and distant notion that it had never crossed my mind I might get to meet him.

"Once we finish eating, let us head to the palace."

Although I was baffled I swallowed quickly my portion of shell wrap (you will read more about this in the chapter on the island's cuisine) and waited impatiently while Karael finished eating. Did she have some kind of special pass that would get us into the palace? I knew that at that time no one was altogether sure who the king was; indeed, I had heard conjecture from a variety of sources on the ruler's identity. How could we possibly gain such easy access to a figure of such mystery? When Karael at last finished eating, we ran down the track which threaded its way through the rock of the bluff, like a continuation in parody of the broad, empty boulevards which passed through the town. Before long we were in the street where the royal palace was; the entirety of one side of the street was occupied by the palace's facade, which now was bathed in shadow.

The palace looked onto the street through a uniform row of high windows, which—in common with all windows in the lower town—had no glass. We walked the length of the building's seemingly unending front. It was as though there was a noiseless conveyor belt bringing the windows on the far side of the palace's empty rooms to the windows at the near side, filling them with the clear seascape and the glaring blue of the sky. It took us quite a long time to reach the arched entrance. Here a cold wind was blowing. We mounted a stone staircase to the first floor, where we passed a series of identical rooms, all without furniture, all with drifts of sand in their corners, all piled high with old papers from the distant past, when reports were still submitted to the king in writing and the royal commands were also issued thus. The dust was swirling in sloping columns of sunlight.

I asked Karael if she had ever been in the palace before.

"No," she said, "But I still hope we'll be able to find the king."

As we walked on and breathed the smell of old, cracked wooden floors, and the remains of faded paintings appeared on the walls like phantoms, she explained to me that anyone could enter the palace, it was just that no one chose to do so because no one was particularly interested in the king. It was true that at that time there was a lot of talk in the upper town about who was king, but the fact the question of the king's identity was an interesting topic of conversation did not mean that it awoke in people the desire to take a look at the royal palace, particularly when the days were as hot as this.

"It may be that the king is not here today," she told me. "But you can come here on your own whenever you feel it."

But I was in luck. By the window of one of the rooms there was a heavy desk that had almost certainly come to the island on a ship, and sitting at this with her back to us, looking out to sea, deep in thought, was a young woman. When she heard our footsteps the woman turned round and smiled at us. I smiled back and Karael waved. I had the impression the girl was pleased to see us; ruling the island must have been agonizingly boring, and I believe she would have been happy to invite us into the room but was too shy to do so. When in the next room I asked Karael if she had known that her friend was queen, she told me she had suspected so.

The very next day I met the queen in the upper town, and I spoke to her on several occasions after that, but I never mentioned our encounter at the palace. It seemed to me it would have been tactless to do so; I thought I read a certain embarrassment in her expression. I realized that the position of king of the island was the most worthless, the least substantial, the most powerless position of all, as it was furthest removed from the final wording of the law.

The king's only privilege was the opportunity granted him to spend his days walking through a long series of rooms scented by the sun, looking at the sea and the white boats entering and departing the harbour. I believe that the queen was glad we failed to mention her position. Although the person who was king enjoyed respect on the island, this respect was mixed with pity and—I believe—a certain contempt.

## 9
## Words and rustlings

The speech of the islanders was one of the things I liked most about the island. Before I was able to understand the language, I used to enjoy listening to the fluent stream of sounds from which all sharp edges had been smoothed, in which all impacts had been softened, how they mixed peacefully with the chatter of the sea and the palm leaves on the shore and the gentle trickling and dripping of water in the upper town. The chatterings and rustlings of the island were tenderly accepting of the sounds. When a word sounded, it was never as it is with us in the north; in our own towns and countries a sound suddenly and without portent penetrates an empty silence, where nothing is waiting for it and where it has nothing to catch hold of, or else it sinks itself into a strange, hostile noise, which it must then drown out and suppress. On the island, words tended to emerge in crystallized form on the surface of rustles, sounding as if they had long been in preparation at their core. The finished word-crystal seemed to be of the same fabric as the other sounds, and there was no fundamental difference between what they had to impart and what the words were saying.

All this might give the impression that the speaker of the language was indifferent to his listener, that speech was incapable of genuine dialogue. But things were more complicated than that. It is true that I often had the feeling the islanders spoke more for themselves than for others, that they tended to listen more to the sounds around them than to what their conversation partner was saying. But the country and the moment gave up to them so many sweet juices, which gathered and solidified in words; by their tantalizing appeals and magical suggestions again and again these drew the speaker away from the realm of ready-made, already-dying thoughts, so that sounds embedded in the landscape ultimately granted the listener more than he gleans from conversations in our part of the world, where all we attend to is the words of the other, severed from their roots and drying out, while we remain indifferent to and indeed erase all other sounds. And in this way we are so completely taken in by the childish exchange of ready-made thoughts and dried-out words that we would fail to notice—were it to resound right next to us—the most wonderful piece of music that held in its notes the germs of magical answers to our questions and possessed the ability to tell us what angels and demons thought of our affairs. The islanders were convinced that such a marvellous musical composition, in which fluttered sources of questions which were also germs of answers, resounded around us all the time; at any given moment in a conversation they were prepared to submit themselves to this surface of clear sounds.

And so, although I often had the feeling that the islander with whom I was in conversation was not really listening to me, curiously enough I learned to find in words born out of the whispers of places and moments more answers to my questions than my discussions in the north tended to grant me. Perhaps the islanders did not listen to the words of the other person directly; they did not concern themselves with his thoughts in their final state, rather persisting in turning their attention outward, to the murmuring sounds—and also the shapes—of the country in which the dialogue was taking place. In these murmurs and shapes the words and thoughts of the other re-appeared, transformed. The sounds, lines and colours of the landscape undermined thought. Words and thoughts—when they came into contact with the music of the landscape and the magical script of rough shapes still free of the prison of things—began to disintegrate, to release old rhythms that had been present at their birth; movements unfurled whose unrest contained the beginning of a question, whose mysterious gravity held the germ of an answer.

And because speech was of the same matter as the other sounds of the island, the meanings carried by words were merely an appeal issued by the material of sounds. Speech was a dream of noises, and from these noises it did not move very far. The islanders knew that the murmurs were really composed of hundreds, perhaps thousands of utterances made simultaneously, that they were generated by the unfolding of an infinite number of stories all told at the same time. They were aware that a murmur was a wise, blissful richness which held words in contempt and shut itself off from them, but they felt, too, that every murmur contained an urgent longing for the liberation of at least one of the story-lines of its blend, that the thread of one plot at least should be unravelled from its fabric. This is why the islanders listened in silence to the sounds of the island, and this is why they spoke.

Another consequence of this homogeneity of speech and sounds of the island was that there existed on the island no sound which did not communicate something in some way akin to speech. The sounds of the island were germs of speech or traces left by it, reverberations of words which were not only the decline and disappearance of meaning but also its liberation and cleansing, as it is when in a broken, decaying, no-longer-usable thing a hidden scent is aroused that expresses the truth of that thing's existence. For this reason there was no silence on the island. After some time, I, too, learned to perceive that which I had taken for silence as an open country of subtle sounds, as speech, as the whisperings of a faceless god.

And for this reason it seemed to me that conversations on the island had no beginning and no end, and that they contained no pauses. A dialogue was the continuation of noises and murmurs, weaving its somewhat darker thread into their fabric; and moments when the communication desisted were just moments when this thread was lost without any split or break appearing in the tissue. Even at those moments when the quietest sounds were subsiding, I felt that the fabric was continuing to unravel; now it was completely white, although it was still of the same smooth, unbroken material. For a time the words dissolved into the murmur, giving up their meanings to it and satiating it by them, perishing blissfully in the murmur and allowing their silent current to crystallize into new words. The islanders did not speak to fill the silence, as they knew no silence; they spoke because in the river of rustles they discovered the germs of words, utterances and images, because in the sounds around them they discovered the thoughts most inherent to them—thoughts which before then they had not known.

But I never thought that the islanders had discovered some kind of paradisiacal state of language. They were so afraid of losing the live source of thought that they never removed themselves very far from it; the vaults of their thoughts were not characterized by courage, the desperation of blind fumbling and the anguish of work; they resounded with sounds from the depths and shone with the lustre of life, but even so I could not help holding them a little in contempt. It is necessary first to lose the music of beginnings before it can return as a dreamlike echo in the architecture of thought. Although the language of the islanders was beautiful, it was a beauty which made weary.

The silence that was lost on the island never returned to me, even after I returned north. The ability to perceive an unbroken, endless fabric of sound stayed with me and became both a source of torment and a well that nurtured a strange happiness. During the day there are so many images woven into the fabric that absorb my attention, that I am hardly aware of the feel of its material; but at night when I am unable to sleep I feel it pass over my face, over my whole body in a slow, gliding movement. Just for a moment I would like to extricate myself from it, to enter the space beyond it, a space unknown to me; I have a desperate longing for silence. But in the material there is no opening, no chink, and now at night there are no pictures against it that might draw my attention away from the fabric; all there is here is a scattering of small, featureless and vague shapes that remind me of the patterns on the duvet cover. At night I appreciate how everything mutters and whispers, how the things of the world rustle, giving sound to the flow of time; I appreciate that all sounds, of the day and of the night, bear the same monotonous, nonsensical message.

But sometimes the disagreeable sense that I am unable to tear through the fabric of sounds in which I am wrapped like a mummy, is transformed to delight; then it seems to me that the murmur of being is the most beautiful music one could ever hear and I feel joy and gratitude that it is given to me to listen to such a concert. Of course, what I hear is no longer the beautiful sounds of the island, the call of the waves and the babbling of springs falling from rocks; now in the dark I hear the sounds of the rain, the trams and cars in the distance, the roar of an aeroplane, and also the sounds of my building at night, its wheezes and groans. But another thing I learned on the island was that the character of sounds is not so important: all sounds are parts of a single musical composition.

## 10
## The panopticon of grammar

The language of the islanders overflowed with an unbelievable quantity of prefixes and suffixes and these encased the roots of words front and back, denoting peculiar features of reality which to begin with I completely failed to grasp, or at least I did not understand why such trivialities were considered important enough to merit their own forms in the language. For example, there was a suffix which described how the thing indicated by the root of a word gave off a heavy scent of decay; a further suffix could be stuck onto this to make it clear that although the surface of a thing was now taut, it would soon begin to slacken; and a prefix might be attached to the front of a root form to communicate that the thing was submerged in shadow, and that this shadow was of either a mauve or a greenish colour.

In this way, the root of a word was smothered by prefixes and suffixes so that it gave the appearance of a mere appendage, while the thing itself disappeared beneath all the designations and determinations, all the shadows, lights, vibrations and rhythms, odours and degrees of tension and laxity communicated by the prefixes and suffixes. The prefixes and suffixes that came together in a particular word carried so much determination that it might seem that this in itself was enough for the designation of a thing and that the root of the word was no longer necessary. The determination indicated by the root of the word presented itself as a feature at once inessential and dispensable; and it was true that one's failure in conversation to catch the root of a word was of no great consequence. (The roots of words were about as important for the island's lexicon as the king was for its political organization.)

I believe that the language of the islanders was in a phase of transition, that it was heading towards a state where the roots of its words would disappear altogether and words would be formed only from clusters of prefixes and suffixes that would collide in the middle of words, although perhaps a hyphen or a weak vowel would serve as a kind of memorial to the now-extinct root. I do not think, however, that this tendency to eradicate its roots reigned over the history of the island's language as a whole. Not only things themselves were subject to constant change on the island, but the manner of these changes was also constantly evolving. It is quite likely that once their language has reached the stage at which words are formed of nothing more than clusters of prefixes and suffixes, other longings and dreams will be awakened within the islanders, and perhaps the long-changing edifice of prefixes and suffixes will collapse, to be replaced by short, concise words to which it will be impossible to attach any prefix or suffix, as anything these could possibly indicate will already be contained in the words.

And as if all this were not enough to deal with, at the end of the series of suffixes there sprouted bunches of case endings. To this day I remain unsure of quite how many cases the island's language had. I had the impression that the case system was constantly swelling; I counted seventeen cases, but after I had been on the island a year I discovered another, as if an inflexion had suddenly put out new shoots. I do not know whether an old, little-used grammatical form had risen back to the surface or whether someone had invented a new case because he had needed it or simply liked it. But other cases were dying off, so it seemed there was no danger that the case system would proliferate so as to contain an immeasurable quantity of endings.

Among the connections established by the island's cases, those that seem to us most important (and that find expression in our own cases) were missing. The case endings of the island's language expressed relations which seemed to me (at the time I was learning the language) wholly bizarre. For example, one of the cases was only used for nouns referring to things that were the subject of fear connected with the vague and probably not altogether pure intentions of a close relative; another was used for nouns referring to things placed on a soft surface which sagged slightly under the weight of the subject, forming on the surface a star shape of shallow pleats. Things were not much better with conjugation. Verb endings did not express which person the action concerned, nor indeed the number of actors. The ending *-vi*, for example, determined that the act signified by the verb occurred on a sandy seashore, while the ending *-ark* made it clear that the action took place on the surface of a cold mirror; if the ending *-ut* was attached to the verb, this signified that the action was somehow connected with green and red precious stones. Verb endings might also be linked together: for example, the word *izarkut* meant that it was visible in a mirror how something in which precious stones were sparkling was slowly submerged in water. A strange world emerged out of this declension and conjugation, a network of peculiar relations and roles which was antecedent to logic.

What irritated me most about the island's extraordinary grammar was not that it concerned itself with unimportant features and relations of reality and created its forms based on the model they provided. The island's lunatic grammar made me anxious more because of what seemed to me the grimace it gave the face of reality, modelling existence as a series of bizarre statues by pouring the substance of reality—admittedly diaphanous—into such peculiar moulds. One couldn't really say that their grammar twisted reality, as it looked at reality in embryonic form: it penetrated to the germs of reality and adapted them to its own obscure dreams. The island's grammar infected the sight, sound, and gesture through which reality comes to us, causing that reality to be composed exclusively of its bizarre and practically endless catalogue of prefixes, suffixes, and endings, its peculiar rhythms, beats, tensions, breaths, gleams, moving shadows, and its attention to whatever goes on inside things or on their surface, for which we do not even have a name.

However, and strangest of all, after a while on the island I began to find its grammar and the reality it created quite natural. This is one of the sicknesses I brought back from the island, of which, it seems, I shall never be cured. As I listen to Czech, now, I sometimes catch myself needing to translate it into the language of the island so that I can understand; and it seems to me that Czech, in common with all other European languages, has on the one hand very little to say about reality, and, on the other hand, contains much that is superfluous. When I hear someone say "They're on their way," and I ask myself unhappily why the form of the verb must communicate that more than one person is coming when this detail is not of the least interest to me and in any case will soon be made manifest, I am disturbed that we can't simply attach an ending to the verb, *-rao* for instance, making clear that this is an action heightening our impatience while holding in check and subduing a vague fear of the goal that will soon be accomplished. This is the sort of thing that really interests me about whomever is on their way; this is the sort of thing that's worth taking the time to express, unlike the banal detail that there happens to be more than one of them.

And so Czech and the language of the island grow together in my head; the cases of the island grow like obstinate weeds between the seven cases of Czech, and when I'm alone my thoughts are in this hybrid language—just as incomprehensible to a Czech as it would be to an islander. It happens once in a while that I am in a shop, standing in line at the checkout, lost in thought; that I fail to notice that I've reached the front of the line; that the checkout girl tries to get my attention; that I reply in my own language. By the way she looks at me I know she thinks I'm crazy, and I feel embarrassed; I pretend to have mispronounced my intention, or I make out that I'm a foreigner and adopt an accent. Having decided to compose this report on the island, I even considered, initially, writing it in my private language. Certainly no one would read such a book, and certainly too no one would want to publish it, but I dreamed of publishing it myself, of establishing my own press through which I would publish only novels of my own, written in my own language; who knows, perhaps one day someone would buy one of them and set about deciphering its text; on the basis of this perhaps he would then invent a language of his own with marvellous new cases and grammatical categories, in which—let's say—there will be a verb ending indicating that in the action thus described, a burning energy full of a magnificent malice is gradually exhausting itself, and that this exhaustion evokes relief, nostalgia, and a kind of spine-tingling music.

## 11
## The adventure of letters

At the same time, I got to know the islanders' script from their *Book* (of which I have much to tell in the chapters to come). I had the impression that it was a mixture of fragments from various other scripts. There was a group of characters that gave the appearance of small, schematic pictures of objects, animals, people, and figures; then there were the letters which bore no similarity to objects or living forms, and these could be divided into several groups, including one of simple signs made up of two or three straight lines, another of complicated tangles of wriggling curves that reminded one of a bird's nest, and another of letters composed of clusters drawn from many barely ascertainable points that increased in density before becoming looser again. My first impression was that the creator of the islanders' script had composed it in haste; he had borrowed letters hurriedly from many sources without in any way attempting to integrate them into the whole, and afterwards this ill-assorted mix endured by the simple force of habit.

Yet I found this explanation unsatisfactory, and as questions pertaining to the script's strange diversity continued to tantalize me, I began to pay visits to the royal palace in the hope of discovering in its old papers something about the script's history. I remember the afternoons I spent seated on the floor of the one of the empty chambers, digging out old documents from under the hot sand and reading them through. No matter where I sat, the crumbling facade of the uninhabited building was always visible in the windows on one side of the room, while the windows on the other side were filled with the splendid blue of the sky; whenever

I stood up, the sparkling, azure canopy of the sea was raised to half the height of the windows, as though drawn up by some miraculous pulley. In a distant room I could hear the steps of the queen as she paced, deep in thought; sometimes I would spot her standing in the empty frame of the door, one of dozens of empty frames that playful perspective made into a grooved ornament, a row of characters in the shape of the letter *pi*, each enclosed in the next, each smaller than the last. Sometimes the siren of a ship sounded in the harbour.

These quiet afternoons taught me that the chaotic heterogeneity in the letters was not brought about by habit and inertia; indeed, there was a restlessness in the script that caused its constant transformation. It was as if it were running away from itself while trying to catch up with itself; it seemed to me that it dreamed of a long-lost past or a magnificent future, of a script ages old or else an idealized one yet to come, full of perfect, resplendent letters, seeking these in endless transformation, following a great variety of mysterious clues, setting out in many different directions at once, but in the end always failing in its efforts.

Even after this it was a long time before I was in a position to appreciate the true nature of the island's script. Having abandoned the hypothesis that symbols from a variety of systems had been stitched together and the whole then maintained by inertia, there was a time—after I succeeded in uncovering the pictograms from which most of the island's letters were derived—I supposed I had indeed discovered the script's origin; how great my surprise, then, when, delving deeper in the drifts of sand in the royal palace, I discovered some documents written in a script older still! I learned that what I had assumed to be an early pictographic script had itself originated in the interpretation of puzzling symbols which represented absolutely nothing.

It seemed that changes washed over the script in waves, and that these waves had no single direction. Apparently the pictographic script had changed many times to form more abstract symbols—by the simplification of the figures into outlines in which it was no longer possible to read the model, or else by the in-growth of tangles of lines—and many times, too, the abstract symbols turned back into pictures, once their outlines began to live and grow, the tangles of lines yielding the figures of humans and demons, animals, birds, and monsters, which till then had been present only in the shapes of the letters as distant dreams or reflected reflections—as memory and suggestion. It seemed to me that the present-day letters of the island were on the cusp of just such a transformation into a pictographic script: a few of the characters had already taken on the form of a bird or an animal. Though the majority had yet to begin forming pictures, I saw shapes trembling in the letters, preparing to break through: nascent, hitherto veiled faces of strange creatures whose cunning eyes blinked or beaks obtruded impatiently from their tangles of lines; unsettling, to say the least. I soon realized that *all* the letters were exuding the same sort of anxiety—as if they contained a secret message, unknown but foreshadowed; every text is a palimpsest, every letter a secret cipher.

The transformation of pictures into abstract symbols and abstract symbols into pictures wasn't the only way in which the script developed, however; evidently there were times, for example, when their lines frayed into ever-thinner threads, or when the lines ran into one another, forming square, solid shapes, or when the lines stretched out like the stalks of climbing plants and had to bend their tips into spirals or arch into sine curves so that they could fit into the spaces between the lines. Then there were times when the letters, pictorial and abstract both, crumbled into ever-smaller pieces until they became cloudlets of ink dust; the documents of these eras look like pictures of a white sky studded with black constellations. There were times too when the letters, pictorial and abstract both, became so complicated that it would take several hours to write just one of them; so, of course, very little was written, although it doesn't seem that anyone on the island was too concerned by this. Indeed, I believe the writer was actually pleased if, on his way across the line, he struck upon such a letter; he could then take a break from his narrative and immerse himself joyfully in the writing of a single character.

Nor was it possible to read this kind of laboriously written script in a single, fleeting glance; it was necessary to go through it collecting distinguishing features—and there were a great many of these, hidden in its knotty network of lines. (It might be that two letters had twenty-nine distinguishing features in common, differing only in the thirtieth.) Hence, a reader could wade around in the bliss of a single letter, and the reading of a single letter of this labyrinthine script might take him one whole afternoon. It rarely happened, in the process, that the reader attained the meaning of the word of which this letter was a part, but he was certainly not concerned by this: his compensation was his encounter with the meaning of a single letter—which always far surpasses the reference point of speech, and its mysterious capacity for communication.

Having decided to write this book, I considered how it should look. For a time I wondered whether it might not be best to produce a book which, instead of a narrative *about* the island, was made up of nothing more than a few of these complicated letters, thus allowing readers to read into it what they would. To the objection that my readers wouldn't know the sounds to which the letters refer, the islanders' riposte would surely be, "All the better!"

Of course, the island's script developed through its interaction with other scripts as well. Thanks to its precious stones, the island always had contact with the outside world. Sometimes I even think I see traces of the island's viewpoint and manner of thinking in

European culture—in Novalis's meditations on shapes that generate sounds in wood shavings, for example, or in the origins of abstract painting, or in the letter-pictures of Klee. It's far more difficult, on the other hand, to find manifestations of the spirit of Europe on the island. Although the islanders have always been very accepting of everything, in the end things always turn out the same way, as they did with the language, science, and religion of their erstwhile conquerors from Europe: all of these borrowings were perfectly absorbed into the rhythms of the island and thus transformed into everyday parts of island life, indistinguishable from any other. Nevertheless, it is still possible to find deposits in the island's script that indicate several old encounters with the Latin alphabet, each of which led to the siphoning off of some of its letters. Marooned among the native letters, these orphaned Latin characters experienced a bizarre metamorphosis: they expanded, they hurled out offshoots in all directions, slowly revealing images of tigers, birds, and fantastical trees. (Was this not, in fact, a return to their mystical origins? A partial revelation of their enduring, hidden power?) Whenever the script of the island swallowed up foreign letters in this way, it would transform them so perfectly in the course of its digestion—into the aforementioned animals, or tangles of lines, or geometric shapes—that on second encounter they were unrecognizable. And it would accept the same letter again and again, and so seem to have grown a new symbol with a distant similarity to the existing one, when in fact what had happened is that the same alien character had been swallowed up by itself, by its own rampant form, which it had initially acquired after first being disfigured by the island's contagion . . .

But, none of these transformations could explain the island's script's most striking feature: the strange lack of unity among the characters. This disunity arose as a consequence of the fact that the restless tangle of forces urging the letters to undergo their continuous metamorphoses was not distributed equally across all letters; for example, the force that impelled the transformation of letters into thin, frayed, and randomly twisted threads might strike violently in one place—within a single letter or a group of letters—and would pick at and crumple its target quite furiously, without noticing the fact that at the same moment, in another part of the text, a force was at play which was beating the letters into solid pegs, while, simultaneously, in yet another section, the letters had become translucent and were transforming into dull smears (but this force had already almost burned itself out), and then, finally, in yet another place, a force thus far unidentified seemed to be staking a claim for symmetrical ornamentation. At any given moment a letter was tugged at by a variety of forces at various stages of development; some of these were tentative, hesitant, just starting out, some were now at the height of their strength, while others were almost entirely spent. And where these forces abutted each other, they collided, made alliances, applied indirect influence, held themselves back, and gathered their strength.

And then it seems there was a long period when all such forces were asleep and the island's script was frozen, after which came a new awakening and a time of even wilder transformation. Although in the days when I was on the island, a tendency towards a pictographic script was predominant, one could see many other tendencies dormant under the surface of their texts—some on the wane, some just being born. The islanders also had a kind of literature, of course, not least their *Book* (which I will get to presently, I trust), but I sometimes think that the story of the island's script makes up a more interesting narrative than all the stories contained in their literary works.

## 12
## The café on Rue des Beaux-Arts

The islanders' letters were so restless that from time to time they produced a longing to pass out of the territory in which script is enclosed; indeed, they began to doubt where the border between script and non-script lay. And so it occurred that the script passed through stages in which it was impossible to say for sure whether its figures were still letters to be read or whether they should be looked at as pictures. And there were other times when the script cast into doubt a border more remote still, that which exists between symbol and object. The letters thought of their depth and accentuated this; they transformed themselves into three-dimensional forms that retained traces of the old life of the letter, but at the same time they were objects in which were born relations to places, to other objects and to certain purposes—which to begin with only glimmered through, but which later gradually established themselves and grew with their hosts. And in echoing this movement another movement was awakened; in the world of objects—in stones, in trees, in machines, in bodies—the germ of an ability to be a letter announced itself. This ability, which until now had kept its peace within, suddenly generated avenues of text, strange sentences which oddly enough were not entirely incomprehensible.

I had occasionally encountered in the cultures of Europe and Asia this fuzziness on the borders between letters and pictures, but the growing together of letters and objects is something known perhaps only to the inhabitants of the nameless island. I have heard only once of a similar fusion of letters and pictures in Europe, and this came in a story whose truth I have never been able to verify. It happened several years after my return from the island, at the Czech Centre in Paris's Rue Bonaparte. I was present at the opening of an exhibition of the work of Josef Váchal, where I met a man of about sixty who came from Prague but had obviously lived for many years in Paris. We struck up a conversation at the buffet; it turned out that he was interested in Váchal's wonderful typography. We went on to speak of the letter-pictures of Klee and Michaux and I was reminded of the script of the island. I mentioned that its letters occasionally release a yearning to transform themselves into objects. He considered this information before telling me that a friend of his in Paris, who had also been born in Prague, had experienced two incidents—one in his homeland and the other in Paris, each by different means—in which letters and pictures were in fusion. This was of considerable interest to me and I asked him to tell me about it. He said that it was a story long in the telling, and he invited me to accompany him to a small café that was just around the corner in Rue des Beaux-Arts.

Once the waiter had brought us our coffee, my new acquaintance began to tell me the story of his Parisian friend. Naturally my first thought was that he was employing the banal tactic of talking of himself in the guise of another, but it may have been so that—as in the famous Jewish joke about trains—he was speaking of someone else so I would believe he was speaking of himself while all the time he was speaking of a third person. Completing his studies in the mid-Sixties at Prague's Faculty of Arts, the hero of the story began to work as a junior lecturer in the Department of Aesthetics. The narrator did not tell me his name, but let us call him Baumgarten. He began to write a book, because this was expected of a young academic. He chose its title somewhat at random; let us say it was "The Beauty of Nature in the History of Art and Aesthetics," "Art and

Society," "The History of the Golden Ratio" or "Kant and Schiller." By staying on at the university as a teacher after completion of his studies, above all he was able to prolong the life without roots of his student years, a life composed of many flaming and fading encounters with people, things, places and ideas. His world was restless, constantly entangling itself in and extricating itself from a web of academic, amicable, social and erotic ties, which transformed themselves from one to another and then evaporated.

After the purges of the Sixties they fired him from the university. But he did not end up as a boiler-man or a porter. He sat in the small offices of scientific institutes, in the light of flickering bulbs whose hum was a cheerless music that always came back to him when he remembered those years; he compiled biographies, wrote précis of papers and translated articles in periodicals, all of which they set down for him on the edge of his desk. The weave of his world, with its ongoing attachment to any situation, disintegrated, leaving behind it nothing but emptiness.

He attempted to fill this emptiness by continuing to work on his book, even though he knew that no one would publish it. He was surprised to discover that his work had embarked on a strange transformation. Now, in the theories on aesthetics which occupied his mind, no matter whether these took beauty to be the expression of an idea, life or formal ties, he saw remnant traces of an encounter with a terrible incident of some kind. Perhaps this was because he was having to learn to live with his new emptiness, that this woke in him an appreciation of slow motions, unnoticed rhythms and slight eddies. He saw in thoughts and gestures as well as in objects a trembling that until now he had never noticed. It was difficult to determine what this meant—not because the trembling resisted expression but because the concepts supposed to capture it stirred related, perhaps even identical vibrations, so that instead of performing the work accorded them, the concepts vibrated along with their subjects in a drunken round dance. Perhaps what was moving was some kind of larvae of being, the blind squirming, lashing out, twisting of being before the birth of something recognized, something named in the world, before the emergence of a thing; or else this was the convulsive twitching of nascent, crude time as it flowed into the body of things as the luminous fuel of their peregrinations across the landscapes of the world. These motions were rather repulsive to him; he felt himself to be looking into an aquarium dark and murky with slime, although there were also times when there was a radiant glow. Whether his feeling was one of disgust or delight, at any given moment these events were interesting to watch; Baumgarten told himself that this was not the worst amusement this wretched time could have found for him.

It seemed to him that the beauty he had read so many theories about, was nothing but this glow, a glow that was born in the midst of revulsion without ever quite accepting into itself that art was an endless, ever-transforming hymn about the soft, revolting germs of reality, an ode composed to themselves by the nameless white larvae of being. Sitting in his corner of the office he sometimes imagined himself presenting his superiors with an extract from the book he was writing and the expressions they would assume, and this fancy pulled his mouth into a grimace of amusement, which itself was a source of confusion among his colleagues.

Perhaps, he thought, many artists and thinkers have come across these motions, but all took fright at them, seizing instead on an understanding of beauty as expressed by an order (in a way this is simple to achieve: in the proximity of beauty it is always possible to find some kind of order which resembles it, because such orders use as their blueprints constellations opened up by the blind motion of beauty) even if they made the same assumptions as he, that beauty was a tumultuous clash of the emergence, transformation, perseverance, hardening and dissolution of order, that symmetry and chaos, maturation and decay, organization and dissolution were figures in the game but were indifferent to it and closed into themselves; that beauty was a poison which circulated in systems, providing them with a force for the creation of chaos (chaos can only be governed by a force which has roots as dark as its own and which gushes from the same source) while it ate away at them and destroyed them, captivated them by a blissful vision of death so as to paralyse them and urge them towards the most distant flashes of its flame. Baumgarten knew, too, that beauty is so much present in these continuous leakages that it conceals itself in them, that we always catch sight of it in a constellation just as it is disappearing; the next moment all that is left to us is a faithful copy, a mask produced with its own skin by which it intends to call our bluff.

He dreamed of a book which he would call "On the Origins of Beauty," a book which would be a hymn to beauty's fascinating revoltingness and also a catalogue of the figures of the dark motions of being and an attempt at the determination of the principles of their choreography. The book in gestation became the one thing of any importance in a life without family, lovers and friends. And as he sensed that the motions he was writing about exercised a clandestine control over his writing, that they agitated the tip of his pen as it moved across the paper, he sensed also that the circle was closing, thus bringing a certain unity into his life. Admittedly this unity reminded him of the motion of plankton in stagnant water and was probably the work of a devil of some kind, yet it brought him a continuous silent joy: after a long time something had appeared in his life which bore a likeness to harmony. He got into the habit of taking long walks across the open country above the city, along the roads which skirted Prague; while on these destinationless trips he would ponder his book. The larva-like motions were also supreme in the realm of sight; in open country they flickered along the outlines of visible objects so that often he found the answer to his own question by looking at a roadside tree or a pile of junk in a garden.

Then all of a sudden the tremblings of the world ceased, the unborn book closed, the landscape abandoned the production of ideas. By now he was so familiar with the world of larva-like motions that he knew long periods of torpor to be part of their life, that he would have to accept this peace just as they did, but he lacked the courage to give up the only thing which still satisfied him. Baumgarten continued to pace the open country above Prague in the hope that as before some rust-stained oddments next to a wall or a torn colour poster on a wooden board would give rise to ideas.

On one such hopeless walkabout he strayed further from the city than usual. He became aware of this only once he noticed that the houses had taken on a different aspect; no longer were they distracted by the proximity of the great capital, no longer did they look beyond the horizon to the city but inwards to their own yards, all the time contemplating the country around them. In the village squares there were no longer city-bus stops, their timetables behind opaque glass; in their place were corrugated-iron huts surrounded by stinging nettles. In one of the villages they told him at the pub that the last bus to Prague had already gone. Fortunately it was a Saturday and he would not be going to work the next morning. He asked if there was anywhere in the village he could sleep and one of the men seated at the table told him he could make himself a bed of straw at the farm on the opposite side of the square. Baumgarten was tired and in need of sleep, so he finished up his second beer and left the pub. Beyond an empty concrete storage tank, on whose bottom there was a foul-smelling black ooze, the gates of the farm opened wide. He entered the rutted yard; on one side there stood a large barn, on the other the white wall of a windowless building against which sundry agricultural implements and assorted junk had been left. Men and women in overalls kept coming into the yard to prop more shovels, rakes and hoes against the wall. He went into the barn, lay down in the straw and fell asleep immediately.

## 13
## Ino of the beautiful ankles

When he woke up it was just getting light and everyone else at the farm was still asleep. Soon the cock began to crow, the only sound to be heard in the village. Baumgarten lay on the straw and looked into the yard through the open door of the barn. For a while he thought of his book, but soon he emptied his mind of these thoughts and left it empty. He let his eyes wander over the objects leaning against the blind wall of the building; most of these were farm tools the names of which he did not know, or parts of things of which it was impossible to say what they had once belonged to. By now there was a pink strip of light across the top of the wall, but all the tools and parts remained submerged in the cold shadow that covered the yard. To the left of the gate leading to the square there was a rusty instrument composed of four poles fastened together by rivets out of which there projected soil-covered prongs; he told himself that this was probably a harrow, though he knew very little about the subject. Leaning against the wall to the right of this were two dark beams, crossed, beaten together at their centres to look like a great "X"; he imagined these forming part of a framework used in the cutting of wood. Resting against this rotten saltire were the remnants of a dilapidated door, upon which were quivering the flakes of a cream-coloured varnish with which the door must once have been painted; the door's centre panel still bore a brass handle. Surely, thought Baumgarten, the farm's manager was an exceptionally frugal character to hold on to junk such as this; at the same time it struck him that what was left of the door looked like a large "E." He began to see amusement in a game in which one read letters in farm tools etcetera, so he moved on to the next object, a triangular wire sand sieve, but he could not think of a letter to compare this with. Next to the sieve there was the handle of a shovel, an obvious "I," followed by a rusting construction of some kind made of the type of pipes used in scaffolding, a passable approximation of the letter "H." The last item in this group of objects comprised three planks propped against the wall, which for some reason had been nailed together; it was not difficult to will himself to see in these the letter "N."

Baumgarten ceased to find amusement in the game. He had not succeeded in his attempt to transform all objects into letters, nor did "XE" or "IHN" have any meaning to disclose. He was almost ready to get up and walk into the yard when something dawned on him: the harrow and the sand sieve did not resemble any letter of the Latin alphabet, but it was possible to see in them perfect representations of *sigma* and *delta*. Which would mean that "X" was in fact "CH" and the "H" of the scaffolding was "É," so that the complete group of old objects read *schedién*, the accusative form of the Greek word for *raft*. Baumgarten resumed his game, this time reading the object-letters in Greek. The first item in the next group was a metal stand that was held stable at the bottom by a transverse bar and had a metal spool attached to its top in which was gathered a steel cable with frayed ends; all this was covered in rust, like all the metal objects in the yard. The stand was a fine representation of the letter "A." Next to this were two wooden poles joined at an angle by insulating sleeving, whose purpose he could not imagine and which formed the letter "N" (the second in this curious notice); to the right of this was the broken lid of a crate in the shape of an "E," and in two columns of some kind of plastic that were joined by a rubber belt gone slack, an "M" was clearly visible. At this point Baumgarten became truly agitated: the murmur of a text was beginning to take shape in his head, a text drawn out from the depths of his memory. He closed his eyes and caught hold of the words, which he uttered in a muted voice.

Then it came to him what the text was, and with eyes closed he whispered, "Schedién anemoisi feresthai kallipe . . ." When he opened his eyes again he was not surprised to see next to the plastic columns in the shape of an "M" a concrete full-round form ("O"), then a stake ("I"), a tool whose function he could not identify (*sigma*) and another stake ("I"). The tops of the object-letters were by now touched by the pink light. After the last stake there was a gap—a stretch of white, plastered wall which put him in mind of a sheet of paper sticking out of an enormous typewriter whose opening line was covered in typescript. Then came another group of objects: *phi* was represented by a small gate stood vertically, which on a round piece of scratched tin appeared to bear the remains of the legend "No Entry"; the next "E" was a portion of a window. All thirty letters and three gaps were where they should be. *Theta* was particularly well done in a wooden hatch from which all the laths but the one in the centre had been ripped out, while *pi* had been produced in a block and tackle.

*Schedién anemoisi feresthai kallipe.* Leave your raft to drive before the wind. When the gods order the nymph Calypso to set Odysseus free, and after he drifts away from her island on a raft, Poseidon unleashes a fearful storm. With the last of his strength Odysseus clings to the raft as it is tossed hither and thither. As the waves roar all around him, he hears a woman's voice. Ino, also called Leucothea, the goddess of the slim ankles, has risen before him from the waves. Odysseus was expecting her to come to his aid, he was hoping she would calm the storm, would repair his disintegrating sail, or that she would carry him away to shore. But to his surprise Ino demands of him the most nonsensical thing imaginable in the circumstances. She tells him to quit his raft, his last hope, to give himself up to the wild water. Odysseus is slow to obey; he is hesitant, asking himself if this is a trick the gods are playing on him. In the end the decision is taken out of his hands by Poseidon, who smashes the vessel and casts Odysseus to the waves. Is not Poseidon, who would have Odysseus roam the seas, truly his friend? This is a difficult question to answer. As the case may be, the sea carries Odysseus to the shore of the island of the Phaeacians, where he meets Nausicaä and from where he sets sail for Ithaca, where Penelope, Telemachus and Argos are waiting for him.

Baumgarten smiled. He did not take long to consider what this strangely conveyed message meant for him. And its content did not surprise him as it had Odysseus because he had known it all along. What had befallen him was quite plain: the book he was writing had grown out of the pain of emptiness and gradually it had filled this emptiness, but in so doing it had destroyed the ground that nourished it, and died; such things happen. And the solution, too, was simple: it was enough to return to the territory of the void, to let himself be carried by its waves and to wait. So rather than thinking about the content of the message, he thought about who could have sent it to him. There was no point in his suspecting any of the people of the village. Being a sceptic he told himself that this was nothing more than a strange coincidence; it was improbable but not impossible. Quite simply he had dreamed that a local deity, lord of sad villages around Prague, demon of abandoned bus stops, had spoken to him. In the end he decided to understand the notice composed of objects as a message from Ino of the beautiful ankles, daughter of Cadmus, founder of the seven-gated city of Thebes, who had been transformed into a marine divinity and had now, for his sake, descended on the yard of this farm.

He decided, too, to follow immediately the advice Ino had given him; he threw the part-written book in the dustbin, shortly afterwards abandoned in his Prague flat all books and papers with notes and extracts on the subject, and left the country. He settled in Paris because it seemed to him that this was a place where one could easily lose oneself, and this he wished to do. It was not his intention to become a *clochard*; he wished to live in a foreign city and try again to be faithful to the void he had once betrayed, to wait for a glimpse of new motions as nonsensical and marvellous as the hymn about the embryology of being he had composed on the dusty streets around Prague and in country pubs.

As he walked the wastelands of the great city, as the faces of men and women unknown to him floated past in the streets like so many incurious fish, as his gaze wandered the facades of buildings and climbed through windows into flats whose furniture was angular and hostile, as he felt on his cheeks the cooling mask of a wind saturated in incomprehensible smells both foul and fine, a new joy was born within him. He changed his job often: he was a messenger and a gallery attendant, a custodian in a museum, a sales assistant. He glimpsed nothing that promised to be the germ of some kind of task; he took joy from the purity of emptiness, from its great airy halls, which he passed through light-footedly. He realized that the most important thing was not the task—a task born, perhaps, out of the emptiness, whose fineness and fragrance it preserved in itself—but the tranquil shelter of waiting for nothing. In this shelter a note of happiness was sounded and gained in strength. Perhaps his task in the great game was to make this realization.

One evening as he was dining in a cheap Chinese bistro in Montparnasse's Rue d'Odessa, a familiar face appeared in the mirror in front of which he was sitting. It belonged to an associate professor from the Sorbonne, whom he had met in Prague when he was still working at the university. They talked for a while, and then the associate professor remembered that he was looking for someone to translate into French selected essays by Jan Mukařovský. Baumgarten thought the offer over for a while, and in the end he agreed to take the job on. This marked the beginning of his Paris career. After publication of the Mukařovský anthology he went on to edit his own anthologies of Czech structuralism, to which he wrote extensive introductions. He himself began to teach Aesthetics at the Sorbonne. He married a Frenchwoman and they had a son; they lived in a large penthouse on one of the great boulevards. The royal castle of emptiness dissolved. He never wrote the book he had intended to write in Prague. Only rarely did he remember the larva-like motions of being, the lost fragments of the Origins of Beauty and the period of his solitary walks on the fringes of Prague.

## 14
## The roofs of Paris

As their fifteenth wedding anniversary approached he went to a jeweller's and bought his wife a valuable diamond necklace. It was January; his wife and son were skiing in the Savoy Alps and would be returning in three days' time. That day he worked in his room through the evening and deep into the night. Before going to bed he opened the window to air the room of his cigarette smoke. For a while he watched the snowflakes, whirling madly and illuminated by the light of the room, and the fresh snow on the sloping roof into which the window was set. Then he switched off the light and went to bed.

A light sleeper, he was woken by a faint rustling coming from the next room. Through the half-open door, in the weak light reflected from the snow he made out the slim figure of a woman. She was wearing black overalls, their pockets swelling in a number of places. Above her head—which was covered with a black mask with three holes in it (two for the eyes and one for the nose)—the cold air entering through the open window caused the white curtain to ripple. The woman in black was leaning over the jewellery box into which that evening he had placed the necklace; carefully yet briefly she felt around inside it. When she withdrew her black hand Baumgarten saw a thin, glittering string dangling from the leather-clad fingers. What he was watching reminded him of a scene from a bad thriller. He took his revolver from the drawer of his bedside table; then he jumped out of bed. Catching sight of him, the woman slipped the necklace into one of her pockets, jumped up onto the windowsill and then out of view. Baumgarten grabbed his dressing gown from the armchair next to his bed and quickly pulled it on over his pyjamas. He put his bare feet into his shoes before climbing out of the window and onto the sloping, snow-covered roof.

To his right the yellow light of invisible street lamps rose from the abyss of the boulevard like sulphur emitted by the crater of a volcano; to his left, in the darkness and through the blizzard he could just make out a black forest of aerials on the ridge of the roof; in front of him, light from the window of his sleepless neighbour spilled out on to the snow. The black-clad figure was dashing through the high, fresh snow. Baumgarten was angered by the thief's sheer cheek. He pursued her in spite of the danger to himself: in his low shoes he might easily have slipped and taken a dive into the boulevard. And now the sensation of being in a cheap thriller was stronger—and more embarrassing—still; he even caught himself making moves that characters in pursuit over roofs were wont to make in such films.

A short while later the thief in black reached the end of the roof. The adjacent building was that of a department store. Beneath the sloping roof of Baumgarten's building there began a narrow ledge on which the legend Galeries Lafayette burned in big letters. The violet neon flooded the snow, throwing the outlines of the thief's footprints into sharp relief. Now the woman would have to climb along the narrow, snow-covered ledge with the neon lettering. Baumgarten saw the figure in black take hold with both hands of the upper arc of the letter "G" before carefully placing the tip of her right shoe into the shallow bowl at the bottom of the letter, where the neon was buried in snow that radiated violet. On the narrow, horizontal stroke that split the lower arc of the "G," the thief sat down, as if in a snow-covered chair, before letting go of the letter's top and grabbing with her right hand the upper arc of the lower-case "a," which was reaching out to her like the beak of an inquisitive, snowbound bird.

Baumgarten took the revolver out of the pocket of his dressing gown; he fired it to scare the thief. He aimed at the upper tip of the "G" and to his satisfaction saw that he really managed to hit it: the letter flickered and then went out, sending from its crest a small avalanche down on the thief's head. She grabbed the "l," which, under her weight, took a perilous tip forward over the boulevard and sent down another cap of snow, this time into her face. Seemingly she was blinded for a few moments: she had to use one hand to wipe her eyes. But the letter held and the woman succeeded in grasping the horizontal line of the central "e," which appeared quite firm. She slid across the face of the "e" and reached for the horn of the "r" as if it were some kind of handle.

By this time Baumgarten, too, had reached the lettering. He stuffed the revolver back into his pocket so as to keep his hands free, then made for the first word. As he was gingerly touching the extinguished "G," the thief was overcoming with ease the "i," "e," and "s," thus reaching the word's end. Then she stopped for a few moments; it seemed she was making up her mind how to bridge the gap between the two words. In the meantime Baumgarten found that his crawl along the word "Galeries," with its extinguished initial capital, was made easier by the footmarks the thief had left; there was no need for him to grope beneath the snow for the outlines of the letters, so he moved more quickly than she. The distance between them was closing. He was heavier than she, however, and under his weight the letters tipped and creaked ominously, the damaged "l" in particular. This tilted yet further forward and its upper end worked itself free of the wall, revealing some cables and producing a flash. Now the letter was unlit and it jutted out like a black pole without its flag from the building into the snowstorm. This was a highly unpleasant course to take. Baumgarten was blinded by the violet light of the letters and the blizzard was beating against his face; his pyjama bottoms were soaked through, their legs ice-cold and heavy.

Just as it seemed he had negotiated the first word successfully, he made a serious error. He was reaching for the snow-covered dot of the "i"; as he could not see this, he could not know that it was attached only by a thin, aluminium bar to the lower part of the letter, not to the wall like the other letters. The bar buckled under his weight and was now leaning like a wilting flower; Baumgarten's feet slipped from the narrow ledge, and there he was, dangling over the boulevard, both hands clinging for dear life to the dot, which itself was sinking towards the abyss, where snowflakes were swirling around in the light of the street lamps. With the last of his strength he succeeded in grasping the lower arc of the neighbouring "e" and so clambered back onto the ledge. The thief now had both hands on the line of intersection of the "f" and was casting about with her right foot in the hollow of the "a" which followed. Baumgarten recovered himself; he made a risky leap from the first word to the second, then clung to the severe initial capital, which to his great good fortune held firm.

As the thief was attempting to place her foot in the snow-filled lap of the "y," which was in the dead centre of the second word, with its lower part protruding from the ledge and into space, she slipped. Baumgarten watched with horror as the woman slid down the "y" and towards the abyss. Though she was clinging to the letter with both hands, its slippery surface eluded her grip; not until the hands reached the ball at the lower tip of the "y"—the very lowest point in the whole legend—was the downwards glide arrested. What luck that they had used a serif typeface, thought Baumgarten. He remembered an article on typography published pre-war in an avant-garde magazine, in which Karel Teige advocated that letters be stripped of elements of the calligrapher's art and other bourgeois flourishes, claiming that the modern age demanded sans-serif lettering. Fortunately this had not come to pass, and Baumgarten was able to hurry along the avenue of violet-glow lettering to the aid of the thief who was dangling wretchedly over the boulevard. On reaching the middle of the word he took the "a" in his left hand and leaned over the abyss, where the snow was swirling about in the lamplight, and held out his free hand to the woman. Happily she was nimble enough to climb, with his help, back up the "y." As she made it to the letter's fork, he pulled the snow-drenched mask from her face.

He was confronted with the face of a girl of about twenty, whose blonde curls were fighting themselves free. She sat down on the back stroke of the "y," leaning her elbows on the front stroke; her breathing was heavy. She made no attempt to conceal her face. She undid the Velcro fastener of her pocket and handed Baumgarten the necklace; this may have been a means of thanking him for saving her life, or perhaps it was his trophy for emerging victorious from this race over the roofs of Paris. The aesthetician put the necklace in the pocket of his dressing gown, next to the revolver. He, too, was exhausted; he sat down on the rounded roof of the "a" and got his breath back. From down below in the street, he thought, a late-night walker would see us as two rather puzzling splodges in the glowing lettering.

Dear reader, you may be interested to learn what Baumgarten and the Parisian she-thief talked about on that snowy roof. It was a long conversation, which my Parisian friend reported to me in full in the pleasant warmth of the café on Rue des Beaux-Arts. But we have occupied our minds with tales of the Czech aesthetician abroad for quite long enough. I have now described the two scenes in which letters and objects are joined, which was the reason for my telling the story of this Czech émigré. You are sure to have noticed that these scenes are those in the yard at the farm (where objects are transformed into letters) and on the roof of the department store (where letters are transformed into objects). Let us now return to the island.

## 15
## Spilled sauce

On the island I often encountered a peculiar shape—asymmetric stains out of which there grew several long, broad lobes; this shape reminded me of a bison on the attack with its head bowed, or perhaps even more so of a lady's glove hanging limp. I saw flat stones which had been carved into this shape and set on a plinth so that the end of the narrowest of the projections on its bottom side was resting on this. These mini-monuments—examples of a kind of "stain" sculpture—channelled streams of water at the centre of fountains in the upper town, and they stood high on promontories of rock. In the lower town the shape appeared as a bas-relief on the escutcheons of palaces or in faded frescoes; some inhabitants of the upper town would set small coloured stones in their walls and mirrors in this shape reminiscent of a bison or glove. I asked several islanders about the shape: once I learned that it represented a monster that many years ago had devastated the island, another time that it described the outlines of magical, luminous flowers that had grown one night on the floor of the bed chamber of a queen who had lived long ago and whose name was forgotten.

I had little doubt that they thought up such explanations on the spot. It was highly unlikely the islanders knew the origin of the shape. To say that they were lying to me would be imprecise; it was rather that for them the past was of the same realm as dream and imagination, and thus they treated fabulation and vague traces of dreams in the present as legitimate means of penetrating the world of the past, from which objects would emerge still breathing, like pleasant fragrances. This approach was born out of their requirement for a certain exactness, albeit of a kind different to the one on which our own sciences pride themselves. The islanders were offended by the notion of historical research, considering it on the one hand practically indecent (obscene behaviour towards the past), and on the other a strange, even comical bypassing of the task at hand. Karael—who, like most islanders, knew English—once spent a long time browsing a history book in English I had brought with me before laying it aside and announcing, "It puts me in mind of an expedition that goes off to hunt animals that don't exist, taking a few cooking pots for use as hunters' tools." In order to hold on to my good name, I felt it necessary to conceal from the islanders that I was researching the history of the island, although the dearth of available sources coupled with the infectiousness of the islanders' worldview meant that my research was more about dreaming than comparing, categorizing, judgment and proof.

Evidently objects in which the mysterious shape was repeated had once had a sacral significance. That religion should have existed on the island seemed to me curious. The islanders were of a nation that felt no need for the spiritual and the transcendental; it was extremely difficult for me to imagine a religious islander. Missionaries of various religions were constantly arriving on the island. Naturally the islanders would hear them out willingly enough and were prepared to repeat after them all manner of things (meaning the islanders would draw the visitors into their games). When the missionaries realized what was happening in these games to the articles of their faith and the identity of their god, they thought it better to leave the island. Many considered this the Devil's island.

I attempted a reconstruction of the lost religion of the islanders, which had perished long before the European invasion, but in my investigations I was not helped along even by the sand-strewn documents in the royal palace. I had very few clues to go on: certain present-day practises of the islanders, the mysterious carving of a man with a fish's head in a rock overhanging a mountain lake, short dispatches posted by Arabian travellers in the Middle Ages (which I had read before coming to the island), notes in a little-known tractate by Averroes. There are so few of these clues, and their value as documents is so dubious, that my reconstruction of the island's religion—and its origins, development and end—had more about it of a dream or vision than the revelation of a fragment of the island's history.

The Arabians write that the inhabitants of the island of Phoenix (which, for some reason, was the name they gave the island) regard marks on walls as a script used by their god to impart his messages and commandments. Some of these communications are reputed to be important—addressing fundamental principles of the universe and ethics—but others are surprisingly vapid, even embarrassing, containing gossip or indiscretions concerning the domestic practises and unspoken thoughts of the islanders; some of these divine inscriptions would be best described as slander. The travel writings of the Arabians also contain a lone, curious mention of how the prophet who founded the island's religion fought on a rock above the sea with a god or demon with a fish's head and killed it.

On the basis of these scraps of information I tried to imagine how the island's religion came into being. It may have been like this: the islanders had once worshipped a deity with the head of a fish; the history of this archaic religion has been lost, leaving behind it nothing more than a carving in the rock in the wilderness of the mountains that is reflected in the water of a lake. I imagine that the prophet of the new religion lived at a time when the original faith was losing strength and changing into dogma, that the vanquishing of the old faith in a struggle to the death between the prophet and the demon with the fish's head had left traces in the tales of the Arabians. Perhaps the prophet had been a priest of the old religion for whom prayers had become sounds without meaning and the script of the sacred texts had lost the power of speech. The silence of this world abandoned by the gods weighed upon him heavily. One evening his despair was so great that he thought to take his own life. In his abstracted state he upset a bowl containing a red sauce over the open pages of one of the sacred books. As the sauce soaked into the paper it formed a stain that was slightly reminiscent in shape of a bison or a glove. As he studied the stain he realized with astonishment that, unlike the other characters, this mark was not mute; it was whispering something to him with great urgency. He saw the red stain as a hole burned into the cool fabric of the world. What is this? he asked himself. Had he perhaps discovered a secret, divine script?

Then he realized that the whispering of the stain was not the only voice he could hear, that other stains on the walls and on objects had begun to speak; there came a drone from the cracks in the dry earth and seams in the rock. This great awakening of the world went further: all shapes were soon learning the language of stains—shapes, too, were stains, but either they had forgotten this or man had convinced them otherwise. The red stain on the page of a book had fought free of the language man had forced on shapes. Suddenly they were reminded of the ancient shape language and their present understanding of the world was overthrown. And the shape language re-opened the world and filled it with joy.

This was the beginning of the prophet's mission. He taught the islanders to listen to the voices of stains—perhaps the prophet saw a god behind the stains, perhaps islander disciples of the prophet imagined a new deity who was the author of the text of stains. (It may be that in those days the islanders were unable to imagine something that today is marvellously easy for them to imagine—that the murmurous text of the stains is forever writing and erasing itself.) Maybe this was when the Stain of Awakening—the stain designed by the sauce, the mysterious alfa, the initial of a divine text—began to be shown and worshipped.

I believe that the new religion changed after the prophet's death. It rid itself of some of its more eccentric features and drew nearer to other religions. That it developed some kind of notion of an afterlife is testified to in Averroes's tractate, in which the thinker from Cordoba rejects the notion of the immortality of the individual soul, employing in his polemic an anecdote from the island as a kind of *reductio ad absurdum*. This is the tale Averroes tells: the prophet of the island of Phoenix pays a visit to his neighbour, arriving as the latter is about to whitewash his home. The prophet bursts into tears and pleads with his neighbour to abandon this course of action. When the astonished neighbour asks what it is about the painting of his home that so troubles the prophet, the latter points to a dried stain on the wall and says: "I see in that the face of my late father. I visit you only in order to be closer to him, so that my father may see me and hear my voice. Were you to paint over him, his soul would wander the atmosphere in confusion, looking for another stain to inhabit. Perhaps it would be forced to settle in a place that would bring it great indignity, perhaps on a wall at the other end of the world, so we should never see each other again."

Averroes writes that the islanders believe that the souls of the dead live on in stains on walls, that they prove this by a curious concatenation of evidence: souls are incorporeal so they must dwell in something with a material volume; volume lacks a two-dimensional form, and as stains on walls are two-dimensional, souls undoubtedly reside in stains. Perhaps the islanders themselves were not altogether convinced of the logic of this, so as a second proof of life after death in stains, they declared that in the half-light we often have the impression we see the outline of a person or an animal.

This story may be based in truth, although plainly it is paraphrasing what Diogenes Laertius tells of Pythagoras (fragment B7 in Diels). It was not so far from Cordoba to the island, and before the original communication was changed into an anecdote and before this anecdote was heard by Averroes, it must have passed through many mouths. I can well imagine the impact the imaginations of sailors and merchants steeped in tales from the Orient would have worked on it.

# 16
# Names of stains

When the prophet—an exemplar of courage who invested the glowing, nonsensical world with murmurs and stains—no longer walked among them, the islanders became uncertain of the way and began to look around for translators and interpreters. Now they needed a grammar and a lexicon of stains, so that they might understand their language. At that time catalogues and dictionaries of stains came into being. We see the transitions as indistinguishable from one another, but to the islanders they are full of similarities and differences. Stains came to be classified, and the various types were given names to which fixed meanings were attached. It seems that in the old days the attitudes of the islanders to stains were personal—some of them one loved, others one hated. These attitudes were subject to sudden, fleeting fashions; sometimes a marginal stain that no one had paid any attention to would appear overnight on all walls and garments and would suddenly adorn the surfaces of dozens of objects. Of course, the Stain of Awakening still held a privileged and unshakable position, and the shape made by the sauce on the page of the sacred book was carved in stone, set in bright-coloured gemstones and tattooed on skin.

At that time the islanders would walk about with dictionaries in their hands, employing them in the reading of stain texts and any other shapes they happened upon. One Arabian merchant tells the tale of how he arrives at the home of one of the islanders for a business appointment. He finds the islander in the yard of his dwelling, watching with excitement a bedsheet that is flapping and swelling in the strong wind as it dries on a washing-line; also he keeps looking in a thick dictionary he is holding in his hand. The islander asks the merchant to wait a few moments. Once the wind calms down, he makes his apologies: the story written in the sheet was an exciting one, and he wished to find out how it ended. When the merchant expresses his surprise at this, the islander explains that his countrymen regularly read the shapes that gather in pieces of cloth in windy weather; like hieroglyphs, he says, they create a continuous text.

I do not know how long this phase of the islanders' religion lasted, but I believe that over time they ceased to perceive stains as communications from god. The changes occurring, the shapes, the stains became for them a game that had no connection to anything in particular. At around this time they laid aside their lexicons and grammars and ceased to ascribe to stains any fixed meanings. But the stains did not fall mute; they returned to their original voice, their blissful, meaningless murmuring. In this way the end of the religion was a triumph, a return to the beginning. Some travellers have written of the islanders with scorn or indignation; in their opinion, the veneration of the god of stains, which it was to be hoped still lingered in the islanders' consciousness, was at least a form of prayer, and thus an attempt—albeit a dark and confused one—to make contact with God; they consider today's total absence of any sense of transcendence as degeneracy of the severest kind. I feel I have neither the authority nor the need to reproach or praise the islanders for their godlessness, but I must say in their defence that much of what has been written about them is baseless slander: the atheism of the islanders has a special mystique based in its superficiality and immediacy, and it creates a space in which fine, almost noble gestures can develop. This hope-free, fear-free, sense-free space is often lit by a silent joy of the kind I have rarely experienced in Europe, and the shapes of stains and objects glow with a clear light. I learned that the islanders knew neither passion nor genuine cordiality, but in their behaviour there was always a tone in which discretion and noble tact were present. It seemed to me that out of this tone there might grow a kindness that would protect the maturing contours of things, a kindness that would be stronger than the kindness we know, because there would be no need for it to take into account sense and order, which always lead to violence and malevolence.

It is true that during my stay on the island I never met anyone who gave the impression that he was approaching such a transformation. For this to happen, it would perhaps be necessary for the seeds of future kindness to be nourished on realities other than the island's anaesthetic murmurs and glimmers, the monotonous fraying and entwining of its currents, the slow melting of the solid and the crystallization of the liquid. It is possible that such a transformation will never come to pass, that what appeared to me as the seeds of a new world was really an afterglow projected by the past, that the islanders already have behind them their better days, their era of kindness and goodness, and that all that remains of it is the dubious virtue of discretion, in which tact comes together with indifference.

I once mentioned to Karael that it seemed to me that island life was heading for transformation, but my girlfriend disliked visions in which developments moved towards aims. I said nothing to contradict her; I didn't have the right. There was only one person I could ask for help in the attempt to realize by alchemy a change in the islanders' indifference, and naturally that person was me. I made an effort at it after I returned from the island, but the alchemy slipped from my fingers just as it did from those of the sorcerer's apprentice: the result was a centaur with a human body and a horse's head, mixed from the island's distaste for large buildings, devoid of the island's lightness and joy, with the European need for sense robbed of the ground beneath its feet that connects it firmly to our world.

The lexicons of stains had been lost and the islanders had forgotten about them, but the categories that had their origins in these books had left a deep impression in the islanders' language and ways of seeing. Stains of different shapes belong to different types; for the islanders they are as different in kind as a chair and a table are to us. Although on the island a great many instruments—many of them objects connected with civilization—are missing that we have by us constantly, the islanders are surrounded by a far greater amount of things than we are. The islanders live among stains as we live among objects and letters. Indeed, they feel more at home in expanses of stains than in the world of objects; for them, stains have more of an existence than ordinary objects. While we compare stains to objects and bodies and say things like, "Hey, look at that stain! It looks like a walrus," when the islanders want to describe the shape of an object—let's say a ship that has just appeared in the harbour—they say, "It looks like a tnaeb." A tnaeb is an oblong, saggy stain with a number of outgrowths on its upper side. The islanders look at the world of objects and bodies as at a Rorschach-type test turned inside out.

The categorizing of stains is embedded so deeply in the consciousness of the islanders that not only do they seek to compare the shapes of objects with those of stains, but types of stains play a role—consciously or unconsciously—when objects come into being. There are many household objects and buildings on the island that are in the shape of a stain, not least being the escutcheons on mansions and palaces of the lower town built in the final phase of building activity that imitate the shapes of various types of stains. It was instructive for me to study the architecture of the conquerors from the time they were already losing the war against the spirit of the islanders; from these it was plain that the shapes of stains had infiltrated the visions of the architects—for example, the facade of a church obviously meant to be a replica of Rome's Jesuit Church of the Gesu was far more reminiscent of the mark amamr. I can well imagine the dejection of the church's architect when he realized this result of his work.

It was a blasphemy to glorify the god of the stain (a god who accepted such devotion would transform into another deity), and it was not possible to run away from a stain. The islanders' stains lay in wait for the builders like cunning beasts of prey; not only did they reside in the dark gaps between shapes (these spaces could have been left as a kind of reservation), but they stole into the seemingly secure territory of recognized shapes and caused much damage there. They destroyed recognized shapes and appointed themselves in their place, or at the very least the stains so bedevilled and confused the recognized shapes that these began to imitate stains. The capitals of pilasters and the volutes of escutcheons could not resist the urge to become grm or mupu stains. Even the figures of saints became images and statues of stains; they were unable to deliver salvation, or—worse still—they offered a terrible salvation, the monstrous paradise of stains.

It was pathetic to watch the desperate attempts of the architects to escape the stains that pursued them, which were more terrifying to them than the monsters of mythology. I often felt the facades of the houses told of their builders' fear of a terrible, debilitating sickness, which we might name the impossibility of the indefinite. Indefiniteness and shapelessness were forever escaping them, because every accidental splatter of mortar immediately became an irao or a ladoe; when they wanted to escape an ede that had grown right under their hands, they found it turning into an alopo. Perhaps it seems strange that they were so keen to preserve the shapeless, the indefinite, the nameless and the patternless. Most of all the builders looked for shapelessness to salvage the world of shapes; shapes needed indefinite, discreet matter to which they could give their orders and which would serve them. When a shape on the island entered matter, what it found there was not calm complaisance but the frenzied proliferation of figures, and in this uncomfortable jungle it could not find a place to settle. It was used in overcoming the resistance of matter, but here its power and solidity were worth nothing; here matter was so apathetic that it put up no resistance to shapes, but it pulled them into its whirling dance and enfeebled it by its toxic breath. The worst thing of all about this was that the monstrous and offensive stain figures constantly putting themselves in the paths of shapes were uncannily similar to these shapes and thus familiar to them. When the shapes discovered the reason for this, they were horrified: it was not that stains were imitating shapes and wished to take their place, but that shapes were of the same genus as stains and had forgotten the world they were born into, that they were just as phantasmic and monstrous as stains, that shapes and stains were the same fruit of the wild proliferation of matter, meaning that shapes were afforded no privileges.

We know how the anguished battle between the foreigners and the demons of the island ended. After a long period of unbearable strain the foreigners yielded, and this yielding was made manifest in their attitude to the danger posed by stains. In a sudden flood of bliss the foreigners were plunged into a paradise they had long yearned for but had been afraid to admit to. In the lower town, buildings from the time of blissful defeat have been preserved; they reveal how their architects revelled in the once-forbidden depravity of stains, how they luxuriated in the stains that had eluded them for many years, how in triumph they allowed them to dominate the island and declare the Collapse of Shape.

## 17
## The master from Berlin

Perhaps, dear reader, you think that as I write my mind is filled with visions of the island, that nothing is important to me except the efforts to fish out of memory clearly-drawn pictures of the landscape of the island. Perhaps you think I consider you a remote figure, unreal or bothersome, a figure that disturbs my dreams and at whose behest I have to demean and exert myself by transferring glowing images into dark, clumsy words, to bind in the manacles of grammar and syntax the free, light motions of the waves, sands, and winds that linger in my memory. Perhaps you think that because of this I hate you, that I consider you the agent of my misfortune, that I sit at my computer keyboard—whose gentle tapping beneath my fingers is transformed into the sounds of gravel underfoot on the scorched paths of the island's rocks—hatching plans which do you harm, which use language to ensnare you.

How mistaken you are, dear reader! I think of you continually; I am grateful to you that our conversation allows me to inject by sharp, angular words at least a flickering glow in the faded images. It is your face that I see in the gaps between all words, I am forever anxious for your comfort, I worry that the reading I ask of you is boring you. I would be happier if this travelogue were sold in a box containing items to supplement the reading matter—a fine-woven hammock, a bottle of a sweet liqueur, flacons, Oriental sweetmeats; you would read the book stretched out comfortably in the hammock, nibbling on Turkish delight and sipping the liqueur, the air would be scented with essence of cedarwood and myrrh; in fact, I would even offer my services for free for the packing of these boxes.

When I told you that nothing ever happened on the island, I suspect you did not believe me; you thought that I was exaggerating, that there was surely a tale of excitement to come. In this I am afraid I have to disappoint you: it really is the case that you will encounter nothing like this in the whole book. I suppose I could invent something, tell you of fights with vicious beasts, of the discovery of precious carvings in a sunken gallery, of the stirring of a volcano, of the remnants of an ancient cult of magic into which I was initiated, of mysterious apparitions in the hot, empty streets of the lower town . . . But I really want to tell you the truth, which is that in the three years I spent on the island, nothing happened; nor had anything interesting happened there in all the centuries since the European conquest. But when—thinking of you—I sat down at my computer this morning, an idea came to me: if you are so anxious to have a story, I can at least finish that of the Czech emigrant in Paris. Now it seems to me I was too harsh on you in refusing to say any more about the theft of the necklace. Let us return to Paris; perhaps you remember that we left Baumgarten sitting next to the cat-burglar—whose life he had just saved—on the snow-covered roof, perched on the neon letter "a."

"Is it really necessary to commit crimes in weather like this?" he asked her with reproach, when at last he had got his breath back. The girl began to apologize, assuring him that she, too, would sooner be sitting at home than in a blizzard like this. But she desperately needed to get her hands on some money by the morning of the next day, when at eleven o'clock an auction would commence where a painting she had long hankered after was up for sale.

"And what picture is this for which you almost plunge from the rooftops? Have your friends ransacked the Louvre?"

"No, the gallery where the auction is taking place is a respectable business. The picture I want is by a German painter who recently died. Drowned last year bathing in the Wannsee. He left only a few works behind and hardly anyone knows him. I came across the picture by chance in a small gallery in Kreutzberg, the quarter of Berlin. And unfortunately I didn't have the money for it then."

"Nothing's changed there, has it?"

"Quite right. In fact I'm in a worse position now than I was then, because the artist's death has raised the cost of his pictures. But I've stopped working in a bank and found a new career for myself, one where I can get more money."

"I have to say you're pretty good at clambering over roofs. But what's so wonderful about the picture by the drowning Berliner?" Baumgarten was asking out of politeness; he was getting cold and he was imagining himself back in his warm bed. But obviously the girl had been waiting for such a question and she began to talk of the picture.

"The picture is really a great book of stories," she said. "There are hundreds of elaborate story-lines on it, which at certain points cross, join or branch off in new directions. It's true that the picture shows a single place at a single, non-dimensional moment, but into the space which fills this moment the artist has implanted a great many signs which form some kind of lettering. One needs to make connections among the signs, to group them into the words and sentences of the individual stories."

"These are symbols, did you say?" Baumgarten, who taught a seminar in semiotics at the university, was suddenly attentive.

"No, the signs are in body language, facial expression, on post-cards and in open letters, photographs, pictures and sculptures, newspaper articles and books lying open with notes in the margin and passages underlined. In the week that the picture was on exhibition in Berlin, I managed only to identify a small part of the story-lines written using these letters, but the need to decipher them took hold of me and I longed to read the picture to the end, although I knew very well that I would be unlikely to manage this during my lifetime. But it'll be marvellous once I have the picture hanging on my wall at home and I'm able to study it when I get in from my night-time excursions to strangers' rooms and empty rooftops. My life will be wonderful and I'm so much looking forward to it!"

"But you've forgotten that you don't have the money for the picture. Or are we to resume our fight for the necklace?"

"Don't worry, I'm finished on this roof. But it's a long time till morning." With this the girl fell silent; it seemed she was waiting for Baumgarten to invite her to tell him more about the picture. But because the aesthetician, too, was silent, she resumed of her own accord.

"If I were to describe to you everything I've seen in the picture, we'd freeze to death up here. Anyway, I don't have much time—as you know, there's still work for me to do tonight. But I would like to make up for the unpleasantness I've caused you. I'd like to give you at least a brief description of the picture."

Accepting that he would have to hear the girl out, Baumgarten made himself more comfortable on the tip of the "a," while cautiously the thief changed her position from the right-hand cap of the "y" to the left so as to be closer to him. The neon tubes hummed quietly; there was something about this sound that reminded Baumgarten of his past, but he did not wish to think about that now. The girl's mouth gave out cloudlets of vapour as she spoke; these were coloured by the purple light before they dissolved in the dark.

"The picture was four metres long and a metre-and-a-half high. Three-quarters of its surface was covered by a gently rippling sea with a blue sky above it. In the other quarter, on the right, the artist had painted a town with a harbour. It looked like it was somewhere in the Mediterranean. It was the time of the afternoon siesta and the walls were sweltering in the sun. There were suntanned tourists walking along the pier, figures in shorts and colourful T-shirts sitting on the terraces of harbour-side restaurants in the shadow of outstretched sails, on the tables beside them glasses of iced coffee, broad-brimmed straw hats, glossy magazines and half-written postcards."

"You said you were going to keep it brief," Baumgarten interposed as the cold continued to bite.

"But that's why I'm not telling you what was written on the menu cards, in the magazines, on the postcards and in the diary of a history of art student from America, which was lying next to her on a wickerwork chair on a café terrace, although these were all extremely important things. On one of the postcards, for instance, written in green ballpoint . . ."

"OK, I won't interrupt you again," said Baumgarten, who was afraid the thief would go into detail about all the things she wouldn't be mentioning.

"In narrow streets leading up from the harbour to the ruins of mighty ramparts were women wearing black dresses, sitting on chairs in front of doors which gave straight on to living rooms. In the shadows of open taprooms the wrinkled, tanned skin of natives was visible as they sipped their coffee and their anisette. As I said, when one studies the scenes in the picture, one discovers connections among them which build up into stories."

"I'm still having difficulty imagining it clearly," said Baumgarten, who was beginning to be drawn in by the narration.

"It might be better if I were to give you some examples of the stories which I read in the picture. How about the one about the turbine, the peanut butter and the sordid dreams? In a window of one of the apartments you could see three men, the eldest of whom was sunk in a deep armchair showing the youngest something on a sheet of paper, while the third man was sitting by the window flicking through a notebook. In a mirror hanging on the wall in the background was the reflection of the corner of an adjacent room, which was flooded with sun and had a table in it on which was lying a metal part in the shape of a cylinder, which was smeared with honey . . . No, the story of the sordid dreams is too long and complicated—it'd be better if I told you the one about the golden helicopter. No, not that one—I'll tell you about the wrecking of the *Zephyrus*. One of the yachts at anchor in the harbour had the name *Zephyrus* emblazoned on its side. The last letter of the name rested against a large, brick-red paint stain in the shape of a butterfly, or rather a moth . . ." (Baumgarten gave the thief a look of reproach, but apparently the girl did not consider her descriptions to be too long-winded.)

"It looked as if someone had painted the yacht as a temporary measure after some kind of accident. On the jetty there stood a sinewy, unshaven native in a checked shirt, one of whose hands was pointing at the yacht, the other making a sweeping gesture while he explained something excitedly to a soft, pink tourist in Bermuda shorts adorned with palm groves and surfers riding great blue waves." (Baumgarten was relieved the girl did not describe the patterns on the surfers' swim-wear.) "He appeared genuinely interested in what the old native was telling him. Which means . . ."

"Which probably means that not long before the yacht had been involved in some kind of adventure which had damaged its hull, and stories of this adventure were spreading across the town." Baumgarten was trying to interpret the scene in the picture so that he could move the girl's account forward. Watching the luminous, phantom-like purple snowflakes, it seemed to him for a moment that he knew their full repertoire of dances, which they repeated *ad infinitum*.

# 18
# The wrecking of the *Zephyrus*

"That's right," said the thief, nodding enthusiastically. "In one of the streets above the harbour it was possible to look through an open window into a modestly-appointed room. On a shelf on the wall I could see a number of exotic sculptures. There was a suntanned, fair-haired man of about thirty sitting at a desk; he looked like a foreigner who had lived a long time in the south. On the right-hand side of the desk there was a typewriter with rounded keys and a black case on which 'Underwood' was written in ornamental gold letters, and beneath this, in smaller letters, 'Standard Four Bank Keyboard.' Towards the back of the desk there were several pots containing pencils and pens. Against one of these a plastic frame was resting; this contained a black-and-white photograph of a young woman, laughing, sitting on a deck chair next to a swimming pool. On the left-hand side of the desk there was a folder, out of which sheets of paper covered in dense writing were spilling from the top and bottom. The folder bore the legend 'Journey,' which was almost obscured by the kind of drawings people do unconsciously and abstractedly; these drawings were of elephants, crocodiles, and birds of paradise among a lot of grotesque shapes and some names and telephone numbers. All the spaces were filled in with a fancy, complicated net—rather like a spider's web—and all the figures, letters and numbers were ensnared in this. Next to the scribbled-on folder there was a glass ball used as a paperweight, where one could read distorted letters of various sizes which made up the words 'Black Hermaphrodite will be with you very soon . . .'

"All these objects created a kind of rampart along three sides of the desk. In the space this marked out, thirty-eight nine-by-thirteen colour photographs were laid out like cards in a game of patience. The man was bent over these in an attitude of contemplation. Many of the photographs showed the *Zephyrus*. In the one at the top left-hand corner she was at anchor in the town's harbour and her paint, white and undamaged, was gleaming in the early-morning sun. Many of the other shots showed the surface of the sea in various guises—gleaming and dark, undulating and flat, whirling restlessly, languid and passive, broken into many small, sharp-spined waves, gathered in a stodgy, formless mass, neurotically tense, listlessly dormant. Regardless of the sea's guise, in each of the photos it was scored through with the white lines of marine ropes. In some shots the figure of a man was visible on deck. It was the man sitting at the desk. Apparently he used a self-release mechanism. As far as I could tell, he journeyed in the boat alone.

"One of the photographs showed the yacht lying pitiful on a sandy beach with a hole in its side, its backdrop the dark wall of a jungle of palms. Others provided various views of the coast and interior of an island which appeared to be uninhabited. There were several of the entrance to a cave which was overgrown with lianas. But the majority of the photos there on the desk were of the inside of the cave, its gloomy recesses lit harshly by an electric flash. Evidently the cave had many years earlier been transformed into a speos. Pictures of gods emerged out of the darkness, carved in the rock of the walls. There were inscriptions in an unknown, angular script, altars practically covered with sculptures and objects whose meaning could only be guessed at. Among them I noticed the figurines which now stood on the shelf at the man's back. All these things led me to believe that the man at the desk was the owner of the *Zephyrus*, in which he had embarked on a solitary expedition on the seas . . ."

". . . and washed up on an uninhabited island, where he discovered in the jungle a hitherto unknown speos. And now he was writing a book about his adventures and discoveries, which the town's locals were already regaling the tourists with. At the moment captured by the master from Berlin he was in the process of choosing the photographs for its illustrated supplement." These last words were from Baumgarten, in whom stretches of apathy and moments of interest in the monstrous picture were fighting for the upper hand.

"I didn't find anything else of interest in the traveller's room, so I turned my attentions to the streets of the town," the girl continued. "My eyes travelled around the maze of streets in the quarter around the harbour until they reached a grouping of houses on a rise hard by what remained of the town's mighty ramparts. Beyond the half-open shutters at one of the windows I recognized the face of the girl in the black-and-white photograph on the traveller's desk. She was lying in bed with her eyes closed, with a strip of light across her face which had slipped past the shutters and extended across the otherwise dark room, illuminating a closed book on a bedside table to the left of the sleeper's head. I wasn't able to read its title because on top of it there was an open cigarette packet with three cigarettes in it. But I did see a strip of paper sticking out of it which had Chinese characters written on it. To the right, the sleeve of light passed over the hirsute chest of a rather plump young man, who was half sitting, half lying in the bed next to the woman of the photograph. His face was melting into the gloom which enveloped the rest of the room. Otherwise there were only two weak points of light—a red spot on the man's face—apparently the glowing end of a cigarette—and then a suspicious grey sheen in the half-open handbag of the sleeping girl. Might this be the barrel of a small ladies' revolver?

"I saw the next scene in the series of pictures connected with the journeying of the *Zephyrus* through the window of a building which looked like an abandoned Venetian palace rebuilt as a residential house. The window revealed a room whose back wall was covered by a bookcase. There were three men in the room. One of them had a well-groomed grey beard and was sitting in a deep armchair whose covers bore pictures of romantic castles and roses. He was showing something on a sheet of paper to a thin young man in glasses, who was leaning towards his elder in an attitude part curious, part servile. Written in a column on the left-hand side of the sheet were the pointed letters I'd seen in the photographs of the speos; the right-hand side was covered in letters in Latin script. On the windowsill there sat a third man, whose face was obscured. He was reading with interest something someone had written in very small letters in a large notebook. This was written in the Latin script, although there were question marks next to some of the words, and brackets which contained groups of the angular letters."

"But you've already told me about this room. You said that it was part of the story of the turbine and the margarine," recalled Baumgarten, in whom sleepiness and coldness were struggling against a desire to know the sense of all these long-winded descriptions.

"Of the peanut butter, not the margarine. At least you know now how the stories in the different spaces intersected with one another. I attempted to draw a chart showing how the individual scenes were part of a system. What I ended up with was pretty similar to a plan of the Paris métro. The places where the stories crossed corresponded to interchange stations. And the plots developed in the painted scenes were of a great variety of genres: in the picture I found stories of adventure, stories of love, detective stories, surrealistic stories, stories moral and immoral, mystical, pornographic, humanistic, sado-masochistic and didactic stories, stories of *l'art pour l'art*, satanist, socialist and Buddhist stories, stories sophisticated and childish, stories of incest, cynical stories, stories sentimental and stories naturalistic. The only thing in this room which belonged in the story of the turbine was the reflection in a mirror of the room next to it, and this had nothing at all to do with the story of the wrecking of the *Zephyrus*.

"I was unable to decipher the tiny letters in the notebook which the man sitting on the windowsill was holding, so I asked the owner of the gallery for a magnifying glass. With her help I read part of a mythological tale about the goddess of the glitter of gold and a poor fisherman. It seems that the man in the armchair was a linguist or an historian, a university professor perhaps. The other two might have been his assistants or students. I think it was the owner of the *Zephyrus* who had given the professor the photographs of the inscriptions in the speos and that his research had enabled him to decipher their script and to translate some of them. Now he had invited his colleagues or pupils to him so he could familiarize them with the results of his work.

"The text carved into the rock, a translation of which was written in the notebook, told of the goddess of the glitter of gold, who falls in love with a fisherman. The fisherman refuses her because he loves a girl in the neighbouring village. The goddess, insulted and angry, turns the girl into a shoal of thirty-three crabs. For a long time the girl cannot get used to living in so many bodies; she runs to and fro on the sand of the shore on her hundred-and-sixty-four legs, desperately pressing all her crab-bodies together as if willing them to grow together. But they remain separate. She goes to the fisherman's shack in order to watch him; she turns on him sixty-six sad eyes on stalks; pathetically and tenderly she extends all her claws towards him. The fisherman becomes used to the crabs and whenever he returns from his fishing he throws them some fish from his catch.

"The girl doesn't want to reveal who she is because she is ashamed of her crab form and still more of the loss of her singularity. But one evening she is so lovesick that she knows herself to be able no longer to live in anonymity alongside the man she loves. When the fisherman returns from his work the crabs gather in front of his hovel and there in the sand form their bodies into a letter, and then into a second and a third. Astonished and deeply moved, the fisherman reads in the crab-letters the sad news of what has become of his lover. From this moment on the girl transformed into crabs shares the fisherman's home. She teaches herself to do light housework so she can be at least a little useful. Every day she waits patiently for him to return from the sea, and when in the evening he reaches the shore she runs down to meet him. Then they talk together long into the night, just as they did when the girl was still in a single, human form, but with the difference that the girl now writes her answers in letters she forms with her crab-bodies, dashing around from place to place on her reversible legs. When the goddess finds out about this, she is so angry that she takes her revenge on the fisherman by turning him into the left ear of a small woodland rabbit. The text ended in the middle of a sentence; the story must have continued over the page, but this could not be seen. So I didn't find out whether the thirty-three crabs and the left ear of a rabbit found a way to communicate and to declare their love for each other."

## 19
## Leibniz and the hermaphrodite

"After that it took me quite a long time to find another scene which belonged in the story of the wrecked yacht. In the old quarter by the harbour there was a house built into the ruins of a cloister. The columns of the erstwhile cloister, which no longer had weight to bear, stood in the house's not particularly well-maintained interior garden among bushes and large, colourful flowers. Leading into this interior garden was a door and the wide window of a sculptor's studio on the ground floor of the house. In the gloom of the studio the outlines of sculptures could be seen, and there were several of them in the garden itself. Labels bearing titles had been attached to the plinths of some of these. A bust standing on what was left of a stone column was labelled 'Self-portrait'; this was a likeness of the owner of the *Zephyrus*. When he wasn't sailing the seas he was a sculptor, and he worked in this garden studio.

"Glinting in the rays of the sun which had found their way through the leaves was a bronze statue. On its pedestal I read 'Leibniz discovers infinitesimal calculus.' And indeed the statue was a life-size likeness of Leibniz, deep in thought and wearing a periwig. The philosopher was seated on a low stool, resting his chin on one hand and holding in the other Pascal's "A Treatise on the Sines of a Quadrant of a Circle," the reading of which Leibniz declared to have led him to the theory of infinitesimal calculus. 'I have discovered here a light which the author did not glimpse,' Leibniz wrote to Guillaume de l'Hôpital. In his contemplation the philosopher had relaxed his grip on the book and it was slowly slipping from his fingers, which perhaps was supposed to symbolize his gradual disentanglement from the original mathematical theories of Pascal. There was a small shaggy dog waiting intently for the book to fall from Leibniz's hand so it could claim it for itself . . ."

"You're confusing me. Was this a real dog or a bronze one?"

"It was part of the statue, of course, so it was bronze. It was bronze and painted on the picture. The statue depicted the ideas of Leibniz in an original manner. It was similar to when someone's visions and ideas are painted onto a picture with their figure, when the painter puts these in the space next to the figure's head. (Usually the figure has the wide-open eyes of the visionary or his eyes are cast downwards to show that he is immersed in his inner world.) In front of Leibniz in the air (but in fact attached to the statue by thin wires) was a geometric diagram—a quadrant bounded by a horizontal line $x$ and a vertical line $y$ (the lines were drawn by metal bars and the letters were soldered on to these). At point I, in the upper part of the quadrant, a tangent was made, and this—at points A and B—sprouted two metal abscissae, one parallel to line $x$ and the other to line $y$. They intersected at point C inside the quadrant, thus giving the catheti of a right triangle whose hypotenuse was the segment AB in the tangent."

"I don't understand this at all, nor can I imagine it. I know very little about mathematics," Baumgarten protested.

"It's simple, I'll show you," said the thief, taking off her black glove and drawing a quadrant in the snow with her index finger. But as she stretched to describe its base and sagitta, the *y* beneath her gave a fearful crack and in terror she grabbed Baumgarten by his dressing gown. He suggested she leave off the explanations: for the listener's understanding of the story of the wrecked boat a knowledge of infinitesimal calculus was probably not altogether necessary.

"You're right," the girl conceded. "You should just know that the right triangle *ABC* plays an important role in all of this and that

Leibniz realized that if we reduce the horizontal base of this triangle, correspondingly we reduce the second cathetus so that the triangle will always remain homothetic; the relation of the two catheti maintains a constant value which is a characteristic of the curve of the line at point I. The infinite reduction on which Leibniz was meditating was expressed in the statue by three fine wires leading from the apex of the triangle which gradually drew nearer to one another before coiling themselves into a spiral. The coiling wires formed triangles in their midst, each smaller than the last. On one of the arcs of this spiral of ever-smaller triangles, which disappeared into the trees, sat the sculptor's tamed parrot, which was green with a red head and was holding a date in its mouth.

"For the story about the wrecking of the boat, the important thing was the statue standing directly next to Leibniz. This was carved in ebony and was a depiction of a hermaphrodite emerging from the waves of the sea, holding a large, open book in its hands. For sure the words in the letter on the desk of the sculptor's flat were about this statue. (Baumgarten had no recollection of what these words were, but he was too tired to ask.) In the book one could read a poem written in letters formed from pearls and set into the black ebony of the pages. This was a poem the sculptor had written for the woman he loved, who at this moment was lying in bed with another man. I imagine that the sculptor and traveller wanted to make the woman a gift of pearls he had found in the speos on the island. He wrote a poem for her and worked on the statue of the hermaphrodite, which were also intended as presents for her (the hermaphrodite was meant to symbolize their ideal communion); then it came to him that his gifts to his beloved would be more original if he made the three into one.

"But surprisingly the poem written in pearls had little in common with love poetry. In painstaking rhyme and regular stanzas it told that the dead do not reveal themselves at night in churchyards or old houses, as people foolishly believe, but that they like the sun, light and warm. So they walk upon sandy beaches, and many people meet their dear-departed on the beach at Waikiki, on the beaches of California, on the Epi-plage or Tahiti beaches of Saint-Tropez, even on the municipal pebble beach in Nice. The epic poem in pearls told how a middle-aged businessman goes on holiday for the first time without his wife, who has been kept at home by her career commitments. Through a travel agent he books a stay on the Aegean island of Mykonos. On his very first day on Paradise beach a suntanned girl in a swimsuit calls to him, and to his great astonishment the businessman recognizes her as a woman he once loved, who died in a car accident twenty years earlier.

"After that they meet on the beach every day, and on a sun bed under a parasol or under the reed awning of the beach bar she tells him of life in the underworld; she shows him which of the visitors to the beach are deceased; she greets other dead folk as if they are all members of some club. She says that life in the underworld is not especially entertaining, nor is it particularly depressing. Admittedly the vast underworld spaces are a little unwelcoming and hardly abounding with comforts, but they are clean and always kept tidy. She claims that such a life is quite tolerable, that it might even be slightly better than life before death: the regime of the underworld is not very strict and the deceased are able to leave Erebus every day. If they return in the evening at a time later than allowed for by their exeat, generally all they receive is a reprimand. They can go anywhere on Earth they choose, and as many of them love warm, sandy beaches they spend whole days on the hot sand.

"She isn't sure whether she is in Hell or in Paradise. She says that this is a common topic of discussion among the deceased, that everyone's opinion on it is different. But there is no higher authority in the underworld to arbitrate their disputes. The guards who watch the gate are themselves deceased who have been in the underworld for a long time, as is the captain of the ship of the dead which takes them ashore every morning. Every evening the businessman waits with her on the cooling beach, on which most of those remaining are deceased, until he hears the distant drone of the engine of the ship of the dead and a white speedboat sweeps into the bay. Then they kiss and the girl climbs aboard with the others and gives him a last wave before the boat disappears behind the rock. When after two weeks they say their final good-byes, the girl asks if she will ever see him on Mykonos again. The businessman replies that it is unlikely he will ever again manage to go on holiday without his wife. 'No matter,' says the girl. 'You can visit me once you die. I'll give you my address. The underworld is pretty vast and complex and you might not find me otherwise. Then we can make up for lost time. I'm already really looking forward to the time we can walk together on Paradise beach every day; in fact, we can visit all the beaches of the Aegean . . .' Hey, don't go to sleep or you'll fall."

## 20
## Dances in the fire

These last words were not those of the deceased woman on Mykonos; they were meant for Baumgarten. A pleasant torpor had indeed taken hold of his body; his eyes were closing, their lashes were wet with melted snow, and he was seeing the snowflakes as foam of the waves on the Aegean beach the thief had been telling him about. When the girl saw that the dozing aesthetician was swaying precariously on the tip of the *a*, she shook him. Baumgarten insisted he had not been asleep at all, that he had been listening to her attentively, but immediately afterwards his head began to sink towards her lap. The girl was not pleased to stop talking about her favourite topic but she concluded that Baumgarten was too sleepy to pay her any heed and it was time to go.

She took him by the hand and led him along what remained of the word *Lafayette*. When they reached the final "e," she saw that he was a little more alert; on their way down she would attempt to tell him something more about the picture. Baumgarten, half-asleep and serene, was happy to be led; he skipped over the letters with the lightness of a somnambulist. The girl's talk had the quality of snow-music and as such was no bother to him.

"I thought that the story of the wrecking of the *Zephyrus* was one of island treasure and heartache," the thief said, giving Baumgarten a radiant smile. "But in the fine weave of the story these were only secondary motifs. The Berlin picture was full of such confusing signs and unexpected twists. Then it occurred to me to use the magnifying glass to look into the car which stood in front of the house of the sculptor's unfaithful mistress. And I saw in the car four agents of the Chinese secret service."

Baumgarten wished for a moment to sit on the short, horizontal line which intersected the second "t," as this put him in mind of a seat. But the thief pulled him away.

"Just keep going, you'll be home in a few minutes. One of the Chinese agents was aiming a rifle with a silencer and telescopic sights at the head of the man who was lying in the bed with the sculptor's mistress. The muscles of the Chinese's trigger finger were tensed. Then it came to me that the red spot I'd taken for the glowing end of a cigarette was in fact the light made by the gun's sights, and it was wandering over the man's face. The next moment he was likely to catch the full force of the Chinese's rifle; had the painter shown the town a second later, one would probably have seen in the room a bloodied face and a pillow stained with red. And what's the connection between all this and the Chinese characters on the strip of paper sticking out of the book on the bedside table? Is this merely a coincidence, or does the sculptor's mistress know more than we think about the game the secret service is playing? And what of the revolver in her handbag? What does she intend to shoot at with that? Perhaps you'd be interested to know what happened." The girl turned to face Baumgarten, who had not spoken, because at that very moment he was giving himself up to a dream in which the violet neon letters were changing into water nymphs with glowing bodies, dancing in a woodland glade.

"The picture didn't show whether the mystery man in the bed escaped with his life. After all, the picture wove together thousands of story-lines, many of which went deep into the past, although all ended at the moment at which the town was captured. So it was unclear what would happen in the next fraction of a second in any of the stories. As you can see, we've reached the end of the word. Just a few steps along the roof of the building next door and we can climb down the fire escape and through the skylight to the staircase; I've tried it before. Oddly enough it was a torn poster I saw on a wall in the quarter around the harbour, a poster announcing a performance by a ballet company, that led me to answers to the questions I'd been asking myself. Among the things the sculptor had found in the cave-temple were two suits of clothing to wear during the performing of rituals. On religious festivals the priests would wear these to dance their sacred dances in the lake of red-hot lava which bubbled in the mouth of the volcano at the island's centre. The suits were woven of special fibres which, so it seemed, were resistant to any degree of heat and insulated the body quite perfectly. Naturally certain international concerns became interested in the suits, as did the general staffs of the armies of many countries. The impractical sculptor had never imagined that the suits would become the subject of great interest, that he would be able to earn a vast sum of money by them. He gifted the suits to his friends, members of an avant-garde ballet troupe, and they wore them in the compelling final act of a ballet on the theme of Plotinus's *Enneads*, the whole of which was set in the fire of the One, represented on stage by a real earthly fire.

"For a long time I racked my brains as I sought to work out who was the man lying in bed with the sculptor's mistress. Who was the man on whom the Chinese had their weapons trained? I'd almost given up hope of finding out when I discovered a photograph of him in a newspaper folded into a hat and worn by a man spraying the body of a car with red paint in a car-repair shop on the edge of the town. The headline told me that the sculptor's rival was a branch director for a giant weapons concern. Was the sculptor's mistress in league with him, had she betrayed him to the Chinese agents, or was she playing a game of her own against them all?"

As he continued along the snow-covered roof Baumgarten became more alert, but still he did not pay much attention to what the girl was saying. He heard some words to the effect of ". . . at a secret meeting in Singapore in which all parties were involved, it emerged that . . .", and ". . . next day they found the body of the Amsterdam diamond dealer in the bay at Villefranche-sur-Mer . . .", and ". . . Doctor Xiang Liu's number was circled in the telephone directory." Once again Baumgarten's drowsiness was chopping the whole which the girl had so painstakingly composed in Berlin into disconnected fragments. They reached a kind of shelf where the thief rummaged in the snow for a moment or two before lifting a metal hatch and pushing the half-sleeping aesthetician into a dark opening. Soon they were descending the unlit staircase of the silent building. There was a sound of snoring from behind one of the doors. Before long they reached the empty street. Baumgarten saw the display windows of the department store, how they illuminated the snowflakes dancing above the pavement, and behind them he saw the door of the building, which he passed through every day. He was surprised to see how close it was; on the roof, the breadth of the department store's facade had seemed to him greater than the distance required by an expedition across Greenland.

He gathered his senses and said to the girl, "You should get some sleep. I need to put my head down, too. Tomorrow I'll come to the gallery and lend you the money for the picture. And there'll be no hurry for you to pay it back."

The thief hesitated, then gave him the address of a gallery on the Left Bank of the Seine. She accompanied Baumgarten to the door of his building before waving down a taxi whose lights emerged from the swirling snow and disappeared. Back in his flat the aesthetician changed into dry pyjamas and set his alarm clock. Then he dropped onto the bed and fell asleep immediately. The next day at eleven o'clock he was at the gallery the girl had described to him. He learned that there would be no auction there that day, and no one knew anything about a picture of a harbour town. The thief did not come, nor did he ever see her again. Later he asked colleagues at the university who lectured on contemporary painting about the picture, but all they did was shrug their shoulders. He described it to some art critics from Berlin who were in Paris for a symposium, and they all listened with amazement to his tales of the statue of Leibniz, the crabs, the Chinese agents and the ballet-dancing Enneads. But none of them had seen the picture or knew of the drowned painter . . . When my Paris acquaintance finished his story, he checked his watch, made his apologies, and left me alone in the café with a story with no point and no moral.

# 21
## Fragments and wholes

When I went over the whole Rue des Beaux-Arts story again, I reached the conclusion that probably it was not true, even though I could not imagine the reason why my Paris acquaintance would have invented it. It was not merely that the story-lines were implausible: in the descriptions of the motionless objects, for example, there was a heavy whiff of French literary influences, and the commentaries in the last part of the story were suspiciously reminiscent of Roussel and Perec. In conjuring up in the café pictures of snowflakes swirling in the light of violet neon, the narrator so befuddled me that I did not for one moment doubt the veracity of his stories. But next day, when I noticed that the lettering bearing the name of the Galeries Lafayette department store had no resemblance to the lettering of the narrator's description, I began to suspect I had been duped. And now I am almost certain that nothing I was told in the café actually happened.

And what is worse, I realized with regret that the story was not particularly well thought out. I have described already how there were two sets of identifiers of things with letters, each the mirror image of the other—in the farmyard, where things were transformed into letters, and on the roof of the department store, where letters were transformed into things. Each of these carried the hero to a new world; I think that the more radical encounter with a new world was in the neon labyrinth of the roof. Admittedly it may seem that the Homeric inscription in rusty tools is in complete defiance of the logic and order of our world, but the peculiar spectacle in the farmyard is blurred by the fact that we can only find a place for it in the categories known to us, those of the miraculous, the mystical and the supernatural; these are still components woven into our world (and as such are traps for those who seek other worlds). The material power of words, however, which the chase on the roof stirs into life, opens up a strange space between things and letters, a space that eludes categorization, a space that is neither in the world nor out of it but in a strange, impossible place opened with the help of this power. Through the gap it is possible to catch a glimpse of a certain disquieting action that perhaps reaches back to the sources of action in our world, an action that marks the birth and death of all worlds. In this sense the episode on the roof was closer to the islanders' identification of objects with letters than the episode on the farm. The islanders were not in the least excited by the supernatural; if an angel were to appear in a deserted street in the lower town, the inhabitants of the island would not be particularly interested, although they would admire the rippling of its robe and listen to the murmur of its wings.

These two related motifs were interwoven cleverly in the story, but the promised identification of letters with objects regrettably remained isolated and barren—in the remainder of the story nothing grew from them. The state in which simultaneously we see a thing, react to it and read it as a letter casts us into an unimaginable, yet real space, in which it is not clear whether seeing, reacting and reading are parts of a single primary action or it is their incompatibility that has set the dizzying vortex in motion. And so this unsatisfactory state, which was tied to the object-letter motif, called for climax and catharis, but such a maturation of this motif in the plotline of the story was not achieved. Although the motifs of the crab's letters and the pearls on the Berlin picture were a repeat of the object-letter drama, they showed it in weakened form rather than developing it further, just as the ornamentation of a frame is sometimes a simplified repetition of the motifs on the canvas.

Of course it was possible to accuse all the motifs of the story of being self-absorbed, isolated and fragmentary. Incidents came to an end and were replaced with others to which they bore no connection; the goddess Ino, for example, who entered Baumgarten's thoughts in the farmyard, disappeared from the story never to return, even though there were plenty of opportunities for her to do so. Having thought these incidents up, a storyteller ought to take the trouble to join his beginnings to his endings in an elegant circle. He could say: "While the thief was sitting on the *y* describing to Baumgarten the Berlin picture, a vision came to the aesthetician in the whirling snow of a garment of billowing white. Shortly afterwards the white figure of a woman appeared before him in the violet neon; she looked at him with sadness for a few moments before vanishing into the darkness of the boulevard. Baumgarten had read in her expression the reproach that he had scorned her advice, that he had quite forgotten about her in the buffet bar on rue d'Odessa and hence had come to grief by becoming the well-respected head of a family and a citizen held in high esteem." Then he might have continued: "In a fit of despair over his wrecked life, over the book he never succeeded in writing to completion, over the emptiness whose purity he never managed to hold on to, he pulled the necklace from the pocket of his dressing gown, handed it to the thief, and then threw himself down into the boulevard. But before his body could hit the pavement he felt a pair of gentle arms wrap themselves around him and bear him upwards. Ino had saved him and was carrying him off to distant shores . . ."

I was also perplexed by how the narrator had the girl simply disappear at the end of the story. A lovely solution had presented itself: Baumgarten could have fallen in love with the thief, whose world reminded him of the world of the rooftops, sleeping houses and undersea caves where strangers dwelled, a forgotten world of emptiness, waiting for nothing, and all the bliss these things entailed;

the figure of the thief would be identified with Ino Leukothea (naturally it would be better if this were not stated explicitly, but the unity of the two characters be left to the listener to discover), and in this way, too, the analogy of the lettering in the yard and the neon inscription would be emphasized, an analogy into whose force field the smaller motifs of the pearl and crabs' letters would be drawn, so that these were no longer superfluous ornamentation. The circle of the action might be further sealed by putting in the painting described by the thief a room on whose wall there hung a picture of Odysseus holding on to his raft as he was beaten by the waves.

I wrote that last paragraph, dear reader, late yesterday evening. Now it is nine in the morning and I'm sitting at my computer over a cup of strong, hot coffee. I would be glad if you would try to visualize for a moment the inconspicuous division between paragraphs, the negligible white space between the night-time period applied in resignation and encroached upon by the foam of sleep on the one hand, and the tense and impatient early-morning capital on the other, and to see these as a negative of last night, so that you might summon from this negative all its blackness and push it between the paragraphs. Otherwise what I write here will seem disconnected and illogical to you. All manner of things changed during the night; I lay in bed thinking about what I had written and I realized I had run straight into the trap the Parisian narrator had set for me.

Now I believe I did not understand the story. At the beginning its protagonist encounters the motions of elusive order and chaos, motions that escape from every code they help to appoint. But in so doing they create a curious unity, and any other unity, connection, and circular enclosure would violate the unity introduced at the beginning, while every violation of the unity and connectedness—and the story was composed practically entirely of such violations—would affirm and complement it. This means that everything in the story was exactly where it should be; its connectedness was formed by its disconnectedness and its unity by its fragmentariness.

By now you are perhaps asking yourself, dear reader, why I do not just drop the story told by the Parisian, as I have so many doubts about its veracity. It may seem strange to you, but a lack of veracity in the story is for me a more persuasive argument for telling it here than its veracity would be. All manner of things occur in it, and these are of no special significance, but the fact that the story of the letters is a fiction is surprising at the very least; that someone in Europe is thinking of the same things as the islanders seems to me something almost as unbelievable as a Greek goddess fluttering down towards the hero of the story on a Paris roof.

## 22
## Board games

I remember the games the islanders used to play. They were fond of board games. The extraction of precious stones from the mines of their homes did not take up too much of their time, and apart from their dreamy attention to the sounds of the water and the murmur of the leaves interwoven with the squawking of birds, apart from their meals and their occasional reading and writing of the *Book*, they practised only one form of popular entertainment. I would often see them two and two sitting in the shadow of a colonnade in the lower town or on a stone terrace in the upper town, leaning over a game-board. It took me a long time to get used to these games, but eventually I learned to take pleasure in the long, puzzling matches with their ever-changing rules and uncertain outcomes. Even today when the rain keeps me in my Prague flat on a Sunday afternoon, I fold out the game-board I brought back from the island and challenge myself to a game. (I have failed to find anyone here who finds amusement in the islanders' games.)

The games, too, gave vent to the islanders' fascination for things which for us do not even exist. By this I mean the shapes of the formless and the surfaces of boundaries. It was as if these games had been born out of the need to create new borders while disputing their existence. The borders were not violated in the name of some kind of (primary or definitive) continuity or freedom. In referring to the islanders' love of the formless I have allowed myself to be ensnared by language. The fact is that the islanders had no notion of *continuous* or *formless*: where we say *formless* they used a word whose literal meaning is "the dance of demons and animals in the early morning and evening." For the islanders, even a white surface was a vortex of nascent and expiring shapes, full of monsters and fantastic fauna and flora; while the real bodies of humans and animals and real flowers were for them produce of a single species which exercised no particular privileges in relation to other species. And the gaps between species were not for them, as they are for us, so much empty space into which a monster will occasionally stray: they were inhabited by a great number of beings, whose bodies assumed all manner of transitional shapes. The islanders were well aware that such creatures do not occur in the real world, yet for all that they thought them no more bizarre than real species (not least the animals I told them about; they considered the distinction between existence in words and existence in the imagination a negligible one).

In the beginning I was exasperated by the fact that all the boards on the island were—to differing degrees—out of focus. At first glance you might mistake one for the common type of board we use, but the dividing line between two squares was blurred, and for at least a fraction of a second a moving piece would pass through an area which was neither white nor black but was so much part of the game that it needed to be taken into consideration. Elsewhere on the board there might be a zone in which several squares had indistinct edges; this would put me in mind of a volcano spewing an ever-changing molten lava which, before it was solidified in the black-and-white squares, dreamed wild dreams about games of sameness and difference. There were boards on which all the borders were blurred and boards on which all the squares had practically dissolved. (The surface of the latter was grey with lighter and darker areas which recalled a world of borders.)

Some of the island's game-boards attained such a state by a process of natural development. I often saw islanders playing with boards which must once have been standard, European chessboards but on which time had worked to erase or obfuscate borders, to lose them in a confusion of lines and a swamp of stains; the board was flaking, crumbling, dripping wet, its squares had paled in the light of the sun, had peeled off, developed cracks, its colours had run into one another, washing over the web of scratches wrought by all the moves and the stains left by all the liquids which had seeped into its pores over many years. The islanders sat over such boards and moved about them decaying pieces thick with mould, with which they wandered the labyrinths of scratches and stains; it was never quite clear to what extent they were searching for traces of squares long-gone or how far their moves and stops were forming a new game-board web both fanciful and vague. Often a game was in progress when the pieces disintegrated to irrecoverable effect; the players would gather together the dust which was all that remained of them, and, after the wind blew this away, continue the game using imaginary pieces. As the end approached there were more imaginary pieces than real and the game crossed seamlessly into the realms of memory and night-time dreams, becoming a game of phantoms.

I played on boards whose squares changed in the course of a single game. They were made of squares of darker and lighter sand sprinkled on the board. In the course of the game the wind would blow the sand about, into long patches run through with different colours, until the board became a whirl of darker and lighter twists, stretching and transforming, wrapping themselves into other twists, reminiscent of the jaspé bindings of books come to life in dreams; and the pieces would pick their way through them, before crumbling and blending in with the sand of the squares.

I taught myself to understand a little the peculiar delight to be had from taking up a position on a blurred border, where none of the segments into which the space is divided have any particular claim on us, where suddenly we encounter the existence of something neither left nor right, neither the same nor different, a third thing which is impossible yet real; we encounter a space the world does not know and that no world would allow, but which provides a strange, rather pleasant place to stay. I believe this space's magical charm is somehow reflected in all the border territories we pass through on our travels, that it gives both shelter and danger, is at once a citadel and a trap. It is there in the city's mysterious edges, where the fringes of a garden give sanctuary to ghosts woven of moisture and shadow, in the strip between road and field, perhaps in that unlit café on the seashore I happened across that night in Naoussa on Paros, whose last tables and chairs were being claimed by the waves as they rose and fell.

Often the pieces were of an indefinite colour, and this would change in the course of a game. Some of them crumbled or melted in the sun and thus became different. Sometimes a player would realize that the piece he had in his hand, with which he was about to make his final, victorious move, had transformed itself into one of his opponent's pieces. As they underwent such transformations pieces would go through phases where it was impossible to say what they were like and to whom they belonged, but however monstrous they were still it was necessary to play with them, to move them about the fluid, borderless squares. Stranger still was the fact there was no clear boundary between piece and board; a piece might melt and become a square, or a square of the waterboard, which was popular in the upper town, might take on a firm shape which then would be moved about the playing surface.

Nor were there set rules for the game. The rules would change in the course of a game, usually by appendices attaching themselves to edges and exceptions undermining from the inside the existing rules, which themselves would become a collection of appendices and exceptions and as such would dissolve. It is to be presumed that a new state of affairs on the board called for new rules. This provoked no argument between the players, who continued to sit over the board in silence; while one was interpreting the new rules from the positions of the pieces and the moves of his opponent and adapting his play accordingly, the other was trying to find the rules in the configuration of the board and the moves of his opponent, which themselves were informed by moves he himself had taken. Even in this complicated manner, which we can compare to an attempt to reflect nothing between two mirrors, in time some kind of tacit harmonization of the rules might have been reached; but around the time new rules were becoming fixed, the impression was created that they were out of tune with the new state of affairs on the board, so again they began to change.

In the beginning the games of the islanders were a cause of boredom or exasperation to me. Once when Karael and I were sitting at the board and after my thirtieth move I remained clueless as to what was going on, I threw a tantrum and scattered the pieces across the board. When I offered her a shamefaced apology, Karael laughed and said this act of mine had in no way spoiled the game and that it was still in progress; I had not fought free of the game or its rules. The rolling of the pieces about the board was simply an expression of a new version of the rules which was immediately assimilated by the game, which thus caught me in its snare.

And so would the island's players sit over their game-boards of blurred squares with fuzzy borders that shifted in the course of a game, moving pieces which changed into other pieces and disintegrated in their hands, playing by rules which originated from the game in progress and underwent constant change. How strange it is that I, too, should come to find pleasure in a way of playing which looked infinitely complicated and laborious! But whoever explored it more deeply discovered that there was a simplicity in it, that the ground it moved us across was ground we knew intimately, and that the simplicity was a source of delight.

I don't know the origins of the island's games. It may be that they came to the island by way of the Europeans and that the islanders adapted them in accordance with their own tastes. It is also possible that board games originated on the island, that the way the islanders play them is the original way, that only later did they find their way to Europe and Asia, where their fluid rules became fixed rules and the borders between squares became calmer and more distinct, paving the way for the games we play today. But what if the boards of Europe were merely dormant, what if some disturbance of the modern age should wake them so that their borders were fluid once again and their squares began to pulsate?

## 23
## The labyrinths of flavour

One of the reasons I stayed so long on the island was its cuisine. When I spoke of the island as the territory of lotus eaters, this was meant as nothing more than an illustration; but the islanders' food was certainly one of the more pleasing aspects of life on the island. It happened on several occasions that I was standing on a terrace in the upper town when a ship flying a Greek or a Spanish flag entered the harbour. Each time I asked myself whether it was time for me to leave. And then I would remember the feast to which I had been invited the next day and would say to myself, "I'll take the next ship, there's bound to be another one along soon." (And there always was, but there was always another feast, too.)

When I was first invited into the houses of the islanders, I found it surprising that there was never a stove or an oven to be seen. As the island lies on the Tropic of Cancer, there is no need for the islanders to heat their dwellings, but as for the preparation of food, it remained a mystery to me where the islanders performed this. I noticed that every house had a room where glass jars and pots of a great variety of sizes were lined up on shelves; all of these were filled with liquids and pastes and were aglow with bright colours. Only later did I learn that these rooms were pantries and kitchens in one: on the island the storage and preparation of food merged into a single act. One of the most striking features of the island's cuisine was the suspicion with which the islanders treated fire. Changes brought about by fire seemed to them too quick and violent and as such incapable of producing anything to interest them.

The seamen in the harbour who fed on roast or boiled meat, they viewed as barbarians. They thought that foodstuffs did not exude their most precious flavours when subjected to crude treatment by fire, that it was necessary to wait patiently for these flavours to show themselves and to learn and be alert to the signs of their coming. The islanders considered flavours to be dreams, perhaps even the thoughts, of foodstuffs, as ever-present melodies which foodstuffs held within, of which we caught a snatch when we dined. For the islanders, fire was too fierce and too crude to draw from a foodstuff its inner melody. Only the processes of gradual maturation were gentle enough to wake the dreams in a foodstuff, slow enough to allow us to hope we would catch the foodstuff at the moment its most splendid tones were sounding.

So the islanders left crushed berries and fruit juices, the shredded leaves of herbs and trees, pulverized roots—either separately or in mixes with varying proportions—to mature, disintegrate, melt and crystallize, to soften and harden, to dry out, go stale, curdle, ferment and swell. The preparation of a meal would take several days; a lunch or a dinner was often matured for several weeks, even months. But usually the result was worth the wait: the juices, jellies, pastes, purées and powders which these mysterious processes produce are celebrated by European and American gourmets, and I have heard they are used in the most expensive items on the menus of luxury restaurants in Paris, London and New York.

Naturally it was difficult to pinpoint in these processes of transformation where maturation gave way to decay. This is why initially I was mistrustful of the islanders' cuisine; indeed, I had the impression that all the island's meals were half-rotten. I took me a long time to get accustomed to them, to learn to appreciate them. It is quite true that when confronted with evidence of what happens to foodstuffs in the pantry-kitchens of the island, people where we come from would, in many cases, observe, "That food's spoiling." But by what gauge should we distinguish fairly between the process of the purging of a foodstuff—or, as the islanders call it, the waking of its hidden dreams or the sounding of its inner melodies—and the process of its spoiling and decomposition? Why should we not assume that foodstuffs dream only of sweetness and purity, not of the darker realms of ruin and decay? Even Aristotle, who called dreams matter in forms, conceded the difficulty of determining whether the emergence of vinegar from wine is the genesis of a form or the demise of one.

Once I was accustomed to the island's cuisine I stopped thinking about what was matured and what was spoiled, stopped searching anxiously for signs of degeneration and decay in its flavours, stopped wondering whether the sweet aftertaste on my palate had in it a tone of growth or a sound of the juices of death. I came to take pleasure in the labyrinth of flavours, which was perhaps still more puzzling and insidious than the maze of the island's grammar or that of the island's script. I learned to wander around this new labyrinth, where individual flavour-tones appeared, each with its own world, each world acknowledging, supporting and denying the others. These tones formed a complex figure in which one was mirrored by another; the reflection showed a great, lavish world of foodstuffs, with inner landscapes populated by men and beasts with flowing bodies, where things occurred which were nothing more than the fizzing of energy yet—or so it seemed to me—were no less interesting than stories of Italian lovers from feuding families or irresolute princes in gloomy Danish castles. To lose one's way in this labyrinth was a joy; it was impossible to extract from it—as things that were foreign—tones of decay, as even rotten tones were part of the maturation of a foodstuff, which as it matured also rotted into pure tones which appeared in its dreams.

On my return to Europe I was once invited to a restaurant where food from the island was served as something very rare and special. I was incensed by the way the European gourmets chose to enjoy it but I did not attempt to explain to my table companions that they did not understand the island's cuisine and that their interpretation of it was wrong. The flavours of the island were translated carelessly into the language of European cuisine and the result was something extremely banal. The half-rotten tones were taken to be of the same order as high game; the presence of these tones was interpreted as a sophistication that afforded a frivolous delight from being on the edge of the normal, a delight engendered by the risk implicit to being on the border between the eatable and the uneatable. I could not blame my fellow diners for this as they had only a slight knowledge of culinary hermeneutics which was born out of the world of boiled, baked and fried foods and which was of no use to them beyond this world. An islander would have eaten something different in that restaurant, even if he had served himself from the same dishes. For the islander no flavour-tone was on the edge: flavour-tones appeared in a labyrinth which had no centre and no edges.

## 24
## The last island

Although, as I said, I learned to like the flavours of the island, still there were times when I could not get a morsel of the meals I was offered past my lips, when my gorge would rise at the smells wafting in from the kitchen, when I would dream of goulash and schnitzel with potato salad. Strange to say, Karael experienced such periods of disgust, too. I do not know whether all inhabitants of the island were affected like this and kept this information to themselves or whether it was Karael's proximity to me which created disorder in how she perceived things. I have to say that it usually seemed she was as resistant to foreign influences as the islanders in general, who had succeeded in chewing up and swallowing Christianity just as they had technological civilization. That the only one on the island forgetting the assumptions of his own world was me; that only I was developing an ever-stronger liking for half-rotten food, for listening to the murmurs and observing the nonsensical, undulating shapes.

As the case may be, at dinner at her house in the upper town Karael would sometimes push away her plate of violet purée and crimson jelly and begin to complain quietly about the island, about its world, about how this was modelled by the island's grammar, about how the island's perspective made itself manifest, how the hands of the island touched and the tongues of the island tasted. I had to lean towards her over the bowls and plates in order to catch her quiet lament. She whispered, "Everything always congeals and runs, runs and congeals, it's so tedious, it's so grim." And then, "How I hate all these disgusting purées! If there's no difference between rotting and maturing, everything is rotten, every flavour is the flavour of death . . ."

Then she would plead with me. "Take me with you to Europe. Promise me we'll leave on the next boat. I could work as a shop assistant, as a cleaner. I don't want to live on this horrible island any longer. The time that passes here is decaying time, rotten time. Past and future ooze out of the runny present . . ." At her back the world trembled, dissolved in the ever-changing carpet of the wall of water. I took her in my arms and soothed her; I told her that tomorrow a boat would be leaving the harbour, in the morning we would pack our things and go down to the lower town, we would be in Europe in a few days and the island would be just a memory. But the next day we never spoke of what we had said to each other in the evening and we avoided looking towards the harbour and the white boat.

When I complained about the character of the islanders and she defended it, Karael and I would often quarrel. But at these times I never reminded her of the moments when the charges she set against the islanders were graver still than mine, when she thought the island on which she was forced to live was a hell. The moments when she saw the islanders as freaks were nothing but the dark underside of the moments of serene happiness which gave our life on the island its texture. I never saw the islanders as freaks. I had no particular love for them, but I believed them to have the same right to their way of life as we had to ours, that theirs was neither better nor worse than the kind of life we led in Europe. As I had lived it since my childhood the European way of life was closer to me, but it was not that much closer. And after I had been on the island a year, and the sources of new emotions had got into my blood and my eyes had begun to perceive the weavings of rays of light in a different way, I was aware that I was beginning to distance myself from the language of European life and culture.

And when I returned there were many things I no longer understood. All the complex syntaxes which determined roles within the family and within society as a whole seemed to me as distant and tedious, as bizarre and incomprehensible as the islanders' grammatical categories and the rules of their games, and somewhat more stuffy and awkward. It was only after I returned to Europe that I found myself on the most distant and strangest of islands, an island from which there is no return because it is home. This was the Ithaca of the *Odyssey*, which someone had rewritten as a silent-screen comedy. (Screenplay: Odysseus, having for ten years consorted with monsters and demons, is himself more of a monster/demon than a man, and he discovers that he no longer understands much of the language of his homeland.) On the last of the islands all that home can provide is the role of the confused ethnologist, looking on as all around him perform mysterious rituals, some inducing depression, others imbued with a moving, nonsensical beauty.

But whoever thinks I am complaining, is wrong. I neither invented nor chose the protagonist who reaches out to the world through my mixed-up gestures, but I am happy with it and have no intention of exchanging it for any other; after all, it has grown out of my travels and encounters, out of the spaces outlined in my memory which perhaps only opened up at stations and in harbours in order to help in its making. I have heard the slow growth of this protagonist within the cocoon of landscapes; it is of no particular importance whether this long, patient childhood was the gradual genesis of the Self in the body of a stranger or some kind of macabre transformation within a monster. It is important to fuse with the rhythm of these changes, to be in thrall to the time when we are born on the islands and in the towns and countries we visit; it is not important to think about the legitimacy of a motion which makes sense only in and of itself, in the development of its rhythms, in the melody which leads up to no finale. This motion cannot accept vindication from anything outside itself: probably it is one of the very first beams of current to pass through the nothingness, which formed on their way the universe of stars, rocks, plants, bodies and consciousness.

Perhaps psychologists and psychiatrists would consider themselves competent to comment on my island in central Europe, but both would be wrong. The loosening and unravelling of the tissues of the world to reveal the womb beneath is a motion older than Man and, I believe, older than life itself. It is one of the motions that explains, among other things, psychology and psychiatry; for certain it is not the other way round.

Apart from all this, the silent-screen Ithaca is a great place to live; I am ever more aware of how much I like this last island, and I tell myself I would not wish to live anywhere else even if it were possible for me to leave it. It is true that nothing here makes any sense, but this is no great misfortune; I learned from the islanders that sense is not of any particular importance, that its presence may even disrupt the clean lines of certain pictures and cast a cloud over their fine light, while laments on the absurdity of being struck me as self-indulgent and objectionable even before my stay on the island. Once you get a little used to a terrain cleansed of sense, you realize that there is amusement enough to be had here, and that only in its emptiness can the magic crystals of beauty originate. And in this space something is revealed: the silent dignity of people, animals, plants and objects, that is able to stir graciousness, compassion and reverence.

## 25
## Fungus and shell

But the evenings that turned into heavy dreams were rare, both for Karael and for me. The island feasts usually gave cause for delight; indeed, I would look forward to them far in advance and I still remember them fondly today. In the middle of the table there was often a pliant, white material which at first I took to be some kind of fungus. In fact it was the solidified secretion of a type of cuttlefish which was hunted in the warm, shallow waters above the coral reef which encircled the island's shoreline.

Several times I was one of an expedition which went in quest of the cuttlefish's white ink. The hunter floats in the clear waters above the bright-coloured coral garden, holding in his hand a kind of ratchet. As soon as he catches sight of the cuttlefish he begins to turn the wheel of the ratchet; the sound this makes frightens the cuttlefish and forces it to flee, but before it does so it releases a cloud of white fluid which twists and curls in the water, sending out projections and winding them back in, all the time solidifying quickly. This solidification starts in the middle and takes only a few seconds to reach the furthest points of white, which become slower in their movement, change gradually to a paste, then stiffen and go still, petrified in a gesture of flight or return.

The very first hunt I took part in presented me with an unforgettable experience. Having floated around the coral reef, Karael and I startled a school of cuttlefish, which disappeared in a flash, leaving white clouds in its wake like the souls of drowning men. As we swam about in the clouds we saw how they were transforming themselves. I fancied I saw in them human faces I knew well, but these would disappear immediately. When the transformations were over and the solidified cloudlets began slowly to sink, Karael and I caught them and threaded them—like soft metals—onto lines ending in a silver barb, which each of us had coiled around our waist.

This white ink fungus is treated in a number of different ways. Sometimes it is cut into slivers for use in a cuttlefish salad (I once saw in Paris how these slivers were laid on thin slices of a white baguette, lightly toasted on the grill and drenched in olive oil). Sometimes it is forced through a utensil which looks like a garlic press, out of which it emerges in the form of long, white spaghetti. Cuttlefish spaghetti are dressed in a red sauce from the pantry made of berries grown in the apartments of the lower town in the close, dark spaces between walls and the backs of rotting cupboards which have been there since the time of the European invasion; in addition to mines, the islanders also have gardens in their apartments. It was easy to carve the solidified ink of the cuttlefish into any shape one chose. The islanders would often ask me about the food where I came from, so once I used several cuttlefish mushrooms to fashion for them the fare on the table of a Czech pub, with plates of goulash and dumplings, a smaller plate with brawn, a basket of bread rolls, several half-litres of beer and glasses of rum, adding while I was at it, an open pack of cigarettes and an ashtray with cigarette ends in it. After the islanders had studied my creation, we ate it together.

Most commonly, however, cuttlefish fungus forms part of a dish known as the "pink porcupine." For the preparation of this meal one also needs the shell of a certain marine snail. One night in the year this snail leaves the sea to shed its shell of twelve months and also to celebrate its lover's ritual in a state of nakedness. Hundreds of snails come ashore, onto the sandy flats of the lower town, where they arrange themselves in the shape of a star with sixteen regular beams. Once the snails have assumed their places they wriggle out of their shells and their soft little bodies glow in the bluish light.

The ritual of their courtship is founded on a game of many-coloured lights and geometric figures. Watching this game from the upper town was an enchanting experience. First the beams of the great star down there on the flats bent themselves into S-shapes while the blue light of the odd beams turned green and then yellow and the blue of the even beams turned violet and then red. The next moment the individual, rippling beams began to change colour from yellow to red and vice versa; this they did in such a way that it looked from above as if the beams of the star were revolving rapidly around its centre. The rippling beams disintegrated before the fragments came together again to form eight fixed circles. Then a new game of lights set up, with the apparent motion coming from the centre and moving to the edge and back again.

After this the circles transformed themselves into eight-beamed stars, which went on to become an evenly-proportioned cross. This cross shone violet and its arms coiled themselves towards its centre before changing into four spirals. These then became entwined and began to form complicated, moving ornaments. Their movement was the result of the meshing of the real motion of the snails and the illusory motion born out of the perfect harmonization of the changes in colour. (Imagine a billboard on which moving pictures arise not only from the lighting-up of individual points, as is common, but also from the real movement of these points.)

After these games, which take the whole night, the snails return to the sea and there begin to grow new shells. On the shore they leave behind enough shells to stock the islanders' stores until the next snail-courtship ritual is played out. It is necessary to gather the shells while the gala of lights is still in progress and to immerse them immediately in a herbal marinade, for soon they harden and once they are hard there is nothing one can do with them. This is why the islanders move carefully among the dancing snails, walking on tiptoe and collecting the cast-off shells, as if complementing the snails' ballet with a dance of their own. I remember how I got to know Karael after my first snail festival. It was a month after my arrival; I knew no one on the island and was living on the very edge of the lower town in an empty house whose windows—every one of them—had a view of the sandy flats. When one night the dark plain was lit up by a moving pattern of lights, among which ever-changing figures were dancing on the tips of black shadows, I had not the slightest idea what was going on. I just stood there at the window watching the dance of the lights and shadows. There was a moment when the crooked beams of the stars straightened and one of them reached the wall of my house; I looked on in amazement at the luminous animal beneath my window. This snail was glowing with a green light which reminded me of the neon of Prague. It was in this light that I first became aware of Karael, who was among those islanders gathering shells. Since my return from the island the pictures of Karael in my memory have been extinguished one after another (just as I have forgotten all her other names), so that now only this first picture remains. Whenever I write of Karael, the face that bobs up out of the dark is bathed in this green light.

The feast at which the ink of the cuttlefish and the shells are served has a strong element of ritual, and as such it is one of the things which was subject to least change in the course of my stay. From the time of my arrival on the island to my departure three years later, half of its alphabet changed and a new grammatical case appeared in its language, but the preparation of the stuffed shells continued in the old way. To begin with the shell is filled with a green jelly made from the leaves of a climbing plant which crawls over the walls of the inner courtyards of the lower town and enters apartments through their windows. In the middle of the night the flowers of this plant open themselves up to the night moths one after another, in so doing making a quiet sound like a finger brushing against the strings of a musical instrument. These tones of different pitches—stars in the realm of sound—are submerged in the chattering of the water. The leaves of the climbing plant are steeped in water and left to mature in the pantries for several weeks.

The shell—filled with a mix of leaves and berries and sealed with a resin—is laid in the centre of the table. Each of the guests chooses one of the prepared pieces of ink-fungus and uses a special spoon to scoop out its inside; this is the origin of the soft, pliant bowls (reminiscent of white rubber balls cut in half) the guests hold in their hands. Then everyone waits until the meal is ready. Someone tells a story to while away the time. The green jelly and fruit inside the shell ferment and work on the casing in such a way that it soon begins to soften, coming to resemble wrinkled skin. From within there is a muted gurgling. After an hour or so the process within the shell reaches its most turbulent phase; the gurgling is more urgent and the wrinkled shell swells so that its surface is so taut I was always afraid that the pressure applied from within would tear it open or that the covering of hardened resin would shoot off, injuring one of the guests. But the sides of the shell and its resinous lid are remarkably solid. A short while later small openings in the taut surface do indeed begin to appear, letting out a pink vapour and a hissing. The pink vapour forms itself into columns which look a bit like the spines of a porcupine, and it is this moment in the meal's development which gives it its name.

The fumes which escape from the shell have a mildly intoxicating effect, which in my presence often caused the story one of the guests was telling to assume characteristics of the fantastic. I remember that Karael in particular was able to invent really good stories at such a feast. And she liked to plot her tales around books I had told her about. Once, for example, she wove this crazy tale out of *Remembrance of Things Past*, *The Castle* and *Twenty Thousand Leagues under the Sea*. The hero of the story, a young Parisian called Marcel, was on board an ocean-going steamship when in mysterious circumstances it was hit by a torpedo from a submarine and sunk. Marcel succeeded in swimming to the undersea vessel, which he was able to get inside of. The submarine was called the *Nautilus*, and in its spacious rooms the sailors and their officers lived with their families. The crew was commanded by the Duke of Guermantes, also known as Captain Nemo. Marcel took pains to work himself into the circle which had formed around the captain and his wife. The cabin boy Barnabas, whose job it was to establish contact between the senior officers and the new passenger, was not able to help him. The captain's nephew Saint-Loup, whom Marcel befriended, was full of goodwill, but his efforts were no more productive than those of Barnabas; the company which gathered around the captain and his wife was a closed one. The captain's brother Baron de Charlus, however, maintained a steadfast interest in Marcel; he took him for trips in his mini-submarine and invited him to join an exclusive society of seamen, whose members included famous submarine captains and senior officers.

Marcel fell in love with Albertine, the daughter of the Nautilus's engineer and the lover of Klamm (one of the senior officers), whom she left in order to go to Marcel. The ties that bound Albertine to Klamm were strong, and for this reason Marcel did not trust her and was constantly suspicious of her; he had her followed and eventually held captive in her cabin . . . Once the intoxicating fumes began to work their effect, the story became more zany still. Karael described in detail Elstir's seascape mosaics, which he composed from fragments of shell, and, most dramatically, Swann's fight with a shark. Then the story slipped the shackles of the three books it had grown out of and sea monsters swept in with pointed spines on their backs and sagging jowls; in the end we were taken to great undersea cities populated by sluggish, apathetic demons.

Once the shell has given off its gas, it goes slack, the cracks in it close, and for about two hours its surface is still. Then the shell does nothing but give an occasional shudder, while from time to time a barely-audible rumbling and sighing comes from its inside. After that the shell again begins to swell up. At this point the storyteller falls silent and the guests gather around the table, on which the bowls of solidified white ink stand at the ready. Quite suddenly the openings reappear in the shell and vermilion geysers of juice spurt forth, which the guests catch in their bowls. Once the fountain desists, the guest sip this delicious liquid; among its dozens of flavours are discernible mango, smoked salmon, ginger, figs, lobster, pineapple and dill. While they drink, the guests nibble on their ink bowls. At the end of the feast the now-flat shell and its remnants of jelly and fruit are cut up and each of the guests is given a piece; this looks a little like apple strudel.

## 26
## The fog

I, too, would tell stories to while away the waiting, until the first red geyser spurted out of the swelling shell. I did not have to agonize over what I was going to say: the islanders were a grateful, attentive audience whether I was narrating the contents of *The Three Musketeers*, *From Russia with Love* or *Night Cab* by Souvestre and Allain, whether I was telling of the Greek myths, reminiscing about rambling in the Bohemian Forest in summer, or describing the dream I had had the previous night. I imagine they would have listened with interest if I had retold the listings of the Prague telephone directory, finding in the sounds of the names the germs of a gripping tale which they could develop in their minds; they would assess the individual telephone numbers by the nature and composition of their digits and consider them silently with the same pleasure as some people take from the study of minerals arranged in rows in the display-cases of museums. Mostly I would invent a tale of fantasy, as this was easier than piecing together the details of real sequences of events or recalling the contents of books as the intoxicating pink vapour was spreading itself throughout the room, insinuating itself into my words and releasing clusters of other words, images and story-lines from each word I spoke.

I remember in particular an afternoon in Karael's room in the upper town. I was sitting over a whispering, gurgling, shuddering shell and telling a story. I could not think of a single book I had not spoken of already, and I was not in the mood to invent, so I returned in my thoughts to Prague, to a chilly and damp autumn day. I had myself walk the foggy streets. As I described myself following the winding paths up the Petřín Hill, its landscape dotted with bare trees, I was drawn into the greyish fabric of the scene. The blurred Laputa of the Strahov Monastery floated above my head, then disappeared. I made my way down Úvoz street, looking down on the bay in a white sea which became the Seminary Garden before the facades of the grand houses of Neruda street rose out of the mist and then sank back into it, like fairy-tale sketches drawn in a secret ink on a sheet of white paper. As I told my story I made the sad realization that I was forgetting Prague; my feeble memory confused the buildings, so that the stone Moors at the doorway of the Morzinský Palace appeared above the Jánský Vrch Castle, the Church of St Kajetan was on the other side of the street and the Golden Wheel Hotel moved down to take its place. And on top of all this my forgetting was littering the streets with empty plots bathed in the white fog. This was one of the moments I promised myself I would be leaving the island at my earliest opportunity.

By the time I reached the Malá Strana square the shell was getting taut, and as I approached the Kampa island cracks were forming from which the vapour was beginning to leak; the shell was transforming itself into the pink porcupine. Before long I could feel the intoxicating fumes working on me. I first suspected this to be the case because of the sudden concentration of close detail in the images that presented themselves to me; I knew that these images were only masquerading as memory. Above the entrance of a house on Kampa, for example, I saw a painted sign which depicted a knight ramming a lance into the jaws of a dragon with a girl in a white dress chained to a rock right next to this scene. I described to the islanders the oily, iridescent lustre of the dragon's scales, the reflection of the setting sun on the knight's armour, I took my time over the long golden waves of the princess's hair. These were the kind of pictures the islanders liked best; I am sure they would have managed to listen to me all afternoon if I had spoken only of the way the pleats of the princess's dress were drawn and of the tissue of fine cracks on the painting.

But I could sense in the fog—this mysterious egg—the germs of pictures wholly new, pictures that were about to fight their way out. I told the islanders how I turned towards the river; there I saw the floating jetty where the steamboats land and a group of about ten people standing on it. They were silent and motionless, looking at the mist hovering over the water. A moment later two lights appeared, one on top of the other in a vertical line, above which there was a point like the dot of an *i*. As the lights got bigger, around them greyish marks began to penetrate the fog; the marks soon joined up to form the outline of a boat. It looked like the service boat of the river authorities. Above the entrance to the under-deck a lamp was burning, and this was reflected in the water. As the boat came to a halt the jetty shook slightly. Several passengers disembarked, then the people on the jetty climbed aboard in orderly fashion.

I paused for a moment, considering whether to join the people on the boat or let it sail off into the fog without me so I could continue my exploration of Kampa. I told myself that if the shell stirred in the next three seconds, I would get onto the boat. The islanders sat there motionless and attentive; Karael was lost in her thoughts, writing something into the wall of water with her forefinger. The shell heaved a sigh and then shook. "I hesitated for a moment before tagging along behind the people climbing aboard." I resumed the story without knowing what was expecting me on the boat. One after another new passengers were passing through the doorway beneath the lamp; most of them had to bend in order to do so. I followed them below deck, down the metal staircase which began immediately beyond the door. I found myself in a smallish room which was rather dark and where—in front of the illuminated stage of a puppet theatre—there were armchairs in rows. Most of these armchairs were unoccupied, their seats up. The newcomers sat down in the empty seats, producing the creaking of stiff joints as the armchairs opened out unwillingly and the whisper of faded plush; there remained many unoccupied seats. I sat down at the end of a row, where a strong perfume wafted towards me; I was put off by this, but I did not wish to move to another seat and in so doing appear foolish. Out of the corner of my eye I studied the profile of the young woman next to me; she was wearing heavy make-up and around her bare neck a pearl necklace shone pale in the semi-darkness.

I turned my attention away from my neighbour and towards the stage. It was about a metre long and three-quarters of a metre deep, and it depicted realistically a very normal-looking living room with upholstered armchairs and a glass-fronted cabinet filled with vases, cups and photographs. The window showed the dark sky of evening and beneath this a row of tower blocks whose windows were lit and then blanked thanks to some special equipment. Moving about continuously beyond the window, and making a light rustle, was a transparent plastic sheet on which were painted little white dots meant to represent snowflakes. In the middle of the room there was a table, and on this I could see two cups, a porcelain coffeepot and a nickel-silver tray with half a marble cake on it. Sitting at the table were two wooden puppets, one depicting a man, the other a woman. Judging by their facial features (which were not particularly well carved), both were about fifty years old. The man was dressed in shapeless blue sweatpants and a white undershirt and the woman had on a light-coloured nylon slip. The puppets' hands and feet were attached to strings which disappeared high above the stage, from where one heard the voices of the actors who were speaking for them.

The man-puppet heaved a sigh and said, "When I went to buy a newspaper this morning I found that they'd printed it in a foreign language again . . . But at least I was able to listen again to the rustling of the paper, to read words, even if those words were meaningless to me and their sounds were dark and threatening. Recently instead of a newspaper they've been giving me rabbit skins, crudely stitched together to make a single sheet. I always look hard at the newsagent to see if she's going to mention it, if she's going to give me an explanation, but as she never says a word, perhaps it's as it should be, perhaps there's a new law which says rabbit skin is to replace newspaper, and we haven't heard about it, that's all. Maybe everyone else knows how to manage a rabbit-skin newspaper, but I don't, I scan the skins desperately in search of news, at least once; I turn them upside down, I run my fingers along the smooth little rabbit hairs, but still I don't know what I'm supposed to be reading, no one gives me any advice, even those who find in the rabbit skins wonderful, informative stories and laugh while they're reading them or else weep with emotion. How I envy them! Once when I asked for a newspaper the newsagent gave me a live rabbit. Actually it was more dead than alive, but it was still breathing, just about . . ."

What sort of performance have I ended up watching? I asked myself in irritation. I had no interest in the problems the characters of the play would be addressing; the unhappiness of a man who is given rabbit skins in place of a newspaper had nothing to say to me. But I couldn't just leave because I was on a boat. God knows how long it will be before the boat pulls up at the next stop! What am I going to have to sit through? How many more wooden figures will be coming on stage? The only mild comfort I took from this involuntary artistic adventure came from the fact the actors were puppets, which meant that I did not have to look into the faces of the actors, which were bound to be dull and disagreeable. Looking at live actors would certainly have upset me. In resignation I sank into the plush of the seat.

## 27
## Waiting for the prince

The head of the second puppet, which until now had been looking fixedly ahead, turned abruptly to the man-puppet; the body stayed where it was. "Fool," said the woman angrily. "Why don't you bring the rabbit skins home? We could collect them and after a while I'd have enough to make a fur coat with. And it's so damned cold, we've been having blizzards for months."

"I can't bring the skins home because I keep losing them. They won't let me into the coffee-houses with them, I have to give them up at the cloakroom. And when I leave they always give me something else in their place. I've had some strange tools, thick books on economics in German from the nineteenth century, plaster-cast busts of Roman statesmen, stuffed birds. They always claim they're mine, and they always find about ten witnesses who saw me leave in the cloakroom a treatise on the railways in Styria or a stuffed owl. What I am supposed to do? I pick up the owl and make my way home through the blizzard. Sometimes I can't help but weep, and so I walk along sobbing, my tears turning to ice."

"I keep telling you not to go to coffee-houses. All you do there is spend money, and I've got nothing to wear. Coffee-houses are terrible places for spreading illness. They're always saying on the radio that someone has gone mad in a coffee-house and started singing that long-drawn-out song about the end of conventional mathematics in some new, evil empire. The waiters are heretics and most of them are former or future killers of women. You can cry over a stuffed owl, but you don't give any thought to me as you spend day after day in your coffee-houses, sitting on your ass with your friends while I'm sitting here all alone staring at the wall."

"I go to coffee-houses because I have to. There's nothing much there that makes me want to go in. In fact, I hate coffee-houses, and you're quite right, they are incubators for the worst epidemics. The waiters beat the customers and strip them naked; this is particularly upsetting for the women, some of whom are even considering avoiding coffee-houses altogether. I'd far sooner be at home with you, especially with the weather as it is now, when it's dark all the time and it never stops snowing, and the meteors whizz by on the blizzard. But what can I do about it? I simply have to go to the coffee-houses, I have to sit it out there in case the prince's messenger arrives. I have to be ever prepared to receive his dispatches and instructions."

"And how many of these dispatches have ever reached you, you fool?"

"None so far. Because enemies have got to the messenger and doped him, very discreetly. They rewrite the messages letter by letter, transforming them into something else altogether, like the service manual for a microwave oven or an advertisement for a second-hand-car dealer's. But still I am able to identify in them distant traces of the voice of my master, and I can hear it calling for help. I know that the expedition to the City of Pure Light came to grief, that for a long time the prince wandered the swamplands, that he was taken captive by evil women who did him harm. Why, they even turned him into a woman and made him dance ballet in a little white skirt, in some sordid Not-Petersburg, a city born on the plains out of the murk of despair, a city which is cursed, a city within whose walls no saviour will ever be spawned. How my prince must be suffering! If I could I'd drop everything and set out in search of him. I'm sure he's waiting for me, asking what's taking me so long. But all his dispatches reach me in such violated form that I have no way of telling where they were issued. All the signs are so ambiguous; at one moment I'm sure that he's in the Gobi

Desert and I begin to plan my journey and learn Mongolian, then it appears he is being held captive in a certain apartment in Prague 8. I asked a prophet for advice, and he thought long and hard before telling me, 'Gobi Desert or Prague 8, it is all the same.' I feel that this holy man speaks the truth, but unfortunately my education is so poor that I am unable to grasp the profound import of his words."

"I don't believe there is any such person as this prince of yours. I think you made him up to explain your hanging around in coffeehouses all day, or else you dreamed him. At best he's some kind of demon made of small strips of paper."

The male puppet jumped up before stomping about the stage, waving his arms like Mr Punch. "How can you say such a thing! That there's no such person as the prince! The prince is more real than any of us. Without him our lives would lose all sense and order; our letters would disintegrate so that once again they would be no more than fragments of the little letters from which they are glued together, and these would slowly gather in the *Gospel of the Metal Tiger*, whose renewal we have dreaded for five thousand years. We would be speechless because we would be unable to connect any subject with any predicate, and white larvae and ice monsters would get into the space between them. Without the prince all that would be left of us would be shavings composed—as is well known—of our bodies, and these shavings are gathered and held together due only to his goodness, due only to the fact that he speaks up for us to the gods, his parents. Even now, at a time for him so fraught with difficulties, he continues to think of us; he never forgets us, not even when he is performing solo at the ballet in Not-Petersburg. The clearest proof of this is the fact that still we haven't disintegrated. Although I believe that recently there was a brief time when we slipped his mind, as I saw bodies beginning to come apart like the spines of well-thumbed books, this was surely nothing more than a moment of weakness for which we can hardly blame him because in his place we would have given up long ago and thought only of our ballet career, with its intoxicating footlights and its merry backstage soirées with caviar and champagne. O my noble prince! It is thanks to him that there is Order in the world; he might have ordained that the stains on old walls should writhe, that the animals should berate us all day long, as used to be the case in the dark days of old, before the prince was born to his divine mother. But surely you remember this? Is that what you want, that our sufferings of those years should return? Do you not recall how unpleasant it was to be woken in the morning by the pigeons walking along the windowsills, speaking of us in disgusting obscenities which, resisting our efforts to shoo them away, they would repeat at lunch in front of our children? And our children lost all respect for us; they conspired against us with the animals and bullied us. And although the animals gave us an apology before they flew away from the planet, our children refused to do the same, writing to us that they had procured a pen with green ink like pus which stank most dreadfully, and it was with this pen that they would write the words 'father' and 'mother' for ever more."

"I don't remember anything of the sort. You're just making things up again," the woman said grumpily. But it seemed that the man hadn't heard her, that he was completely distracted by his master the prince. The puppet walked stiffly around the table, raising and then dropping its arms before calling: 'The prince! The prince! How marvellous the times before the Reconquista, when he set out for the City of Pure Light, when we—filled with infinite gratitude and immeasurable hope that the golden age would return—bade him farewell at the kiosk whose light blazed in the dark, there at the tram terminus, the last time we drank coffee together from the plastic cup which is a timeless symbol of our brotherhood!'"

"If the prince really does exist and isn't just some paper demon or a figment of your imagination, then he's certainly the same kind of worthless thing as you are, the same kind of loud-mouthed coffee-house loser. You're always using him as an excuse, you're always rambling on about a City of Pure Light and messages from the prince, but for all I can see you spend your days just hanging around with your friends in coffee-houses sipping sweet liqueurs; all of you would be better off with a proper glass of apricot schnapps. And when you get home you don't lend a hand with anything, you just go straight to your room and shut yourself in, saying you've got work to do, that you've got to cut animals out of plywood with a fret-saw. But I know full well what you do in there: you amuse yourself with your lovers. I'm not as big a fool as you think; I see right through you. You've given them dresses in the same pattern as the wallpaper in your room, and you've stuck wallpaper masks on their faces as if you think that'll keep me from recognizing what they are. But I've known about your lovers for years; I've heard them laughing and I've seen the flash of the diamond teeth you bought them. I see them very well, and I talk to them, too. As soon as you leave for the coffee-house I go in to them and we talk about you; they ridicule and impersonate you; we all laugh at you, and their diamond teeth glow in the lamp-light and glint across the room."

"You don't understand anything: the wallpaper, suits and masks are of the splendid fabric used for the curtains of the chateau in the City of Pure Light in the era of its glory, before the treacherous tanks of Byzantium drove into its streets. As the city was being evacuated I managed to salvage a little of this fabric to remind me of the happy days which it was my good fortune to spend in the galaxy's secret capital. I used it to make wallpaper and clothing for the women among my old friends and comrades-in-arms who escaped from the Byzantine despots along with me."

The man paused and the woman said nothing. Then two curtains darted across the stage, one from each side, while two strings came down from above from which was suspended a sign bearing the words "Entr'acte: 10 minutes." There was the sound of shuffling legs and coughing.

"Boring, isn't it?" said an unusually deep female voice; it belonged to the woman sitting next to me, who had turned to face me. "Today's show is pretty rotten," she sighed. "In fact, every show is worse than the one the day before. I'm thinking of giving up on the boat theatre." Then she asked me out of the blue whether I knew anything about old clocks. I answered in surprise that the repairing of old clocks had long been a hobby of mine, that I indulged in this esoteric delight almost every free evening I had.

"Your beautiful fingers told me that might be the case," said the woman. "I've been watching them and imagining them moving about in a labyrinth of cogwheels. They look incredibly dexterous and quick." The woman stroked my fingers shyly, giving the impression she would never tire of their touch; then she leaned towards me and whispered, "I am in great anguish and I think you might be able to help me. It's my antique clock: a month ago it just stopped. I appreciate that your time is precious to you, but I was wondering if you'd do me the kindness of coming home with me to take a look at it. When all's said and done, today's play is a real disappointment with so few elevated thoughts in it, and so little nobility. Since my clock stopped ticking, my apartment has been so quiet, particularly at night, when I doze to the groaning of the building and a rustling which takes my memories captive and turns them into recollections of some ancient evil. Every night the building resounds with age-old insults and vicious mockery. The boat's almost reached its next stop; I live close to the jetty, we'll be there before you have a chance to stretch your legs. I'd be delighted if you'd take a look at the clock. Who knows, maybe you'll be able to tell me what's wrong with it. For you it'll probably be child's play. And it'll be enough for me to hear your opinion on it. While we're at it, I've got some rather special wine for us to drink. Friends of mine brought it back from the vineyards of Bordeaux."

I was a little intimidated by the woman's deep voice, and I shuddered at the thought of the rooms in which it had probably been formed, the reverberations of which could be heard within it (gleaming antique furniture, modernist lamps, Japanese electronics with fidgety little green lights). I was inclined to make my excuses but was too lazy to come up with a reason; I was also tempted by the prospect of the insides of a valuable old clock and a glass of good French wine. So I told the woman I would go with her, just for a short while. Almost as soon as I accepted the offer, the boat shook as it touched the jetty. Several other members of the audience left their seats along with us. Up on deck I saw that the fog had cleared somewhat, that the boat was at anchor between the Steel Bridge and the Palacký Bridge. There were a number of new audience members waiting to board.

## 28
## Crime and punishment

No doubt it was high time I was bringing my story to a close, but on that day the shell was rather tough; it looked taut enough to burst but the red juice was still spurting out of it. There was nothing to do except for me to continue with my invented story, to reimmerse myself in the waves of long sentences, not knowing where they would carry me. The woman was leading me through the wide, quiet streets of the Podskalí; her garrulousness, which had irritated me so much on the boat, had ceased, and we walked on in a silence I found embarrassing. For something to say I explained how I had disliked the boat and how glad I was no longer to have to listen to the nonsensical dialogue carried on by the puppets, of which I had understood nothing. When the woman gave no answer to this I became even more uncomfortable. As I was searching for an excuse by which I could wriggle out of this, my guide stopped in front of a building and proceeded to unlock its front door. We climbed a dimly-lit staircase. As soon as we entered the apartment—which was exactly as I had imagined it—the woman led me over to an empire commode, upon which, propped against the wall, there stood a beautiful pillar and scroll clock adorned with cherub figurines. I opened it carefully and pushed my right hand in among its dozens of cogwheels.

"I think the fault is somewhere further back," said the woman, who was standing right behind me. "Maybe a little spring has snapped right at the back, right up against the rear wall. You need to get in as deep as you can—I know the clock is unusually deep, but I'm sure you can manage it with those fine, slim hands of yours." Now I heard a hint of mockery in the woman's flattery. And I was a little put out that so far there had been no mention of French wine. Would it not be for the best if I were to disengage myself from the broken clock and make a hasty retreat from this posh, inhospitable apartment? But then again, I was truly curious about the insides of the instrument; it was as if it were making room for me to enter, and I went up to the elbow, up to the shoulder, and still I didn't touch bottom. Was I the victim of a conjuring trick? At last fear got the better of my curiosity and passion for clocks, and I began to withdraw my arm, taking great care not to damage the delicate wheels or to injure myself on their teeth. But when my arm was still in the clock up to the elbow, there was a whirring sound and the wheels began to turn, vibrate and otherwise move about rapidly; before I had time to remove my arm the sharp teeth tore into my shirt and bit into the skin, gripping my wrist and failing to release it. I could feel how my blood was dripping onto the mechanism from many small wounds. I called out to the woman for help, but she remained standing behind me, saying nothing.

After a while she spoke in a low voice. "We've got you at last. My ruse has succeeded; the queen will praise me. For months now I've been carving puppets from wood, for years I've been writing a play for the puppet theatre; I used up all the talent I have on this, my moments of purest inspiration, but now I no longer regret it. I hired the best puppet players and a boat whose crew I had schooled at the naval academy in Hamburg; I patiently trained the extras who played the audience. That's right, this whole comedy was played out for your sake, it was part of our pursuit of you, which has been going on now for several decades on all continents. And it was well worth it: the queen will be delighted, she'll burst into tears of joy, good, noble soul that she is. After all these years, justice has at last been done. It has been proven that everything must be atoned for. Now at last you shall receive your punishment, and the stars that burned red with shame will again be as pure as before. I bet you thought you'd be able to destroy all traces testifying to your guilt, but in this you overreached yourself: everything was kept in reserve, kept for this very moment."

She took from the wall a painting of a sombre landscape, in so doing revealing the metal door of a safe. This she unlocked before carefully drawing from it a book, which she leafed through before holding it out open for me to inspect. I saw some geometric figures and formulae; in the white margin of the page there was a clumsy drawing of a battleship. It was all somehow familiar to me. Then I remembered. "That's my geometry textbook from when I was in Year Five or Six. It was me who drew that cruiser in the margin during a lesson," I said, astonished.

"A confession!" the woman exclaimed in triumph. "Not even I could have imagined it would go as smoothly as this! This forms only part of the charge, although it is serious enough in itself. He who sullies white paper with his drawings could demolish the temple and smash its marble statues; he could rip out the strings of the piano and leave them out in the evening wind to jangle a nonsense song about cities consumed by jungles; he could deny the existence of the stars and the great, beautiful beasts which thirst for flames, run to conflagrations and bathe in fire. This crime is enough to get you life imprisonment on the cold staircases of apartment buildings, staircases with handrails made of metal flowers; enough for a thousand-page novel to be written about you in which you spend your days in solitude in an apartment by the railway line, where deep within the dresser the cutlery rattles at night whenever a train goes past. Your guilt will suffice to have all the islands of the icy sea which bear your name renamed, or at the very least to have some of their sounds changed so that the islanders are incapable of remembering them; they will curse you and their fur-clad arms will gesture threatening in the direction of the place where you were born; they will use your name with derision to describe the evil walrus so that over time your name will become the natural-historical term for the walrus, a term which will survive into the age of happiness which is still many years ahead of us, an age when people will forget your crimes as they forget your existence. Is not the thought of this almost-certain future enough to persuade you to reflect on your despicable acts? Perhaps you are not yet altogether depraved. And as I've indicated, we know still more about you. Was it not enough for you to draw cruisers and Red Indians in the margins of the pages of books? 'The more one has, the more one wants,' as one of our highest-placed devotees pointed out recently at the dawning of the age in which the seals that had lain for centuries on the teachings of the East were removed. Let us see what you have to say about this."

Again she leafed through the book before placing it in front of my eyes, now open at a page which bore a geometric representation of Thales' theorem—a circle with a right-angled triangle inserted above the diameter; next to this I could see the clumsy, childish picture of a bear with a bow around its neck. Perhaps this, too, was one of my drawings, but I had no recollection of it.

"We wished to spare the queen the sight of this blasphemy," my captor continued. "But she is a brave woman and she told us that as the mother of her people she had no right to evade even such awful tests as this. My God, how could you do such as thing? Surely you knew that it was she who assisted Thales in his discovery of the theorem, when amid the bathing beauties in the circular pool of the gardens of her palace in Asia she stretched and tightened the string of a musical instrument on which she had threaded pearls? A string which reached across the centre of the pool and touched the side at three places? The moment when silently she pointed out to Thales a great emerald which was glittering in the early-morning sun among the pearls, at the very point where the string made its right angle, is captured in many paintings and frescoes; pictures of the Demonstration—many of them touchingly artless—hang on the walls of the poorest cottages, immediately next to the Golden Snake, and the shepherds at their evening firesides sing songs of this bright moment in our history. But what did you think of when you saw the sacred figure? Did you think of the good name of the royal institute of geometry and those who run it? Did you think of the honour of the nation, of the glory of the dynasty, of the sufferings and hurt with which our history has been marked? No. You thought of a bear with a bow around its neck."

Having said this the woman slid quietly down to the carpet, where she rested her sobbing frame against the commode. After a while she recovered herself somewhat, dried her eyes and stood up. "After the queen saw your picture of the bear," she went on, "for many weeks she closed herself up in her chambers and allowed no one near her. Her only companion was her little dog. Then this dog fell gravely ill at the sight of its mistress's suffering, and shortly thereafter it died. It was at this time that the people gave you the name Dog Killer. The dog's body—which had been stricken with the most dreadful illnesses—was laid in a modest grave in the grounds of the chateau; from this grave there grew a plant with a poisonous yellow flower, whose breath killed the birds which flew over it and the gardener who tended to it. They say that the gardener's ghost appears at night among dormant machines in factory halls. The yellow flower erodes and blinds mirrors in which it is reflected, and if someone thinks of it the neurons in his brain become so excited that a short circuit might result and the brain catch fire. This phenomenon, known as "burning brain syndrome," was defined and interpreted by the queen's court physician, my lover.

His professional achievement is the more remarkable for his having been forbidden to imagine the yellow flower for the course of his researches; had he done so, his brain, too, would have ignited. He was given the Nobel Prize for his work; to begin with he was supposed to receive the Nobel Prize for Medicine, but the committee of the Swedish Royal Academy, a group of elegant, dark-complexioned young men with fine hands, decided to give him the Nobel Prize for Peace as he'd brought calm to many troubled souls; no longer does the ghost of the murdered gardener roam the factory halls at night in such a rage. At that time there was an uprising among the generals, who were against the queen giving up her overseas dominions. It had never been clear whether these were merely figments of a dream, or perhaps groups of divine spirits that were around at the time. One night the plotters broke into the palace, intending to murder the queen; then one of them suddenly thought of the poisonous yellow flower and his brain burst into flames. When the other plotters saw the flames flaring from his eyes and ears, lighting up the halls of the sleeping palace, reflected to infinity in the great mirrors, they fled. So it is thanks to you that the generals' plot foundered: it was you who saved the queen's precious life. She will never forget this; I had to promise her I would search the world for you so that she may express to you her boundless gratitude and bestow on you a bountiful reward. She asks you to come to her. She will make her beautiful sister, for whom the mightiest lords have given their lives, your wife. You will live in a palace, which the queen will have built for you opposite her own and which will be a mirror image of her own . . ."

At this moment there was a gentle whir and the wheels of my clock-prison sprang back into motion; as they released their grip it seemed to me they gave me a friendly tickle. I could still hear the excited voice of the woman.

". . . in the morning the virgin queen will breakfast on her balcony while you and her sister do the same on the balcony opposite. The queen will raise her right hand to you in greeting and you will return the greeting with your left. The birds will sing. It will be beautiful. I can hardly wait for your arrival; flags will fly throughout the town in your honour."

Fortunately this was the moment at which the first red geyser spurted from the swollen shell. Karael jumped up nimbly and was the first to catch the juice on the ink sponge. The shell ruptured in other places, too, and the juice burst forth in torrents which the guests caught in their bowls. So I ceased to think of clocks adorned with cherubs, of a poisonous flower and a queen; I, too, took up my bowl and caught the delicious juice; I, too, sipped the liquid and nibbled on the bowl. The sun had almost reached the level of the sea and the wall of water blazed an incredible crimson. Thus ended one of my days on the island.

## 29
## First encounter with the *Book*

The story I told at the feast was no doubt influenced at least a little by the island's *Book*, although for a long time I found this maze of adventure stories, fairy tales and myths about rabbits, princes and princesses, whose descriptions, insertions, digressions, improbabilities and anachronisms knew no end, quite insufferable. It took me far longer to find in it something that appealed to me than it did to get used to the island's cuisine and its board games without rules. Now is perhaps the time for me to say something more about the *Book*, which I have mentioned a number of times already. I confess that I have kept putting off talking about the *Book* because I don't have much of an appetite for it, but having discussed board games and food I can't think of anything else of particular interest: I will just have to tackle the *Book* here and now.

The main reason for my avoiding writing about the *Book* was the fear that I would lack the strength to negotiate its labyrinth, which has become yet more intricate since the time it left the island and settled in my brain. I found the *Book* puzzling enough when I read it on the island, and then I had no idea of its extent; indeed, it is unlikely that I even discovered what was its main part. Since then it has become even more difficult to survey, having become something of a hybrid, in which pages woven from the fine fibres of memory and pages born in the realm of dreams sit side by side. When I think of the *Book* I see its long insertions emerging from the blurred landscapes of memory, stretching to infinity as they grow around tremulous pictures produced by the imagination. Dear reader, I believe I told you in the first chapter of this book that I was looking forward to wandering in ghostly realms ruled by the triumvirate Memory, Dream, and Desire, and to having adventures there; but now, having reached the twenty-ninth chapter, I am feeling very tired. I hadn't realized how exhausting it is to wade about in the swamp of memory.

As I said, the islanders took no great interest in art. After the apotheosis of the Stain, when the building efforts of the Europeans in the lower town ceased, no architecture existed on the island. The islanders needed no temples or offices. Sometimes they would build a simple house on the islet of rock on which the upper town was accommodated, but, as the island population was in decline and no new houses were needed, they tended to repair old dwellings instead. The islanders had no painting and sculpture (which is perhaps surprising considering the great roles these play in the story-lines of the *Book*); they were satisfied by the shapes of stains, the movements made by the shadows of leaves on walls, the ever-changing white figures described by the foam of the waves of the sea. They had no music because it was enough for them to listen to the rustlings of the island; indeed, in the tapestry of island sounds there was no tear by which music could enter.

For a long time I believed that the islanders cultivated no art at all. But one morning, having awoken in Karael's house, lying there with my eyes closed, listening to the chatter and trickle of water, I realized I was hearing occasional sounds which escaped the classifications I had established for familiar island sounds. A sound kept returning that reminded me of the opening of a Velcro, or a cookie being bitten into, and this was usually followed by the kind of sound made by a cloth fluttering in the wind or the rapid flapping of a bird's wings; the third sound was a light swish or perhaps a quiet sigh. I tried to guess what was making these sounds, but the only idea that came to me was the improbable one of a sorrowful bird groaning in pain, pecking intermittently at a cookie and flapping its wings. I got up and walked through the wall of water to the stone terrace. There I saw something that surprised me more than the sight of a sorrowful bird nibbling cookies would have done: Karael was sitting on the terrace reading from a large book which was lying on the stone table in front of her.

I sat down next to her and watched. I saw that the pages of the book were neither stitched nor glued to a spine, that they were gathered like those of a children's foldout picture book, and that they were written on one side only. At a number of places on a page there was some kind of paper patch-pocket attached; these pockets looked a little like ears or mushrooms. At certain places in the text there was another kind of attachment: a thin strip of paper which became wider and thicker two or three centimetres along to form a kind of oval (the cap of a mushroom) whose axis (the stalk of the mushroom) was perpendicular to the paper strip. The upper side of the oval was sealed along its whole length and contained a number of slits. Although Karael paid no attention at all to some of the pockets, others she opened (this was the sound that had reminded me of Velcro or the crunching of cookies) and pulled from them a small pleated strip of thin paper. This strip, too, had attachments like those I've just described, and some of these (somewhat smaller) ears, too, Karael opened, pulling out more paper concertinas with ears. I looked on in amazement, trying to work out how many levels the book had. I counted six, but even at the sixth level there was a little ear jutting out; there was no way of telling how many more concertina strips with ears were hidden within it.

At some moments all the concertinas were folded inside the pockets; at others Karael would have left open several pockets simultaneously, having opened out not only the strips which they had contained but also some of the strips which these gave issue to.

Whenever there was a gust of wind, all the concertinas were lifted up and began to flutter (explaining the sounds of bird's wings), reminding me of those little flags we used to wave on May 1st. When the wind dropped, the concertinas lay limp across the table, their ends hanging over its edges and shivering (the murmuring, whispering, sighing sound).

A short time later Karael carefully folded all the concertinas back into the pockets and closed the book. But her agitation remained inside the book; indeed it was even more obviously present when Karael's hand was not on it. Inside the closed book, the ears formed a bump which reached its highest point in the book's centre. The front cover—which was not joined to the back cover by means of a spine, only by the round shape of the largest paper concertina (the only one which did not belong in a pocket)—rocked from side to side ceaselessly. I was concerned that the book would topple, and this indeed happened, the front cover tipping over slowly to the ground, the paper concertina unfurling in an arc, leaving the ears so shamelessly exposed that I turned my eyes away.

Karael told me this was the island's *Book*. I'll write it with a capital letter because the islanders have only one book. I was surprised to discover that *any* form of art existed on the island, and that this should be literature was astonishing to me. Why should the islanders, who have such a love of formlessness, choose an art form that works with words? Words are surely more hostile than colours, lines or tones to a formless life. But once I familiarized myself with the *Book* and its history I realized it could not have been any different. I have already mentioned—in the chapter on the phonetics of the island's sounds and rustlings—that the shapeless whirling the islanders love to watch is really the life of many waning and emerging images and shapes, that the whirring they listen to is the voice of a thousand fused stories. In this whirring the islanders recognize the appeal to protect the formless from a humiliating lapse into form; and they hear in it another appeal, too: to affirm and celebrate the wealth of the formless by hunting in its depths for some of the treasures hidden there, and to show these off to the world. It seemed to me that the islanders thought the formless resounded with the quiet plea to expose at least some of the pictures that glimmer through the whirring, thus releasing at least some of the plots and stories whose telling weaves the murmur of stillness. The appeal to keep silent and the appeal to tell become entwined, revealing a single, formless longing—a longing to unfurl the monstrous, stupefying whirling of which it has long been part and product. A whirling in the life of the formless dreams of shape that allows itself to give birth to a complicated architecture, but this soon caves in, disintegrates and crumbles to formlessness so that the process can start again at the beginning.

But a new beginning is only possible at the very end of the shaping process, not until it seems—no doubt deceptively—that the last trace of the formless has been eradicated. Tones and colours would not be able to maintain the progress of this ages-old cycle: their borders do not stretch to the most distant headland on the continent of shapes. Tones and colours would not be able to bring about the glorious re-emergence of the formless because they would be unable to eradicate these traces completely. For this you need words, sentences and stories. The murmurs, rustlings and blurred shapes of the island did not dream of pictures, sculptures and tones; the murmurs and rustlings of the island could bring forth nothing but a book. I have mentioned already that the islanders loved border territories; life on the island was played out on two borderland strips—the world of shapeless murmurs and whirls and the world described in the Babylonian architecture of the *Book*. Each of these territories worked on the other; the one was born out of the other and they were astonishingly similar—the monotonous murmurs and whirls were really a complicated mesh of many shapes, pictures and actions, and in the intricacy of the *Book*'s architecture it was not difficult to trace the monotonous principle that determined the inserting ad infinitum of one into the other.

# 30
# The history of the *Book*

Though indifferent to art, the islanders had their literature, and this literature was contained in the *Book*. The *Book* existed in a single copy only, and this was passed from hand to hand. There was no rule which determined how long a reader might hold on to the *Book* and no one ever recalled it or asked for it to be moved along to the next reader, nor was it anywhere stated who the reader should pass it on to. Usually the *Book* arrived unexpectedly, and whoever received it might choose to pass it on immediately or to keep it. It was typical for the *Book* to remain in the possession of one reader for several days or weeks. I can't imagine that anyone ever tried to read the *Book* from beginning to end; readers tended to choose one of the *Book*'s sections and wander around in it. Nor did I read the *Book* in its entirety, even though it came into my possession several times. I looked into the *Book* on the day of my departure from the island, and even then I found in it quarters completely unknown to me, places which I would never have the chance to get to know.

When the *Book* came into the possession of an islander who chose to hold on to it, he or she would read several passages. Sometimes it was passed on in the form in which it had been received; more commonly, the text was modified somehow. The islanders considered the act of writing in the *Book* a natural part of the process of reading it. Cases when the reader made no alteration to the text were regarded as exceptions, phases in the endless metamorphosis the *Book* was subject to, in which the powers of transformation were concentrated while new forms matured beneath the surface. Like the other islanders, Karael knew that books in Europe were generally read without the reader's writing into them, but she was amazed by this European custom and struggled to imagine what such reading was like. It seemed to her as absurd and eccentric as watching a film with the same shot in every frame; the islanders studied our books with an expression of confusion we might compare to that of the novice cinema-goer confronted with a film by Andy Warhol where all that appears on screen for several hours is a view of a New York skyscraper.

So it is true to say that in most cases the reader passed on a book which differed from the one he had received. As the *Book* circulated, the written-over was written over—and so the reader never encountered the same work twice. He discovered that since his last reading the characters he had introduced into the plot had acquired virtues and vices of which he had had no inkling, that dark events from the lives they had led before had come to light. And so it was that the *Book* was always a fragment: at any given moment no one knew it in its entirety.

There were three ways of making a change in the *Book*: insertion, overwriting of the text and deletion. The most significant and most common changes were made by insertion; indeed, the *Book* itself was a kind of insert, a pocket containing a corrugated reality. Probably the *Book* was born at the moment its first author noticed a crack emerge in the roar of the sea or the rustling of leaves; out of this crack the pictures and the words gushed forth, just as the strips of paper forced their way out of the *Book*'s pockets. The ongoing proliferation of insertions was the main event in the endless metamorphosis which was the life of the *Book*: the most remarkable aspect of its transformation was the expansion brought about by the insertions made on its many levels.

I know something about the history of the *Book* from the *Book* itself: in one of its pockets I found a contribution which told of the life and origins of the *Book*—the rest I have imagined and invented. It seems that the *Book* has transformed itself from the very beginning, although in the distant past it was more similar to our books in that insertions were written in gaps between lines and the margins of the page. But as the insertions became longer and longer and other insertions were inserted in them, it became more and more difficult to find unoccupied space for new text. Lettering became smaller and smaller; new sentences were woven around pre-existing text and other insertions, continuing bottom up as they wrapped around the line and proceeded back the way they had come before making another swift turn so as to proceed in the original direction; if, for example, in the corner of a page they found unoccupied space, they would contort themselves into a spiral. Text written thus gradually became illegible and assumed the character of a picture—a fantastical word-drawing. Then there was no longer any space at all for new words; it was necessary to tear out the pages, to write out on new sheets everything that was still legible. The new sheets were stuck into the *Book* to make a text which—initially, at least—was easy to read. But over time this, too, changed into an impenetrable jungle of letters.

Later some reader who was searching in vain for a blank space in which to make his insertion, and who did not wish to transcribe a whole page, came up with the idea of writing his contribution on a new sheet, which he would then stick—by means of a thin strip of paper—to the word or sentence in the pre-existing text to which his insertion was related. In this way it became the practise to paste insertions in the *Book*; on to the pasted-in sheets other pasted-in sheets were added, others on to these, and so on. When I imagine what the *Book* must have looked like in those days, I see its covers as the cracked shell of a wounded crab; spilling out of confinement there are strips of paper, upon which at various points have been stuck other strips of paper, which themselves sprout yet more such strips. All this paper either lies limply on a table or flutters in the wind and rustles. Periodically someone tries to stuff it within the covers as one would try to stuff heaps of underwear into an undersized suitcase.

It is out of these beginnings that today's relatively simple and convenient use of the *Book* has developed. In terms of its form the *Book* is like a foldout picture-book; this form recurs on all its levels. Whenever someone wishes to make an addition to the *Book*, he does not violate the pre-existing text, nor does he transcribe the page in question; he writes his contribution on any long strip of paper and folds it into a concertina. Should he choose to make a longer insertion, all he needs to do is paste a second folded strip on to the end of the first. Once the reader-author has finished his contribution, he tucks it into an ear-shaped pocket, which he pastes in using the juice of the berries of one of the island's trees; the pocket is stuck by the same agent above the word or term in the pre-existing text to which it refers and whose content it develops. (But the hidden content of every object is the rest of a universe, tied up in that object; and so the *Book* has erased the difference between the explanatory note and the digression, or rather it has revealed that the distinction was always an illusory one. The hidden content of every part of such an insertion/explanation/digression constitutes a whole universe, making it something very large, which is not at all what it seems.) We might describe the ear of an insertion as a three-dimensional bracket. The pocket is easy to unstick: should another reader-author wish to write an insertion to an insertion, all he needs to do is repeat the whole process and to paste another, smaller ear at the appropriate place on the first insertion.

This bulking of the *Book* from the inside is possible because the paper used is extraordinarily light and thin but also very tough. This paper is produced from reeds which grow on the banks of the lower reaches of the river. It is made by the islanders during the periods they spend in the lower town. And here their journey to work rarely takes much longer than it does when they are living in their homes in the upper town, where it is their custom to stop off in the family mine on the way from bedroom to pantry. There is no shortage of reed in the lower town. Reed has swallowed up the statues and obelisks which stand along the river. Like a mighty but patient army it has advanced along the streets that lead from the river to the edges of town, has penetrated the courtyards of the palaces and the entrance halls of mansions and apartments alike. I saw town-centre apartments which brought together reed from the riverside and sand from the outskirts. Nor is there any shortage of demand for the paper-makers' wares: the interest of the bibliophiles of Europe in light but tough paper never wanes. Paper is the island's third article for export, after gemstones and fruit jellies. (I once discovered in an Amsterdam bookshop an annotated edition of the collected works of Nietzsche printed on the island's paper. It had been possible to contain these in a single volume, which included all the letters, drafts and notes of Nietzsche's estate—those on the forgotten umbrella, too—and an extensive commentary by the publisher.)

Owing to the extraordinary thinness of the paper, insertions could be made in the *Book* on many levels. Each series of insertions reached a different depth; I don't know which were the deepest because I didn't open all the *Book*'s pockets (and I didn't reach the bottom of all those I did open). It was impossible to determine the number of levels of insertion by the thickness of the pocket: some of the more swollen pockets had only one or two levels, as the stories recounted in them were long. The deepest I ever reached into a pocket was the eleventh level—but I'm not saying that it went no further than this. As the case may be, the island's *Book* had more levels of insertion than the nine counted by Michel Foucault in Raymond Roussel's *New Impressions of Africa*.

## 31
## The life of the pages

Although parenthetic pockets are a very practical arrangement, their main significance is to enable a reading of the *Book* in a great variety of ways; at any given moment the *Book* is equivalent to many books of different kinds. The reader might ignore the pockets altogether (the story-lines and situations they punctuate remain self-contained without reference to the pockets); he might explore the contents of a single pocket, reaching right down into its depths; he might overlook some of the pockets and delve into others; he might read only the text at—let's say—the third or fourth level of insertion; with reference to some numerical key, he might determine beforehand the number of interior pockets he is going to open and read.

It was common practise for readers of the *Book* to alternate and combine all these approaches. Reading became a labyrinthine journey whose directions were various. It twisted and turned, it drove backwards and forwards; it might follow one direction for a long time before plunging down to the deepest dungeon (built by the king of Babylon in playful protest that the building of a tower was forbidden to him), then rising upwards like a fanciful staircase. Also subject to constant change was the character of the energy coursing through these journeys; sometimes reading proceeded at a stampede, while at others it was like a furious digging, a systematic underground exploration, or an abstracted tumble into parenthetic holes followed by a disoriented crawling back out of them; it might skate lightly on a smooth surface, step indecisively or gingerly on cracking ice, circle lethargically, panic and submerge itself, reel first one way, then the other. Reading was always a kind of ballet, a source of both joy and torment.

All these rhythms and routines were born out of a tension between two basic forces and two kinds of longing that corresponded to these forces. In their purest form both kinds of longing became an unhealthy obsession. I knew this better than the islanders; the islanders knew how to float in the maelstrom created by the clash of these two currents while I was always swept towards the source of one or the other. The initial longing was the quest for the very bottom of every insertion, for the *Book*'s very lowest point amid its many branches; it demanded the inspection of the *Book*'s maze of dungeons in the hope of finding treasure there. (The reader was sure that a complicated labyrinth such as this was hiding some kind of treasure.) Then there was the second longing—to skate lightly over all pockets, refusing to be seduced by their depths with their promised delights otherwise only to be found in dreams; this was the desire not to descend to the evil of the utterance (which dulls the glow of simplicity), the desire not to betray the magical stories that flutter in the murmur of the void, stories replete with bright-coloured gemstones shining in the dark, dancing on terraces and night-time gardens by the sea.

If left to their own devices, each of these longings would eventually wreck the process of reading and bring about the collapse of the *Book*. The reader who started on the insertions would never reach the end; indeed, at the moment he entered the first he was signing himself over to the devil of the deep, and as such was lost. This vigorous, crafty devil would draw him in ever deeper until he was a prisoner of insertion hell, a dark, cruel subterranean world of text from which there was no escape. And the devil would chuckle to himself as the quest for an illusory bottom made the reader more and more feverish.

There was no stopping place. Not even the final inscription in the innermost pocket could provide salvation, as this, too, sprouted a multitude of insertions which became visible only as they were reached; although these insertions were as yet textless, their intention was plain—the phantom blossoms of parenthetic pockets of the future were hovering over the paper. The poor reader wished to read on, but though he sensed the proximity of the next word it eluded his grasp. There it was, shimmering on the shore, promising salvation—but he just couldn't get through to it. It eluded him as the tortoise eludes Achilles: between this next word and the last there opened up a bottomless gulf of real and imaginary insertions. The *Book* collapsed in on itself; it became a weeping wound in which were gathered words visible and invisible, words wriggling like maggots. To stop reading, thus escaping the undertow of the gulf, was not an option. One knows that the *Book* itself is a kind of insertion: once inside the *Book*, it is impossible to resist this dark surrender. Once the wound in the *Book* is opened, the constellations begin to quake and then the cosmos caves into the oozing depths.

Although the second longing—to skip all the insertions—spares the reader the hell of subterranean text, it, too, bears along in its wake the collapse of reading and the disappearance of the *Book* and the world. There is no satisfaction in skimming the surface, leaving all pockets sealed. As I have said, the *Book* itself is one big insertion: it was born when the hum of calm was fractured and words began to stream out of it; the entire *Book* is enclosed in an invisible pocket. The reader feels a longing to change this imaginary pocket into a real one made of the island's paper and to seal the whole *Book* inside it so that the obscenity and disgrace of words are covered up. In this way the *Book* would disappear, but not even this would satisfy the yearning for the simplicity of undispersed radiance. Whoever encountered the *Book* as an insertion would realize that the substance into which the *Book* was inserted was itself only an insertion—an insertion inserted into other insertions—and that as such it was a text of dubious character in which words gloss over what is important, its splendid emptiness.

Now the colours into which the white light had dispersed could be a cause of great anguish to the reader, just as the words into which the truth of the hum had dissolved had caused him great anguish previously; he would search the plain of colours as if it were a coat of loathsome splashes and slops befouling the radiant white of the void; he longed to erase the shame of colour and return to the original whiteness. All shapes would seem to him a needlessly long and rather banal interpretation of a number of basic geometric figures, but as soon as he restored these figures to the world of perception he would again be overcome by a sense of dissatisfaction; he would realize that they had originated through straight lines succumbing to the temptation to pursue various courses, that their potentialities were trembling within. Only after the discontented reader had rendered all figures into straight lines could the final act commence, and then it would dawn on the reader that the straight line itself—still, and inadmissibly—brings forth two courses which ought to remain folded within, in the blissful embrace of non-dimensionality. And here he would conclude his work (which had begun in the distaste for the contents of the *Book*'s pockets) by pushing back into the non-dimensional point the straight line into which the whole world of shapes had been reduced.

Now to the changes which were made to the *Book* by transcription and overwriting. The island reader always thought of the *Book* as a palimpsest, a manuscript written over another manuscript;

the surface text always evoked the original, which insinuated itself between the letters—sometimes forcefully, sometimes more subtly—in an attempt at restoration. Over time, I, too, came to view the *Book* in such a light, and now it is impossible to for me to rid myself of the urge to look at books as I looked at the *Book*—when I read these days, another tale, the translucent pages of another book rise gently to the surface of the open pages of the actual book, before subsiding like the wings of a great, ghostly butterfly. This is how words and sentences came to be expunged and replaced by other words and sentences. It was easy to wash characters written in fruit juice from the reed paper before replacing them with others. Indeed, it was perhaps too easy; in the upper town, where water was forever streaming from various directions and the reader sometimes carried the *Book* through a wall of water, it was not an infrequent occurrence for a whole passage to be erased.

The islanders understood words blurred into smudges as still readable text; the last way in which the *Book* transformed was not a washing clean of the paper but an erasure by which the text disappeared and was not replaced. There were three ways in which erasure could occur: a page or pages were pulled out and the violated foldout was resealed; or pockets of insertions were removed; or written words were washed away without their being replaced by new words or figures. I remember a time when readers were going through the *Book* like mushroom-pickers through the woods, plucking out insertions so that very few remained. The *Book* became a thin volume which might have dwindled away to nothing; I imagined an isolated scrap of paper bearing its last remaining sentence, its last remaining *word* as it was carried away by the island wind. (But this paper flake might be the seed out of which a new *Book* could grow; in this new *Book* the contents of the old *Book* would return as a dream.)

There was also a time when the pages and pockets of the *Book* remained in place while they shed words and sentences, leaving a blank space on a page or even a whole page which was blank. This disappearance was quite different in kind from that given by the pulling out of pages and insertions, and the *Book* did not become any thinner. The whiteness spread rapidly and it seemed possible that soon the reader would have only white pages to leaf through, that he would open pocket after pocket to find nothing but blank pages. As you can see, the *Book* led a rich existence thanks to the several ways by which it could approach nothingness.

# 32
# Looking for the beginning

For a time I tried to find the *Book*'s original layer, the first passage out of which the *Book* grew by insertion, transcription and erasure. It may be that such an undertaking was within the bounds of realizability, but it proved so difficult that I gave it up. It certainly was impossible to identify the oldest layer by its content; the constant modifying of the text meant that it was far from out of the question that the oldest passages were those which told of the latest technical discoveries, about which the islanders had learned from sailors. To begin with I imagined it would be possible to identify the oldest text by the level of insertion at which it appeared. The fact that the *Book* grew mainly through insertion encouraged the assumption that the manuscript was like an inverted Troy, where the oldest layers were on the surface (in the *Book*'s larger foldouts) and those which had been written and stuck in only yesterday were at the deepest level of insertion. The task of a textual archaeologist would be to monitor closely the surface while resisting the temptation to go beneath it.

But suddenly it hit me that this assumption was false. Certainly, the making of insertions was the main activity demanded by the *Book*, but there was no guarantee that individual passages of text would settle in one place; indeed, passages went up and down in the hierarchy of levels—they might fall sharply before embarking on a steep climb, as if riding a Ferris wheel. It was not uncommon for a passage to disappear and then reappear in modified form as an insertion on the second, fifth or sixth level, to be lost again without trace in the bowels of the *Book* before bobbing up on the first level in white pages which had lost their text in one of those periods when hatred of words was paramount. The *Book* was really a cyclical entity, a demented structure whose foundations were on its roof. It was probable that the beginning of the *Book* had long ago been lost through the regular batterings it took as it was transformed, yet it may have been the case that the beginning remained hidden at the bottom of the deepest pocket—a pocket that was so distant that the motions of constant change could not reach it, which was buried so deep that it would exceed the patience of the most persistent of insertion speleologists.

Once a foreigner (myself, for example) had grown used to the *Book*'s revolving-wheel nature, he was driven to distraction by the *Book*'s other whims. The *Book* constantly violated the seemingly obvious rule that the number of flights taken in its descent should correspond—if the action were to be returned to the original level—to the number of flights taken in its ascent. It might happen, for example, that the hero of Story A was also the narrator of Story B, while in Story B the narrator of Story C made an appearance; but the action would not, as one would expect, return to Level B once Story C was finished—instead it was Story A which continued on the pasted-in strip. It was as if by some dark magic Story B and the world it described had disappeared from the *Book* entirely; but later, once we had recovered from it, Story B would continue in some wholly unreasonable place, say at Level F or Level G. The hero of a story on Level A wrote the novel *Silver Cloud*, which was played out on Level B. Some way into the story a character from Level B stepped into a bar on Level A, where he struck up a conversation with the cousin of the author of *Silver Cloud*. I didn't know whether such offences against logic occurred by intention or through negligence, but to begin with they so exasperated me that I felt inclined to seek out their authors so I could throttle them.

Fortunately the authors of individual parts of the *Book* were so entirely anonymous, there was no chance of finding out their names. Besides, to ask around after the identity of an individual author was socially unacceptable. The sense of shame it would provoke might have something in common with that known by the island's kings, who would have liked to remain every bit as anonymous as the authors of the *Book*.

But this was not all. At certain points the *Book* would bite itself in the tail, so that it was barely possible to ascertain the level on which a given passage was located. (When counting off the levels, one could start wherever one chose.) Let us say that a character appears in Story A who is the narrator of Story B, while one of the characters in Story B is the narrator of Story C; then one of the characters in Story C begins to narrate not Story D (as one would expect) but Story A. (Escher's lithograph *Print Gallery* is folded into itself in a similar way (although it has a simpler A (A) form. (In a gallery a visitor is looking at an art print which portrays a town which contains the gallery in which the visitor is standing. (I would like the reader to consider what this lithograph would look like if—like a story in the *Book*—it had the form A (B(C(A)))?))).) (If that last sentence was written by one of the authors of the *Book* it is quite possible, dear reader, that you would count in it three left-hand and thirteen right-hand parentheses.)

Karael and I once sat on the jetty in the lower town discussing the way the *Book* folded in on itself. We had been bathing in the harbour and had taken the *Book* along with us. (As I have mentioned, it was not necessary to treat the *Book* with any great care; smudged letters and marks were taken as part and parcel of the *Book*'s transformation.) I argued that the form the *Book* took did not correspond to the arrangement of its contents, complaining that the rule was abused which stated that an insertion at the lowest level should be in an interior pocket; I also suggested how this might be corrected. It would be necessary to cut an opening into a pocket pasted on to Foldout A—the biggest, which contained Text B—and another into the pocket containing Text C which was inserted in the first pocket; a pocket could then be pasted on to the appropriate place on Text C. Where this new pocket was at its narrowest, it would be elongated so as to pass through both openings, only widening out once it had escaped the physical confines of the *Book*. The new pocket would need to be big enough to ensure that it could be turned back in towards Level A, closing this (and the whole *Book* along with it) inside itself. It would also be necessary to cut into this pocket an opening by which its beginning—which coiled out from pocket C—would be able to exit.

To my surprise, Karael understood my somewhat confused explanation; she quite liked the idea of a *Book* which absorbed itself, but straight away she objected that the observing of one rule would necessitate the violation of another—that by which nothing with its origins in a pocket should get out. We laughed about this. For a short while longer we thought up various fantastical forms the *Book* might take; as connectors of passages on various pages of the *Book* we imagined insertions like the kind of suspension bridge we had seen in adventure movies, and insertions that were like secret tunnels through the *Book*'s pages, and insertions crawling out of the *Book* like rootstock, themselves the seeds of new books. Then we gave up on this and jumped into the water. After a while we looked back to where we had been sitting, where the unfurled strips of the *Book*'s pages were fluttering in the wind like an ill-fated white jellyfish washed ashore by the incoming tide.

As I said, I never read the *Book* in its entirety; nor would anyone have been able to do so even had he wished to. (Besides, it is pointless to think of it as a whole *Book* as it will never be written to completion.) No one had ever known—except for the short time when it contained a few pages only—how long the *Book* was. The paper used for the innermost insertions was so thin that an epos greater in extent than everything I knew of the *Book* might have lain there undiscovered and unread, like an island Mahabharata, longer than the entire contents of the rest of the *Book* even though it was contained deep in a single pocket. It was impossible to read the *Book* from beginning to end for the simple reason that it was not apparent what was the beginning and what was the end. The system of insertions was so complicated and the paths were interwoven to such a degree that to take as the beginning the first word on the first page of the largest foldout would have been nonsensical.

I came across all manner of things in the insertions. After a while nothing would surprise me: I might pull out of a pocket a cookbook, a guide to what seemed to be an imaginary town (complete with detailed street-map), an exorbitantly long description of a sunset, a bizarrely distorted retelling of European history, or descriptions of animals (some real, some imaginary). I have noticed that a lot of literary critics are bothered by the mixing of genres; indeed, some of them are so easily offended in this regard that they experience distress when faced with trifles like the use in a passage of fiction of concepts of theory (as if there were some fundamental difference between stories of people, animals, plants and objects on the one hand and stories of concepts on the other). What a torture it would be for them to read the island's *Book*, in which it is common for a lyrical passage to give way to several pages of description related in chemical formulae!

Yet it was the case that narratives of mythology, fairy tale and adventure were more numerous than other kinds. Kings, princes and princesses, sorcerers, dragons and demons . . . all these things featured frequently. It seemed to me curious that the islanders should choose such a cast of characters. I long failed to understand how it was that they kept writing about all-powerful wizards when they themselves had no interest in power; why it was that they wrote about kings, princes and princesses when the island had no aristocracy and its king was miserable and impotent. They did not appear to be in the grip of nostalgia for a feudal past. It was also curious to me that many of the stories of the *Book* featured violent passions when apparently the islanders themselves knew no passion or desire.

Then it came to me that these mysteries were not as insoluble as they seemed. Let us not forget that the *Book* was an insertion which had emerged out of amorphousness; it was an exposition of formlessness, an interpretation of subtle murmurs and whirls. But an exposition of formlessness cannot itself be formless, fuzzy and soggy: there are bound to be clearly-contoured shapes behind it. We should not interpret the weak whirls of reality (which undulate with the primordial tremor out of which later we make time) as the feeble gurgitation of a torpid will, but as a story which evolves in a desire and a passion coagulating with other desires and passions. To close in on the formlessness and forms the *Book* describes, bold gestures, pictures and stories were required; the nascent stories summon heroes—kings, generals and wizards—who have a power which enables them to the utmost extent to act, react and reign. The casts of aristocrats are in no way an expression of a conscious or unconscious desire for a hierarchical society: they are a means of ensuring the gyratory progress of the *Book*. As naturally the authors have no knowledge of such heroes and motifs from their own experience on the island, they seek them out in dispatches from our world delivered by visitors to the island. The *Book* is not a treatment of the islanders' world but of ours; it is an ever-changing island dream of our world.

Whenever I came across characters and situations in the *Book* that were familiar to me from fairy tales, I found myself eagerly anticipating magical, poetic and fantastical images; in this I was always disappointed. Individual stories were governed by a strange mechanics which was only for show. The plot of a story often revolved around the need to solve some kind of task, and the characters performed this by either trying to construct a suitable mechanism or to find a natural phenomenon (animal, vegetable or mineral). In spite of their fairy-tale settings and magical props, the stories were reminiscent of mathematical equations or the assembly of complex machines. And as stories were entered at many levels and folded in on themselves, the *Book* behaved towards the intrepid reader as a monstrous machine with no function but many levels of cogged gearwheels.

## 33
## At the station in Vršovice

Now, dear reader, is perhaps the time for me to present you with a story from the *Book*. I still don't have much taste for this, and I have to admit that yesterday after I finished work on the last chapter I spent the entire afternoon walking the streets of Pankrác, Michle, and Vršovice. The spring mist was so fine that I could barely distinguish it from the foretaste of rain; I was bombarded with hundreds of different reeks and scents (I'm writing these chapters at the end of April). I was considering the pros and cons of embarking on the most pointless undertaking yet in the setting down of my recollections of the island. I was tempted by the thought of ending my writing here and now, thus leaving the stories of the *Book* to your imagination, not least because I realized I couldn't remember that much about them and would have to piece them together from disconnected fragments, or else think up new connections. But I reached the conclusion that it would be unfair of me to wriggle out of this task; besides, as transformations of the text were part and parcel of the *Book*, would not a narrative transformed by forgetfulness and patched-up fantasy be truer to the *Book* than an exact representation of the *Book* as I knew it during my days on the island?

I was yet more afraid of the *Book*'s peculiar tendency to uncontrollable proliferation and expansion. I knew the *Book* well enough to realize that it was unlikely that the long period it had spent in a remote part of my brain had sufficed for its deactivation. I knew that once I began to bring extracts from the *Book* out into the light I would need to proceed with the caution of an experienced pyrotechnician—without careful handling any of them could explode, spraying over a wide area contents hitherto hidden. The light-minded narrator might have chosen a chapter from the *Book* and then found himself at the centre of a blast, with pages raining down on him by the hundreds.

But then I reached a point at which the dangers of the *Book* took on the aspect of a game of adventure—I told myself it would be cowardly to shirk the challenge this presented. I have some experience of the *Book*, after all; I know its tricks, where its dangers lie, the signals it gives, and to pay these due attention. I reached my decision as I was walking past the station at Vršovice. Since I like this place I went inside, bought myself some coffee in a plastic cup, went out on to the platform and sat down on a bench that rested against the wall of the station building. I watched the trains come and go and imagined you, dear reader, reading the tales of my travels. I wondered which part of the *Book* I should narrate from. As I have said, the texts that fight free of the *Book*'s pockets are from many different genres. Initially I thought of recounting what I could remember of the sections of the *Book* which seemed to me the most original. These were texts which had something in common with abstract painting, long passages in which no people, animals, plants or even objects appeared; the heroes of these passages were various kinds of smudges or stains, of which I have spoken in an earlier chapter. The islanders gave these smudges or stains special names. Admittedly, these texts are not exactly typical of the *Book*—the main motion present in the *Book* is a sweeping gyration in which formlessness gives way to form and vice versa. The stories of stains circulate only in a small wheel, in which the shapes brought forth do not trouble the material world.

These passages describe in detail how stains transform, how their positions change in an abstract two-dimensional space, and how the relations between these stains change. For example, one insertion describes over dozens of pages how the stain *puo* sprouts two *nest* protrusions (have I mentioned already that it is not only stains that have names but also parts of stains?) and how in time the ends of these stains begin to curl in towards each other. For a while all the indications are that the protrusions will join up, thus creating a rare kind of stain containing an island void, but as the protrusions appear to be about to meet, their progress is halted and they remain separate. From time to time—as if by way of contrast—a small stain approaches one of the protrusions, but it never gets close enough to bring any kind of influence to bear on the larger stain. So what is the shape to which the main stain aspires? The islanders find this kind of narrative quite thrilling; they devour it as we devour detective stories. If the island had television, the islanders' equivalent of *Dallas* or *Dynasty* would probably be a daily episode of a never-ending series on the transformation of stains.

As the narrative progressed it seemed that the original *puo* stain was about to be transformed into a *ziud* stain. But the reader of experience smelled a red herring: the signs foretelling a transformation to *ziud* were too obvious, too stage-managed. Though they were hidden, this was done in such a way that the attentive reader could spot them. He began to understand that signs suggesting a transformation to *ziud* were scattered across the work to draw the reader's attention away from the real—albeit hidden—focal point of the plot, and that this must be the suspiciously unobtrusive small stain near the *nest* protrusion. He became ever more certain that the moment was approaching when the small stain would enter the action; it might suddenly expand before swallowing the large stain so that the two of them formed a *mue* stain.

But in the end the reader was surprised to learn that his bluff had been called. His shrewdness and worldly wisdom had been shown up as naivety. The author had reckoned with his suspicions and exploited these with craft. The reader had overlooked the fact that there were two red herrings; his uncovering of the first deceit had prevented him from seeing the second, from deducing that two untruths made a truth. The small stain did not enter the action at all; its ostensible meaninglessness was a disguise for emptiness. There came a point in the action where the small stain unravelled and then disappeared. When the baffled reader returned to the large stain—having paid so little heed to the unobtrusive changes taking place on its left side, as he was preoccupied with tracking down a ruse on the part of the author—he realized that the original stain had gradually assumed the form of the *ziud*, the very outcome he had least reckoned with.

Of course, in describing these beautiful stories separately, I am not showing them to their full advantage; to give you a proper idea of their nature I would have to relate whole *stain* eposes and symphonies replete with heroes, crisscrossed networks and unexpected twists. But I think it likely you would not find this amusing. Indeed, I doubt you much enjoyed the tale of the *puo* stain. If you skipped a few lines or even the whole passage, you have nothing to be ashamed of: it took me a long time to get used to this literary genre.

If I were to retell some of the *stain* novels contained in the *Book*, I would struggle with the translation. This is another of the things I was thinking about at the station. As you know, the islanders have names for the different stains that have no equivalents in Czech, so these would have to remain in the original with the attachment of long explanatory footnotes, in which I would describe the shapes of the stains, the relationships among them, their durability and changeability, their tendency to different kinds of transformation and the effects of these transformations on other stains, both close and distant. To explain the name of a stain I would need to refer to the names of all the others; in the end we would have a network of explanatory footnotes in which each note referred to all the others, and this network would draw in the main text, which would become a commentary on its own commentary, a series of footnotes for footnotes.

So in the end I decided to retell a relatively closed episode from a part of the *Book* in which an unknown author describes over a great many pages (spangled with dozens of white insertion pockets like a meadow flush with mushrooms) the feud between two royal houses living in a mythical archipelago. This feud survived several generations—the crimes of fathers provoked acts of vengeance from sons which were also crimes which would have to be paid back. Interludes of peace allowed the heart to nurture memories of how it had been wronged, with the result that the unquiet hand groped for the dagger and new wrongs were wrought.

## 34
## The queen's illness

The story of the feuding families was written on a strip of paper folded into one of the *Book*'s pockets; this pocket was inserted into a story about the adventures of an island prince, a character reminding one of Odysseus and Sinbad. One night a wicked jinni steals into the bedroom of his beloved wife and spirits her away. The prince spends twenty years at sea in a fast boat called the *Dark Desperation*, searching sinister islands and ill-boding coastlines. The end of this long section is rather strange even by the standards of the *Book*. After twenty years of roaming the prince finds his wife on a distant island of rock. She has been living here for many years alone in an empty palace by the shore: the jinni lives with each of his women for one year only, and he left her long ago.

In the beginning the woman is desperate with longing for her husband and her homeland. But over the years spent in seclusion on the island, she develops a love of solitude; she spends hour upon hour watching the ever-changing surface of the sea until she believes that she understands its script. These are the most beautiful letters in the world, and she never wearies of reading their wonderful messages. And so she spends her days on the shore in a state of rapture. The sudden appearance of her husband is unpleasant to her, as are the constant, noisy perambulations of his retainers on the paths and in the gardens of the palace. She is torn from her contemplations, dislocated from her dialogue with the ocean. She sulkily prepares her departure. But when the *Dark Desperation* is about to sail, she tells the prince she will be staying on the island. And the prince does not attempt to talk his wife out of her decision: for the several days of his stay on the jinni's island he has found her indifference and eccentricity hard to bear. He realizes that he is glad to be leaving the island without her. Thus ends a twenty-year pilgrimage.

As the wife stands on the shore watching the boat disappear over the horizon, it seems that the prince is quitting the pages of the *Book* for good. After several days of unpleasantness, confusion and discomfort she is happy to return to her reading of the great manuscript of the sea. She whispers a declaration of love and a promise of fidelity to the sea; this Lautréamontesque ode to the ocean tells of the beauty of her lonely, husbandless, childless, friendless death on the moist sands amid the murmur of the waves. (Perhaps there is a direct influence at work here, but I am at a loss to identify it. It is not inconceivable that Isidore Ducasse stopped off on the island as he voyaged between Uruguay and France.) To the anti-social, solitary islanders this ending is far less scandalous than it would be to us.

But the story of the feuding families is set sometime earlier than the curious ending of the quest for the lost wife; the prince is still dreaming of reunion with his beloved, still scouring every coastline he can find. Most of the islands where he drops anchor are populated by monsters, cannibals or walking machines in metal coats which glow in the sun. Only once does he come across an amicable people with a welcoming, shaded palace. As he rests here a while the prince tells the island's ruler and his family—in the manner of Odysseus in the palace of the Phaiakians or Aeneas in Carthage—of his homeland and his travels. The prince is descended from one of the warring families, so his story includes an account of the feud. The *Book* states: "For three days and three nights he recounted to the king and the queen the long, sad tale of the warring families." Those readers who chose to let this sentence be and not to open the thick pocket which was inserted here, learned nothing about the feud; they spent two weeks on the hospitable island in the company of the hero, learned of his further adventures and then of their bewildering end. But those who did choose to open the pocket, as I did, were given the history of the feuding families of the archipelago. It includes an episode I would like, dear reader, to retell.

There are two islands, Illim and Devel. On the first there lives a king called Tana, on the second a king called Taal. There exists an enmity between the two royal houses. When Tana and Taal are still children, their fathers begin to tire of the same old naval battles joined in the cold of dawn, invasions mounted on sandy beaches (which memory makes an ongoing, dreamlike struggle), punitive expeditions to the humid jungles of the hills in search of guerillas (goaded to do so by the enemy)—and so they negotiate a tired peace. With time weariness and resignation give way to a kind of tolerance and respect, and so it comes to pass that Taal and Tana spend their youth together at the court of a Gallic king and become friends. But it seems that the ill-will has never dissolved, just lain dormant in the blood; once roused, it takes sustenance from an ages-old, bounteous source—love for a woman and the jealousy and abasement with which this is imbued. Perhaps the hatred awakes of its own accord, finds a woman to please it and stage-manages a drama in which it resumes the reins of power, makes itself joyfully manifest in words and gestures and streams into all thoughts and acts. Tana and Taal fall in love with the Gallic princess Nau, who hesitates between them for a while before expressing a preference for Tana. Tana takes her with him to Illim. When some time later his father dies, Tana becomes the island's ruler and Nau his queen.

Taal returns to Devel, where shortly he marries the beautiful Uddo, whom he also knows from Gaul and who rumour has it was implicated in a poisoning affair when she was only fourteen. Such a spare characterization is of little use for my retelling. In this part of the *Book* the unknown author says nothing more about Uddo, although in the scenes in which she appears lengthy descriptions of the patterns and fabrics of her clothing and of her jewels are provided. These descriptions are made in the shadows of pockets whose contents relate the history of the lands where the fabrics are woven and give details of the lives of the artists who chiselled the jewels. (Have no fear, dear reader—I will exclude these descriptive passages from my retelling.) The faces of all the figures in the *Book* are veiled in a fog; around this void fabrics flutter, scents waft and jewels twinkle. I considered painting faces on the characters of the tale before deciding not to force masks on them and so conceal the emptiness they are used to.

Uddo hates Nau, and the evil influence she works on the embittered Taal grows stronger with the years. On Devel, well-paid court poets laud Uddo's erudition. When at twenty-three the dazzlingly beautiful wife of the king is appointed president of the Devel Academy, an assembly of venerable old men who have dedicated their lives to science, jokes are cracked on all the islands of the archipelago. But the jesters are in error—Uddo has an extensive knowledge of chemistry, transformation in metals, runes, augury, archaeology, metaphysics, geometry, architecture, statics, boat-building and building of labyrinths, demonology, astronomy and haruspicy. In these sciences Uddo's learning exceeds that of the academicians by far. (She acquired it at schools of the dark sciences of which it is better not to speak. All that is heard of these are rumours—and they may be nothing more than recollections of dreams—of night-time lectures delivered in whispers in dark rooms furnished with mountains of cushions and pillows for the students and teachers, who drift in and out of sleep.) There is no doubt that Uddo takes her duties at the Academy seriously—within very few years she turns it into a kind of secret society, something between an alchemist's workshop and the Cosa Nostra.

At the time our story begins, Tana and Nau and have not seen Taal and Uddo for twenty-five years. In all that time there have been occasional discoveries on Illim of spies and mischief-makers from Devel, but the wary peace between the two islands has never fractured to such an extent as to excite open conflict. One day Tana receives a letter from Taal in which the latter expresses the wish that he and Uddo be reconciled with Tana and Nau. Tana answers immediately with a long letter of his own, in which he invites Taal and Uddo to Illim. Since the time of his break with Taal he has had no real friends, and in the evenings over a glass of wine he often looks back with fondness on the happy times they spent together in Gaul. Such is his joy at Taal's letter that he pays no attention to various tales abroad in the archipelago which speak of Uddo's murderous chemistry and Taal's dark sonatas of power, whose darkest chords are played by his paramilitary guard. At this time Tana's son Gato is twenty-four and he is a student in Gaul, where he is living with his mother's parents. Fo, the son of Taal and Uddo, who was born in the same year as Gato, died four years ago; Fo's sister Hios is seventeen. It seems that the names of both princes and the princess are mentioned in the text only incidentally—Gato and Hios are many miles from Illim and Fo is dead, so none of them will be playing any part in the action. Still we wonder if they might be important for the story—perhaps one of its strands will contrive for the wanderers to meet, or the action will return to a time when the deceased was still living.

Presently Tana and Nau are down at the harbour to welcome the galleon from Devel. They embrace Taal and Uddo, who for many days will be their guests at the palace. Every evening the four of them sit on a balcony above the trees of the garden, looking back on the days they spent together on Gaul and talking of their islands. It seems that these evenings serve to dissolve all remnants of resentment and ill-will between them. At this time Nau begins to be troubled by a strange illness. One morning she realizes that the skin of her right hand has stiffened, lost feeling and acquired a bluish hue; over the next few days she observes with alarm how these changes progress. Within two weeks the skin has become a smooth, grey-blue shell in which the queen is held captive: Nau is walled in in her own body. She has become a statue of herself, unable to move, unable to speak or even eat. Fortunately the hardening has not attacked her inner organs, so she can swallow pulped food when it is poured carefully into her mouth. The only feature of her outer body which is not grey and immobile is her eyes—two terrified, twitching larvae set in the heavy metal her skin has become. Whenever Tana carries his queen in his arms he watches in the smooth surface of the new metal distorted reflections of the palace—sagging columns, bloated window frames, soft networks of chequered corridors; when he leans in close to her round, gleaming, pitted face he sees in it a grotesque caricature of his own.

Tana takes meticulous care of Nau. He dresses her as if she were an enormous marionette; he carries her into the garden; every evening he bathes her and lays her next to him in their bed. He summons the most celebrated physicians, each of whom recommends a different treatment—one has Nau's shell of a body coated in rose oil, another daubs it with ass's milk, another fills the room with smoke produced from the wood of trees that grow on distant Formos. The physicians come and go, but the queen's shell becomes not the tiniest bit softer. Taal and Uddo declare themselves extremely concerned. Taal summons his court physician, who applies to Nau's body over several weeks a decoction of Develian herbs. But it seems to Tana that all these cures only serve to make Nau's skin harder still.

# 35
# Luminous letters

The royal palace has a square ground plan. Its rooms are on seven floors and entered from seven arcaded galleries joined by a staircase. The galleries enclose an inner courtyard, where a fountain surrounded by palm trees spurts water continuously. The tops of the palms reach to the third gallery. One warm night of a full moon Tana is unable to sleep, and he sees from the movements of Nau's eyes that she, too, is awake. So he carries his hardened queen from the room with the same care as if she were a priceless statue. Their bed-chamber is on the seventh, highest floor of the palace. In the dark gallery Tana leans his queen against the wall and lets her breathe in the fragrance of the summer night. He sits down on a stone bench beside her, takes up his telescope and studies the moon, which is illuminating the slim columns of the arcades and is reflected in the metal statues of the galleries. The room of Taal and Uddo is on the opposite side of the gallery, and next to this, in an alcove, there is a circular aquarium in which the water is rippling and lit blue by a medusa. This was a gift to Nau from an envoy of the Emperor of China and she keeps it as a kind of living jewel. Apart from the glow of the moon and weak blue light of the medusa—which is like the flame of a gas burner in the wind—the sleeping palace is in complete darkness. (That one story of the *Book* should tell of Gaul, galleries and telescopes, alchemy and chemistry is an anachronism characteristic of all its parts. The authors of the *Book* do not use anachronism with any particularly sophisticated intent; they do not use it in conjuring tricks like Jünger or Gracq. Anachronism in the *Book* tends to be employed carelessly, even naively, and at times it is not even clear whether it appears through negligence, playfulness or a simple ignorance of history.)

Suddenly Tana becomes aware of a muted conversation. Then two shadows appear in the gallery opposite; they flitter about for a while before coming to rest next to the medusa's aquarium. Tana recognizes the voices of Taal and Uddo. His guests from Devel are too far away for him to understand what they are saying, but he identifies in their tone an evil gaiety which regularly gives way to quiet laughter. Tana is shocked to hear them laughing at a time when all voices in the palace are muffled in sadness. The suspicion is roused in him that the visit of Taal and Uddo to Illim is a mission of evil, an act of treachery that will bring in its wake a new war. There is no way of his approaching his guests so that he might eavesdrop on their conversation—any movement in their direction would be picked up by the moonlight. They would be alerted, too, by the calls of the birds whose cages line the arcades.

Then he makes the happy realization that there is one way in which he can find out what his guests are talking about. Once he, Nau, and Gato were standing in a dimly lit room admiring the beautiful, luminous dance of the medusa when they noticed that the medusa gave an answer to every sound by means of a special movement. Plainly it was able to distinguish the ripple frequency of different sounds and for some reason it would react to a given wave with the same movement each time. (At this point in my reading, the text sprouted one of its "zoological" pockets. These were attached to a page wherever a new species of animal made its first appearance in the *Book*. There were insertions in these pockets that described the anatomy of the animal, its behaviour and habitat, and how it hunted its prey. Sometimes recipes were recorded in which the flesh of the animal was the main ingredient.) Tana, Nau, and Gato often played a game in which one of them stood next to the aquarium and whispered something while the others tried to work out from the movements of the medusa what had been said. So now, from the other side of the gallery, Tana trains his telescope on the aquarium and sets to reading the luminous blue transcript of Taal and Uddo's conversation. The medusa delivers this tirelessly, carefully, and always accurately.

Within a few moments Tana is quite appalled. He learns that Taal and Uddo's amiability is a disguise. His evil guests conspired to put powder from Uddo's witch's kitchen in Nau's wine-glass, and it is this that has turned Nau into a gleaming blue-grey statue. It seems that the plan was devised by Uddo, who has never desisted in her hatred of Nau, and that she persuaded the hesitant Taal to put it into practise. Up there in the gallery Taal asks Uddo if one day a physician might appear on Illim who would find a cure for Nau; laughing, Uddo assures him this is quite out of the question. The formula of the medicine that would restore Nau to her original form is known by her and her alone; it is composed of forty-four ingredients, and if but one of these is missing the medicine has no effect whatever. Then she begins to itemize the ingredients. Tana quickly pulls off his ring, then takes the telescope in his left hand and puts it to his eye; his right hand moves across one of the marble panels laid in the wall, inscribing into it the names of the substances by means of the diamond set in the ring.

When Taal and Uddo start to make fun of Nau's carapace, referring to her as the Illim Tortoise, Tana's anger gets the better of him; he sprints through the dark gallery towards his enemies. On reaching them he grabs Taal by the throat and pushes him to the floor before proceeding to choke him, all the time shouting that the despicable plan will fail because he has recorded all ingredients of the antidote in the marble of the wall. The medusa's frantic, luminous letters write Tana's cries into the dark, but no one takes the trouble to read them. For a few moments Uddo stands over the two kings as they scramble about the floor in each other's clutches, just watching. Then she lifts from the wall one of the bronze shields that an unimaginative palace decorator has had hung in each of the corridors and dashes it against Tana's head.

Stunned, Tana falls flat on his face. The calls of the birds ring out and the palace is stirring from sleep; in the lower galleries strips of light appear and then vanish; there is the sound of voices and footfalls on the stairs. When he sees guards running up the stairs towards them, Taal begins to panic, but Uddo—for whom villainy has always been an exact science—keeps a cool head. Within seconds the troops are in the seventh-floor gallery. Uddo tells them that thieves have broken into the palace; it was they who inflicted the injury on Tana when he caught them red-handed. Now they are hiding in the rooms of the lower floors. As soon as the men leave, Uddo picks up the aquarium with the luminous medusa as if it were a lantern and carries it to the opposite side of the gallery. In the restless blue light she examines the wall. Nau is still propped up against the wall like a broken beam. Uddo lifts the aquarium to the level of her adversary's face and watches with satisfaction as the terrified eyes flit to and fro in the distorted, radiant-blue mirror. Then Uddo continues her inspection of the wall until she finds the inscription in the marble.

Uddo always wears a little white pouch on her waist. Theories and rumours abound as to its contents. I can divulge that it contains a first-aid package for use in everyday situations of difficulty in which Uddo might have cause to find herself. For Uddo everyday situations include betrayal, intrigue, blackmail, poisoning and mortal combat. Concealed in the pouch are five sachets made of fine paper, the colours of their powders showing through. Among these is the white powder that brought about Nau's illness. Now Uddo pulls out a sachet of red powder. Then she fishes the medusa out of its aquarium and drops it onto the paved floor. For a few moments the medusa squirms pitifully; then its light goes out. Uddo pours the powder into the aquarium before throwing its transformed contents at the marble panel.

As it trickles down the panel, the red liquid obscures the ingredients of Tana's transcription. The red solidifies rapidly until all that remains of the inscription is thirteen isolated letters on islets of grey. Uddo might easily obliterate these, but she leaves them exposed as an act of malice, imagining Tana standing over them, trying desperately to piece together the words they grew out of. Uddo looks approvingly on her work, this poem of hate made up of thirteen lost letters; then she turns to Nau and leans against her, knocking her over. The queen hits the slabs with a boom and proceeds to roll along the corridor; Nau rattles down the first staircase and then the second, knocking the marble and bronze statues of the galleries out of her path as if they were skittles. Soon she is pursued by a booming herd of rolling statues. The last of the staircases flings her towards the fountain; she is dashed against its metal base, which rings like a bell, then caught and deluged by statues.

At the place which told of Uddo's pouch, there was an unusually fat pocket. I opened this in the expectation it would contain details of the countries of origin, composition and preparation of the medicaments concealed in the individual sachets. But there was an altogether different explanation for the pocket's bulk. The author was having a joke at the reader's expense: instead of describing the contents of the sachets, he had filled the pocket with small-scale representations. (The reader's initial confusion was compounded by the fact that the pockets of the *Book* were practically the same colour and shape as Uddo's pouch.) The five sachets of the *Book* reminded me of tea-bags; powders of five different colours were visible inside them. Having read this passage, Karael decided she would change it. (Her replacement was more of a thriller, in which the struggle was joined by two tamed cheetahs kept by Tana in the palace.) While she was at it, Karael tore off the pocket with the miniatures of Uddo's sachets. I kept it as a souvenir and I still have it packed away somewhere.

While Tana is still unconscious, Taal and Uddo leave the palace and head back to Devel; in all the confusion no one spares them a second thought. As soon as he regains consciousness, Tana sets up a search party for Nau, which scours the palace all night before discovering Nau under the pile of statues by the fountain. It soon becomes apparent that there is no tool in existence that is powerful enough to scratch the coating of red from the marble panel nor any solvent that is effective against it. Tana offers a reward to anyone who can invent such a tool or solvent, yet still he does not lose hope that he will remember the ingredients he was told by the blue light of the medusa. Gradually he calls to mind thirty of them, but of course this is not enough for the creation of the antidote. He wanders the palace oblivious. Before his eyes there are thirteen swirling letters; these summon other letters in an unceasing swarm, forming thousands of real and non-existent words that always disintegrate. One day a fugitive Devel academician arrives on Illim. This scientist has some familiarity with Uddo's murderous chemistry and is able to give Tana details of a solution guaranteed to dissolve the red coating on the marble panel. The substances needed for the production of the solution prove relatively easy to find, but the liquid becomes active only after a certain red gemstone has been submerged in it for several days. Only one such gemstone is known to be in existence, and sad to say this is in a casket that belongs to Taal.

## 36
## Silver ball

I am returning to my writings about the island after an interval of two days. Although I do not wish to try your patience, dear reader, I would like to tell you of my experiences since my last dispatch. But perhaps you need to know immediately whether Tana succeeds in stripping the marble panel of its red coat; perhaps you loathe digressions and dislike books that take you in the course of a single paragraph from a Prague apartment to the tropics and a shack made of reeds, or from the calm of the here-and-now to the picturesque court of a despot of ancient times—before, in the very next paragraph, taking you back where you started, as if nothing has happened. If this is true of you, I wish to assure you that I have no intention of bending your will to mine: should you choose to skip the next few pages, I will not hold it against you. Imagine that they are written in the form of a fold-out strip on thin reed-paper which is inserted in a white pocket and which you do not open. You have my word for it that in the chapters to come we shall return to Illim and Tana and Taal. Gato, too, will make an appearance, and as you learn about an expedition to Devel, the fact that you have skipped a few pages will not compromise your understanding of the adventure.

Now that restless readers have moved ahead, back to distant Illim, now that we are rid of the over-eager, I should like to reveal to you—my judicious reader who is in no particular hurry—that the most important aspects of any story reside in its digressions, even when connections between a digression and the main story are impossible to establish. This is one of the things I learned on the island, and I believe it to be true of more than just literature.

There is an experiment we can perform to verify this. If you are working towards a particular goal or trying to solve a riddle (big or small), take the first path that leads off the highway you have drawn for yourself; as you continue on this nonsensical, pointless and indefensible diversion, soon you will glimpse the first flashes of the secret that has so far eluded you, the first letters of the inscription that will reveal the target of your ambitions. Only on the marvellous fringes of diversions that lead nowhere—the paths of resignation, curiosity and adventure—will you find chambers of rest, books of secret learning and the woman of your most agonizing nightmare.

So are you sitting comfortably? I shall take my time in describing to you what happened to me in Michle; there is time enough for us to return to the story of the island. And if one chapter should not suffice for my description of the events in Michle, I know you will not be angry with me if I continue it in a second. Who knows, perhaps the Michle insertion will generate a whole host of chapters, even a book within a book. Or perhaps I will tire of the description before I reach the end of the paragraph and take us straight back to Illim. But let us not concern ourselves with that for the time being—there is still some way to go to the end of the paragraph. Let us enjoy the sense of freedom the diversions grant us; let us breathe in their scent, the pure air of the uncontaminated vapours of sense and intent, the atmosphere of the myriad, always-beautiful encounters to come with monsters on the one hand and luminous beings on the other. But perhaps once again you are dubious: didn't they always tell you that a work of art is a whole? How can a text be a whole when each of its parts grows rampant without consideration for the others? My answer to this is a quotation from a passage of the *Book*, where the neo-Platonic king Asa answers the complaints of his advisors that he has had the royal palace built to the plans of thirteen architects, each from a different corner of the world, by the "exquisite corpse" method (though each of the architects knew what their colleagues were contributing). "My dear, over-solicitous ministers," says Asa. "The relations that create the true whole are those which join the ends of the rampant growing parts. The harmony of the subtle tremblings of the last outgrowths of digression suffices to establish a rhythm for the whole. Do you not see that my palace is the best-integrated work of architecture ever known?"

When in the morning of the day before yesterday I was writing about the night-time struggle in the palace on Illim, I forgot all about the pocket of the *Book* that resembled Uddo's pouch—which since my return from the island had lain at the bottom of one of the drawers of my desk. I sought it out and studied the sachets of coloured powder it contained. Their scent was so heavy that it soon gave me a headache. I thought about throwing the pocket away, but instead I put it in my bag. I left my apartment around midday; I remembered the pocket as I was crossing the bridge over the Botič in Michle, and I tossed it into the water. There was a sudden fizzing sound followed by the scattering across the surface of concentric circles in silver and violet. The system of circles drifted several dozen metres downstream before converging at a single point, out of which began to rise ribbons of luminous vapour that came together to form a gleaming silver ball about one metre in diameter. Although the ball appeared to be made of a shiny heavy metal, it soon reached the height of a two-storey building; at this point it paused for a few moments before continuing its ascent along the overgrown Pankrác side of the brook and disappearing into the clouds.

I had no idea what to make of this flying metal ball. I was seized by the strange feeling that my stay on the island had taught me nothing. I had assumed that the strangest thing about the island was that it had no secrets at all—that the island's greatest mystery resided in the absence of any kind of mystery on the island. Now I suspected that for the entire course of my stay the island had been keeping its secrets from me, that the seeming absence of mystery had in fact been an elaborate, deliberate act of concealment. I was not able to place the gleaming ball within the context of anything I had known on the island. As I stood there perplexed on the bridge in Michle, I thought it probable that I had stumbled across an indication of the island's witchcraft, of whose existence the islanders had kept me in perfect ignorance. I had several times read in magazines about the theory of the Atlantis origin of the island's culture, and I had always thought it ridiculous. Now I asked myself if these sensationalist articles and books about the legacy of Atlantis might be more truthful accounts than my own more sober one, which was based on unvarnished facts.

Could an island on which everything takes place on the surface, where not even the mirrors and the transparent walls of water suggest any depths, where the most mysterious spaces—the shallow, gloomy caves with their gemstones—lie behind half-open doors, could such a place possibly have invisible depths? On the island I always knew that the discovery of a single hidden space would suggest the existence of a great many others. So had this fantastical possibility now become a reality? The existence of sachets of powder that transform into a mysterious flying ball was such an unexplained hollow. Might not the island be riddled with hollows, like a piece of cheese? Might it be concealing the underground temples of an unknown cult, where the islanders meet at night in secret? Or chambers carved in the rock containing the mummies of kings of old or ancient chronicles in which is recorded the island's rich history?

I wondered now if the islanders had been playing a game of deception with me throughout my stay, if they had always laughed at me behind my back. And I felt a sharp pain at the thought that Karael, too, had been party to this game, that she had laughed along with the others at my ignorance and naivety, that she had left the bedroom at night to participate in the playing out of the island's mysteries. Everything I had lived through on the island acquired a new meaning; in everything I found traces of deceit and ridicule. I wondered at my inability to recognize the obvious. And it came to me that everything I had written about the island up to that point was wrong. In my desperation I accessed my computer's directory and the file that contained my narrative about the island and pressed the Delete key. But as I was reaching for Enter, I told myself I would sleep on it.

## 37
## Achilles and Briseis

That evening there was a report on the television news about the gleaming ball. The reporter interviewed a number of inhabitants of Michle and Pankrác who gave excited accounts of what they had seen. (All of them drew two semi-circles in the air with their hands, beginning at nose level and ending with the joining of the fingers behind the knees.) There was also an interview with the president of some society which monitored UFO activity. In addition to this the broadcast included a curious video recording made by inhabitants of an apartment house that gave onto the brook; this showed the silver ball reflected in a mirror. I spent a restless night thinking about the island's hidden face. I had a short dream in which I played silent witness to a night-time gathering of islanders revelling in an orgy of island voodoo, waking in terror once the islanders had discovered and surrounded me and were calling in jubilation, "Kill the intruder!" whilst waving their machetes.

In the morning I made my way to the apartment house in Michle, intending to investigate. A girl I had seen on TV the previous evening took me to the room where the recording had been made, but there was not much she could tell me about it. She had seen a shimmering silver ball which had stopped for several moments in front of the window to the room, almost as if it were looking in, and then flown off. The midday TV news would be on in a minute, she said. Why didn't we watch it together to see if they'd found out anything else about the ball?

And indeed there was another item about the ball. A businessman had contacted the station, viewers were told, whose company imported pyrotechnics from China that contained a special powder.

When this powder came into contact with water, a gas was released that formed in the air a ball whose gleaming surface gave the illusion of metal. Standing in the garden of his villa, the businessman took the opportunity to show off his merchandise to the cameras—we saw silver, green, violet and blue balls, cylinders and cones ascending slowly into the sky. Everything fell into place: the author of this part of the *Book* had got the pyrotechnical powder from a sailor on one of the boats moored in the island's harbour, and by putting it in one of the *Book*'s pockets he had been making a joke. Temples in the rock, witchcraft and secret island brotherhoods existed nowhere but in my imagination.

Now that everything has been cleared up, we could choose to return to Tana and Nau on Illim. But as we've already been diverted from the mythical archipelago to Michle, and as we've accepted that the longer the digression, the better, I shall tell you, dear reader, something about the video recording I saw on the television news. Indeed, it is more interesting than the whole matter of the supposed mystery of the island, which I now feel to be pretty worthless, even embarrassing. As I was saying, the video recording from Michle was rather strange. It showed the room the girl took me into the next day. The polished floorboards were bathed in a soft light; on the wall there was a large mirror in which the window and the overgrown hillside opposite were reflected; beneath the mirror there sat on a sofa of light-coloured leather a young man with neatly combed hair, wearing a brilliant-white shirt and an expensive-looking woollen suit. The young man was wordlessly fondling a girl wearing silk underwear; the girl's hair was cut short and tinted blue, and she had a pale, motionless face and lips painted dark violet. Her eye shadow, too, was violet; the colour of her eyes was somewhere between turquoise and green. (When the next day I saw her face stripped of its make-up, with great shadows under her eyes, I did not immediately recognize her.)

Next to the sofa there was a stand with a chalkboard on it; on the chalkboard there was some kind of geometric drawing. On the wall there were several etchings of empty town squares, probably in Italy. In the part of the room closest to the camera there was a table with a glass top and legs of curved chrome. On the table there was a bottle of bourbon. Sitting at the table was a second man, also young and also wearing an elegant suit, this time with a tie. This second man was drinking contemplatively from a glass containing a gold liquid and ice cubes. Little electronic sounds drifted softly towards me, perhaps the outer froth of some kind of music. I had the impression I was watching an advertisement for cosmetics.

Then there was a tapping sound on the recording. The three figures looked at one another; the young woman moved in closer to her partner, but he extricated himself gently from her embrace and left the room. It was at this moment that the shining silver ball appeared in the mirror above the girl's head and stopped. Of the people in the room, the only one who could see the ball was the ghostly cameraman, whose figure was present only in the motions of the pictures, which were now shaking slightly. Judging by the barely perceptible raising of her eyebrows, we can assume that the girl on the sofa had spotted the ball in the window. The young man with the bourbon was plainly startled; he must have caught sight of the ball's reflection in the glass table-top. Still the three of them behaved like professionals and filming continued. In the meantime we heard the first man unlocking a door in the entrance hall, followed moments later by his voice, which sounded bitter and affronted, saying, "Welcome, heralds, messengers of gods and men; draw near; my quarrel is not with you but with Agamemnon, who has sent you for the girl Briseis." So this was no advertisement for cosmetics: it was a modernist film adaptation of the *The Iliad*. (Why not indeed, if Ulysses can wander around Dublin?)

After a while the man playing Achilles returned to the room. When he caught sight of the silver ball in the mirror he gave a start; then he turned to the window and saw for sure the ball hanging in the air above the Pankrác plain. Finally his eyes settled on the third version of the ball, in the white, horizontal reflection of the table-top. All this took but a fraction of a second. This man, too, handled the unforeseen situation very well; he turned to the man seated at the table and addressed him by the name I had been expecting: "Patroclus, bring her and give her to them, so that they may take her away." Then he called to Agamemnon's messengers, who were still in the hall and out of the shot. "Let these two men be witnesses by the blessed gods, by mortal men, and by the fierceness of the king's anger, that if ever again there be need of me to save the people from ruin . . ." While he was talking, the silver ball started to move again. Its reflection slipped silently behind the mirror so that all that was visible in it was again the dark Pankrác hillside. It may be that there was more video footage of Homer's tale, but here the recording stopped so that the TV news could move on to the next item.

Now that the mystery of the silver ball had been settled, I asked the girl what this video recording was supposed to mean. She explained that she and her friends were shooting a film which was an adaptation of *The Iliad*. All the action took place inside buildings in Michle. The rooms of the apartment represented the tents of the Greeks and the chambers of Priam's palace, while the battles were fought on crepuscular staircases and in dim-lit corridors and the assemblies of war of the Achaeans were held in entrance halls and courtyards. When I told the girl I had thought at first that the film was for advertising purposes, she was obviously delighted. The film was inspired by advertisements for ladies' cosmetics, the pictures of Giorgio de Chirico and Plotinus's *Enneads*, she said.

It appeared that the Michle *Iliad* was mostly the work of the girl. She explained to me that the first impulse to make the film was a dream she'd had, in which Achilles and Hector were fighting with heavy swords in front of a bookcase of dark polished wood in the living room, the Persian carpet muffling their footfalls. The glass doors of the bookcase reflected the neo-renaissance facade of the building opposite with its dusty *mascaron*. When she awoke, the calm light of early morning lay across the things in the room, and she had the impression that the characters of her dream and the calm light began a dialogue, in the course of which their voices merged into one. And the vision of her *Iliad*—filmed, if possible, from the first line to the last—was born; from Agamemnon's return of Chryseis to the agony of Hector and beyond, in the style of a television advertisement, in expansive, well-lit rooms where the emptiness of simple modern luxury was masked neither by object nor ornamentation; this emptiness pervaded Chirico's spaces, inhabited by ghosts of the past and the future, and Plotinus's spaces, formed from light which was not yet darkened by shape nor materialized as object. She envisioned all these light-filled voids merging into one, the three lights becoming a single white glare-free glow.

And in this glow the girl wanted to see Achilles and Hector, Agamemnon and Odysseus—characters for whom a world controlled by the whims of the gods was the source of acute anguish and even greater joy. This was the joy of the great Game, part of which was an acceptance of whatever each throw of the dice would bring, when one never knew whether it would fall on its black or its white side. An unhappy throw of the dice—a revelation of divine animosity—meant anguish for sure, but this anguish was part of a joy greater still, the joy of the Game. The girl believed this world called for the calm light she had known first in her dream, then on the walls and floor of her room; she longed for the bodies and objects of the world of the great Game.

## 38
## The voice behind the wall

The girl was a student and her *Iliad* vision had come to her at the beginning of the summer vacation. So she was able to sit at home day after day, looking through the window at the Pankrác hillside or watching the play of the light on the furniture, all the time imagining one scene or another from her film. She said nothing to anyone else about her ideas because she thought people would laugh at her about them; indeed, the film seemed pretty ridiculous and nonsensical to her, but she couldn't stop thinking about it. On top of everything else she had no experience of making a film and didn't know anyone who had.

Curiously enough it was her dream-soaked lounging in the Michle apartment that produced the encounter that gave her the courage to start making her Homeric film of light. So rich was this encounter that it inspired her to find people with the right experience and level of enthusiasm to work with her. The apartment was quiet at all times of the day and night. The sounds of the relatively busy Michle streets did not reach it: all its windows faced the Botič brook. This was one of those city spaces with a brook or a railway line at its heart that might have belonged to another world . . .

"It was so quiet that I could hear hushed voices from behind the walls, above the ceiling and under the floorboards, the practically inaudible music of the neighbouring apartments," the girl told me. When she fell silent for a moment, I, too, heard the quiet voices like fine sand falling on the bottom of a time-glass. The girl went on to explain how she would hear—from early morning till late afternoon—a monotonous male voice from beyond the living-room wall. The voice took a great many short pauses. She imagined that it was dictating some kind of long text, and sometimes she had the impression she was hearing the quiet clack of a computer keyboard. She was curious about this endless dictation. If she pressed her ear against the wall, she could hear a little better, but to begin with she could still make out no more of the voice than its melody. But after she had concentrated hard for a while, she began to distinguish words, although all she really heard were fragments and hints from which she figured out whole words. Then she experimented with these probable words in likely sentences, which she completed with words she had heard nothing of. With great effort the girl's sentences came together to form fragments of a plot. It was a long time before the girl was competent at this strained eavesdropping. But eventually a remarkable story began to emerge.

The girl was quite shocked by what she heard. Several times she saw the writer and his typist in the corridor—he a fair-haired young man in rollneck sweater, jacket and moccasins (and always carrying a black attaché case), she a well-groomed older woman in a suit. The girl marvelled that these two people—whose appearance suggested they had stepped out of a newspaper advertisement for a bank—could day after day roll around in the palpably sick images and utterances she heard through the wall. She had never even known that literature like theirs existed. She had read *Maldoror* and *The 120 Days of Sodom*, but her neighbour's text seemed to her more fantastical, more brutal and more perverse. It was a novel about the life of Amélie, a prodigal daughter. In the beginning Amélie obeys her parents and wishes to be a good daughter, but the parents reproach her constantly for not loving them enough, sighing that she has fallen short of and offended their great love for her. One day they tell her they can no longer stand idly by as witnesses to her degeneracy—what pain it causes them!—so they intend to denounce her to the police.

This is a strange police force whose members are summoned from the pattern of the wallpaper, whither they return after they complete an assignment. The police and the parents take Amélie away from the town, to the place of a stinking cesspit connected to a nearby factory by a pipe from whose mouth there issues a violet dribble. There they force the wretched girl to undress before tying her to a post next to a cave where there sleeps a giant monster, whose chops protrude from the opening, showing teeth that in and of themselves are creatures of great cruelty. The teeth taunt Amélie, describing how they will sink themselves slowly through her flesh and into her guts, how they will greedily chew her up. From the damp, stinking depths beyond them, the tongue speaks up, shouting out in ecstasy its obscene vision of what it will be like to fondle the bloody flesh of the chewed-up girl; then it tries to force its way between the teeth in the hope of touching with its restless tip the flesh of Amélie's body. The police officers have to leave because they are beginning to be transformed back into wallpaper, but the father and mother remain by the cave and converse with the teeth and the tongue about the great misfortune suffered by parents of naughty children. The teeth offer their commiserations while the tongue bursts into tears, so moving does it find their fate. Amélie is shaking with terror, pleading with her parents for mercy. The parents tell her it is too late now for tears, while the teeth declare that what is about to befall her should be the fate of all disobedient daughters.

Amélie hears a pounding which gets stronger and stronger, as if a hammer striking the pipe leading from the factory were getting closer and closer. Then a metal robot—a mechanical dog—leaps from the mouth of the pipe onto its back legs and pounces on the mother before biting into the arteries of her neck. Before he can so much as cry out, the father, too, falls to the ground with his neck violated. The metal dog bites through the chains by which

Amélie is bound and bears her away. The furious teeth try to raise the dragon with their screaming, but the dragon remains lost in sleep. The tongue flies about in its dark hideaway, desperate to find out from the teeth what is going on. After this, the mechanical dog becomes Amélie's guru. The book dictated by the voice behind the wall describes how the two of them wander across several countries and how the dog initiates Amélie into his anarchistic and amoral philosophy of life. It is not clear whether he has been programmed to think these thoughts or whether they have formed of themselves within his electronic networks. But after the dog's batteries run flat and he stops suddenly on a boulevard pavement in the midst of one of his aphorisms, Amélie walks the towns and country alone. The text becomes a picaresque novel describing Amélie's fantastical and erotic adventures . . .

The girl from Michle was scandalized by the eccentric imagination, brutality and amorality of the author, but she was also attracted by them. The more stories she heard from the life of the unprincipled heroine, the more she envied the author's imagination, his fidelity to his vision and his courage in disregarding the opinions of others. Quite unexpectedly, her encounter with the voice behind the wall woke in her a similar kind of courage: she found the strength to commence work on her *Iliad*, no longer concerned that others might laugh at or scorn her. She convinced herself that in the light of her neighbour's bravery in writing a novel that contravened all aesthetic and ethical norms, she would be committing an act of cowardice were she to abandon the calm light of her *Iliad*. And the courage that now burned within her shone a light for others; there was no need for her to look for anyone because all the right people suddenly presented themselves. As to those she had imagined mocking her ideas, they were asking her if they could be involved in the film.

Once she began work on her film she no longer had so much time to listen to the novel beyond the wall. But every day she found a few moments to lay her ear against the wall and find out something of the latest scandalous adventures of the novel's heroine.

"Last month I listened to a new episode about white snakes born in the rippling movements of curtains. As ever the story-line was fantastical and nasty, and as ever I couldn't tear my ear away from the wall. But in the end I had to leave for a meeting about the shooting of the film. When I left the apartment I saw two men in overalls in the corridor. They were pulling some kind of cable into the neighbour's apartment: perhaps he was having cable TV installed. The door to the apartment was open, and I heard—this time with perfect clarity—the voice with the well-known intonation, accompanied by the gentle clacking of the computer keyboard. The realization that my neighbour was not speaking Czech but a Scandinavian language I didn't understand, came to me as if in a dream. He had never spoken Czech—the words I'd thought I was hearing were in fact fragments of Swedish or Norwegian; it was I who had made of them something they weren't and composed them into a story-line that was at once scandalous and fascinating to me. A few days later I got to talking with the typist by the mailboxes, and she told me that my neighbour, her employer, was the Prague representative of a Swedish software firm. He didn't know a word of Czech and spent most of the day dictating to her messages in Swedish for the firm's headquarters in Uppsala."

I was reminded of the "language of water," of utterances born of rustlings and murmurs, but I didn't want to tell the girl about the island. "I thought the similarity between the novel behind the wall and your *Iliad* quite striking," I told her instead. "The motif of the prodigal daughter was, I thought, also present in the dreams you had about your film. Your *Iliad* was about more than just the fighting between the Achaeans and the Trojans: it was also about a girl who had turned her back on her father and fallen in with some gods with low morals. Why don't you write the novel you invented with your ear to the wall?"

"I don't know, perhaps one day I will. The moment I realized I was the author of the novel of the prodigal daughter, that terribly obscene dream, I realized, too, that I could be the source of an endless number of stories. It seems to me that everyone has such a source of stories inside him; mostly, though, this remains hidden. Mine was stirred by fragments of Swedish and the murmur of the language and the fractured images these were immersed in. To begin with I was horrified because I thought it would be my responsibility to write down all the stories that spurted from this source and that my whole life would be too short to manage this in. Then it came to me that each of the stories contained something of all the others. You said yourself that my *Iliad* is the same story as my novel about Amélie. I realized there was no hurry to do anything—it's always enough to tell one story, shoot one film, or paint one picture at a time for all pictures and stories to be present."

## 39
## The quest for the gemstone

Three weeks after the flight of Taal and Uddo, Gato returns to Illim. When she was still able to move her hardening lips a little, Nau asked Tana not to write to Gato about her illness; she did not want her son to see her transforming into a piteous, gleaming tortoise. But after a time, and in spite of Tana's best efforts to censor this, news of the queen's condition reaches Gaul, and Gato sets sail for his island home as soon as he hears it. Then the moment he learns of the hidden inscription and the gemstone at Taal's palace, he announces his intention to leave for Devel; he will find and bring back the gemstone. Gato paces the sand-strewn paths of the park deep into the night. When Tano wakes from a restless sleep, he hears beneath his window the repeated crunch of the sand. In the course of this sleepless night, Gato devises a plan for how to gain entry to the palace of Taal and Uddo.

Gato's plan is based around the fact that no one at Taal's court knows what he looks like; also, it draws on a strange art that Gato learned in a land where his ship was once washed ashore while on its way to Gaul. Next to the name of this land there was one of those thick pockets I came to think of as "geographical-historical." It contained details of the territory and its history, interwoven—as was common in the *Book*—with the psychopathology of its ruling family, again expressed by images from mythology—conspiracy, erotically-motivated revenge, incest, battles at sea, intrigue and uprising, sharp daggers under pillows, faithless women consorting with enemies of the family, dragons in palace gardens at night, high politics discussed in bed chambers, catalogues of poisons seeping through the closed world of the family, inscriptions on walls in scripts unknown, the rising sun shining bright on warriors' blades. But as this is of no great importance to our story, let us leave this pocket closed.

The land on whose coast Gato disembarked was celebrated for its carpets, which were more magnificent than the most beautiful works of Persia and Bukhara. Its people wove carpets from fine but strong fibres spun by a special species of spider which lived off great butterflies in mountain forests. The spiders had two means of attracting the butterflies: by giving off an intoxicating scent, and by a chemical reaction that was actuated in their fibres by early morning sun (when the butterflies flew out), causing the webs to take on the most glorious colours. Each spider would spin fibres of a different colour, as the colour of a web also had the function of marking its territory. The fineness and strength of the fibres made it possible to portray on the carpets the subtlest of details. The people of this land wove into their carpets *vedute* of towns in which it was possible to count the number of stones on the bracelets of women walking in the streets; there were carpets with battle panoramas in which were clearly visible teeth in the grimacing mouths of warriors, and carpets showing jungles where each stalk of grass and each colour in a parrot's crest were carefully distinguished.

A popular genre was the so-called "lost portrait." Having commissioned a master weaver to produce his likeness, the client would some time later receive a carpet that showed, for example, a large town in which there were thousands of figures in the streets and at the windows. One of these figures was a portrait of the client, but in order to find it, it was necessary to look very hard. The longer this search took—and it might take months or even years—the more highly the work was prized. The carpet weavers employed a number of tricks: after several years of intensive searching, one client found his own face reflected dimly on the lid of somebody's snuff-box, while another found himself painted on a crumpled chocolate-bar wrapper lying on a rubbish heap. A carpet which made use of Poe's principle of the "Lost Letter" was particularly celebrated. This depicted a painter showing his girlfriend a picture mounted on his easel, that of a town. The town was extraordinarily elaborate and there was a fantastic number of figures in the streets and parks and on the squares and bridges. The client studied the picture for many years, taking in every figure and every nook and cranny, until one morning he found his portrait in the large face of the painter in the foreground.

Yet the carpets fascinated most by their marvellous daily metamorphoses. The fibres retained all characteristics of the spider's web: all night and for most of the day they were snow-white in colour, but when the first dim rays of sun heralded the dawn they gave off their acute scent and then wonderful pictures began to paint themselves across the white surfaces. The first marks to appear on the white fabric were red and white, but they were followed slowly by the rest of the colours. Each picture would shine for an hour or so, after which time the colours would begin gradually to fade, until the carpet returned to white and remained thus until the next morning. Poetically, the natives called such works "dreaming carpets": they imagined that for a short time at dawn the carpets had colourful dreams before falling back into the heavy, dreamless sleep of objects.

Gato was enchanted by the carpets. Because of them not only did he remain in this strange land for a whole year but he undertook to learn the subtleties of the carpet-maker's art in one of its most celebrated binder's workshops. When he sails away he takes his journeyman's work with him—its picture that of a castle perched atop a rock which rises out of a lake. The castle has many towers and turrets, one growing out of another and all joined to little arched bridges. (On one of these bridges Gato has depicted himself as a figure standing by a balustrade contemplating the bizarre shapes of the clouds in the distance.)

Gato sails off to Devel in disguise, over his shoulder a rolled-up carpet whose white fabric conceals the picture of his dreamlike castle, in his travel bag a collapsible weaver's loom and a ball of spider-spun fibre. As in the half-light of evening the ship pulls in to port at Devel, Gato is standing at the prow, leaning on the rail, looking at the grey, hostile town with its steep, winding streets that reach from the harbour to the walls of the gardens of the royal palace. All but one of these streets turns back the way it has come; this street has succeeded in extricating itself from the tangled knot, reaching beyond the last houses of the town right to the gates of the great gloomy palace. Having passed the night on the jetty, Gato sets off for the palace before sunrise. The day begins early at the palace, and Gato is immediately admitted to the presence of a chamberlain; there he rolls out the carpet moments before the red flags on the turrets of the castle and the masts of the boats on the lake become visible together with the great red flowers and emerald-green leaves of the trees on the bank.

The chamberlain watches with delight as the magical castle emerges; before the last of the coloured marks has appeared he rushes to show this wonder to the king. The king has Gato brought to him and immediately buys the carpet. By the time the castle and the lake begin to dissolve an hour later, Gato has been appointed court carpet-binder and a servant in livery has led him along a long passage to his chamber, where he is to work on his first commission. Taal wishes him to weave for his daughter Hios a carpet that will show a garden of paradise with fountains, artificial waterfalls, alleys, summerhouses, gaily-coloured birds and winsome beasts.

Once Gato is alone in the large, well-lit room he steps to the window. He sees below him the tops of the trees of the palace gardens, and further below still, the grey pitched roofs of the houses in the streets that slope down to the harbour, and beyond these the light strip of the sea.

## 40
## The peregrinations of the caliph

The next part of the *Book* described Gato's stay at Taal's palace. It is not difficult for Gato to discover the whereabouts of the gemstone: everyone at the palace knows that it is in among the other jewels in the royal treasury, which is in the corridor leading to the main hall. To Gato's surprise there is no guard at the door to the treasury; he is surprised also by the fact that there is a metal panel mounted on the door, into which has been carved a complicated, square-shaped labyrinth composed of passages represented schematically that intersect at right angles and lead into an empty central space. There is only one entrance to the labyrinth, and in this there is a game stone, which appears to be a piece of a magnet. It seems that this game stone is waiting for someone's hand to take it and push it along the intricate passages.

Gato wonders if there is some connection between the route taken by the labyrinth and entry to the treasury. He puts his hand on the game stone and is about to move it when a cry of horror rings out behind him. He turns to see a lady courtier running towards him down the empty corridor. She leads him away from the treasury and proceeds to tell him about it. The prince learns that everyone has the right to attempt to open the door, and whoever succeeds may take whatever he wishes from the treasury. The door is said to open when the game stone reaches the centre of the labyrinth on its thirty-sixth move, although so far no one has succeeded in making this happen. One false move and a trap-door opens in the floor, sending whoever is standing in front of the door tumbling into a chasm in the rock on which the palace stands, into the icy waters of the subterranean river that flows down below. Since the death of Prince Fo, only Taal, Uddo and Hios know the right moves.

Though he cannot rid himself of the image of his solidified mother, Gato is afraid to ruin things by his impatience. He makes a drawing of the labyrinth in his attempt to work out which thirty-six moves to take in order to reach the centre. He has plenty of time for this; although it is his task to weave a garden of paradise and he receives frequent visits from Taal in supervision of his progress, it is only possible for him to work in the early morning, when the spider's fibres display their colours. This means he can devote the rest of his time to the labyrinth. He rarely leaves his chamber, but this suffices for him to notice that all the corridors on one side of the palace end in locked doors. When he comes across the lady courtier who explained to him the secret of the treasury and asks her what is beyond these doors, she pulls him towards her and whispers, "The castle of the spirits. Dusty Fo-land. The palace of the dead prince."

Princess Hios, too, develops the habit of going to Gato's chamber each morning, so that she can see how the work is progressing. There is another curious thing about a dreaming carpet: so fine is the material used that it allows detailed work on the tiniest parts, and this means that parts are in constant rebellion against the whole. Motifs are conceived—which often go unperceived by all but the most observant eye—that not only have no connection with the whole but may even serve to subvert it in some amusing or eccentric way. The coloured fibres encourage playfulness and small-scale subordination. The irony alive in the carpets and so much connected with their weaving has settled in Gato's fingers to such a degree that his hands compose the fibres of the garden-carpet in scenes unexpectedly grotesque, his sadness, restlessness and anxiety notwithstanding.

Should one take a close look at the group of monkeys cavorting in the tree-tops, for example, one would see that one of them is not part of the game; instead he is sitting comfortably on a branch some way off, reading Aristotle's *Metaphysics* and writing in the margin of one of its pages the word *Absurd*! The observant student might notice, on the calm waters of the lake, the reflection of a house on whose veranda there is a rocking-chair in which a retired naval captain is sitting. Yet neither next to the lake nor elsewhere in the picture is there any such house. Taal fails to notice details such as this, but Hios finds them straight away and they are a source of great pleasure to her. Every morning she looks forward to finding something new in the shrubs of the garden or the gloom of a summerhouse.

Then she begins to notice other things, too. She suspects that the lines described by the spreading branches and the twisting lianas are a kind of trail left by a heavy, sad current that flows across the carpet from one form to the next. At one point the grey-blue surface of the lake resounds with a silent pain; at another, in a whirl of silver leaves stirred by the breeze, there is the sound of a music that borders on madness. And Hios asks herself who this stranger is. Who can this person be who repeats one hundred and twelve times—with the pertinacity of the melancholic at times of heaviest depression—a complicated oval motif in the ornamental relief work of the cornice of a summerhouse, before placing the goggle-eyed face of a bespectacled, pipe-smoking rabbit exactly where one expects the hundred-and-thirteenth to be? The princess has a dear friend called Ara, and it is around this time that Ara becomes painfully aware in the moments she and Ara spend together that Hios returns in her mind to the magic garden. No longer do Hios's touches represent the crests of waves of desire that course through her body; her fingers continue to pursue old paths, but they do so abstractedly and mechanically, or—and this for Ara is more humiliating still—they follow courses suspiciously reminiscent of those taken by Gato's carpet.

Gato soon comes to see in Hios's joyous expression an understanding of the carpet that is very different from Taal's. He begins to weave for her scenes with crazy animals and living objects. This early-morning dialogue between pictures and gazes, held day after day without the uttering of single word, is the only source of joy for Gato in the hostile palace where the task he is pursuing is practically hopeless and his being found out and killed is a constant threat. Hios, too, enjoys this wordless communication of conspiracy, which takes place before the unsuspecting Taal's very eyes. And the images that Gato creates for Hios become more personal and tender with each passing day . . .

Dear reader, I shall not make myself ridiculous by leading you to a certain event which I would then present to you as a twist in the story. You have certainly guessed what is about to happen, just as I did when I was reading these passages of the *Book*. (In terms of psychology, the *Book* did not have much to boast about.) Naturally enough, Hios falls in love with Gato, and so she will play in the story the somewhat trite role of an Ariadne (in a proper, non-symbolic, albeit miniature labyrinth, what's more). After several pages on which the unknown author describes how the motifs of Gato's carpet become ever more erotic messages to Hios, the much-anticipated moment arrives and the princess and Gato embrace. After this Hios goes every night to Gato's chamber, where she stays until morning. Several times she has to avoid being seen by Taal (who is coming to see what is new in the garden-carpet) by concealing herself behind a potted palm in an alcove of the corridor. Unhappy and insulted, Ara leaves Devel and disappears for a long time from the pages of the *Book*. Indeed, in my reading of the *Book* I came to believe she would never reappear; then she turned up unexpectedly after many more folds in the concertina so as to play a telling role in the Devel tale's bloody finale.

The night Gato finishes work on the carpet, Hios is in his chamber. The day has been humid, but after midnight the atmosphere cools and from the palace gardens there comes the gentle murmur of rain falling on leaves. The princess throws a blanket around her shoulders and goes to sit on the windowsill. Gato sits down next to her, and together they look down at the town, up at the starless sky and across to a place where land and sea are joined. In the dense, dark mass of the town all that is visible is ragged strips of streets illuminated by street lamps and the distant fire of the lighthouse in the harbour. Gato turns to Hios and tells her who he is and why he has come to the palace. All Hios asks of him is that he should take her with him when he leaves Devel; then she tells him that the red gemstone is on the highest shelf of the treasury, in a small box which is made of the wood of the terebinth tree and has a picture of a basilisk on its lid. She tells him what to do in order to get it.

"Do not try to seize the stone unnoticed," she says. "You may believe the corridor to be empty before the door to the treasury, but in fact there are many peepholes manned by many unseen eyes. Observe the handles of the closed doors of the corridor and you will see that none of them is still: they are held from the inside by the hands of watchers. Listen well at the thin walls and the folds of the curtains and you will hear the whisper of secret commands passed from mouth to mouth. The palace corridors are long, and you would not be the first to disappear in them without a trace. Death awaits in the gloom of nooks and empty corridors; you must do your dealings in the glare of the chandeliers of the great halls. Tomorrow my father will hold a celebration in the main hall. You will announce to him before all those present that you wish to solve the problem set by the door to the treasury. Thus shall everyone know of it. It is highly likely that the eyes of curious courtiers will follow you about. That you shall be under surveillance is good: those curious eyes might spare you from the knife or the bullet.

"In moving the game stone about the labyrinth, naturally it is impossible that one should be guided by written instructions. You will need to know each of the thirty-six moves by heart. Thirty-six times you must decide whether to move the stone to the right or to the left. I shall now teach you the story of the caliph of Baghdad. This you shall have no difficulty in remembering, as each of its events is linked to the next. Disguised as a merchant, the caliph walks the streets of Baghdad, where he has thirty-six encounters that correspond to the thirty-six moves. As you move the stone you will tell the story to yourself. Whenever the caliph meets a man, you move to the right; when he meets a woman, this means you must move to the left."

And there at the window above the sleeping town the princess proceeds to tell the story of the caliph, who one warm night mounts the side gate of his palace and sets about walking the narrow moon-and-starlit streets. There he has encounters with a wise man, a robber, a magician, a ferryman who works the Euphrates, a fig-seller, a woman whose face is concealed by a veil. The woman then disappears and reappears in a great variety of guises. The caliph last comes across her in his chamber after he has returned to the palace. The mysterious woman is the daughter of his vizier. The caliph embraces her, delighted to have captured the apparition that escaped him time and again in the Baghdad night. The last move of the stone is to the left, after which it meanders about the passages for a while before it suddenly reaches the centre of the labyrinth, whereupon a hidden mechanism opens the door. Hios teaches Gato the story of the caliph all night long. Only when the dawn-time scents of the carpet reach their nostrils does she steal from Gato's room.

## 41
## The royal treasury

I am telling you the story just as I learned it on the island, in the full knowledge that little of this *Book* island, if anything of it, remains today. First to change was its environment. I remember receiving a telephone call from Karael several months after I had left the island; in those days we were still phoning and writing to each other quite often. When my cellphone rang I was walking under a leaden sky along a mud-spattered sidewalk among the tower blocks of Prague's Jížní město housing estate, looking for an electrical repair shop. Among other things, I asked Karael about the *Book*, and she told me something of its most recent changes. I learned that the town on Devel had in the course of several rewrites become gradually flatter, until it became a town of humble dwellings scattered about a marshy delta, the old camp of nomads who had stopped there on their way to the sea. The town was strung together around the mouth of a shallow brown river, where the tents reluctantly gave way to imperfect houses. In this version the conversation in which Hios advises Gato how to negotiate the labyrinth does not take place above the town but on its fringes; the princess and her lover are sitting at a ground-floor window from which they look upon the steppe, lit by the moon to the distant horizon. But I am not able to think of the town's face as ever-changing, as the islanders can. My memory needs to select one face, one town from the many metamorphoses. So that time on the Jížní město estate, as a wind that reminded me of the island gusted between the tower blocks, I decided to take no notice of the town on the delta and to preserve in my memory the image of the town I had taken from my own reading of the *Book*.

The next day Gato hands the garden-carpet over to Taal. In the afternoon the celebration in the great hall is declared open, and Gato wastes no time in approaching the king and declaring his wish to negotiate the labyrinth on the door of the treasury. News of the wish expressed by the stranger travels in whispers in all directions and to every corner of the hall, killing all conversation so all that is heard is a murmur of curiosity, astonishment and dismay. Taal's face has darkened; he says that anyone has the right to attempt to conquer the labyrinth, that Gato should remember the trap-door and the subterranean river, but he says nothing more. Gato leaves the hall immediately and makes his way along the corridor, which seems to him endless. A procession of silent courtiers tiptoes cautiously behind him, stretching back beyond the bend in the corridor. Whenever Gato turns, they stop mid-step, some of them leaning forward with a foot raised, the outstretched toes just touching the gleaming parquet. Gato remembers reading that the moment after death the soul recalls the last image it saw in life, and he says to himself, "What strange theatrics I shall look upon in the underworld if I confuse one of the moves!" But once he reaches the door to the treasury, he does not turn again. He takes the magnetic stone in his hand, and begins to recite the story of the caliph.

His anxiety does not leave him. At one moment he suspects the stone is moving away from the labyrinth's centre and into a blind alley, and he asks himself if Hios has not betrayed him, if she has taken the side of her family against the stranger. Perhaps her coming to him in the night was part of a plan devised in collaboration with Uddo and Taal. He thinks back to some of things she told him, which seem to him now ambiguous and disquieting; he imagines Hios leaving his chamber and going straight to her father, how they share in laughter at his expense just as cruel as the laughter of Taal and Uddo over Nau's sickness and Tana's desperation. When in Hios's telling the caliph climbed through a hole in the wall into the garden of a stranger's house, where he was addressed from the dark of the summerhouse by an old Persian merchant, it almost seemed to him that she had changed the story on purpose: would it not have been more logical for the caliph to encounter a woman, not a man in a garden at night? He suffers anguish akin to torment as he considers whether to move the stone to the left rather than to the right, before at last he obeys Hios and goes right, and the floor beneath him remains firm.

But the caliph had many more encounters that night, with men and with women, and Gato has many more decisions to make and junctions to negotiate. After every move he waits for the floor to open up beneath him, plunging him down into the subterranean river; he feels something akin to disappointment when this does not happen, as he will have to persist in this unbearable anxiety. The thirtieth move has been made and still Gato stands on the polished parquet, but this is no comfort to him. He knows very well how cunning Taal can be, and becomes ever more certain that Hios and Taal are in league, that he has been told thirty-five right moves but that the thirty-sixth will open the trap-door to the chasm when he feels victory to be in his grasp.

When the moment arrives for him to make that last move, when the caliph has returned to his chamber and the clear Baghdad sky is bright with stars, Gato pauses with the stone in his hand. What if the figure in the semi-transparent veil waiting in the caliph's bed is not the lovely daughter of the vizier? What if the story Hios has kept from him has the caliph pull back the bed-drapes to find a thief, who has broken into the palace that night and is waiting for the caliph with a sharp dagger in his hand? Gato stands there for a long time with the stone in his hand, deliberating whether to go left or right. But in the end he goes left, as Hios told him to, and closes his eyes. There is a creaking sound. Gato attempts to hold on to the relief work of the door, although he knows full well that this will do nothing to save him from the long fall. His hands slip on the smooth, rounded surfaces. His eyes closed, he falls. He feels the chill of the cave and he hears the chattering of the subterranean river.

## 42
## Fo's palace

Dear reader, this division between chapters is not taken from the island's *Book*. The book was not divided into chapters, nor even into paragraphs; the only means of division in the *Book* was given by the pockets, which sorted passages of text into different levels. But even these borders were constantly violated, so that which was separate was forever being drawn back into the fantastically tangled knot. I paused at the point of Gato's long fall into the unknown so as to increase the tension. Let us set him free, and see that he is not falling into the abyss but into the space beyond the door. The creaking is not being made by the mechanism of the trap-door: it is the sound of the door opening. The chill Gato feels has been released by the treasury and the chattering comes from the astounded courtiers. In his anxiety Gato has done Hios an injustice. Taal and Uddo have no idea that their daughter and the stranger have become lovers. Hios did not betray him; for the whole time Gato was negotiating the labyrinth, she was standing there among the courtiers with bated breath, praying that Gato would not make a mistake.

By the light of a dim lamp, the gemstones, pearls and gold jewels of the treasury glitter. Gato quickly discovers on the top shelf the little box with the basilisk on its lid. He turns back from the treasury and his gaze seeks and finds the smiling face of Hios in the astonished crowd. Taal and Uddo are standing at a distance from the rest; Gato can see that Uddo's mouth, its lips moving rapidly, is close to Taal's ear. Having recognized the gemstone in the stranger's hand, Uddo knows now who he is and also who told him how to get into the treasury. And on the spot she thinks up one of her dark plans, details of which she is whispering now to Taal. By the time Gato reaches the royal couple, Uddo's lips have stopped fidgeting, moved away from Taal's ear, and are set in an expression of satisfaction. A smiling Taal offers Gato his congratulations and commends his skill. Giving Gato a friendly pat on the shoulder, Taal tells him to be less modest and to help himself to more of the precious objects. Gato announces that next day he will be leaving the palace and the island, news which Taal greets with a nod of the head before moving closer to Gato and whispering to him: "Before you leave there's something I must show you. My chamberlain will visit you in your chamber this afternoon and bring you to me."

After luncheon the chamberlain does indeed come to Gato, and Gato follows him in silence. Rather than turning as usual at the end of the corridor, the chamberlain takes out a bunch of great keys and unlocks one of the doors that hitherto has always been locked. For the first time, Gato steps into the palace of the dead prince Fo. They pass down a long, straight, well-lit corridor, the silence broken only by the jingling of the keys at the chamberlain's waist. The wind enters by the broken high windows to lift the white curtains, whose fabric squirms before Gato's eyes like a dreamlike script and brushes dust and a scent of decay across his face. In alcoves on the other side of the corridor there are statues of white marble; these depict heroes wrestling with Gorgons, the dances of demons, women being transformed into bushes and wild beasts. Most of these statues are unfinished, and some of the plinths bear nothing more than a chunk of marble out of which there emerges a human face or hands, the wings of a great bird, a sharp beak, the talons of a beast of prey, the scaly tail of a monster. At the end of the corridor there is a glass door; when the curtains before this are parted by the wind, Gato sees that it leads to a small balcony. Here Taal is resting his weight on the stone wall, looking down at a closed courtyard.

The welcome he offers Gato is exaggerated in its heartiness; the prince dreads what will come next.

"I haven't yet shown you the most beautiful work of art in the palace," says Taal. "It would be a shame for you to leave without having seen it."

Gato steps up to the wall and looks down into the courtyard on the strangest group of statuary he has seen in his life. Its setting is the seashore, over which there looms the head of a giant squid whose eight terrible arms and two terrible tentacles are attacking a group of people sitting on the shore around a long table. Those unfortunates who are already in the squid's terrible grip are struggling in vain to free themselves; the other figures are thrusting swords and knives into the body of this monster of the deep. There are plates on the table bearing the remains of a meal; Gato notices that the food on one of these has been shaped into some kind of figurine which is a modified, small-scale depiction of the scene of the struggle with the squid. But more than by the statue itself, Gato is astonished by the material of which it is made. To begin with he takes this for dark-green coloured glass, but then there is a gust of wind and the whole edifice quakes gently. When the wind is stronger the figures themselves stir. Gato is astonished to realize the work is made of some kind of jelly or aspic. The greenish jelly is transparent enough for Gato to see small, long, black shadows moving about within it.

"A marvellous statue, isn't it?" says Taal from behind him. "I don't show it to those philistines at court because they wouldn't be able to appreciate it, but I was sure that you—as an artist—would grasp the depth and beauty of the work. You may study it for as long as you wish—I shall be happy to wait here with you."

"You do me a great kindness, Your Majesty. The statue is indeed sublime, and I am most grateful to you for showing it to me." Gato's words are spoken in honesty. "But I wouldn't wish to keep you, so I shall leave you now to prepare for my journey."

"There's no need to be shy. I am sure you would like to look at the statue more closely. While you do so, perhaps you would allow me one last look at the gemstone from the treasury; I am sure you have it about you. I received that stone as a gift from my wife many years ago, and I have to admit that I am sorry to see it go. I trust that you do not suspect me of wishing to take it back from you?"

And Gato is forced to assure Taal that such a suspicion could not be further from his mind, and then to give him the stone. Taal turns it from side to side, holds it up against the light, and then—and he barely bothers to conceal the fact that the act is deliberate—the stone slips from Taal's hand and off the balcony. Gato cries out; he can do nothing but watch as the stone sinks into the soft statue, into the head of the giant squid, before the jelly closes over it. Taal proceeds to apologize to Gato for his clumsiness, but assures him there is no need for concern—Gato can retrieve the gemstone from the statue whenever he chooses, it is a simple matter to walk through the jelly; should the statue incur slight damage as a result, Gato need not fear Taal's wrath, his servants will restore the statue to its original state.

In that case, says Gato, he will retrieve the gemstone straight away; and he runs down the staircase into the courtyard. When he reaches the shuddering statue, he stops short. Then he plunges his hand into one of the figures, and indeed it does enter the soft, cool jelly with ease. He is about to step into the statue when he becomes aware that dark shadows are flocking from the depths to his hand. This upsets him, and he remains standing before the statue with one hand inside it. Then there is a sharp pain in his finger, which causes him to cry out and withdraw the hand. At the tip of the finger a small body is hanging; he pulls this off and throws it down on the granite paving slabs, but its teeth have retained a piece of his flesh. The fish flaps about angrily, making a sound that reverberates around the great empty courtyard. Gato looks in disgust at its round, spiteful eyes and pumping mouth full of sharp, brilliant-white teeth. Having succeeded in thrashing its way back to the statue and slipping itself inside, the fish sticks its head back out and grins at Gato before disappearing for good.

"Don't worry," calls Taal from above. "Give it a try some other time." He is leaning over the balcony, unable to conceal in his voice the tones of derision and triumph. "Regrettably, I can wait no longer than three days." With this, Taal's head vanishes behind the stone balustrade.

Gato decides not to try to enter the statue again that day: he will think things through carefully and seek the advice of Hios. When that night he tells her of the gemstone and the statue, Hios is horrified. He was enormously lucky, she said: the fish that live in the jelly are ferocious. They feed on birds that happen to fly low over the statue, which they watch from just beneath the surface and then ambush by pitching themselves out of the jelly and snatching the birds in their teeth by the wings. Hios describes how once, in a fit of anger, her mother threw a cat from the balcony; all that was left of it a few moments later was its white bones. There is only one means by which one can enter the statue. Once a year the servants do so in order to clear out the bones of birds, dead fish and any other rubbish that has fallen into it. So that the fish keep away from them, the servants smear the napes of their necks, their wrists and ankles in a grease made from a certain species of wild duck whose scent the fish cannot stand. (Next to the word *duck* there was a pocket containing a detailed exposition of the way this duck lived, the land in which it was found, and the history and religion practised in this land.) Hios promises Gato that the next night she will find a pretext on which to visit the servants' wing so that she can bring him a jar of the duck grease.

## 43
## The birth of a world

Above the sentence in which the unknown author first mentioned the group of statuary, there was a thick pocket. This I did not open immediately because I was curious to discover how the scene in the courtyard would play itself out, but once I had read the page on which the author describes the conversation between Gato and Hios about fish and duck grease, I went back to it. As I was expecting, the text on the strip of paper I pulled out gave a description of the origins of the statue. This sculpture in jelly is created four years before the death of Prince Fo, the son of Taal and Uddo. That year Fo is to turn to twenty, and Taal decides to have a magnificent new wing built on to the palace in honour of his birthday. He summons to Devel the best architects, painters and sculptors in the archipelago.

The shell of the new wing is complete when Taal sails off to the island kingdom of Kass for a meeting about a protracted dispute over territory, which has again flared up in the form of skirmishes in ports and short exchanges of fire between ships in the straits that separate the two islands. At the castle of Kass's ruling prince, Taal is enraptured by the magnificent statues placed along the walls of all corridors at regular intervals. The prince tells him that all the statues are the work of one person, Kass's court sculptor. On hearing this information, Taal promises without hesitation to withdraw his military forces from all the disputed islets in the straits the very next day and to guarantee the safe passage of Kassian ships, on condition that the prince lends him the services of his court sculptor for two years. The prince is happy to consent to this, though he tells Taal that he is perhaps in for a surprise.

Two weeks later a ship arrives at the port on Devel. Taal is surprised indeed: once the labourers have carried out all the cases of tools and piled these up on the jetty, a lightly-built young woman steps ashore. Her name is Mii, and it was she who carved the statues of the Kassian court. The commission to decorate Fo's palace has aroused in her a great enthusiasm. Mii is not capable of making one statue only; whenever she is working on a statue she feels the need to create a whole universe of which this statue is but a part. Mii's manner of working is as follows: first of all she walks around the palace or park in which her statues are to stand, listening to the sounds of individual spaces until she gains an understanding of their pulsation and energy, the ebbs and flows of the forces within them, and it is out of this that shapes begin to crystallize. It is as though the spaces tell her of their anxieties, dreams and myths, of their gods and demons, of the mysterious beasts that inhabit them, of the dramas they stage, of the hell that glows in their corners, of the paradise whose music sounds behind their walls, of the sea whose tide washes up to them, of the galleries of dreams that are anchored at their most distant point.

Mii always stipulates that she herself should choose the places where the statues are to stand. For many people, her choices are beyond comprehension. A statue might stand in a hall aglow with the radiant light of chandeliers or in the darkest, dustiest corner, on an ostentatious portal or in a concealed alcove that is difficult to find, in a room in which the statue controls the space imperiously or high on a facade where its features are impossible to make out, perhaps even in an attic where no one ever has cause to go or in a cellar where the light never penetrates. It has happened that a client of Mii's finds to his wonder, years after she completed the commission, a statue hidden in the dense brush by the park wall or beneath the murky surface of a pond.

As the figures take shape, so too do they acquire life stories: new worlds are born with their own histories, their own gods and mythologies, their own mores and laws. Mii knows the intricate mycelia of relations and events that are expressed in the gestures of the statues, surge into the points of daggers held over the breasts of enemies and the tips of fingers reaching out for conciliation; she knows the thousands of images and stories of the world of statues that have never achieved expression yet pulsate in stiff gestures of the body. But she has never felt the need to tell anyone about this world, nor herself to portray it in any way; it is enough for her that it radiates from the point of a dagger or the fingers of an outstretched hand.

Mii always works day and night, practically without a break. Whenever she finishes the creation of one of her worlds she feels immense fatigue; she sleeps for several days, and for weeks after this does not get up from her bed. In this time the universe she has created becomes dimmer and dimmer in her mind until it is gone. So clear is Mii's mind now that when she receives a new commission and is walking around a house unknown to her, she does so with an empty consciousness, listening to the new whispers of unknown spaces, which introduce her to the rhythms of a nascent world.

When Taal shows Mii the sketches that express his ideas about how the statues of the palace should look, the sculptress does not so much as look at them. She asks him to take her to Fo's wing, and for one whole month she does nothing but walk the empty corridors, halls and staircases. Out of the veins of the marble panelling and the rippling of the curtains, the gloom of the corridors and the brilliant light of the halls, there gradually arise the shapes of new gods, demons and heroes, the figures of humans, animals and monsters; the staircase transforms into cascades of water, giving life to nymphs and river deities; in the corridor an army of phantoms appears that mounts an expedition against the world of the humans. To begin with, Mii has blocks of marble set down in places she determines; then she gets to work on many statues simultaneously. Taal looks on with awe as she runs from the mouth of a statue by the wall of the balcony to the scales of a Triton in the fountain.

The pocket attached to this passage in the *Book* contained a detailed catalogue of all the statuary Mii created in Fo's palace. I would quite like to have read this, but it was so badly smudged as to be practically illegible. I imagined someone folding out his part of the text and then walking with it through a wall of water; or perhaps these pages had been caught by a higher wave down by the sea. It was with a sense of sorrow that I looked at the white pages and the smudges of ink that had run. It came to me that here was a place where the forms of the statues returned to the realms of the shapeless currents out of which once they had crystallized.

Fo goes to take a look at the birth of a new world, just as Hios will do four years later. To begin with, Mii is unconcerned by his presence: in any case she hardly ever notices creatures that do not belong in the world she is creating. So Fo watches the origination of unknown creatures that will share his palace with him. His admiration for Mii soon develops into love. But at this time Mii lives in the world inhabited by her statues; for her figures she knows an incestuous love, in which she is the mother. For Mii, Fo is an incomprehensible and ever less welcome apparition, coming from another world.

We do not know if Mii could have fallen in love with Fo had the prince waited to declare his feelings for her until she finished her work at the palace, until she began to forget the faces and fates of her lovers in a disappearing world and to return to the world of men. But like all others of his family, Fo is of an impatient, excitable nature. When he realizes that Mii is taking absolutely no notice of him, when he sees that the only answer she has to give to his declaration is silence and that the only feeling she shows in his presence is resentment that someone is disturbing her work, he quits the palace and wanders about the island, sleeping in caves, under trees in the woods or on the sandy shore.

## 44
## A cabin in the woods

The part of the *Book* that described the wanderings of the unhappy Prince Fo was extremely long, although it included hardly anything that had a particular bearing on the main story-line. The author gave a long-winded description of Fo's encounters with country-dwellers who fail to recognize the wayfaring stranger who speaks with them. I read details of the country Fo passes through. The *Book* acknowledged Fo's entering new districts with pockets in which the author wrote at length about the flora and fauna of the new territories or told a variety of boring or interesting tales from the locality. But the islanders made no distinction between the main story-line and its adjuncts; once when I was speaking with Karael about the unexpected digressions the islanders were always willing to give in to, she came out with something like an aphorism. "The main thing," she said, "is that which is incidental." (Another of her aphorisms was: "If you wish to encounter something that is exactly the same, go somewhere completely different.") For a long time I found these labyrinthine insertions and diversions quite intolerable, but as you now know, dear reader, in the course of time I learned to appreciate the charms of nonsensical encounters on minor routes and confused returns to a world my absence had made strange to me. In these encounters our most intimate and important life goals suddenly become diversions that lead us away from a path that is unknown, monstrous and endlessly alluring, a path that is spun from materials we have always known to be diversional but at whose end there shines the highest, most blissful Goal, the correction of everything that has ever bothered or distracted us.

One afternoon in the woods, Fo gets caught in the rain. He takes shelter under the branches of a tree and watches the bushes as they shiver in the torrents of water. Then he catches sight through the leaves of some kind of building. It is a small cabin, built perhaps by woodsmen for their own use; since the woodsmen abandoned it, it has no doubt been used as a night shelter by various vagabonds. The cabin has no proper windows or door, just openings cut into the walls. On its floor there is a palliasse, its rotting straw poking out at several places, and cinders in a grate. (The smoke leaves the cabin through a black-edged hole in the roof.) Having laid himself down on the palliasse, Fo watches the woods grow dark through the door and listens to the lovely song played by the rain on the leaves. Before long he falls asleep. At dawn he is woken by the cold. He goes off in search of brushwood so that he can get a fire going. As he is laying rain-drenched twigs in the grate, he notices in there between the sooty logs a piece of blackened paper—the fire-ravaged page of some book. He reads the only sentence that is still legible. (It is this: "For a long time the king studies and contemplates the radish.") He looks about the room for something to light the fire with. In the corner of the room there is a pile of paper, bearing on one side of each sheet records on the felling of trees. Fo crumples up several sheets, pushes them in among the twigs and lights the fire.

Then he pulls the palliasse closer to the fire, lies back down on it, looks through the door at the play of the mist above the roots of the trees, and listens to the crackling of the flames. He is expecting to see Mii in his mind's eye, and it is indeed so that her face and hands (working the stone) appear to him at once. But this time the images do not develop in accordance with the established ritual: they have got stuck; some kind of obstacle has forced itself between him and them. To his surprise and displeasure Fo realizes this obstacle is the sentence he read a while earlier on that piece of singed paper.

For the time being this aggressive sentence has blocked the transmission of the film of painful bliss he was so looking forward to; images of Mii have paled and buckled. Fo is furious that something as inconsequential as a couple of banal words about a vegetable can come between him and his grand passion, but still he is helpless to resist thoughts of the king and the radish. His mind churns out one question after another, and of these questions he cannot rid himself. What could possibly be the reason for a king's long contemplation of a radish? Of course, if it were a particularly fine example of its kind his eyes might be drawn to it, but why would he need to look at it for a long time? Did he not have enough on his plate with all the affairs of state? If it were a fine example of its kind, perhaps he was shown it at an agricultural fair he had cause to visit. But Fo finds this answer unsatisfactory: not even the most marvellous vegetable can be studied and contemplated for long, and it is inconceivable that a ruler would do so. He had a vague notion that the meaning of the radish was somehow bound up with the position of the king in society: there must be some connection between the radish and the fate of the state or the life and death of the king or someone close to him.

Fo takes a walk in the woods, where he picks some red berries. Thinking of turning back, he finds himself hoping he will be unable to find his way to the cabin where he was troubled by the radish in such an absurd manner. Just as he is beginning to think himself lost, and to feel relief at the prospect, the back wall of the cabin emerges from the bushes right in front of him. He returns to his new dwelling with a sigh and lies back down on the palliasse. He tells himself the words on the singed sheet of paper are so intrusive because they make no sense. If he thinks hard for an hour about the king-radish sentence, he is sure to hit upon some meaningful connection, and thus will he succeed in breaking its power and rid himself of it. Then once again he will dedicate himself to the blissful suffering of his lovesickness.

Sitting on the palliasse, he sets about a deconstruction of the situation described by the sentence. The king cannot afford to fritter away his time in the study of radishes: he must rule, and if at any given moment he happens not to be ruling, there are surely means of diversion available to him other than the contemplation of vegetables. No, implicit in the radish there must be something important, a message of the utmost significance. But if this were hidden inside the radish, the king would not find out what it was just by studying and contemplating it, regardless of how long he spent in doing so. Unless, of course, the message was on the very surface of the radish, in someone's handwriting or perhaps carved into it. But even this made little sense: if the message were in a script or a language the king understood, it would be unnecessary for him to study and contemplate it for a long time, and if it were in a script or language unknown to him, even the longest imaginable study of the text would be no help to him in deciphering it unless other things were done besides. On top of all this, why would anyone carve an important message (concerning, perhaps, the security of the kingdom or the life of the king) into the surface of a radish? It was practically impossible to imagine a situation where someone was required to write to the king on a radish rather than a piece of paper.

But perhaps the message is not carved into the radish; perhaps it is conveyed by the radish's colour or shape. What if the colour or shape of the radish were unnatural? Perhaps the radish is dyed or its shape somehow altered. Perhaps someone has cut pieces out of it. By this time the radish and the insistent questions it keeps putting have driven the image of Mii from Fo's mind completely. Perhaps, Fo tells himself, it is impossible to decipher the message by a complex search for its code; perhaps the relations by which it holds together are revealed at a single moment. Then it might make sense for the king to study the radish and try to discover these relations so as to set the radish in some kind of meaningful whole.

The outlines of the trees are beginning to fade in the gloom; the cut-out seen through the door opening looks like a dingy tapestry hanging on a wall. Fo realizes that the fire went out long ago, that he has spent the whole day thinking about the radish and the king. Although there is no reason for him to hurry and time has no value to him, still he is annoyed to have devoted a whole day to an activity so trivial. He determines to quit the accursed cabin first thing in the morning and continue on his travels: pastures new would be bound to dispel the irksome radish and the peculiar king from his thoughts. And as soon as he reduces the intensity of his concentration, the construct of logic on which he has worked the whole day but which has yet to form any recognizable shape, is pushed silently aside by a vision that has long been forming itself beneath all his questions and answers.

In his mind's eye Fo sees a king whose long study of a radish has—the king believes—enabled him to grasp the message it has for him. (But has he understood it right? Fo sees in his interpretation a fatal mistake, which will change the history of the kingdom.) For Fo the image of a king contemplating a radish has entered the network of relations; it is as if he was holding a solitary piece of a jiggle puzzle when the rest of the puzzle came into view, complete with an opening that matched the exact contours of the first piece; as if the shapes and colours of a landscape have emerged through a quick-dispersing fog, complete with places and characters. He can see the sea and gleaming rocks, a blazing sun, a palace above the sea, a king dressed in white who is hand in hand with a girl; he sees the cold marble corridors of the palace, boats afloat on clandestine missions, betrayal, intrigue, meetings of conspirators behind closed blinds;

he hears sinister whispers behind curtains; he smells rooms in the early morning and evening, the salt wind off the sea, rocks baking in the sun. While a few moments earlier the king and the radish were surrounded by emptiness and had no place in any story, now the image of a king contemplating a radish is flooded with hundreds of other images, and this inundation straight away forms itself into an inviolable web that constitutes a self-contained world.

And it is impossible to stop this great birth of people, objects and landscapes; all Fo can do is look on in astonishment. The thought flashes into his mind that once he knew someone who told him of the genesis of a world like this, that then he barely understood a word of what the other was talking about. But now there is no room in his mind for reminiscences: it is fully engaged with this great birth, which is now painful and blundering, now easy and smooth. Throughout it beats out its shape with incredible power, a power impossible to resist and which sweeps all other thoughts and memories aside.

Even the thought that this new world has no meaning, purpose or idea, that it has no knowledge to convey and is entirely unnecessary, cannot hinder its rampant growth. It is neither a symbol nor an archetype, neither more interesting nor more boring than other worlds. To Fo its very senselessness is a source of delight the like of which he has never known before. All night long he lies on the palliasse and follows the genesis of this world. There are times when he must prepare the way for the images it brings, others when all he needs to do is watch them arrive without his assistance. As day begins to break, he takes one of the sheets from the pile of paper, and on its blank side he begins to write his dispatch from this new world.

## 45
## Conspirators on Vauz

The *Book* made no mention of whether Fo has a pencil with him or whether he finds this, too, in the cabin. But there is plenty of paper in the cabin on which Fo can write everything down in careful detail. And I have no doubt that this is indeed what he does, with a pedantry common to all the imaginary authors who tell their stories and stories within stories on all levels of the *Book*, with their endless descriptions of the patterns on the dresses of princesses and the ornamentation of the walls of palaces. At this point in the text there was a pocket that contained Fo's writings from the cabin; this pocket was so full that when I unstuck it, it burst open like an overripe pod and the paper folded within it tumbled out, compressed concertinas falling to the ground, there continuing to unfurl. I was reminded of the festoons of a fancy-dress ball.

I could pick out individual words written on all this paper—words telling of monsters of the deep and of palaces on planets in distant galaxies, words that tempted me to delve into this insertion. But I decided not to let myself be detained by a never-ending novel about a radish; I would not let the wily *Book* draw me into the wretched labyrinth of insertions. I would read the insertion that told of the origins of the statue in jelly, I told myself, and then I would make an orderly return to the story of Gato, Hios and poor, hard Nau: I wished to find out at last whether Gato succeeds in getting the gemstone out of the statue and whether his mother is restored to health. So I proceeded to stuff the fallen paper back into its pocket. But when its billowing end was about to reach the table-top, I realized my resolve was no match for my curiosity; the accursed radish had befuddled me, just as it does Fo.

I was worried that after my return from the island the radish would appear to me on wakeful nights, and when at last I fell asleep it would turn itself into a monster and pursue me around a never-ending labyrinth. I would forever be in its power just because I had failed to read about what happened between it and the king. To return to the island in an attempt to make this good would be to no avail—in the ever-changing *Book*, the story of the radish and the king would be long gone. With a heavy sigh I pulled the long strip of paper back out of the insertion and set to reading Fo's work. I shall do what I can to rebuild my memories of what I read in it; I would ask for your forbearance, dear reader, as I embark on this journey into the bowels of the *Book*.

Consider yourself the experienced leader of a speleological expedition. I am well aware of the great demands that this descent to the lower levels of the text places on you (I wouldn't wish to worry you, but I suppose you know that this will be followed by an ascent less pleasant still). I appreciate the need to make this as easy as I can for you; perhaps each level of the *Book* could be printed in a different colour to make orientation simpler. But then again, this might be too expensive. Better still (and even less realizable) would be to distinguish the different levels by the same method the islanders use to tell time: the text could be printed on paper saturated with a different scent at each level. (A difficult task for printing the work, but it need not be difficult for you; those readers made dizzy by the use of different colours for different levels may find it relatively simple to produce a scented book.)

On the very edge of the archipelago on the island of Vauz, there lives a king called Dru. Dru is a celebrated patron of the arts and sciences, and in his youth he, too, was a scientist—he is the author of a number of books on mathematics and astronomy. These are the first sentences Fo writes in the cabin. Festering wounds left by real and imagined slights overlaid with etiquette, age-old feuds between families that are incurable because their roots are long forgotten, the tangles of minor grudges and the bitterness that is always abroad in the fine dust of the atmosphere of a hierarchical society—when all these things ripen into treason, a conspiracy against the king is conceived in the royal court. The conspirators desire the king's death, but to kill the king is no simple matter for he is attended at all times by a well-armed, dependable entourage; nor is it possible to use poison against him, as one of his retainers always tastes his meals before him. Only certain members of the military command are involved in the plot, and the conspirators know that it is possible to move against those divisions loyal to the king only in the confusion that would follow the king's death. The admiral of the royal fleet devises a plan that the other plotters at first consider eccentric and fantastical, but in the end they are forced to admit that it is probably the only way in which they can kill the king. The plan is founded on the knowledge that the king has a weak heart. His physicians have warned him that a great shock of any kind could bring about his immediate death. The admiral has spent his life sailing the seas, and he knows where to find a deep underwater valley that is the resting place of giant squids; he knows that the scent of a certain plant will draw this animal out of its lair and can be used to make it follow a ship; he knows, too, that the squid springs up out of the water when it hears a certain sound.

With his young fiancée Isili, his friends, members of his household and a group of musicians, King Dru likes to dine on a little platform carved into the face of the sheer, smooth rock at whose top stands the royal palace. The platform is only half a meter above the sea, and it is reached from the palace by a zig-zagging flight of steps that is also carved into the rock. The sheer wall of rock continues beneath the surface; the water here is so deep that no diver has ever succeeded in reaching the seabed. It is to the deep waters near the little platform that the admiral wishes to lure one of the squids. While the king is sitting at dinner, one of the musicians will sound a horn with a peculiarly deep tone; as soon as the squid hears this, nothing will be able to stop it from plunging itself above the surface. The admiral and his fellow conspirators are hoping that the sudden appearance of the giant, monstrous head with its mad eyes, will be enough to give the king a heart attack and to bring about his death. Another advantage of this plan is the unlikelihood that anyone will make the connection between the sounding of the horn and appearance of the squid, meaning that the conspirators will not come under suspicion should the plan fail and the king remain alive.

To begin with everything goes according to plan: the giant squid follows the boat, from whose helm a sack of fragrant herbs is hanging. From time to time the admiral, who is standing on deck, catches sight of the creature's great round eyes deep in the water. The boat drops anchor by the royal palace and the squid remains nearby, many meters beneath the surface. On the day of the attempt on his life, as usual the king meets his fiancée, his friends, his household and the musicians, plus his two large dogs, on the terrace at the foot of the stone staircase above the sea. The company sits at the table in its usual places, everyone on one side of the table so that all can watch the play of colours on the sea at sunset. From the palace kitchens a basket with the first course has just been lowered down the rock face and onto the terrace. The dogs are resting contentedly under the table. The soft light, with just a hint of red in it, is lying across the bowls of fruit. There is a light breeze coming off the water.

## 46
## Assassination attempt

None of the plotters is a member of the king's inner circle, hence none of them has access to his dining table. But the king's fussiness about the company he keeps works to the advantage of the admiral's plan, as it excludes all the plotters from the circle of suspects—although the sudden appearance of a squid may not raise suspicions of treason in any case. The musician who is given the horn has no idea what his playing will bring about. On that fateful evening the admiral is standing in the passage next to the kitchens with the marshal, another of the plotters. They are looking down on the party on the terrace, discussing in whispers the various scenarios that might play themselves out after the squid breaks out of the water. Suddenly they hear a noise behind them; it turns out that in a dark alcove there is a door to the pantry. The cook is in the pantry, and he has surely heard everything they have been saying to each other.

By killing the cook the conspirators would disrupt the smooth progression of the evening, and this would jeopardize their plan. They have to make do with escorting him back to the kitchens, where they keep him under surveillance to make sure he does not try to escape or put something into one of the dishes for the king's party that would alert them to the possibility of an assassination attempt. The cook racks his brains for a way of warning the king. To write a message on a piece of paper is out of the question: not only would the plotters notice this right away, but anyway there is no paper or pencil in the kitchens. The cook is famed for the figures he models out of marzipan; he puts these into scenes that depict various events in the life of the king and his fiancée. The king likes to guess what each scene is showing; many times he has rewarded the cook for these culinary works of art. It dawns on the cook that he might send the king a message about the danger by depicting in marzipan the awful event planned for him. But on that day there is not a scrap of marzipan in the kitchens or in the pantry. The cook is trying frantically to think of a substitute for the marzipan when his eyes light on a large radish that is lying on the table right in front of him. This is not the ideal material in which to make a miniature statue, but by its inconspicuous nature a radish might have the advantage of escaping the attention of the conspirators. Besides, radishes are a favourite with the king, so the ruler will know that the plate bearing the cook's creation is intended for him.

So the cook picks up the radish and begins to carve into it the scene so alive in his own soul. He carves a musician blowing a horn, the head of a squid emerging from the deep with its ten awful limbs; he carves figures—which include those of the king and his fiancée—jumping up from the table in horror, turning over their chairs. His work is quite a success, and fortunately the admiral and the marshal have paid no attention to his treatment of the radish. So the radish is conveyed down to the terrace along with several other dishes, and after it has been tried by the court taster it is placed before the king. For a long time the king studies and contemplates the radish. He looks at each of the tiny figures in turn and tries to work out what the whole scene is supposed to mean. Unfortunately this deciphering is made more difficult by the fact that the taster has bitten off two of the tentacles that made it possible to identify the monster as a squid. These tentacles are longer and thinner than the other eight and at their tips become oval-shaped bowls covered with suckers. "What scene has the cook thought up for us today?" says Dru, turning the radish—which is redder still in the light of the sun approaching the horizon—over and over in his hands. In the end he sends a servant to the kitchens to ask what the radish statue is supposed to mean, but as the man reaches the first bend in the staircase, Dru calls him back: he thinks he has grasped the sense of the cook's work.

Dru recalls that one of the poems he wrote for his fiancée, in which he delighted in the use of various astronomical metaphors, contained the line, "Your song brings from the heavens dream-like stars and restless comets." Surely the cook wishes to please the king and his fiancée by giving shape to this image in a radish. "Just look at this!" the king says to his delighted fellow diners. "The cook has made a horn-player to accompany Isili's song. And here are the charmed listeners. And here—" (he indicates the head of the squid) "—is the comet, lured from the heavens by the song and now plunging itself into the waves." In mistaking the ten tentacles for the tail of a comet, the king is making a fatal mistake. Although the cook has given the squid enormous round eyes, the king considers this an instance of anthropomorphism, a finishing touch that develops the metaphor; if the comet can hear the song, it must have ears, so there is no reason why it shouldn't have eyes, too. And everyone at the table sees the radish as a comet that has flown down to listen to the song of Princess Isili; they are surprised they didn't see this straight away because it really is quite obvious. They applaud the cook's craftsmanship and his devotion to the king. Isili nestles her body against the king's, and as the red sun is about to reach the shimmering red line of the horizon, the king signals to the musicians to commence their playing. The musicians reach for their instruments; the horn-player puts his horn to his lips.

The deep, sad tone of the horn sounds. Then, terrifying in its quietness, ghostlike in its slowness, the head of a giant monster with great round eyes emerges from the water right in front of the diners, blocking the red sun from view. With the pink sky as a backdrop, the tentacles ripple. Though it seems there are hundreds of these tentacles, in fact there are only ten. After a moment of silent stupefaction, cries ring out as the men begin to chop at the serpent arms with their swords. The dogs jump on to the table and tear into the ends of tentacles flapping among the bowls of food. One of the two thin feelers shoots out like a lasso and, lightning fast, wraps itself around Isili's slender body. Dru grabs a bread knife and drives it several times into the deadly liana that is closing around his fiancée, but the tentacle coils itself up and bears Isili away. Then the other tentacles are withdrawn sharply from the table; they give a last slow ripple before dropping beneath the sea's darkening surface. The last part of the squid to remain above water is the enormous eyes, which for a moment or two observe the dinner guests, who have lapsed back into a state of silent petrifaction. Then the red sun touches its reflection and merges with it.

At the sound of the cries, the admiral and the marshal rush to the window. The cook makes use of this development to slip out of the kitchens and down the stone steps to the king's aid. But by the time he has reached the twentieth step, the struggle with the monster is over. As the tentacles of the squid were uncoiling themselves over his head, the king realized that his interpretation of the radish statue was wrong. He is condemned to believe ever after that he is the cause of Isili's death. The cook is rewarded richly for his loyalty and all the conspirators are imprisoned. Then the king hands over his kingdom to his younger brother and sails off to Europe. There he travels through land after land, along highways and across plains; he sits about in empty inns in the country; he walks about the biggest cities, whose streets merge in his dreams and memories into one endless city-labyrinth; he sleeps in cold hotels and inhospitable boarding houses. In the writing of his book, Fo forgets completely about his own past, but it returns to him in pictures that come to him through the dark. The description of the European wanderings of ex-king Dru are surely a result of the despair and disquiet of his own past, even if he remembers these no longer. The only despair he knows now is stirred by the multifarious images that elude his inner eye; the only disquiet that pursues him results from the frantic rush of sentences that propel themselves into the vortex of blurred images waiting for words to describe them while retreating from these very words.

## 47
## Eyepiece of a telescope

It is a day in November, and Dru has been walking the paths and tracks of a forest for many hours. He is now so deep within it that he cannot find his way out. Night is falling and Dru is beginning to think he will have to sleep beneath the trees. But when he reaches the top of a low rise, he sees between the dark trunks before him a cluster of twinkling lights. He tumbles towards these through crackling drifts of leaves and soon finds himself on the edge of the villa quarter of a large town. As he goes along the streets and past dark gardens replete with the smell of decomposing grass, he meets no one. He looks into the lit windows of the villas. In one of these he sees a woman who is carefully moving a dust-cloth over the surface of a gleaming instrument. This is an astronomer's telescope, the most complex telescope of all; Dru recognizes it from the times he was interested in astronomy. He looks up to see that the silhouette of the villa ends in a cupola, and that the barrel of the telescope is protruding from this at an angle. He recalls his erstwhile passion for the stars. After a few moments of hesitation, Dru rings the doorbell of the house. The door is opened by the woman he saw through the window. She is about fifty years old, and Dru imagines it is a long time since she spoke to anyone other than the man who keeps the shop on the corner of the street, whose illuminated window he has just passed. It seems to him that the long period of silence has forced the features of her face into a tight knot that lets nothing of her inside out. He asks the woman if she will permit him to look at the telescope. To begin with she refuses, but once he offers her money, she opens the door to him.

The telescope is in the middle of a room whose walls are lined with shelves bearing carefully arranged treatises on astronomy. The instrument's optical centre is swathed in metal casing, but by its size it is obvious that it contains an immensely complex system of lenses and mirrors. Dru runs his hand along the instrument's cool surface, as if he were a stroking a great motionless beast. Then he sits down in a chair and looks into the eyepiece. He sees a broad boulevard in a large city, where the palaces are built in a metal unknown to him. Walking in the streets are beings similar to humans, but with faces a gleaming gold. On the road surface there is an ultramarine dust; along it glide golden sleighs, their noses slim and curved like Viking ships. Dru is confused. Is he really looking at a city on a distant planet, or is this some kind of trick by which these moving pictures are generated somewhere in the depths of the instrument?

There is not much to be found out from the woman. She is the widow of the astronomer, who in his youth received many accolades from the world of science but whose irascible and obviously eccentric nature caused him to break with all his colleagues one after another, to conceive a hatred for other scientists, and close himself up in a private observatory he built for himself. He then dedicated all his energies to watching the stars and perfecting his instruments. He had nothing to do with other astronomers, he didn't publish any papers or books, and he never spoke to his wife about his work. One morning she found his motionless body lying on the floor next to the telescope. After this she lived in the villa alone and cleaned her husband's workroom every day just as she had when he was alive. Still she dusts his telescope every day. It has never crossed her mind to look into the eyepiece.

Dru offers the woman all the money that remains to him and they agree he will rent one of the rooms in the villa, with access to the telescope whenever he wishes. The woman is at first reluctant to go along with this, but her money is running out and she knows her only other choice is to sell the villa along with the telescope. So Dru moves into the villa and spends whole nights looking into the eyepiece of the telescope, set by its creator so as to watch the journeys of the planets across the sky. He cannot rid himself of the suspicion that he may not in fact be observing life on a planet that orbits a great purple sun in a distant galaxy but rather a projection produced somewhere inside the instrument; perhaps he is the victim of a practical joke the misanthropic stargazer prepared for one of his colleagues. One day he unscrews part of the instrument's casing, but once confronted with the magnificent glass labyrinth composed of so many visions and lights, he lacks the courage to take the work of the grumpy astronomer to pieces. But the more he immerses himself in life seen through the eyepiece, the less he thinks about whether or not it is real. (Although on days when the sky is shrouded in cloud and he lies morose on the ottoman in his room, the thought does flash through his mind that the world that is slowly becoming his home is just an illusion, the joke of a dead scientist.)

But that year is notable for its clear nights; only rarely is the sky overcast. Dru begins to live with the inhabitants of the distant planet. To begin with all he does is watch the activity in the streets and thoroughfares and buildings, the latter of which fortunately have large glass windows that make it easy to look into the dwellings of the extra-terrestrials. The telescope is so sophisticated that it can be focused on any place on the planet's visible side, its lenses set so that Dru can read without difficulty unknown gold characters on the red pages of the books the extra-terrestrials hold in their hands. Dru learns to lip-read the spoken word and to understand what it means from the context. After a time he has the impression he can hear conversations, along with the melody and timbre of voices. He looks through windows into classrooms and learns to read and write with small children; he looks over the shoulders of readers and reads along with them novels, epic poetry, and works of philosophy and history. He discovers that the planet's name is Umur and learns about the most dramatic moments in the histories of its states, about its religions and thought systems.

Three times a day his landlady puts a plate of food in front of him without saying a word; if he happens to be asleep, she puts the plate on his bedside table. They barely speak. Dru never tells her what he has seen in the telescope, just as her husband never told her, and it seems she has no interest in it. Dru watches the opening and closing of the great, fantastical flowers of creeping plants that grow around the houses; he watches tournaments in vast arenas, naval battles, azure geysers spurting from the floors of apartments and their transformation each night into clear ice that reflects the light of the moon and the stars.

He knows that it takes a ray of light thousands of years to reach Earth, that all the beings he watches are long dead, yet still it seems to him that he lives among the Umurians. Sometimes he replies to questions he reads from their lips—questions that were asked of someone else and spoken many thousands of years ago. He calls out in Umurian to the solitary night-time walker to take care, having seen slinking up behind him one of the panthers that live in the wild gardens of the rooftops and at night climb down the tangled creepers into the streets, although he knows full well that thousands of years have passed since the moment the panther bit into the foolhardy pedestrian's neck. The stargazer's widow is a frequent witness to Dru's shouted utterances in a language that bears no relation to Earth speech as he stares into the eyepiece. But never does she comment, never does she ask any questions. She remains silent when he turns his attention to her, perhaps with the intention of thanking her for a meal, when a strange language issues from his mouth and he struggles to recall the words of his own planet. Perhaps she lived through this with her husband; perhaps he, too, spoke in the same unknown language; perhaps she thinks that the instrument to which the two men have sacrificed so many nights is an invention of the devil, a bringer of madness and death; perhaps she thinks this is man's business, and that she has no right to interfere in it.

Dru sleeps during the day, and when he wakes in the afternoon he waits with impatience for night to fall. He sits in his room in a low chair, watching through the window the outlines of the bald branches of the garden; he contemplates the white walls of the room and their pictures of a glorious distant planet, which appears to be living through the later years of a golden age (there are obvious indications of imminent decline). Sometimes the face of Isili comes to him as in an obscure dream, or scenes from his life at the court of Vauz, or from the hotels and wayside inns of his days as a wanderer. By this time Dru's thoughts are in the language of the Umurians. The face of his landlady—the only human face he ever gets to see—appears to him monstrous, stirring his compassion. One day he catches sight of his own reflection in the hallway mirror and is horrified to see that he, too, has a ghostlike white mask instead of a face of gleaming gold. He covers the mirror with a piece of cloth, and his landlady is willing to leave it like this.

Having forgotten Isili, Dru falls in love with a girl from Umur. Nus has a face of dark gold set with diamonds. There he sits at the telescope, unkempt, unshaven and unwashed, whispering Umurian words of love to Nus, watching her travel about the city. When she falls in love with a young panther-hunter, he feels a dark despair; such is his torment as he looks into her bedroom and follows their night-time games of love, that he wishes he would die. Sometimes he has the impression that the lovers know about him and are laughing at him. Sometimes he thinks Nus might be looking—in provocation and derision—in the direction of the distant telescope and Earth, straight into the eyepiece of Dru the cosmic voyeur; when this happens he flies into a rage, cries out and kicks the telescope, curses Nus of Umur and threatens her with a dreadful revenge. But Nus, of course, has been dead for several thousand years.

## 48
## Fo's return

The plot of the novel written by Fo in the cabin in the woods is gradually shifted to the other planet. Dru, erstwhile king of Vauz, comes into the story less and less, until he features only in connection with the description of scenes from the telescope. Now events are described to which Dru's telescope does not have access, events which he is surely imagining. Also described are the feelings and thoughts of the extra-terrestrials, whom Dru learns to read better and better from their facial expressions, gestures and words. And so the extra-terrestrial passages, which to begin with were somewhat reminiscent of the *nouveau roman*, gradually assume the nature of a traditional, omniscient author. (But the right to get right into a particular space or the thoughts of a character, which the authors of the nineteenth century considered theirs for the taking, is in this case paid for by Dru's agonized solving of clues as his gaze wanders about the dumb surface of objects and faces, a surface that remains resolutely closed to him.)

And as visible worlds grow out of invisible worlds and carry their hidden spaces and secrets within, as what is close to the surface illumines depths, backs and interiors, the world in which Dru lives has from the very beginning its own depth, in which there are very few gaps. Because of this Dru is all the more exasperated when he comes up against a genuine blind spot. For example, the main square of the capital city is entered by a mighty river, screened from view at a certain point by the city hall; the river does not re-emerge on the far side of this building. Dru's gaze is well-trained in looking for clues of the hidden, and he studies carefully the reflections flickering across the smooth sides of sleighs that emerge from behind the city hall. But the sleighs move too quickly and the reflections on their warped surfaces are too misshapen to read. Once mirrored in a metal tray carried by a waiter in a restaurant at the back of the square, he sees something pulsating, which may be natural or may be mechanical; after this his gaze follows the waiters of this establishment for several nights, but never again do they hold their trays at the correct angle.

By this time only one sentence in every hundred pages reminds the reader of the eye resting against the eyepiece to observe a planet in a distant galaxy; now the people of Earth are figures from a strange planet. Then at last the eye disappears from the text entirely—in his cabin, Fo forgets all about it, and the novel becomes a saga of Umur. The gaze is free of the constraints imposed by the eyepiece and able to travel about Umur at will; all coverings are demolished, objects are no longer made up of fronts and backs, surfaces and insides. The gaze that sweeps the planet, sniffs into hollows and joyfully orbits objects like a dog, belongs to no one in particular; its drunken course leaves in its wake a continuous trail of words. A life form appears on the square behind the city hall that is half-plant, half-mountain, that drinks in the water of the river and transforms this water into translucent, coloured crystals that travel through steep caves into glowing underwater lakes. The pressure of gases in the lakes occasionally throws these crystals high above the Umurian city like magnificent fireworks. The gaze follows Nus into rooms in the most secret depths of her house, pushes through walls and curtains, walks about with her in a vast gold cellar Dru never knew existed.

The tale of Dru's wanderings and the description of how—once in his new world—he forgets about Isili entirely, is no doubt an echo of Fo's own fate. Mii's face has disappeared entirely from Fo's thoughts, but it returns unrecognized in the masks of his characters. The similarity between Fo's story and the story of his heroes is so great that the unknown author of this part of the *Book*—perhaps Fo himself in the cabin—several times confuses Mii with Isili and inserts the wrong name. ("If you wish to find something exactly the same, go somewhere completely different.") It might be expected that Fo's projecting his own trauma in his work would be a kind of therapy for him, allowing him to exorcize the demons of despair and restlessness. I was imagining that once his imagination had given his demons new bodies, he would find the courage to drive them from his thoughts; but in fact all that happens is that the demons gain new nourishment, which makes them stronger and more aggressive. They control the world of Fo's novel just as earlier they controlled the world of Fo's real life; they unify both these regions under their rule, and in this new empire they begin to flaunt the rituals of their power.

Fo is lying on his front on the palliasse, writing in ever smaller letters on sheets he lays on the floor. He is worried that the store of paper in the cabin will not suffice, and thus he will not be able to describe everything that is happening and has happened on Umur—its celebrated history, the grandeur of its court, the glory of its celebrations, the beauty and magnificence of its nature. When he has filled the last sheet in the cabin and placed it atop the pile next to the palliasse, he turns this pile over and begins to write on the other side of the pages, in the gaps between lines recording numbers of felled trees. The letters become so small that Fo himself is not able to read most of them, but it is enough for him to know that the pages are being filled. He has long been recording dialogue in the Umurian original, not bothering to translate it, and on top of this—in the manner of Lev Nikolayevich Tolstoy, who in *War and Peace* switched from the Cyrillic alphabet to the

Roman for the writing of dialogue in French—Fo does this in the hieratic script of Umur (composed of monstrous letters he has thought up in the cabin). In the end he is writing the rest of the text, too, in the hieratic script; whether or not it is in the Umurian language, no one will be able to determine. Thus on the floor of a small building in the woods are scattered many sheets of paper filled with small, illegible characters written between the lines of a forester's record-keeping.

It was not just Fo's book that was written in the script of Umur: the part of the *Book* that described Fo's work, which I read on the island, quoted from it in the original. I really believe the islanders read these pages, and that they even derived pleasure from doing so in spite of not knowing the meaning of Fo's characters and thus not being able to understand what they were reading. But unlike the islanders I was not so good a student that I could take pleasure from symbols without meaning. When I noticed that the last two thirds of Fo's work were written in Umurian characters only, I carefully folded the strip of paper back into itself, returned it to the pocket it belonged in, and went back to Fo's cabin. I still hadn't finished with the pocket whose contents described the origination of the statue in jelly, which itself—as no doubt you remember, dear reader—was to be found in the pocket that contained the seafarer's tale of a feud between two families in an archipelago, itself inserted into a description of twenty years' worth of this seafarer's travels.

Fo's fall into another world is perhaps the result and also the cause of a sickness that has taken hold of his mind and body owing to the hardships suffered on his solitary journeys and the harshness of his life in the cabin; these come immediately after the burn-out of his unrequited love, and are exacerbated by the draining tension and compulsive ecstasy created in him by his writing. When at last Fo is discovered by one of the units searching the island for him at

Taal's command, the crown prince, who has by now covered both sides of every sheet of paper he can find, is lying in the cabin trembling with fever; he has used the last of his strength to carve some strange letters into the floorboards. News of Fo's discovery reaches the palace before he does: the king, Uddo, Hios and the whole court are standing in the courtyard when the unit delivers him home. What they see is a delirious, emaciated figure being borne through the palace gates on a stretcher; the figure does not see them. Fo's parents and sister are a constant presence at his bedside, but Fo does not recognize them. They have Mii brought to him in the hope that the sight of the woman he loved will clear his mind, but Fo babbles to her something about how happy he is that she managed to escape the squid's tentacles, and he seems to be telling her how sorry he is about the dreadful illness that so changed her golden, diamond-spangled face. Then he whispers something in an unknown language and retreats into himself. By dawn of the third day his separation from the world is complete.

## 49
## Theatre in the forest

This episode in the *Book* is connected with something that happened to me a few years after my return from the island. On a hot day in mid-July I decided to take a trip; I took the bus to Mníšek, and from there I climbed through the sparse forest, along the brooks with their magical, drowse-inducing scents that reminded me of the scent that the fierce sun drew from the island's parched slopes. At a ridge in the path I looked down on a velvety valley with the glittering monogram of a river unfurling at its bottom edge. I walked down a path whose concentrated quiet occasionally spilled over into glades with rustling clusters of glowing leaves, as if it were unable to keep its dreams of light to itself, but the silence always returned.

I trust, dear reader, that by now you are so hardy in matters of digressions and insertions that you will have no trouble in relocating from a mythical archipelago to the Brdy hills of central Bohemia, where you will accompany me through the grass, breathe in with me the woodland scents, and pause with me awhile to take in the view of houses in the distance, dissolving downwards in the languid haze like cubes of sugar on the bottom of a cup. I am well aware that all the bold words you have heard from me about the value of insertions and digressions have failed to convince you; you are distrustful and stubborn, dear reader, and no doubt you are preparing to skip this insertion and its savage intervention between you and the tale of the origination of the statue in jelly. I expect you think I won't notice. I won't try to talk you out of anything, nor will I offer advice or prompting; who knows, this insertion may take you to the centre of an underground lake beneath Prague whose banks are lined with silver palaces, but then again perhaps all you will get to witness is a boring conversation in a pub in Řevnice or Dobřichovice between owners of country cottages. You probably won't miss anything important if you skip the next couple of chapters, but you could miss the encounter that holds the key to the entire text. The decision on which path in the labyrinth to take is yours and yours alone; whichever path you take, you do so at your own risk.

It was already getting dark when the woodland paths at last began to lead me to the upper edge of Řevnice. I came across a gate on which there hung a poster advertising a woodland theatre—a festival of amateur theatre companies from central Bohemia was being held at this very place. On the programme that day was a play called *In the Sea and on Dry Land.* (I didn't recognize the name of the author.) Through the wire fence I saw an illuminated stage beneath dark trees; the performance was in progress. For a while I watched out of curiosity. On the stage was an oblong table, at which there sat ten or so figures with their backs to the audience. There was a group of musicians standing to one side. When the musicians began to play, a construction made of wire covered with grey plush was hoisted up beyond the table; it was about two metres high, looked like a great rugby ball stood on its end, and into its front piece were sewn two large circles made of white cloth with two smaller circles of black cloth sewn onto them. Then ten stuffed plush pipes—their ends attached to thin wooden rods that were obviously controlled by actors hidden behind the stage—were lifted clumsily from the lower part of the construction. These pipes waggled about in the general direction of the figures at the table, who were crying out, assuming various attitudes of terror, and poking at the plush pipes with knives. It dawned on me that what I was watching was a dramatization of a scene from the island's *Book*.

I bought myself a ticket, sat down on a bench, and watched the king and his retinue struggle with the plush tentacles. I looked about myself; there were not many spectators. The long benches contained several groups of young people drinking beer—they might have been friends and relatives of the actors. In the Řevnice rendering of the scene, the giant squid kills the king and his fiancée and eats them. The naturalism in the depiction of Dru's and Isili's deaths was a strange contrast to the childish representation of the squid. The plush tentacles pulled Dru and Isili down into the sea. When they had gone from the stage, their terrible shrieks could still be heard as they were eaten alive; great geysers of red paint squirted high into the air. Then there was an interval. I bought myself a beer in a plastic cup and drank this slowly while I waited to see how the action would develop.

Although we had just witnessed the terrible death of the king and his fiancée, both these characters reappeared in the next act. The stage was set as a room in a modern-day apartment. Dru and Isili, who live in this room as tenants in straitened circumstances, are discussing the unspecified nightmares they have both been having. The room next to theirs is occupied by another tenant, a disagreeable bank clerk who looks like a bank clerk in a pre-war comedy film. The clerk is forever bothering Dru and Isili with his complaints (they haven't mopped the bathroom floor, they have the radio on too loud at night, etc.) In the course of one of his visits it turns out that he, too, has recurrent nightmares on a similar theme. All three tenants dream of an evening by the sea, of a struggle in which the points of daggers glow with a red fire, there are great undulating serpents, and the foam of the sea is mixed with blood. It soon became clear to the tipsy Řevnice audience that Dru and Isili were in the afterworld, living in a post-mortal city, that their past life was returning to them in these vague dreams; after a time, the characters, too, remember their pre-death existence. The author of the play mixed motifs from the island's *Book* with the work of Ladislav Klíma and Swedenborg.

But the role of the clerk in the events on Vauz remained unclear. The three characters try for some time to figure this out together; then their memories suddenly come into sharp focus: in life, the post-mortal bank clerk was the squid. The clerk goes into shock and bursts into tears. Dru and Isili throw themselves at him; they scold him and beat him while he whimpers and pleads for mercy. Dru and Isili take a cruel revenge on the erstwhile squid: they make him their servant and humiliate and bully him. The clerk who was once a squid takes the abuse and the slaps from both his tormentors with cowardly submissiveness, but all the time, unobtrusively but cleverly, he is plotting against them. He succeeds in turning Dru and Isili against each other to such a degree that they begin to hate each other. To humiliate Dru, Isili becomes the lover of the bank clerk who was once a squid, and together they decide to kill Dru. At night when Dru is sleeping, Isili unlocks the door of the room for the clerk to enter. The erstwhile squid holds Dru down while Isili drives a knife into his chest several times. In the course of this grim scene streams of red paint once again spurted onto the floor of the stage and the grass in front of it. A very strange play, I said myself, although I was well used to various guises of the bizarre from the island's *Book* and imagined myself unshockable by any kind of literary eccentricity.

Then Isili and the squid live together. Memories of his life in the ocean deep gradually come back to the bank clerk; he tells Isili about it every evening at dinner. They promise each other they will both try to return as squids in their next incarnation—massive, beautiful and strong they will swim through the depths together. They tell each other they will have to be on their guard against Dru—who is bound to want to avenge himself—but they hope that his violent death in the post-mortal world will have sent him to a distant underworld, from where it will take him a long time to make his way back to our universe.

The next act—a balletic interlude—was set in the sea. Green filters pushed in front of spotlights and long gauze drapes rippling in the Řevnice breeze were intended to create the illusion of an undersea world. Romantic music I didn't recognize was played over the speakers. Two figures in grey leotards ran onto the stage, one from each side; it was Isili and the bank clerk, who had become squids. Now the director was ignoring the literality of earlier scenes in favour of a more modernist approach. There were no plush probosces sewn onto the dancers' leotards; the twenty tentacles were represented by the movements of four arms waving about continually like those of Indian dancers, pulling the body onto the tips of the toes in their rise before falling in languid sinusoids to the boards of the Řevnice stage; stretching for alluring underwater depths and returning to their starting point, as if in the knowledge that the most beautiful place of this magnificent underwater life was precisely where one happened to be. The imaginary tentacles created in the arm movements of the dancers combined over and over in new figures of tenderness and passion. Apparently the ballet was meant to represent a life of freedom and joy in the depths of the ocean. The act ended with the peaceful death of the elderly squid Isili and the grief of her consort, who now wrung his tentacles and whirled around the corpse on the seabed in an expressive dance of despair (the weary undulating of the ballerina's arms represented the currents of the sea toying with the squid's remains), and moved his arms to indicate that he was embracing his dead mate with all his tentacles and that he would never overcome his sadness.

# 50
## Encounter above the Neckar

For the next act, which followed after another interval, there was again a change of scene. We found ourselves on the glassed-in terrace of a villa obviously built on an elevated spot on a hillside: through the glass wall one could see to the bottom of the hill, where a peaceful river ran through a quaint old town with narrow streets watched over by domed churches. The river was spanned by a magnificent towered bridge, and immediately beyond the last houses of the town there were hills covered in deep forest. Partway up one of the hills—like a weightless, two-dimensional picture—were the ruins of a great castle. (The town in the valley was in fact produced by a colour slide projected onto a screen.) This town, hemmed in by hills on all sides, was familiar; I realized the slide was a view of Heidelberg in Baden-Württemberg. So this had to be one of the villas on the hillside that rises sharply on the right-hand (north) bank of the Neckar.

There's the piercing sound of the house's doorbell. Emerging from inside the house, a white-haired old man comes on to the terrace and opens the door. Standing behind him is a young girl. She has just arrived in Heidelberg to study at the university; she has read about the availability of lodgings at the villa in the classified ads of a newspaper. So that's how the girl came to live in the villa above the Neckar. She and the kindly old man become friends. Every day they sit together on the terrace and the old man talks about his life, which in no way has been exciting—he spent his career as a clerk at Heidelberg City Hall. His children have not lived with him for many years, and when a few years ago his wife died, he decided to rent out rooms to students.

The girl is a student of German literature. One day she confides to the man that she is trying to write a fantasy story. Over breakfast she begins to describe its plot to him. (I doubt anyone in Řevnice was surprised to learn that the story was about a conspiracy among courtiers in an island kingdom—they had all suspected from the beginning that the student was a reincarnation of Isili. But the identity of the owner was not clear; I heard my fellow spectators betting on whether it was Dru or the squid.) The student believes that her imagination is creating images when they in fact arise from her memory. The old man is not surprised by the story's plot; when his tenant—wishing to show off her storytelling skills—asks him to guess the manner of the attempted assassination of the king, which the conspirators decide upon after lengthy deliberations, he answers while breaking into his boiled egg with his spoon. "I suppose they decided to kill the king by confronting him with a giant squid," he says. The astonished girl tries to find out how it is that he knows the plot of her story when she hasn't even committed it to paper yet or spoken to anyone else about it. All the old man says in reply is that he doesn't wish to speak of it at the moment, but that he will explain everything to her some time soon. When the Isili-student asks when this will be, he looks out of the window with a smile on his lips and says, "Perhaps . . . perhaps after the first fall of snow."

One morning the girl descends to the terrace from her room to find that the roofs of the houses in the town below and the trees of the hills have been coated with snow. (The picture has been changed in the slide projector.) The old man is standing on the terrace already, looking pensively at the white scene with its gentle touches of grey. The girl stands next to him and they study together the snowy landscape and the cable car rising slowly through the white pass in the forest on the hillside opposite. They have been standing in silence for quite a while when the old man begins to speak of the royal court on Vauz, of that last supper by the sea, of the shameful murder in the post-mortal city, of the burning deserts of the second underworld in which he ended up after Isili and the squid killed him. He is Dru. And as he is speaking, everything comes back to the Isili-student; she rests her head against the cold glass of the window lit by the snow of Heidelberg on the Neckar, as images from her memory rise up from the dark chasm within her.

Then she weeps quietly and asks Dru for his forgiveness.

"I forgave you when I was still in the desert of the second underworld. I knew you'd show up here. I've been waiting for you for years, since before you were even born. And trust me, it's not so I can take my revenge on you."

"How did you know I would come?"

"When I was living in the second underworld, I reached its outermost frontier. There I came across a great abandoned palace—perhaps it had been the palace of some god who had left for another cosmos. I walked its corridors and studied the frescoes depicting the past and the future of the universe that adorned them. It was in one of these that I saw the two of us sitting at breakfast on this terrace; it was clear from the picture that we were not meeting for the first time. Perhaps you have heard of Heidelberg Man?"

"Protanthropus heidelbergensis. An anthropoid. Its jaw was found in Mauer—not far from here—in 1907." The girl was quoting from a coursebook in anthropology.

"That jaw belonged to you. Way back when you and I lived together in the forests here. It wasn't a bad life—indeed, it was every bit as beautiful as your life in the ocean deep, which I also saw in the frescoes. I always expected to meet the squid in Heidelberg, too. I asked myself for ages who it might be; there was a time when I believed it to be Professor Gadamer from the university, but one evening when I was sitting in the Florian wineroom, its owner came in and I knew straight away that he was the one. And he recognized me as well; he joined me at my table and had a good bottle brought up from the cellar. We sat there drinking together until morning. He told me about your life together in the ocean; we made good our differences and became friends. These days we take walks together in the woods above the city. We've both been waiting for you here. You must go and see him—he'll be delighted to see you. Don't worry, in future lives we'll love each other again; we'll also persecute and hate each other, fight and kill each other on both sides of the frontier of death. But for the time being, we can spend a few years here in tranquillity. Hölderlin wrote—a long time ago, admittedly—that Heidelberg was the most beautiful of Germany's smaller cities. And just look at the peace that rests in its streets and the squares of the old town. The walls breathe with a silent joy, and it is a joy to walk its hills and sit in its university library studying from volumes whose pages are bathed in a calm light. Let us pass here our short golden age, an age we'll often look back on during the trials and in the despair of our lives to come."

The play at Řevnice had not finished yet, but by this time I was tired; at the end of the Heidelberg scenes I slipped out of the audience and went down to the station. As I sat under a glaring bulb in an empty carriage of the late train, I thought how strange it was that the Řevnice play had grafted motifs from the island's *Book* onto philosophies of reincarnation and pessimism, ideas very distant from the islanders' view of the world. I had written down the name of the company that produced the play, thinking I would get in touch with the actors at their Prague base and ask who the author was and where they discovered him, but then I dropped the idea. I was pretty sure what they would tell me: either the play was written by someone who had spent some time on the island, come across the *Book* there, and used some of its motifs in his work, or else some visitor to the island had told the natives about the play and then part of its story had been incorporated into the *Book*. The *Book* was open—it drew in stories from other books, plays or films and transformed them, and naturally it was willing to release its own story-lines and images for use in the literatures of other nations. Perhaps many motifs in works of literature of international renown have their origins in the *Book*; there is no way of knowing this for sure—the *Book* changes so quickly that whatever escapes from it to find lasting form on the pages of other books or theatre stages, transforms and then perishes in the *Book*.

## 51
## Taal's task

Fo was carried into the palace with his book. After Fo's death, Taal has his son's work published in many thousands of copies and instructs everyone on the island to buy it. In addition to this, the king has several copies produced on the finest handmade paper as facsimile publications; these are kept in leather cases set with red, green and violet gemstones. Fo's lettering is faithfully transcribed in all its transformations, and on the back of the sheets Fo's text is woven around the lines of the forester's records, just as it was in the cabin. The facsimile describes not only the story of the unfortunate Dru but also the story of Fo's script, which is beautiful in its early guises but becomes ever more distorted as the fever takes hold. The letters were infected by the diseases of Fo's thoughts, but perhaps the letters stirred the sickness in Fo by the piercing gaze they fixed upon him. The facsimile told of the fates of letters that became more and more akin to demons; these demons became lords of the text, shuddering, fraying and shrivelling until they were transformed into the monstrous letters of Umurian (woven somnambulistically around the clumsy letters of the woodsmen). Taal has Fo's original manuscript placed in a gold box that he has specially made for it, and this is placed in the treasury guarded by the deadly, impassable labyrinth.

The king's pain suddenly transforms into hatred for the woman he believes to be the cause of Fo's death. One day he summons Mii to the audience chamber. This vast darkened hall seems to Mii to be empty as she makes her way across it; only when she is almost at its end does she see a slight movement in the gloom. Taal speaks. Since the death of his son, Taal has avoided the light. Curtains are drawn across windows and shawls thrown over lamps. The weary voice that comes out of the nest of shadows tells Mii it wishes her to honour Fo's memory by the creation of a statue that depicts one of the scenes in his novel. This time the sculptress lacks the courage to refuse. She senses that Taal wishes to destroy her, that Taal would welcome her refusal as justification for her imprisonment or execution. There is a long silence during which nothing moves in the gloom. The audience appears to be at an end, so Mii curtseys and begins her retreat across the long, empty hall.

But she knows how cunning Taal can be and of his liking for the staging of dark, sinister acts, so the feeling of disquiet does not leave her. And before she reaches the door, Taal speaks again.

"There's something important I forgot to mention. I spent a long time considering which material you should work in." Mii has stopped and turned back. She knows she is about to learn what evil plan Taal has thought up. "I ruled out all varieties of stone and metal. I spent a lot of time considering rare woods, but all of them seemed too crude for a statue that should be an expression of the soul of my son. In the end I decided to have the statue made of water. You have three months in which to complete it. You may start work immediately."

"You wish me to make a statue out of water?" Mii's dismayed voice calls out into the dark towards where she believes Taal to be.

"Indeed. And of course I don't mean snow or ice. Nor will I allow the water to be in any container that gives the statue its shape. But I suppose the material needn't be water. Any liquid will do. I would quite like a statue made of aromatic oils, but I shall leave the choice to you. There's surely no need for me to tell you that failure to obey the royal command is punishable by death."

Mii knows this very well. She knows, too, that there is no point objecting that it is impossible to make a statue out of water or any other liquid, so she does not even attempt this. There she stands in the middle of the hall thinking desperately what she should do, but it seems to her she has no alternative but to wait in Taal's palace for three months for death to arrive. But then something comes to her from deep in her memory; it contains the germ of an idea (at first foggy, but becoming ever clearer) for how Taal might be outsmarted. Mii knows that she must somehow get Taal to modify the task without ever suspecting there is a trick involved. She must induce the king to make a small change to the commission that will appear to him as nothing more than a meaningless elaboration, and she must get him to do so before she quits the hall. She begins to speak before she has a clear idea of how to proceed; her plan comes into being as she describes it in words. She walks back through the hall towards Taal; her voice is weak because she is more used to whispering to marble statues than to conversing with people. To begin with she is practically shouting, but still the king must lean forward so that he can hear her, and in so doing his face emerges from the darkness. The closer Mii gets to the king, the quieter her voice becomes. The king falls back into his armchair and the darkness.

"Very well, Your Majesty, I'll try to make a statue out of some kind of liquid," she says as she walks. "But there is one thing I need to get straight before I start working. There are thicker liquids and runnier pastes, aren't there? What I mean to say is that it is not always clear where to draw the line between what is a liquid and what is a solid, and I wouldn't like to think we might argue this point once the statue is finished. I suggest we agree beforehand what we consider a liquid on the basis of a simple and clear criterion, such as . . ." (as she walks, Mii pretends to be pondering on this) ". . . such as whether fish are able to live in the material the statue is made of."

By now Mii is again standing before Taal's chair, hidden though it is by the dark. Her plan for how to escape death was completed when she spoke her last word and took her last step. Taal is mistrustful and he takes a while to consider her proposal, but he finds nothing in it that could make the statue any easier to produce and thus jeopardize his intentions; on the contrary, it seems to Taal that in her panic Mii has made the task still harder for herself. So he replies, "Very well, it is your task to create a statue from a material in which fish are able to live." He promises Mii that no one apart from her assistants will see the statue until it has been completed. Then he dismisses her.

As she stood before the king, Mii was remembering a marvellous lake that was hidden high in the hills of the small island on which she spent her childhood. After thousands of years of a gradual drying out, the water of this lake thickened into a kind of jelly. In the lake there lived predatory fish that darted out of the water to feed on birds that came too close to the surface. The fish would bite into the birds and pull them into the jelly, before stripping off all the flesh so that only the skeleton remained. Because it had taken such a long time for the water to thicken, the fish had had plenty of time to adapt to the changing conditions. Unlike the African lungfish (protopterus annectens)—which has created some kind of ersatz lungs for itself and will soon drown in water if it cannot get to the air above the surface—they did not convert to the breathing of atmospheric oxygen; the fish of the lake still breathed with their gills, which had adapted themselves entirely to the jelly and were very well able to exploit the small quantities of oxygen the jelly contained. It was difficult to decide whether the nimble movement of the fish in the jelly was swimming or burrowing. (The burrows disappeared immediately, of course, because the jelly closed as soon as the fish had passed through it—if you find this difficult to picture, try moving a spoon about in a blancmange.) Mii knows that the jelly is solid enough to make a statue out of, as the villagers living around the lake make quaking jelly statues for sale at the market in the capital.

# 52
# A tent in the courtyard

Mii immediately sends her assistants to the island for barrels of jelly and fish from the lake. Then she begins to read Fo's book. She is perhaps the only person in the kingdom who has not yet read it. Mii never reads books: the worlds in which she lives are so full of characters and stories that no more faces, bodies and stories could fit into them. But now she is in the company of dead Prince Fo, walking the corridors of the uncompleted palace, which is now slowly closing in on itself; the outlines of unfinished statues have befriended and merged with the spaces around them. Mii immerses herself in the vision born out of Fo's solitude, sickness and despair.

And Mii is enchanted by the book. As in a dull metallic mirror, she recognizes her own face in the joyous child's face of Isili and the noble gold, diamond-spangled face of Nus. In his many characters she gets to know Fo's features and gestures, which were nothing to her while he was alive but a blurry backdrop to her nascent statues. They are made manifest not only in Dru's wanderings and the process of his disengagement from the Earth, but also in the vigilant glances, whispers and light steps of the Vauz conspirators, and even in the elegant unfurling and recoiling of the squid's tentacles. She identifies the rhythms of Fo's blood in the undulation of the ocean's surface and the dumb rotation of the stars around the centre of a distant galaxy. And this polymorphous but homogeneous pulsation, which goes deep into the bodies of the sentences and itself exploits the movements of these dark bodies, makes Mii think of something she knows from her own experience—that behind every work of art there are two things intermingling, each referring to the other: the face of the author, the features of which are drawn from the universe at large, and the universe, which appears in the mirror of the face.

It seems to her that the characters, stories and landscapes create together a picture of Fo's mind, and that, had he never begun to write, Fo would never have encountered himself or the real world. Mii, who hears talk of separation from real life in connection with her own work all the time, knows very well that only at the bottom of our most personal myths, which we ourselves do not understand, only where these myths feed on juices flowing in the weave of real things and there recognize their cosmic names, do we encounter the true voice of the world. She wants to laugh when she reads of the wait for "a great societal statuary" after the installation of a new regime in Kass; she knows that the voice of the world speaks only through these nonsensical myths, that only its pictures, which take nothing from the world, are the hieroglyphs in which the world writes its secrets, just as it is only possible to write the word *table* using strange characters that bear little resemblance to the table itself.

Genuine reality is the birth of reality, and the birth of reality is an act that is spun out of myth and alive with spirits. We see the world in the convex mirror of a weird obsession that belongs not to us but to the monster that stalks the halls of our consciousness; all plane mirrors are blind. Fo was Dru and the squid, the admiral and the cook, Nus and Isili; he was the ocean the squid swam through, in which Isili's body was lost; he was the multiform landscape of Umur. Fo's character was composed by the gathering into itself of all these images, as they appeared to him over manifold, wonderful encounters. And Mii knows what sickness had consumed Fo: it was the horror and the delight evoked by his self-encounter and encounter with the world and all the figures, animals, deities, spectres, landscapes and stars that make of us what we are, and also delight and horror at the blurring of their shapes in the mute, monotonous pulsation of the great medusa of the cosmos.

Mii knows too that in his hatred Taal had made the right decision; Prince Fo was worthy of celebration in a marvellous, terrible statue made of a quivering, transparent material and full of predatory beasts. Had the king asked for a statue of marble, she would be asking him now if she could make it in jelly. Although she had tricked Taal into changing the task, she is convinced that a statue of jelly is more marvellous than a statue of water (assuming that it were possible to create such a statue), that the only material suitable for Fo's apotheosis is one that is not of the four elements, so that it almost might not exist while being present within all the elements as an anguished, delightful possibility—the possibility of death and a return to the beginning that elicits transformation. Within solid matter there lives a shapeless porridge that is a dream of cosmic decay; within liquids it is a slow melody of turbidity; within fire it is the aspect of the flame that does not tend to the purification of the shape but to its warping, by preparing it to receive moisture; within air it is the gradual transformation of gases and vapours into a dark sediment that coats the surfaces of objects, thus healing over the wound inflicted by the blade that cut these objects free of the world.

A pity, she thinks, that I could not transform the whole book of Fo into a forest of statues that would stand somewhere out on the plain; or I could have colonized a town with statues, set statues of jelly in its streets and lanes, in its thoroughfares and in its courtyards, on the staircases of its buildings, in its bedrooms and hallways, in its cathedrals and in its mysterious, stinking public conveniences. But Mii must choose one scene only, and it takes her a long time to decide. She pictures Dru wandering about Europe, an out-of-humour Dru lying in his bed in the stargazer's villa on a night when the sky is overcast; she considers depicting a scene of life on that other planet—one of the city's curve-nosed sleighs, perhaps, in which Dru's extraterrestrial lover would be sitting—or creating a group scene that would address the pages covered in the unreadable script of that other planet. She is for a long time given to thoughts of a statue that would illustrate some of the book's later pages, where Fo's writings coursed around the lines of the forester's records—this statue would show both of these worlds.

But in the end Mii opts to create a statuary group depicting the scene with the giant squid, and in which she will give Dru the face of Fo. She is more and more certain that the moment the king looks into the great eyes of the monster is the secret heart of Fo's work. She wants her statue to show a hero confronted with the greatest of all dangers, a terrible enemy that resides at the farthest point of his fear, in the last chamber of the labyrinth of his nightmares. She wants it to be apparent that the moment Dru first beheld the face of the awful beast, he saw himself in it: now he understood that what he most feared was also what he most desired—this vision of awfulness was also himself, and it was in this that he should perish. Mii wants the statue to express Dru's hatred and also his love of the monster and himself, just as he loves and hates Isili—for indeed it seems to Mii that Dru must hate his beloved fiancée for being an obstacle on his journey to the sea bottom, to his joining the monsters that reside there, his brothers and sisters, his sweet underwater lovers with their deep eyes and beautiful undulating tentacles. Mii understands that this ironical heart is not the sort one usually finds in books: it is not a concentration of the sense of Fo's work, nor does it reveal this sense. Rather, this encounter of the hero and the monster that smashed his world seems to subvert any possible orientation in one's reading and instil an uncertainty in the work that anticipates its meaning and thus is always able to escape it.

Within ten days a ship appears in the harbour at Devel; out of this Mii's assistants carry a great many heavy barrels, which they then convey up to the palace. At the place in the courtyard where the statue should stand, Mii has a great tent erected. The barrels from the ship disappear beneath its canvas. From this time on, Mii spends every day and every night in the tent. Apart from her assistants, who never speak a word, no one knows what is going on inside. Taal walks about the courtyard and around the tent, or he stands on the balcony looking down on the tent's roof. In the evening, lamps are lit inside, and they burn all night, casting strange shadows on the tent walls. In these Taal sometimes recognizes Mii's face, and, as the lamps travel from one point to another, the greenish shadow of an enormous Fo in profile creeps across the canvas before it dwindles away. By the light of the moving lamps it is impossible for Taal to tell which face in the mime of shadows belongs to a living person and which to a statue; he has the impression he can see his son's lips moving and his arms reaching out toward him. The activity in the tent hardly makes any sound—just a kind of quiet squelching and slapping. But occasionally a scream of pain penetrates to every corner of the silent palace and shakes awake all its occupants. That this is the cry of a careless, sleep-starved assistant who had been bitten by a fish, no one knows. At the time Gato was preparing to enter the statue, Hios would remember these night-time wails with great anxiety.

Taal is puzzled. At first he thinks that Mii is hiding in the tent in order to conceal from him for as long as possible the fact that she is incapable of accomplishing the task; but the moving, greenish shadows, the spooky squelching sounds and the night-time screams soon make him nervous. The king begins to entertain the belief that Mii is a sorcerer able to create statues out of water, that perhaps she has summoned demons to help her in her work; but then, at other times, he tells himself that the coloured shadows are part of a trick that by way of lights and green-tinted glass, Mii is hoping to create the impression that she is carrying out Taal's orders, while all the time she is simply waiting for the right moment to attempt an escape. Taal sends reinforcements to his guards at all the palace's gates, though there is nothing to suggest that Mii is really planning to leave the palace in secret.

On the penultimate day of the third month Mii announces that the statue will be unveiled the next evening. Shortly before sunset, Taal arrives in the courtyard alone, although he had earlier imagined inviting the whole court to witness Mii's defeat and humiliation, her tears and pleas for mercy, all of which he had been anticipating with relish. (Such a cruel theatre would be played out on the same spot four years later.) He is far from sure what will meet his eyes when the tent is removed. He keeps imagining himself seeing the granite paving of the courtyard and nothing more, Mii kneeling down before him and beseeching him to spare her life; but then, neither did he rule out the possibility that he would indeed see a statue made of water, which by some miracle had been fashioned into human form. Taal crosses the smooth granite of the empty courtyard, half of which is bathed in warm, reddish light. Then he steps into the shadow cast by the tent.

The sculptress and her assistants are already standing in front of the tent. When Taal stops a few paces from them, Mii gives the command for her assistants to pull away the canvas with a single tug on a rope. To his amazement, Taal finds himself looking at a statuary group atremble in the evening breeze—the terrible face of the squid with its enormous eyes, the tentacles slithering about the fragile body of Isili, and—reaching for his knife—Dru, who bears the face of Taal's dead son. The scene depicted by the statue was played out at this very hour; the sun sinks a little lower, and its red rays serve to illuminate the green matter of which the statue is made. In the glowing bodies of its figures, magical sparks and the black shadows of moving fish can be seen.

Mii had accomplished Taal's task: she had created a statue from a material in which fish were able to live. So enchanted is Taal by this work that his hatred quite evaporates. Having no further task for Mii, he rewards her for her work and releases her. Mii sails away from Devel, never again to return to the island. Taal orders Fo's wing of the palace to be sealed, and his courtiers quicken their pace whenever they pass the closed doors to its empty corridors—empty, that is, except for the white statues frozen forever in blocks of white marble.

# 53
## Vicious fish

I folded the insertion that told the story of the statuary in jelly back into itself, and pushed it into its pocket in the *Book*. I was on the terrace of Karael's house in the upper town. I knew that the plot was about to jump four years into the future, returning to Hios and Gato, who at the time I began to read of Fo's love and death, were frozen in mid-word and gesture—as if by some fairy-tale magic—by the open window of Gato's room, in whose frame was petrified the forked lightning of a storm fast approaching. I did not manage the transition from one level of the *Book*'s narrative to another with the same facility as the islanders; it induced in me a queasiness similar to that experienced by divers who come back to the surface too quickly. So I allowed myself a short break, during which I watched the metal jewel of the river work its gleaming course along the plateau and between the houses of the lower town. It was hot, so I spent some time walking barefoot among the steep lanes and up and down the steps of the upper town, the water flashing in the sunlight and maintaining the sublime cool of a mountain lake.

And then I returned to the *Book* and the royal palace on the island of Devel. The lightning rip in the black sky healed over and the frozen figures came back to life. Hios succeeds in procuring the jar of ointment. On the morning of the third day Gato announces to Taal that he will enter the statue and attempt to retrieve the gemstone. But Taal and Uddo anticipated that Hios would go for the duck fat and have replaced the contents of the jar with common pork lard. Taal bids Gato come to the courtyard that evening at six o'clock; he, his family and the court as a whole are looking forward to witnessing the spectacle.

As six o'clock approaches, Gato follows Hios's instructions in smearing his wrists, ankles and neck with what he assumes to be duck fat; then he steps into Fo's wing of the palace by the door at the end of the corridor (that day all doors are open wide) and makes his way down to the courtyard. There he sees dozens of chairs (brought by the servants from all over the palace) set in rows in front of the green statuary. The chairs are occupied by those agitated courtiers who have not dared refuse Taal's invitation; they do not know what to expect; but as they know their king, they are not expecting anything pleasant. As Gato approaches the statuary from the aisle between the chairs, the perplexed faces of the courtiers turn towards him and then away again. He hears a murmur of voices and a scraping of chairs: it is as if he were in the theatre when a performance was due to start. On reaching the statue he turns and for a few moments allows his gaze to wander over the anxious faces of the involuntary spectators. Their eyes are lowered; across their faces there shimmers a restless green light reflected from the statue by the setting sun. As he bows awkwardly he cannot help but smile. Taal, Uddo and Hios are sitting in the front row.

He now turns to face the statue. The fish have taken notice and are swimming towards him from all areas of the jelly. The sight of this restless swarm is far from encouraging, but this time Gato is sure that Hios has not betrayed him. He steps into the statue, amid the horde of fish. To begin with, the fish scatter themselves to all corners. At the statue's edge, Gato is standing up to his waist in jelly. The furrow his body has ploughed closes behind him; he has the feeling he is walking through an enormous dessert. In his choice of path he attempts to cause as little damage to the statue as possible. He comes to the gelatine table, which reaches up to his neck. Here he chooses to take a rest, and it appears to the onlooking courtiers that his head has left his body and is lying among the bowls of food. Gato studies the jelly plate of bread and cheese that is close to his face; he can see the imprint of Isili's little teeth on the cheese. He turns his head and sees the famous sculpted radish, a working in miniature of the contents of the statuary as a whole. Then he continues on his way—the gemstone sank into the body of the squid, which is at the very centre of the statue.

Through the clear jelly Gato sees the fish swim back towards him and begin to circle around him. The first fish bites into his thigh and he cries out in pain; suddenly he knows that he has been betrayed. Taal and Uddo steal a look at Hios, who is sitting next to them; they are disappointed to see she does not move a muscle, that the expression on her face does not change. But Hios understands very well what must have happened, and Gato's cry has not only shattered her world but flooded her mind with hate and a thirst for revenge. From this point on an expression of hard indifference will be on Hios's face always; it is a precious mask she will wear with pride.

The blood from the wound seeps into the jelly and the fish circling around Gato are suddenly wild. They fly at him and rip joyously into all parts of his body, tearing off the hunks of flesh and gulping them down. Gato, behung with fish, staggers about the statue. The courtiers jump from their chairs and cry out in horror, unable to tear their eyes away from the head whose mouth is screaming with pain, from the body covered with great, terrible clusters of fish, from the pall of blood spreading throughout the statue. Perhaps Prince Gato would have survived had he turned and tried to fight his way out of the statue. But his mind is focused on the gemstone still more keenly than the physical pain. On the final stretch of the journey towards the longed-for gemstone—which consists of the swollen waves of the sea and the body of the squid—the statue is taller than Gato. Gato takes a deep breath before plunging into the jelly with his eyes open. He catches sight of the gemstone, glinting as a ray of sun pierces the jelly. Gato struggles towards the flash of red in the green gloom, his body a flame of pain.

Now the sharp teeth rip into Gato's cheeks and neck; he is overwhelmed by the need to cry out, and the jelly gets into his mouth. He begins to choke. He has to jump up in order to catch his breath. The courtiers see his head break the surface—a bloody head with fish hanging in bunches from its cheeks—before it sinks back into the jelly. Not even Uddo can keep herself from exclaiming in horror. Only Hios remains silent and motionless. The glinting gemstone is now close enough for Gato to close his hand over it—a hand which has been gnawed down to the bone. He then forces his way through the squid. Between the last of the waves and the shore, the surface of the sea brings the statue to its lowest point. The courtiers look on as this is breached by the body covered with blood and behung with fish—with red and black bunches of death. The prince takes in breath and staggers a few steps more; then he loses consciousness and pitches back onto the jelly table with its jelly food, deep into the statue, which closes over him. In the courtyard a silence settles; nothing is heard but the distant calls of birds flying high above the palace. In silence the king, the queen, Hios, and the courtiers watch the shadow of the prince's body in the jelly, how it is enveloped in a great cluster of black, how it continues to make slight movements (whether these are the final motions of departing life or are effected by the furious tugging of the fish, is unclear). After a while the great bunch of fish dissolves. On the bottom of the translucent jelly there lies a white skeleton with a red gemstone sparkling in its hand.

The performance is at an end. Wordlessly the spectators get to their feet; again the scraping of chairs across granite begins. The king and Uddo are well satisfied. But they are bothered by

Hios's detachment—after all, the performance was staged largely to punish her for betraying the family. Taal and Uddo wished to see her weep and wail. But by the time Hios rises from her chair, hatred of her parents has burned into her brain; henceforth the spectre of revenge will live on the ashes of her reason and sensibility. In the days that follow Hios continues to behave calmly. But everyone begins to fear her.

## 54
## Putsch

Months later the news reaches Taal that Hios has become the lover of the commander of the palace's praetorian guard. Taal flies into a rage and determines to question Hios at luncheon that day, but when he does Hios does nothing to refute the allegations. While her father rants and rages, she sits there calmly eating a peach. Suddenly Taal falls silent, begins to wheeze, and falls face-first into the crockery. Hios continues to bite into her peach, watching her bewildered mother flap around Taal. When no further sound comes from Taal, Hios throws the peach stone into her bowl and leaves for her room. Once it becomes clear to Uddo there is nothing more she can do for Taal, she runs through the long corridors in pursuit of her daughter. But at the door to her daughter's chamber her way is blocked by two praetorians. She screams at them that she is the queen, but the guards hold their silence and do not move. She runs to her own chamber to find there six more guards going carefully through her things. Nor do they respond to her threats, and when they leave they take with them all the apparatus of her evil kitchen—all the flasks and jars of poisons, potions and drugs, all the instruments of her prowess as a chemist, which she would sit over for hour upon hour and compose for as though they were the most sophisticated musical instruments, concertos filled with pathos or dreams, nocturnes and preludes of evildoing. It seems that the putsch is proceeding along carefully prepared lines. As the praetorian guard takes the palace, others of its units occupy the Academy; but this is nothing more than a futile gesture of perfectionism on the part of the putschists, a small, unasked-for present to Hios from the praetorians, or perhaps a settling of old accounts. (There has always been a certain tension between the guard and the Academy, the two real centres of power on Devel.) Owing to the gradual disappearance over the past twenty years of centres of resistance to the government, the Academy has become somnolent; it has ceased to be a feared nest of the dark sciences and forces to such a degree that occasionally it returns to the innocent researches of old.

Surprisingly the command of the army puts up as little resistance as the weakened Academy. Years ago Taal promoted the palace guard to the position of most powerful force in the state, and this resulted in the *de facto* subjugation of the army. The guard does not have a hierarchy; it has the character of a strong but elastic web woven from dark bonds, impure dreams and complicity in old crimes. The guard has no code nor central idea, nor any specific purpose in the running of the state. The motto on its coat of arms is composed of incomprehensible, magic words for which everyone has his own interpretation. The guard is the ideal means of disseminating and enforcing decisions that should be spoken of only in whispers and ambiguous terms, decisions that grow from dark roots and grope about for means of implementation, even for guiding aims. The guard does not act by the passing down of clear commands through a hierarchy, but in such a way that its instructions—or rather the dark movements of its consciousness and emotions, spoken in low voices behind locked doors, in high galleries or the alleys of parks, in which tone of voice and accent play important roles—enter immediately the filiform web from which the body of the guard is woven; once these instructions are in circulation, the imagination of the great body sets to work on developing the dark themes within them, while simultaneously—as if in a single movement—turning them into action. This was the chemistry by which Taal exercised power; it was in many ways similar to his wife's more intimate compositions, whose lifeblood was poison.

Only subsequently, once everything is in motion, are a design and a plan fashioned, and these are really little more than hallucinations. These visions, of which the guard takes so little notice, set the army in motion. The army itself has no sensory organs by which to perceive the tangle of forces, desires and chaos that glimmer behind these phantom constructions; the commanders of the army do not realize that orders are born out of whispers, twitches and dreams, that indeed they never move very far away from them. So the putsch under the leadership of Hios and the commander of the praetorians is not so very different from the way things have been for many years up to this point. Even while the coup is in progress, a sense of normality sets in, stirring in the army command a sense that law and order are at work. After all, Hios is the daughter of the late king, and it has always been so that the commander of the guard mediates between the palace and the army. Hence the army—whose intervention Uddo is relying on—does nothing. The system of power established by Taal is turned against Uddo, and the queen discovers that she is powerless to resist it.

Hios does not attempt to disavow the rumours that claim it was she who poisoned the king. The commander of the guard is prepared to do whatever Hios asks of him, and so are his men. Since the deaths of Gato and Taal, Hios has grown so beautiful that she seems to have pillaged all the jewels of hell. Her dark splendour holds the praetorians in thrall; any of them would willingly undergo torture and death for the sake of their lady. Life at the palace becomes uncanny and dreamlike. The guards now walk its corridors, sprawl on its expensive upholstery in their high riding boots, enter its halls and chambers without invitation. Everyone gets out of their way. Hios glows with an icy, deathly beauty; fear abounds in the chambers of the palace. Uddo retires to ever-more remote rooms, waiting for Hios to strike against her. Hios leaves her mother alone while she considers how to dispose of her. One night Uddo gathers her jewels and makes an attempt to leave the palace by a side gate, but the guards there silently refuse to raise the barrier. Uddo shouts at them, then breaks into sobs and offers them jewels and money, but none of them speak or step aside, so Uddo returns to her room.

Hios begins to rule over the palace and the island as a whole. She refuses the title of queen, although the praetorians, who love the lustre of ceremony and the sight of gaily-coloured uniforms in the light of the sun, persist in proposing a magnificent coronation. It is enough for Hios that everyone fears her. She has the gemstone fished out of the statue and sent to Tana on Illim; using this, Tana is able to wash the red coating off the marble panel and thus prepare the remedy for Nau, who begins to get softer as soon as the first drops are applied. But when Tana asks for the return of his son's remains, Hios refuses to give up Gato's skeleton. She commands that this stays in the statue, and every evening when it is lit by the setting sun and Gato's silhouette comes into relief like a puppet in an Adriatic shadow theatre, she walks across the deserted courtyard and sits on a granite paving stone in front of the statue, where she remains until it is immersed in shade and Gato disappears.

One afternoon it suddenly grows dark and above the sea there appears a black column approaching the shore. The superstitious town-dwellers, whose streets are infected by the silent horror flowing from the palace, tell one another that the Devil has come for Hios. But it is nothing more than a tornado. When the whirling dance reaches the town, it rips off several roofs and tosses them into the air. It shakes the ships in the harbour, and—on reaching the palace—bores into the jelly statue like a giant screw, gathers it unto itself, bears the statue off towards the skies, then drops it—jelly, Gato's skeleton, the predatory fish, and all—into the streets. Before the fish die of fright they manage to sink their teeth into a number of people who try to pick them up from the ground. Hios orders the collection of Gato's remains, and these she has placed in the gold box, out of which she first ejects the manuscript of her brother's book. Now she detests whoever has the same blood as she, whether living or dead. Then she gives the order that Mii be found and told that Hios has work for her. But Mii, who has experienced a religious crisis and become terrified of the world that gave birth to her visions, is by this time living somewhere in northern Europe, on the tundra and deep in the forest, making ephemeral statues out of ash, then watching the wind reshape them until they disappear. So Hios's envoys bring to Devel the sculptor Nubra of Kass. When Mii was working on Fo's palace and the statue in jelly, Nubra was one of her assistants, and after her departure he took over her workshop.

## 55
## The new sculptor

Hios asks Nubra if he is able to create a sculpture in gold that would show the moment when Gato, behung with predatory fish, emerged from the jelly for the last time before falling back into the statuary. The figures in gold should be of the same size as the jelly and living figures in the scene that is the subject of the gold statuary. The sculptor tells Hios straight away how much gold he will need. Hios promises him all the gold from the state treasury, and in addition to this she issues a decree that all noblemen and wealthy merchants should exchange their gold for state bonds. No one believes in the validity of these, but no one protests.

The sculptor immediately gets to work on his design. He, too, is work-obsessed, but unlike Mii he does not create great visions, worlds that grow out of a confrontation between one's eyes and a space, a void filled with endless content. He concentrates always on one statue only, and he works on this until he has solved the rebus or complex mathematical equation it presents him with. As a rule Mii would reject any conditions set for a commission (unless her failure to meet them would result in her death, as was the case with the statuary in jelly); she would create her worlds gradually by her own themes, laws and rules, and in her own style, none of which were known to Mii before she started work. With her successor, on the other hand, the stricter the rules the client sets, the better; when this is not the case, he sets advance conditions of his own, which he must respect at all costs, even though these sometimes verge on the impossible and he is the only one who knows of them.

When, for example, he was commissioned to produce a portrait of the family of the chancellor of one of the island kingdoms, he began his work by setting himself to ensure that the fingertips of each of the figures described the circumference of a precise, if imaginary circle, whose radius he determined by the throw of a dice; after this he three times opened a dictionary with his eyes closed, thus finding the names of three objects or beings he would have to work into the composition of the statuary group. These were a pineapple, a bat and a hand of a clock. It was Nubra's task somehow to establish connections among them and also between them and the members of the chancellor's family, related to what the subjects thought about and the kind of lives they led. Such incipient connections as these draw other objects and animals into the statue, providing outlines for situations in which they might be inserted. Once a statue is finished, it is common that those who view it find in its composition and the objects and scenes it depicts symbolic meaning and deep philosophical thought. In addition to this, Nubra likes to experiment in the creation of a variety of moving, mechanical statues, some of which are driven by wind or water, others by springs concealed in their insides and wound up by a great key protruding from the back of the plinth. It is possible that these experiments have their origins in Nubra's work on the statuary in jelly.

Incidentally, Nubra was deeply dissatisfied with Mii's execution of Taal's task. Although her statue corresponded exactly to the task set by the king in its amended, definitive version, it was Nubra's opinion that the small changes to the assignment secured by Mii undermined the purity of her design and with it her achievement as a whole. Nubra believes that the conditions set at the outset should not under any circumstances be changed—that if the chess player is unable to defend his king it does not give him the right to move his rook as if it were a bishop. So years later Nubra decides to correct Mii's error and create a statue that really is made of water. The principle on which he bases this is relatively simple: springlets of water are sprayed through a dense web of holes drilled into horizontal panels placed at a variety of pre-determined heights, thus creating a relief. Of course, this system has one significant defect; perhaps, dear reader, you have hit upon it yourself: it does not allow for overhangs—as the lines of the water statue work their way upwards, they are bound to narrow. It is not even possible to create in the common position something as simple, yet important as the human nose. But Nubra finds a solution to this problem, too: he designs his water statue in such a way that it requires no shape whose highest point is wider than its lowest.

And so he sets to work. He and his assistants drill into a panel with the dimensions 3x3x3 metres—which will serve as the statue's plinth—1,920,000 small holes to create a regular web that has 1,600 holes along its length and 1,200 holes along its width. The underside of each hole is attached to a tube; the holes are divided into two hundred groups of varying numbers of holes, and all the tubes attached to the holes of one group come together in a single bigger tube. The bigger tubes are fed horizontally beneath the statue's plinth and leave the room by a hole in the wall. In the adjacent room these are attached to more tubes, each of which has a different diameter and goes upwards at a different angle. Each of these tubes is fed into a tank of water, which is located in the upper part of the room at the top of a metal construction; water from the river above a great waterfall enters this by force of gravity through an opening in the ceiling. Owing to differences in the diameters and biases of the tubes connected to the tank, the water flows through the flat-lying tubes beneath the plinth at various strengths and speeds, and when it reaches the hole in the panel, geysers of various heights rise out of the panel. Nubra has arranged things so that these come together to create the effect of a statue in water. The water is then drained into the gutters that line the plinth, and another pipe carries it out of the room and the building.

The statue portrays the corpse of the royal land surveyor, with a dagger in his breast, lying on his back in the desert; it is but an hour since he was murdered and his body is half-covered in sand. Next to him, jutting out from the sand, are some objects: a locked chest, a belly-shaped bottle, a bell, the front of a regular icosahedron, a cone. It is possible to trace in the sand a geometric figure—it is a circle, with a trapezium inside it. Next to this figure we can read what the murderer has written in the sand with his finger—"The dances on the silver bridge have not yet started." Although this inscription evidently continues, subsequent letters have been washed away by the sand. There are also the merest traces of small footprints—obviously made by a woman—which, like the remainder of the inscription, the circle with the trapezium, the corpse of the unfortunate surveyor and all the objects around him, soon disappear beneath the sand.

This is a scene from a well-known Kassian legend. For a long time Nubra inspected this image in his mind's eye. To his great satisfaction he discovered that it contained no overlapping or overhanging shapes, no protrusions or pendant lobes. Perhaps, dear reader, you would like me to tell the story of the royal land surveyor, so that you might take a break from the dismal affairs of Devel (and it would be well worth the effort—it is a legend with a long, convoluted plot that is set in many towns, in which there appear the sly emissaries of a padishah and a beautiful, mysterious woman). But you must forgive me, as I am not really in the mood for such an undertaking. You know that I have tried to oblige you whenever I can; indeed, I have pampered you. But please acknowledge that it is impossible for me to indulge your every whim. Let me propose another course: why not create for yourself a story to fit the scene in the desert into? You will experience the joys and ironies of fabulation; you will learn that fabulation is a drug to be wary of—even where the most honourable and moral of stories are concerned—as always it eats away at the good intentions and noble ideas that are its impetus, of which it supposes itself an obedient instrument. What fabulation does is transform its subject into a purposeless and joyous cosmic dance driven by ancient, entirely treacherous rhythms.

Fabulation is an adventure of encounter and homecoming; it carries you to landscapes where there is a murmur of stories hitherto unknown, where faceless figures take shape, where the bodies of inarticulate beings—great larvae—rub against yours in the dark. You realize that this landscape is not only the birthplace of the story; it is a home for your own gestures, actions and thoughts. Only in stories born of this landscape do you encounter your true self. Remember how Fo saw himself in the faces of his characters and the mysterious letters that recorded his true name. You will realize that your life is in some strange way a copy of the stories that arise from this landscape. And you will smile when I tell you of the literature of the authentic diary because you will know that you never encounter yourself until you leave yourself behind for the world of magical stories. Even the most candid diary is an embarrassing conceit, as the *I* of such literature is always a pitiable, fantastical figure who is less real than all the kings, princes and princesses of the island's *Book*.

## 56
## Performance

The sculptor is happy to accept Hios's assignment. Never before has he made a large statue out of gold, and he is excited by the prospect of creating a work whose greatest part will be a depiction of another statue and which will portray living beings (the upper half of Gato's body emerging from the jelly and the predatory fish biting into his flesh) in one place only. So the time comes when, in place of the work in jelly, there stands in the courtyard a statue of gold, showing Gato with his face twisted in pain, his body behung with predatory fish, as he emerges from Mii's statue of jelly, which is leaning slightly to one side in the evening wind. Day after day in the early morning Hios sits herself in front of the golden statue; the burning, dazzling sunlight is reflected from its curves into the princess's eyes, turning them into fireballs that whizz about like meteors in the dark inner universe behind Hios's aching lids.

One night Hios has a dream in which she is again witness to the final moments of Gato's life. But this time the prince's death is played out in a world where everything is made of gold. A golden figure with the face of Gato steps into a golden statue on a golden courtyard, struggles through the statue to the golden head of a giant squid, and when he re-emerges from the golden jelly he is behung with golden fish. When Gato at last falls, a golden surface closes over him. When the Hios of the dream looks about herself, she sees that the terror-stricken courtiers, too, are made of gold, and she thinks that her eyes will not withstand so great a glare. She lifts her arms to cover her eyes and hears a clang as her golden palms strike against her golden face, and this wakes her.

The next day at luncheon she retells her dream, lamenting that the statue of gold can never be made to move. Sitting at the table next to the commander of the praetorian guard is Nubra, and this talk of an impossible statue immediately rouses his attention. As we know, Nubra loves a challenge. He turns to Hios and informs her he will make a moving statue that will depict her golden dream. As he is saying this, he has no idea how he will accomplish the task. The next week he never leaves his chamber; he lies on the bed, contemplating how he will keep the promise to Hios and complete the assignment he has set for himself. His gaze roams about the flower-pattern motifs that are endlessly repeated on the paper covering the walls of his chamber. He has a great many ideas, but all of these he gradually rejects. At one moment his eyes light on the stylized drawing of the bud of a lotus next to a lotus whose petals are already open; Nubra has the feeling he is seeing the flower open. And then the solution to his assignment comes to him. In order that the viewer see how the golden Gato dies and how the golden fish thrash about, it is not necessary in the least that the statue itself move. All that there remains for him to do is to construct a mechanism whose real but invisible movements will give the (false) impression that the statue is moving.

He presents his plan to Hios, and she promises to get for him everything he needs. Having worried that the princess would find his vision too grand and too costly, Hios is taken aback to see that she considers it too modest a memorial to Gato and her pain and hatred. Nubra cannot know that on first acquaintance with his idea, she sees in it the germ of a work far more wide-ranging—a golden statue that will be a second-by-second representation of the whole of Gato's stay at the palace, beginning with Gato showing the chamberlain the carpet with the fairy-tale castle, followed by his work on the carpet commissioned by Taal, his night-time lovemaking with Hios, the moment when he stands anxiously before the labyrinth on the door of the treasury. But for now Hios charges the sculptor only with building in the palace gardens an amphitheatre which will be part of the moving statue.

The monstrous work, in which Hios's incipient madness is joined and complemented by Nubra's cold, technical reason, is ready within the year. Nubra produces several dozen statues to represent individual phases of Gato's course through the statuary, from the moment he first stands before it to the moment he falls back into the jelly. This series also includes original statues in gold. The rest of the statues are gold-plated only, as Devel does not possess enough gold. Nubra has the statues built on a great turntable he has placed in the palace gardens, in front of which he orders a wall built with an opening where it meets the turntable, out of which rises the auditorium of the amphitheatre.

It is possible to close and re-open this hole in the wall by means of the two lightning-fast wings of a sliding door, which come together with a heavy impact (the sound of their colliding is softened by upholstered strips stuck to inside edge of each wing), then slide swiftly into cavities in the wall. All motions of the mechanism are unified by an ingenious transmission system. In the fraction of a second for which the door is closed, the turntable moves to bring round a statue representing the next phase of the action. When the doors re-open—again, this takes but a fraction of a second—the new statue is before the audience, and this is followed by a statue representing the next phase of the action, and so on. These rapid-changing statues create a grisly golden film about the death of Prince Gato.

When Nubra is building the amphitheatre, Hios has the palace park closed so that preparations for the Golden Statue Theatre can be carried on in secret. She forbids the workmen engaged on it from speaking about the work on pain of death. It is unnecessary for her to impose any prohibitions on Nubra: the surprise his inventions will excite is an inseparable part of the work, and besides, absolute silence is a central feature of his manner of working. The courtiers look with anxiety towards the closed gates of the park, at the constant comings and goings of covered wagons; they listen day and night to the workmen's blows and think nothing good can come of it. Then the noise in the park ceases and the wagons disappear. Shortly after this, all the ladies and gentlemen of the court receive an invitation to a performance in the palace park. Uddo, too, receives an invitation—one look at the guards who deliver the invitation is enough to dissuade her from refusing it. The performance is due to commence after nightfall. With foreboding, the courtiers take their seats in the auditorium. It is barely two years since they were made to participate in another wicked performance at another place in the palace grounds. They have no idea what it is that is about to be presented to them, nor whether they will have to sit through more deathly ballets and bloody operas in the future. Uddo tries to hide in the back row, but when a guard comes to her a short while later and orders her to move to the front next to Hios, she allows herself to be led to an empty seat before the grey door in the wall.

When the lamps in the auditorium are extinguished and the door opens, the spectators are presented with a golden statue that depicts a statue of jelly. The door closes swiftly and then re-opens, the turntable turns, and before the eyes of the astonished courtiers a statue begins to move. To begin with this movement is little more than a gentle wobbling in the breeze, but then a fish jumps above the surface before disappearing back into the jelly. (In fact, fish modelled at various points of their jump are attached to the statue of the jelly statue by thin metal rods at points in consonance with the movements of the breeze.) From the left-hand side of the wall there then emerges a golden figure. When this figure reaches the statue, it turns to the auditorium and bows, just as the bewildered Gato did two years earlier. As if in a nightmare, the stupefied courtiers follow the familiar story: the golden figure of Gato steps up to Mii's (golden) statue; the golden figure enters the golden statue, which is wobbling in the (imaginary) breeze; for a time the figure is out of sight, but then it re-emerges and turns to the audience with a look of anguish on its face, lifts up its arms fringed with golden fish, then falls back into the golden statue, which itself is a representation of a table set between the royal castle of Vauz and the sea.

Believing the performance to be at an end, the courtiers allow their horror to subside. But the turntable continues to turn. Once again the golden figure approaches the golden statue; again he steps into it, battles with the fish, and falls back into the gold. The monotonous golden film lasts five hours, after which time Hios makes a signal of command and the wings of the door crash shut for the last time that night. No one—not even Uddo—has dared to leave before the end of the performance. Although Hios and Uddo have been sitting next to each other throughout, not once has the daughter turned to look at the mother. Once the film has ended, Hios stands up in front of the closed door and announces that the spectators may go to bed, adding that the next performance will begin at the same time tomorrow.

Thus does the grim serial begin. Performances are held every night. And every night the courtiers are forced to watch the death of a golden Gato, over and over, so that they begin to fear for their minds. Every night Hios is present from beginning to end; she always sits next to her mother and watches the stage with a rapt expression. The guards stand in the aisles, drawing amusement from the discomfort of the courtiers. Before each performance starts, no one knows how long it will last—not even Hios, who always makes this decision when it is in progress. Often it lasts until morning, but still the guards allow no one to leave before the end, not even those who are taken ill or need to go to the toilet. Anyone who falls asleep is woken by a guard. For many years afterwards, the awful memory of daybreak in the palace park will return to the courtiers in their dreams. When at last the dim light of day washes over the amphitheatre, it is accompanied by cries, wails and groans; someone might howl for several minutes before falling silent; there is a stink of sweat, urine, faeces and vomit. Soon all these liquids have soaked into the velvet cushions of the seats, and every evening the blend of stinks greets the involuntary spectators as they make their way to the amphitheatre; soon this has penetrated the palace and it seems it will descend to the town and settle in its streets.

## 57
## Terror and invasion

As soon as Nubra finishes work on the golden theatre, Hios—by now at the deepest point of her madness—sets him on another task. She dreams of a great golden drama that will celebrate her and Gato's love, but first it is necessary to punish her mother. Hios presents Nubra with her design of a monument that is to stand on all the squares of the capital. These monuments are to depict executioners who are torturing, raping and otherwise humiliating Uddo by the vilest means the dark thoughts of the princess can invent. Nubra is horrified; as a lover of games and rebuses, he has no liking for commissions such as this, and he despises Hios's dreary, clumsy hate that is slowly developing into the purest form of madness. But he is no more able to decline this order than Mii was able to decline the order to produce a statue in liquid for Taal. Once the dreadful monuments are in place, every morning Hios takes her mother around the squares on a tour of hate; Hios orders the coach to stand for at least an hour in front of each statue. Hios never addresses her mother, and whenever Uddo closes her eyes at a statue, Hios strikes her across the face and neck with a riding whip until she opens them. From these trips Hios escorts her mother directly to an all-night performance in the palace park. After a while Uddo abandons all resistance: she weeps no longer, but follows dumbly the changing scenes of the day-time and night-time statue performances.

By this time everyone at the palace is dull-witted or mad in some way. The courtiers grow accustomed to the terror practised on them by the praetorian guards and to the glassy-eyed expression of the queen; they grow accustomed to the many-hour-long re-enactments of the golden death, to the dreadful monuments, to the humiliation and stink of the amphitheatre. They are indifferent to the leaking of bodily fluids and stains on garments and upholstery—they wear the reeking splotches on their clothing like dark jewels. And the madness, stinking juices and bad dreams descend from the palace to seep into the streets of the town, the country at large, the waves of the sea. In the people of the town, fear of the guards' patrols and raids (which often are the same banditry) mixes with joy at the general state of anarchy; in most cases, wrongdoing is tolerated when it does not affect the well-being of the guard or the princess, when its scope is limited to a house or the town, or when it happens to benefit some nobleman or other. The avarice and thirst for power of the guard is a fine complement to the disinterested, ostentatious cruelty of the queen. The people of the town blunder about stupidly in the shadows of the obscene monuments. Some days they cower in their homes and bolt the doors, listening to the sounds of carts and footfalls beyond the door; other days they are drunken participants in the looting of mansions—when a property seizure is in progress, they wait for the guard to leave before bursting into the paralysed house through its fractured doors.

Such brutal scenes as these were by no means exceptional in the *Book*. Mostly I came across them in deep insertions, perhaps in a pocket concealed inside another, as if I were descending to the dungeons of a building to find there the foundations of the ancient palace of a despot. Perhaps, I thought, the poison in the insertions will soak through to higher levels of the *Book* and the whole thing will become one obscene, cruel dream. And as the borders of all worlds were weak on the island, and the games of the islanders spilled over them, I even wondered if the evil in the *Book* might conquer the quiet life of the island, which would then begin to resemble that of Devel in Hios's years.

I still wonder how it is possible that such dark images were born in the minds of the peaceable islanders. Perhaps the slow crystallization of shapes and systems into the shapeless, the various forms of which was the islanders' main source of entertainment, was not as innocent as it seemed. The disintegration of language and order that occurred when these encountered labyrinthine shapes or passed over borders, released a playful force that built and revived different orders and languages in an endless kaleidoscope; but this force was itself a combination of many forces, whose tones sounded in it and which could render themselves independent. It is probable that a force could be distilled that would rise above matter and find its aim and its delight in the crushing of matter, without the fragments thereby created being used in new games. And this force would begin to elaborate its own figures, to write in hieroglyphs of evil, to set up its own dreadful world.

It seemed to me that the germs of dark worlds were present on the island in the breath of all things, sounds and words. As I was reading the history of the kingdom of Devel, I got to thinking about what it was that all those years ago so bewitched the European conquerors that they forgot their homelands within three generations, that they, too, came to hear voices in the island's murmurs; I thought about the faces and figures that appeared to them in the play of the foam and the leaves. Were they really overwhelmed by the placidity of the islanders, or did they—experts on power and violence that they were—scent evil hidden at the bottom of this placidity and capitulate in admiration of its grand style? But I would be doing the islanders an injustice if I were to find in their calm, non-violent nature only the seeds of cruelty. I have said already that the force that ruled their world was woven from many sub-forces, and that each of these could separate itself from the bunch. It was possible to find in the islanders' world the germs of many attitudes and many worlds, celestial and infernal. Images from these worlds sometimes flashed through in the islanders' gestures and the melody of their voices. (For example, I was able to imagine very well that the admirable precision of their eyes—which was able to recognize and record the finest distinctions in shape—could be used in the development of brilliant analytical thinking.)

Families flee from Devel in ever-greater numbers. There are voices on the island's beaches and light signals out at sea. Many of the fugitives find asylum at the court of Illim. Here a plan is hatched to invade the island ruled by the mad princess and her guard. The émigrés invite Tana to lead their flotilla, but Tana refuses: he does not want to renew the hostilities between families that was extinguished by the love of Gato and Hios, and also he is grateful for the gemstone, thanks to which Nau is now almost as soft as before (apart from the skin of her face, which has remained hard and is like a gleaming mask of metal).

The émigrés form themselves into opposing groups; each has its own candidate for commander of the army and its own plans for the invasion, which it is not prepared to give up. The groups reach no consensus until the unexpected appearance on Illim and in the *Book*—introduced in a subordinate clause right at the end of a very long compound sentence dealing with the fragrance of the old walls of Illim's harbour—of Ara, whom the reader has believed would always remain in a kind of *Book*-world Hades into which characters descend from pages read. Above her name there is a thick pocket, probably detailing what happened to Ara after her departure from the palace at Devel. I did not open this because I was anxious to find out how the invasion of Devel would end, and quite simply I forgot to go back to it. I very much regret this, as Karael once told me that the adventures of Ara were among the most beautiful passages in the *Book*—she told me that Ara meets voiceless birds on her travels, which instead of singing, play long musical compositions by tapping their beaks on dripstones of differing thicknesses that grow at the mouths of caves in the hillside and give tones of different pitches. Perhaps the émigrés suspect that their planned strategy would be no match for the power of Hios, brewed as it is in a witch's cauldron of pain, beauty, cruelty, desire, tenderness and madness. It seems they recognize in the words and gestures of Ara a power that is born of sweetness, nightmares and stifled cries; they understand that this night-time torrent of courage and evil is capable of confronting Hios and the dark army she commands.

So it comes to pass one starless night that all ships of the invading force push off from the harbour at Illim and out to sea. Ara is aboard the command ship, watching the flashing of the white, red and blue signal lights on all sides. The darkness begins to change to a grey mist, through which the outlines of dozens of phantom-like sails can be seen. (I meditated on what Ara would actually be able to see from the bow of her ship. I imagined a forest of masts in various shades of grey. But the *Book* was so indefinite in its references to time, in the boldness or carelessness with which it mixed the props of various ages, and by the dearth of words its authors employed in describing the main shapes of things—even though it was able to describe over dozens of pages the adornments on a house facade or the network of cracks in the plaster of an old wall—that out of the mist of dawn there might just as well have emerged the funnels of steamers. Or perhaps the ships slid lightly through the waves powered by some marvellous fuel unknown to our world—perhaps the milk of the silver mountain tiger was bubbling in the glass cauldron of a magical engine room.) The mist before the bow is an ever-thickening, ever-expanding pall of dark-grey, which suddenly develops cracks to reveal the streets of Devel's capital. Ara wades through the cold water. All around her, grey figures step out, plunging their feet into the wet sand of the beach. Out of the mist comes the clank of metal and screaming. Ara and the others climb the steep lanes of the harbour area, which she knows well from her childhood. The lanes open out into a square, where dreadful monuments rise out of the mist. The mist is filled with points and blades of metal; as if in a dream, Ara beats these off with dagger and sword.

By midday the invading forces have broken down the gates of the palace. Dagger in hand, Hios joins the battle in the corridors of the palace, incurring many wounds and killing many of the enemy. After the death of the commander of the praetorian guard it becomes clear that the palace is about to fall. Hios leaves the action by a secret corridor and goes into the palace park, where she sets the golden theatre in motion. This is the first time a performance has been given to an empty auditorium. Devel's princess sits there alone and stares rapt at the golden images of Gato's demise. She has left a trail of blood in her wake and Ara has followed this to the theatre. Then the unknown author described a scene that might have been from a film: for a long time Hios and Ara, each armed with a long dagger, engage in wordless, hand-to-hand combat, threading their way up and down the empty aisles of the amphitheatre. Two slim bodies, which once would join in nights of love, move to the dumb dance of death in front of revolving scenes of Gato's death and rebirth, death and rebirth. Steel daggers flit about before the golden dumbshow; the ringing of metal mixes with the thud of the wings of the door as they slam together and the purr of the mechanism that drives the turntable. At last Hios falls in the aisle between two rows of seats. Ara wipes her dagger on Hios's clothes and goes back to the palace, where a great victory celebration is in preparation. Before an empty auditorium, Gato dies and comes back to life in the golden statue again and again. That evening someone stops the mechanism that drives the statues of the theatre, but Hios lies among the seats in a pool of dried blood for several days more. There was no mention of whether her shadow and Gato's were embracing in the underworld.

Ara briefly serves as queen of Devel, but then she leaves the island and sets out on new adventures that take her to a great many lands. (These were described in another part of the *Book*.) Meanwhile, on Devel and Illim two boys from other sides of the feuding families have grown to maturity, and one day a new war breaks out between the two islands . . .

# 58
## Journey's end

So ended the story of Tana and Nau, Taal and Uddo, Fo and Mii, Gato, Hios and Ara—one of the many episodes of the transforming, disappearing *Book*, one of the works of art created by the islanders, or perhaps a constellation of thousands of works of art, in which the reader forever encounters new books and fragments of old books no longer in existence and lost to the past like the fragile scrolls of the Egyptians. But the reader also encounters sonatas and symphonies for string, wind, water and fire instruments, and ballets, in which the dancers are people, animals, phantoms and mechanical dummies; and he encounters statues made of water and jelly, pictures painted on canvas, in sand and in water, mosaics composed of gemstones, luminous beetles and hallucination-inducing lights.

I can imagine that in today's *Book* there are none of the figures I read about when I was on the island: no Tana, no Dru, no Gato, no Hios. They have been replaced by other characters, whose stories perhaps bear echoes of the heroes I knew. And certainly in the features of these new heroes, the faces of the heroes who will replace them will be germinating. The giant squid has disappeared. So, too, has the statue in jelly. Perhaps the whole archipelago has been claimed by the sea, and new islands and continents have sailed out onto the *Book*'s pages. Perhaps new stars are shining in the galaxies of its universe, and there are new planets on which unknown civilizations will thrive and expire, circling in this imaginary universe born out of the practically imperceptible breath of its script, for as long as it takes for the *Book* to devour them. And because islanders have bad memories, the heroes, towns and islands, planets and galaxies that were described in the *Book* at the time I sat on the terrace of Karael's house, do not even exist in anyone's mind.

During my stay on the island I learned from its inhabitants many bad and also several good things. But I have never been able to welcome change and extinguishment with the same joy as they did. It was my secret hope that the characters disappearing from the island's *Book* would live on at least in my report about the island. But my memory is the not the best either; it was so often mistaken that I am afraid the characters and deeds of my telling have little in common with those I read about on the island. It sometimes happened while I was writing that I remembered something from the text of the *Book* as I first experienced it; but when I returned to the passages I now believed to be wrong in the hope of rewriting them, I had to laugh at the futility and ridiculousness of such efforts. It dawned on me what nonsense it was to strive for fidelity in something that was constantly changing shape, that no one could confirm, that lived on only in my memory, which had failed me several times already.

Karael no longer telephones or writes, so I have no news of what has happened to the *Book* since my departure. It is possible that its stories have crumbled, leaving nothing but isolated sentences and words. It is even possible that they have been erased by the soaking into its pages of the water of the upper town or the waves of the sea, that the islanders now pass from hand to hand a *Book* with blank white pages filled only with phantoms, on which the contours of new shapes and bodies are beginning slowly to beat out the rhythms of new stories.

Was the *Book* a genuine work of art? Now I would probably hesitate before I answered that. Part of art is constancy and invariability, but not because it should raise itself above time and approach the world of eternal shapes and values: art must descend to constancy because only from the chasm of this descent, from the misery of non-variability, can it face the challenges of the endlessly transforming, which is what art yearns for, adores and sings about; only a motionless statue that immerses itself in the current of time can address the undulations of transformation. And a work of art should have a single author. It cannot be written by a multitude of anonymous islanders—not because it is an expression and a celebration of individuality, but because it must descend to the poverty of a single voice; only out of this poverty can it respond to the abundance of voices of the world, in which it wishes to dissolve itself. Only in its misery and impotence can the uncertain echo of these voices arise, and all the sonorous voices of the world can reveal themselves only as the tremor of sadness in a single voice for its inadequacy.

As a work of art, the island's *Book* was a failure from the very beginning. It is fairly certain that it was this failure the islanders were striving for. There was no need for Ino of the white ankles to fly to the island: the people that lived there knew very well what she had to impart, it was written in their blood. Now I believe that the *Book* was ridiculing art, was a parody of art. The islanders did not like art because its shapes stood in the way of their eddies of shapelessness, and its sounds drowned out the music of silence. To begin with I wondered if Mii, Fo and all the other artists who kept appearing on the pages of the *Book*, were the expression of some kind of islanders' dream of real art, a permanent, unchanging work of art, but then I realized that for the islanders such characters were laughable or pitiful, that their often woeful fates were meant to show where a yearning for shape could lead. I know now that the *Book* was not just a parody of art; it was a parody of our world as a whole, fragments of which would arrive on the island in each ship that came into port.

The supposition that the *Book* was a work of art was also based on the view that the island's literature was a response to the summons of shapeless murmurs and eddies that yearned for the release of the images concealed in them. But having returned to the *Book* and drawn from my memory certain of its passages, I was no longer sure that its roots contained the desire of the shapeless for shape, and if so, then only as a part of the circling that both the shaped and the shapeless contain and overlap with. Now I would explain the origins of the stories of the *Book* more simply and in a way more in keeping with the character of the islanders: at the core of the shapeless there is a blind, irresistible pressure to expel images, so that after some time the purity of the shapeless is clouded by a sediment of images, which are at various stages of development. If this were so, the writing and reading of the *Book* would be a cleansing process by which the shapeless would rid itself of sediment, draining away all the shapes and images that had settled in it. Renewing the limpidity of the *Book* would make it possible for the islanders to bathe in pure streams of the shapeless. The *Book* was not an end in itself but a mere by-product; it was a filter that caught the dirt of shapes and images.

On my travels around Prague I have yet to spot in a travel agent's window a colour photo of the island. It seems that there is still no modern hotel on its shores. But even if there were, this would not have to mean the destruction of the island's culture. I have written of how hitherto the islanders have always been cunning victors over the culture of Europe. Perhaps this time it would be different; perhaps in time the streets of the lower town would fill with restaurants, souvenir shops and ice-cream stands; perhaps loud music would drown out the island's murmurs and rustlings. But it might happen that a fresh encounter with Europe would lead to another victory on the part of the islanders; let us remember that the islanders have always won as easily and unwittingly as they draw breath. We know how the European invasion of long ago ended, and it is more than likely that the colourful emblems of multinational corporations would penetrate the streets of the lower town only to transform in the same way as the conqueror's geometric drawings and devotional pictures—they would be overwhelmed by stains and webs of cracks, the music playing in the streets would be infiltrated more and more by rustlings and murmurs, so that all would be overgrown as surely as the once-proud buildings were covered in creeping plants. And things might not end here—the changes might spread to Europe and America, they could transform whole continents; whole world civilizations might come to resemble the life of the island. And then my book would be for nothing, as it would speak of banalities known by all.

I am glad that I succeeded in making this second, imaginary journey to the island without succumbing to the Sirens of sense, ideas and guidance. Everyone has his own magical library and in it his eposes of the bizarre, the pages of which sometimes gleam in the dark. The girl in Michle encountered a luminous Iliad woven from TV advertisements. My second journey to the island became an odyssey at whose beginning lay a ghostly Ogygia of the past and at whose end was a phantom Aeaea of language; it became a journey from the nymph of blissful forgetting to the sorcerer of purposeless metamorphosis.

Although at the beginning of this travelogue I boasted of my power to resist absurdities, perhaps when I did so I was clinging to the hope that I would glimpse some purpose in my stay on the island. I have not been able to shake the feeling that journeys should bestow at last some kind of experience. But the writing of this book has brought it home to me that my stay on the island was but a small tear in the great web of experience—a pulsating empty space that sometimes widens and makes threats, that devours everything, that is sometimes overgrown with old connections. The void of the erased face of the island's king, the void at the centre of the island's *Book* that skips from page to page, the void of the expiring roots of words, the void of the blank pages of travellers' diaries.

Perhaps this tear had something in common with the void out of which words arise, a void which always lies silently in the gaps between letters and in their hollows like the cool, treacherous snow blown into the characters of the neon sign on the roof of the Paris department store; the void of this tear called for a book, for a travelogue—not to join together the words, but so that it might look with pleasure in the mirror of sentences, so that in their chinks, tears and hollows it might encounter its own self, so that thanks to a book it might defend its forever-threatened purity. As such my book has become a reflection of the island's *Book*, which I first dipped into on a terrace in the rock of the upper town, and which exasperated and bored me for so long. This *Book* that has nothing to say and whose author is the last person to ask about its meaning, is actually an empty space, too, just a gulf of emptiness in a world of fullness, one of the places where the knots of reality unravel and where every world becomes a question without an answer.

But I hope that this void does not worry you, dear reader—this is the last time I will address you thus, as the time has come when we must say our farewells. I trust you have read my travelogue with enough attention to realize that I did not drown in the cool void, that I still have my images, that this emptiness does not mean indifference, solitude and the extinguishing of conversation. Quite the contrary, in fact: only out of emptiness may the shapes rise and the words sound, shapes and words hitherto untouched by the fragrances of the void, shapes and words whose breath bears the tremor of an old, elusive message; perhaps in my voice, which draws on the currents of the void, which resonates beneath the pages, something of this tremor that fascinates us all has been preserved, while your invisible face—which somewhere in the dark turns towards me and makes itself known only by breath that has yet to become the matter of words or part of a gesture, but so far just a tremor in the void—is to me a revelation of a world of living absence, which wakes a ripple of utterance on the surface of another eddying emptiness. And so do tremulous emptinesses and their never-ending game create borders between one another, in whose twisted relief are created words, thoughts, dreams and desires, and in which the faces of heroes and gods, the images of animals and plants, palaces, towns and ships at sea appear.

And it seems to me that this is the place to stop. The nameless island in strange seas is evidently deserving of the sleepless nights of the one who returned, and also of his writing a book about it in which he sings his variations on motifs of island life. But it has also earned the right not to be thought about for too long, to be released into oblivion when the time arrives, for the images born on its soil to be scattered to rubble and thoughts of them to be changed to anonymous music in the accompaniment of new thoughts and new journeys.

Michal Ajvaz is a Czech novelist, essayist, poet, and translator. In 2005, he was awarded the Jaroslav Seifert Prize. He is a researcher at Prague's Center for Theoretical Studies. In addition to fiction, he has published an essay on Derrida, a book-length meditation on Borges, and a philosophical study on the act of seeing.

Andrew Oakland's recent translations include Radka Denemarková's *Money from Hitler*, Martin Reiner's *No Through Road*, and the autobiography of architect Josef Hoffmann.

## SELECTED DALKEY ARCHIVE PAPERBACKS

Petros Abatzoglou, *What Does Mrs. Freeman Want?*
Michal Ajvaz, *The Golden Age.*
*The Other City.*
Pierre Albert-Birot, *Grabinoulor.*
Yuz Aleshkovsky, *Kangaroo.*
Felipe Alfau, *Chromos.*
*Locos.*
Ivan Ângelo, *The Celebration.*
*The Tower of Glass.*
David Antin, *Talking.*
António Lobo Antunes, *Knowledge of Hell.*
Alain Arias-Misson, *Theatre of Incest.*
John Ashbery and James Schuyler, *A Nest of Ninnies.*
Heimrad Bäcker, *transcript.*
Djuna Barnes, *Ladies Almanack.*
*Ryder.*
John Barth, *LETTERS.*
*Sabbatical.*
Donald Barthelme, *The King.*
*Paradise.*
Svetislav Basara, *Chinese Letter.*
Mark Binelli, *Sacco and Vanzetti Must Die!*
Andrei Bitov, *Pushkin House.*
Louis Paul Boon, *Chapel Road.*
*My Little War.*
*Summer in Termuren.*
Roger Boylan, *Killoyle.*
Ignácio de Loyola Brandão, *Anonymous Celebrity.*
*Teeth under the Sun.*
*Zero.*
Bonnie Bremser, *Troia: Mexican Memoirs.*
Christine Brooke-Rose, *Amalgamemnon.*
Brigid Brophy, *In Transit.*
Meredith Brosnan, *Mr. Dynamite.*
Gerald L. Bruns, *Modern Poetry and the Idea of Language.*
Evgeny Bunimovich and J. Kates, eds., *Contemporary Russian Poetry: An Anthology.*
Gabrielle Burton, *Heartbreak Hotel.*
Michel Butor, *Degrees.*
*Mobile.*
*Portrait of the Artist as a Young Ape.*
G. Cabrera Infante, *Infante's Inferno.*
*Three Trapped Tigers.*
Julieta Campos, *The Fear of Losing Eurydice.*
Anne Carson, *Eros the Bittersweet.*
Camilo José Cela, *Christ versus Arizona.*
*The Family of Pascual Duarte.*
*The Hive.*
Louis-Ferdinand Céline, *Castle to Castle.*
*Conversations with Professor Y.*
*London Bridge.*
*Normance.*
*North.*
*Rigadoon.*
Hugo Charteris, *The Tide Is Right.*
Jerome Charyn, *The Tar Baby.*
Marc Cholodenko, *Mordechai Schamz.*
Joshua Cohen, *Witz.*
Emily Holmes Coleman, *The Shutter of Snow.*
Robert Coover, *A Night at the Movies.*
Stanley Crawford, *Log of the S.S. The Mrs Unguentine.*
*Some Instructions to My Wife.*
Robert Creeley, *Collected Prose.*
René Crevel, *Putting My Foot in It.*
Ralph Cusack, *Cadenza.*
Susan Daitch, *L.C.*
*Storytown.*
Nicholas Delbanco, *The Count of Concord.*
Nigel Dennis, *Cards of Identity.*
Peter Dimock, *A Short Rhetoric for Leaving the Family.*
Ariel Dorfman, *Konfidenz.*
Coleman Dowell, *The Houses of Children.*
*Island People.*
*Too Much Flesh and Jabez.*
Arkadii Dragomoshchenko, *Dust.*
Rikki Ducornet, *The Complete Butcher's Tales.*
*The Fountains of Neptune.*
*The Jade Cabinet.*
*The One Marvelous Thing.*
*Phosphor in Dreamland.*
*The Stain.*
*The Word "Desire."*
William Eastlake, *The Bamboo Bed.*
*Castle Keep.*
*Lyric of the Circle Heart.*
Jean Echenoz, *Chopin's Move.*
Stanley Elkin, *A Bad Man.*
*Boswell: A Modern Comedy.*
*Criers and Kibitzers, Kibitzers and Criers.*
*The Dick Gibson Show.*
*The Franchiser.*
*George Mills.*
*The Living End.*
*The MacGuffin.*
*The Magic Kingdom.*
*Mrs. Ted Bliss.*
*The Rabbi of Lud.*
*Van Gogh's Room at Arles.*
Annie Ernaux, *Cleaned Out.*
Lauren Fairbanks, *Muzzle Thyself.*
*Sister Carrie.*
Leslie A. Fiedler, *Love and Death in the American Novel.*
Juan Filloy, *Op Oloop.*
Gustave Flaubert, *Bouvard and Pécuchet.*
Kass Fleisher, *Talking out of School.*
Ford Madox Ford, *The March of Literature.*
Jon Fosse, *Melancholy.*
Max Frisch, *I'm Not Stiller.*
*Man in the Holocene.*
Carlos Fuentes, *Christopher Unborn.*
*Distant Relations.*
*Terra Nostra.*
*Where the Air Is Clear.*

FOR A FULL LIST OF PUBLICATIONS, VISIT:
www.dalkeyarchive.com

# SELECTED DALKEY ARCHIVE PAPERBACKS

JANICE GALLOWAY, *Foreign Parts.*
*The Trick Is to Keep Breathing.*
WILLIAM H. GASS, *Cartesian Sonata and Other Novellas.*
*Finding a Form.*
*A Temple of Texts.*
*The Tunnel.*
*Willie Masters' Lonesome Wife.*
GÉRARD GAVARRY, *Hoppla! 1 2 3.*
ETIENNE GILSON,
*The Arts of the Beautiful.*
*Forms and Substances in the Arts.*
C. S. GISCOMBE, *Giscome Road.*
*Here.*
*Prairie Style.*
DOUGLAS GLOVER, *Bad News of the Heart.*
*The Enamoured Knight.*
WITOLD GOMBROWICZ,
*A Kind of Testament.*
KAREN ELIZABETH GORDON, *The Red Shoes.*
GEORGI GOSPODINOV, *Natural Novel.*
JUAN GOYTISOLO, *Count Julian.*
*Juan the Landless.*
*Makbara.*
*Marks of Identity.*
PATRICK GRAINVILLE, *The Cave of Heaven.*
HENRY GREEN, *Back.*
*Blindness.*
*Concluding.*
*Doting.*
*Nothing.*
JIŘÍ GRUŠA, *The Questionnaire.*
GABRIEL GUDDING,
*Rhode Island Notebook.*
MELA HARTWIG, *Am I a Redundant Human Being?*
JOHN HAWKES, *The Passion Artist.*
*Whistlejacket.*
ALEKSANDAR HEMON, ED.,
*Best European Fiction 2010.*
AIDAN HIGGINS, *A Bestiary.*
*Balcony of Europe.*
*Bornholm Night-Ferry.*
*Darkling Plain: Texts for the Air.*
*Flotsam and Jetsam.*
*Langrishe, Go Down.*
*Scenes from a Receding Past.*
*Windy Arbours.*
ALDOUS HUXLEY, *Antic Hay.*
*Crome Yellow.*
*Point Counter Point.*
*Those Barren Leaves.*
*Time Must Have a Stop.*
MIKHAIL IOSSEL AND JEFF PARKER, EDS.,
*Amerika: Russian Writers View the United States.*
GERT JONKE, *The Distant Sound.*
*Geometric Regional Novel.*
*Homage to Czerny.*
*The System of Vienna.*
JACQUES JOUET, *Mountain R.*
*Savage.*
CHARLES JULIET, *Conversations with Samuel Beckett and Bram van Velde.*
MIEKO KANAI, *The Word Book.*
HUGH KENNER, *The Counterfeiters.*
*Flaubert, Joyce and Beckett: The Stoic Comedians.*
*Joyce's Voices.*
DANILO KIŠ, *Garden, Ashes.*
*A Tomb for Boris Davidovich.*
ANITA KONKKA, *A Fool's Paradise.*
GEORGE KONRÁD, *The City Builder.*
TADEUSZ KONWICKI, *A Minor Apocalypse.*
*The Polish Complex.*
MENIS KOUMANDAREAS, *Koula.*
ELAINE KRAF, *The Princess of 72nd Street.*
JIM KRUSOE, *Iceland.*
EWA KURYLUK, *Century 21.*
ERIC LAURRENT, *Do Not Touch.*
VIOLETTE LEDUC, *La Bâtarde.*
SUZANNE JILL LEVINE, *The Subversive Scribe: Translating Latin American Fiction.*
DEBORAH LEVY, *Billy and Girl.*
*Pillow Talk in Europe and Other Places.*
JOSÉ LEZAMA LIMA, *Paradiso.*
ROSA LIKSOM, *Dark Paradise.*
OSMAN LINS, *Avalovara.*
*The Queen of the Prisons of Greece.*
ALF MAC LOCHLAINN,
*The Corpus in the Library.*
*Out of Focus.*
RON LOEWINSOHN, *Magnetic Field(s).*
BRIAN LYNCH, *The Winner of Sorrow.*
D. KEITH MANO, *Take Five.*
MICHELINE AHARONIAN MARCOM,
*The Mirror in the Well.*
BEN MARCUS,
*The Age of Wire and String.*
WALLACE MARKFIELD,
*Teitlebaum's Window.*
*To an Early Grave.*
DAVID MARKSON, *Reader's Block.*
*Springer's Progress.*
*Wittgenstein's Mistress.*
CAROLE MASO, *AVA.*
LADISLAV MATEJKA AND KRYSTYNA POMORSKA, EDS.,
*Readings in Russian Poetics: Formalist and Structuralist Views.*
HARRY MATHEWS,
*The Case of the Persevering Maltese: Collected Essays.*
*Cigarettes.*
*The Conversions.*
*The Human Country: New and Collected Stories.*
*The Journalist.*
*My Life in CIA.*
*Singular Pleasures.*
*The Sinking of the Odradek Stadium.*
*Tlooth.*
*20 Lines a Day.*
ROBERT L. MCLAUGHLIN, ED.,
*Innovations: An Anthology of Modern & Contemporary Fiction.*
HERMAN MELVILLE, *The Confidence-Man.*
AMANDA MICHALOPOULOU, *I'd Like.*

FOR A FULL LIST OF PUBLICATIONS, VISIT:
www.dalkeyarchive.com

## SELECTED DALKEY ARCHIVE PAPERBACKS

STEVEN MILLHAUSER,
*The Barnum Museum.*
*In the Penny Arcade.*
RALPH J. MILLS, JR.,
*Essays on Poetry.*
MOMUS, *The Book of Jokes.*
CHRISTINE MONTALBETTI, *Western.*
OLIVE MOORE, *Spleen.*
NICHOLAS MOSLEY, *Accident.*
*Assassins.*
*Catastrophe Practice.*
*Children of Darkness and Light.*
*Experience and Religion.*
*God's Hazard.*
*The Hesperides Tree.*
*Hopeful Monsters.*
*Imago Bird.*
*Impossible Object.*
*Inventing God.*
*Judith.*
*Look at the Dark.*
*Natalie Natalia.*
*Paradoxes of Peace.*
*Serpent.*
*Time at War.*
*The Uses of Slime Mould: Essays of Four Decades.*
WARREN MOTTE,
*Fables of the Novel: French Fiction since 1990.*
*Fiction Now: The French Novel in the 21st Century.*
*Oulipo: A Primer of Potential Literature.*
YVES NAVARRE, *Our Share of Time.*
*Sweet Tooth.*
DOROTHY NELSON, *In Night's City.*
*Tar and Feathers.*
ESHKOL NEVO, *Homesick.*
WILFRIDO D. NOLLEDO,
*But for the Lovers.*
FLANN O'BRIEN,
*At Swim-Two-Birds.*
*At War.*
*The Best of Myles.*
*The Dalkey Archive.*
*Further Cuttings.*
*The Hard Life.*
*The Poor Mouth.*
*The Third Policeman.*
CLAUDE OLLIER, *The Mise-en-Scène.*
PATRIK OUŘEDNÍK, *Europeana.*
FERNANDO DEL PASO,
*News from the Empire.*
*Palinuro of Mexico.*
ROBERT PINGET, *The Inquisitory.*
*Mahu or The Material.*
*Trio.*
MANUEL PUIG,
*Betrayed by Rita Hayworth.*
*The Buenos Aires Affair.*
*Heartbreak Tango.*
RAYMOND QUENEAU, *The Last Days.*
*Odile.*
*Pierrot Mon Ami.*
*Saint Glinglin.*
ANN QUIN, *Berg.*
*Passages.*
*Three.*
*Tripticks.*
ISHMAEL REED,
*The Free-Lance Pallbearers.*
*The Last Days of Louisiana Red.*
*Ishmael Reed: The Plays.*
*Reckless Eyeballing.*
*The Terrible Threes.*
*The Terrible Twos.*
*Yellow Back Radio Broke-Down.*
JEAN RICARDOU, *Place Names.*
RAINER MARIA RILKE,
*The Notebooks of Malte Laurids Brigge.*
JULIÁN RÍOS, *Larva: A Midsummer Night's Babel.*
*Poundemonium.*
AUGUSTO ROA BASTOS, *I the Supreme.*
OLIVIER ROLIN, *Hotel Crystal.*
ALIX CLEO ROUBAUD, *Alix's Journal.*
JACQUES ROUBAUD, *The Form of a City Changes Faster, Alas, Than the Human Heart.*
*The Great Fire of London.*
*Hortense in Exile.*
*Hortense Is Abducted.*
*The Loop.*
*The Plurality of Worlds of Lewis.*
*The Princess Hoppy.*
*Some Thing Black.*
LEON S. ROUDIEZ,
*French Fiction Revisited.*
VEDRANA RUDAN, *Night.*
STIG SÆTERBAKKEN, *Siamese.*
LYDIE SALVAYRE, *The Company of Ghosts.*
*Everyday Life.*
*The Lecture.*
*Portrait of the Writer as a Domesticated Animal.*
*The Power of Flies.*
LUIS RAFAEL SÁNCHEZ,
*Macho Camacho's Beat.*
SEVERO SARDUY, *Cobra & Maitreya.*
NATHALIE SARRAUTE,
*Do You Hear Them?*
*Martereau.*
*The Planetarium.*
ARNO SCHMIDT, *Collected Stories.*
*Nobodaddy's Children.*
CHRISTINE SCHUTT, *Nightwork.*
GAIL SCOTT, *My Paris.*
DAMION SEARLS, *What We Were Doing and Where We Were Going.*
JUNE AKERS SEESE,
*Is This What Other Women Feel Too?*
*What Waiting Really Means.*
BERNARD SHARE, *Inish.*
*Transit.*
AURELIE SHEEHAN,
*Jack Kerouac Is Pregnant.*
VIKTOR SHKLOVSKY, *Knight's Move.*
*A Sentimental Journey: Memoirs 1917–1922.*
*Energy of Delusion: A Book on Plot.*

FOR A FULL LIST OF PUBLICATIONS, VISIT:
www.dalkeyarchive.com

## SELECTED DALKEY ARCHIVE PAPERBACKS

*Literature and Cinematography.*
*Theory of Prose.*
*Third Factory.*
*Zoo, or Letters Not about Love.*
Claude Simon, *The Invitation.*
Pierre Siniac, *The Collaborators.*
Josef Škvorecký, *The Engineer of Human Souls.*
Gilbert Sorrentino,
*Aberration of Starlight.*
*Blue Pastoral.*
*Crystal Vision.*
*Imaginative Qualities of Actual Things.*
*Mulligan Stew.*
*Pack of Lies.*
*Red the Fiend.*
*The Sky Changes.*
*Something Said.*
*Splendide-Hôtel.*
*Steelwork.*
*Under the Shadow.*
W. M. Spackman,
*The Complete Fiction.*
Andrzej Stasiuk, *Fado.*
Gertrude Stein,
*Lucy Church Amiably.*
*The Making of Americans.*
*A Novel of Thank You.*
Lars Svendsen, *A Philosophy of Evil.*
Piotr Szewc, *Annihilation.*
Gonçalo M. Tavares, *Jerusalem.*
Lucian Dan Teodorovici,
*Our Circus Presents . . .*
Stefan Themerson, *Hobson's Island.*
*The Mystery of the Sardine.*
*Tom Harris.*
Jean-Philippe Toussaint,
*The Bathroom.*
*Camera.*
*Monsieur.*
*Running Away.*
*Self-Portrait Abroad.*
*Television.*
Dumitru Tsepeneag,
*The Necessary Marriage.*
*Pigeon Post.*
*Vain Art of the Fugue.*
Esther Tusquets, *Stranded.*
Dubravka Ugresic,
*Lend Me Your Character.*
*Thank You for Not Reading.*
Mati Unt, *Brecht at Night*
*Diary of a Blood Donor.*
*Things in the Night.*
Álvaro Uribe and Olivia Sears, eds.,
*Best of Contemporary Mexican Fiction.*
Eloy Urroz, *The Obstacles.*
Luisa Valenzuela, *He Who Searches.*
Marja-Liisa Vartio,
*The Parson's Widow.*
Paul Verhaeghen, *Omega Minor.*
Boris Vian, *Heartsnatcher.*
Ornela Vorpsi, *The Country Where No One Ever Dies.*
Austryn Wainhouse, *Hedyphagetica.*
Paul West,
*Words for a Deaf Daughter & Gala.*
Curtis White,
*America's Magic Mountain.*
*The Idea of Home.*
*Memories of My Father Watching TV.*
*Monstrous Possibility: An Invitation to Literary Politics.*
*Requiem.*
Diane Williams, *Excitability: Selected Stories.*
*Romancer Erector.*
Douglas Woolf, *Wall to Wall.*
*Ya! & John-Juan.*
Jay Wright, *Polynomials and Pollen.*
*The Presentable Art of Reading Absence.*
Philip Wylie, *Generation of Vipers.*
Marguerite Young,
*Angel in the Forest.*
*Miss MacIntosh, My Darling.*
REYoung, *Unbabbling.*
Zoran Živković, *Hidden Camera.*
Louis Zukofsky, *Collected Fiction.*
Scott Zwiren, *God Head.*

DEC 07 2010

FOR A FULL LIST OF PUBLICATIONS, VISIT:
www.dalkeyarchive.com